ROYAL MAGIC

STORYTELLERS
BOOK ONE

JANEY FEINGOLD

Cover Illustration/Design by Samantha Aliferov

Copy Edit by Joe Badore

First Edition Jan 28 2026

ISBN: 979-8-9936272-0-5

EPUB ISBN: 979-8-9936272-1-2

For the storytellers.

And the people who have supported me in telling mine.

Thank you.

PROLOGUE

"...and so the Old Gods and the New Gods reached an agreement: they would share the *Forest In The Sky* and leave *Gaia*, our planet, and the Humans who lived here behind. But life is filled with checks and balances, and as one conflict found its resolution, another problem was born..."

The familiar sound of Grandma's honeyed voice mixed with the distant crash of waves and the steady rhythm of trotting hooves. We were making good time on horseback as we traversed the cliffside trail which ran the entire length of the seaside kingdom of Kadneria, the Kingdom I called home. Hazardous as it might be, this trail was the most direct path from our village to the Kingdom's capital, and we had been summoned to visit the Palace immediately.

I glanced back at Mother riding behind me, admiring the soft, emerald silk of her finest dress peeking out from beneath her dark travel cloak. We had all donned our best for a visit with the Royals.

"Still listening, darling?" Grandma called from where she sat proudly on a gray and white mare before me. I loved how the salt and pepper streaks in her otherwise rose gold hair matched her horse. I tugged at my own hair, a nearly petal-colored shade of that same rose gold. I wondered if my color would change one day, just as hers had.

"I'm still listening!" I called out, my voice battling the wind. A strong breeze rolled against the cliffside and I raised my hood to protect the careful braid I had woken up early to plait with my favorite green ribbons, the ones we saved for special occasions like this one. Grandma and Mother received the summons from the one and only King Godwin Raines last night. All of the Storytelling families of Kadneria were being called for an audience with the King's Council, and we were eager to make a good impression.

Grandma told me that before ruling Kadneria, King Godwin Raines was a celebrated Alchemist by trade. Upon taking the throne, his first order was the creation and distribution of many tonics and medicines for his Kingdom, at no cost to his people. Mother once said the real brains behind the King's kindness was his wife, Queen Lydia. I was eager to learn more about these Royals, they seemed like good people.

"Good. After the Gods and Goddesses left Gaia, the Humans suffered..." Grandma fell right back into the easy cadence of her storytelling. "We had become reliant on their power. Keep in mind, Gods and Goddesses — both Old and New — used to live amongst Humans, sharing their magic to aid in the growing of crops, innovation, healing, and so much more. Without magic, the Humans struggled, and that struggle brought conflict. The different human Kingdoms turned on each other, and war broke out." Grandma pulled the reins on her horse, slowing down as the trail before us narrowed significantly. I followed her lead, holding my breath as we entered the most dangerous section of the cliffside trail. Luckily, Grandma continued her story, providing enough distraction to ease my mind.

"But there were those who sought peace, and gathered representatives from each Kingdom to come together and appeal to the Gods and Goddesses, asking for their help, begging that the Almighty not let the rebuilding of their world fuel the destruction of ours." Grandma glanced back to check on me, and I offered her a small smile before she continued. "The Gods and Goddesses listened: they appointed three of their own to watch over the Humans. Do you remember their titles, darling?"

"The Friend, The Foe, and the Frequency!" I responded quickly, keeping my eyes trained on the back of Grandma's head, trying not to look down at the roaring sea below us.

"Their *formal* titles," Grandma urged. She was a stickler for formalities.

"The Friend who Protects, The Foe who Confronts, and The Frequency who connects us to Magic." I recited from memory as Grandma had taught me many moons ago. I loved every minute spent learning about our history, knowing that I was being trusted with sacred truths of our people, that I was meant to carry these stories on and share them with the generations to come. Just like my ancestors had before me.

"Yes. Three Goddesses who were put in charge of the Humans, who gave us magic, but only if we were to be responsible with it. And what did they do to ensure that us Humans would be responsible?" Distracted by her question, I hardly notice the trail widening.

We had cleared the most perilous part.

"Two things," I loosened my grip on the horses reigns as we continued along the smoother terrain, "First, they had the Humans who came to them that day make a sacred vow to keep the knowledge and secrets of their people and carry it on from generation to generation, so that the lessons learned would not be forgotten, to ensure that magic would always be used responsibly! That group became the first Storytellers. Our *ancestors!*" I glanced back at my mother riding behind me. A proud smile spread across her face as her gold rimmed hazel eyes sparkled in the sunlight. With her encouragement, I continued. "Then, they divided us all into three different types of magic, so that we would have to work together peacefully!" With the most treacherous part of the path conquered, the rest of the journey to the Palace would be easy from here and I was growing excited for all that awaited us.

"And the three types?" Grandma asked.

The wind picked up again as we rounded a corner and

I shouted to be heard over its roar. "Stellar, Lunar, and Solar!"

"Very good. So Humans were given magic, but only one type of magic each, so that they would have to work together peacefully. Remember, life is filled with checks and balances." I rolled my eyes: it was the phrase I'd heard her repeat time and time again. Somehow it seemed to be the moral of every story.

Checks and Balances.

A thought occurred to me, one I'd never ventured to ask before.

"What about Eclipse Gifts?" I knew all about how those born during an Eclipse might receive a special magical gift outside of their innate ability, but I had not yet heard how it tied into the history. "Why do some people get them and not others? Is that for balance too?"

"You're asking the right questions, darling." Even with the roaring wind, I heard my mother stifle a laugh at Grandma's non-response.

"That's not an answer!" I huffed, frustrated with the lack of information.

"The Eclipse Gifts are not promised. They are rewarded to those the Goddesses see fit. You must remember that it is a privilege to receive one." She picked up her speed and my own horse followed suit as I called after her.

"I have more questions, Grandma!"

"Good. We can discuss them on the journey home!" Grandma glanced back at me then, I could see her whole face light up as she said this. It seemed she enjoyed these lessons as much as I did.

✳

The Palace was colder than I expected. My teeth chattered as we ascended the sprawling front steps of the grandiose four-story giant which housed the Royal Family of Kadneria. The oversized stone walls were so polished they almost looked silver. Before us, hundreds of perfectly rectangular windows sparkled in the sunlight and the overwhelming sight of it stole my breath away. I'd never seen a home so large. How many people lived here? And why was it so chilly?

Kadneria had warm weather year round. The land was broken up into a collection of tiny seaside towns and villages. I had spent the 10 years of life that I had lived so far in one of those villages, known as Luz. Today, we were visiting Kad, the capital of Kadneria, where the Palace stood proudly in the center of a robust town. Kad was the largest of all the Kadnerian territories, known for both its thriving marketplace and the finest sand beaches. A visit to Kad always promised entertainment, whether that meant spotting a Royal or overhearing the latest Court gossip while shopping for fresh fish at the market. Unlike the rocky beaches back in Luz, the beaches here were filled with the finest grains of soft sand. I had been looking forward to spending a little time at the beach after Grandma and Mother's meeting. Would it be this cold on the beach as well?

As we ascended the white marble front steps of this monstrously large building, I couldn't help but marvel as a delicate snowflake fluttered down from the heavens and landed on my cheek, offering an icy kiss before melting against my warm skin.

"It's snowing!" I needed to make sure Mother and Grandma were aware of this oddly delightful occurrence.

"So it's true then? The Palace is growing colder." Mother's face scrunched in worry as she looked to Grandma who was already a few steps ahead of us. She paused to pull out a large wool scarf from her bag and tied it tight around my shoulders, the familiar sweet and spicy scent of her tomato leaf perfume filling my nose. We hadn't worn coats. We hadn't known it would be *this cold*.

I wondered why not.

Grandma had been the one to prepare us for this visit. She packed our bags and horses. Surely she would have known what to expect. It had always seemed to me that Grandma knew *everything*.

"You can never know everything darling." Her words from a recent lesson floated back into my mind. *"We are always learning. Even the past can surprise us."*

So I guess this was one of those moments. Huh, Grandma was right. Again.

"Come along then, we can't be late," Mother exclaimed as she hoisted up her skirt, lifting the now damp edges up from the light dusting of snow. We were eager to get inside to greet the other Storytelling families and to find out what the King's Council wanted from all of us. I was promised sweets if I stayed out of trouble while Grandma and Mother did their business with the Royals. I found it hard to argue with that.

❄

The dark marble walls were detailed with delicate silver decorations as far as my eyes could see. I nearly hurt my neck gazing up at the impossibly high ceilings of the ball-room I'd been left to wait in. Light emanated from laven-der-hued orbs which floated freely around the room. A few members of the Royal Guard stood at the ready in the doorway, and I took note of a hovering tray of fruit juice and water that made its way across the room of its own accord. Juice and water, but no snacks? Not a cookie in sight? A room full of children and no treats. What type of Palace was this? I knew then I had to escape and find something to eat.

I glanced back at the Royal Guards stationed at the door. They were far too bothered by a drooling blonde boy crying at their feet over a lost toy. Trained for combat as they may be, these guards were clearly not accustomed to watching over children. I smiled innocently and rounded on a little girl with a stuffed bearhound in her hands. "Is this your toy?" I asked her, batting my eyelashes. She didn't have a chance to respond before I called out to the guards. "I think she's got it!"

The little boy then turned and ran at the girl, they began fighting and the guards scrambled to separate them. I would have preferred they talk it out instead of fighting, but distractions are hard to come by, so I seized the opportunity and slipped out of the ballroom, following my nose towards what must be the kitchen. Maybe I would come across a platter of baked goods and return to the ballroom a hero. All the other children would love me for it. Lost in my thoughts of treats, I failed to notice a different young boy racing down the hallway.

An instant later we collided, falling to the ground. I stood quickly, dusting off my precious dress. The boy looked at me, his big brown eyes welling with tears.

"Are you okay?" I reached for him. He flinched.

We heard voices coming and that scared him even more. He eyed a nearby room and ran towards it. Not knowing what else to do, I followed. We made it inside before anyone saw us, slamming the door shut and taking a seat with our backs pressed against the wooden door.

"What are we running from?" My heart was racing from the excitement. I didn't even feel cold anymore.

"I can see what they are afraid of and it's... it's..." Tears welled in his eyes again.

I reached out and gently put my hand on his shoulder. Grandma always did this to me when I was upset and I found it incredibly comforting. My hand was met with softness as I noticed his rich chocolate-colored fur cloak. The same color as his eyes. And his hair. The fur looked expensive but at least he was warm in this frozen Palace. His family must have known about the temperature change. Maybe he belonged to one of the more wealthy Storytelling families gathered here today.

"You can see their fears?" I asked, and he gave a timid nod. "That's not common magic..." I began to search my brain for anything I might know that could help him.

An idea occurred to me.

"It's your Eclipse Gift isn't it?"

He looked at me like he had no idea what I was talking about. This poor boy, had no one told him about Eclipse Gifts? I instinctively felt the need to comfort him.

"Those of us who are Eclipseborn may receive special

gifts, I haven't learned them all yet but yours sounds like you can see people's thoughts... oh maybe you're a Dreamseer! But you can see like, daydreams too? And fears!?" I had just begun studying the history of Eclipse Gifts as part of my Storytelling training and felt very proud of myself for this recollection. I wondered if he had begun his own training yet. He looked about my age.

"It's never happened before today." His eyes fell to the floor in embarrassment but there was nothing to be embarrassed about. I knew I had to help him understand this.

"It must have just manifested! Congratulations! Maybe your family will throw you a party! Grandma said she would throw me a party when I get my gift. I'm Eclipseborn too!"

I wanted him to know that this was a good thing and so I wrapped my arms around him, burrowing into the softness of his fur. He stiffened, before settling into my touch, studying me. Knowing he could see what I was dreaming up, I imagined a lovely party. I imagined Grandma and Mother feeding me chocolate cake and praising me for manifesting a wonderful Eclipse Gift. I imagined this boy there with me. I even shared my cake with him.

"I can see the party you're thinking of...that's a nice thought." A small smile spread on his face and it warmed me to know I had put it there.

"See! You *can* see more than just the scary thoughts people have. You can see what they dream of! What makes them happy! Think about how much easier it will be to give people presents they actually like."

"I don't usually give people presents," he said in response.

"Why not?"

"Usually people just give *me* presents." A dimple formed in his cheek as his mouth bloomed into a self-conscious smile.

"Lucky you. Although I do prefer giving presents to receiving them..." I thought it was strange that he had never given someone a present but I didn't want to make him feel bad. "Receiving them is nice too."

He looked at me then, as if noticing me for the first time.

"Maybe my mother would throw me a party, but my father certainly wouldn't. Maybe I shouldn't even tell them." He glanced away again and my eyes stuck on his boyish profile. He was probably the most handsome kid I'd ever seen. My stomach fluttered the tiniest bit. Or maybe I was hungry.

"Well that's up to you, but it's nothing to be ashamed of, you've gotten a wonderful Eclipse Gift." This seemed to soothe him and I looked down to realize we were still hugging. I took this as my cue to scoot back, creating some space between us. He must have been heating up like I was, because he shrugged out of his fur, exposing his bare arms. That's when I noticed a burn on his forearm, a perfect circle wrapped around him, almost like a bracelet. He quickly pulled his arm away from my view.

"If I decide not to tell them, would you keep my secret?"

Now that was a tricky one. On the one hand, I felt what a privilege it would be to hold the truth of his

Eclipse Gift in my heart. On the other, while Storytellers held secrets, they always shared them when it was needed. For the sake of history. For the sake of knowledge, and justice. And I might be early in my training, but I was still a Storyteller.

Maybe he didn't know this yet. I decided to tell him.

"I would be honored. But you should know, as Storytellers, we believe that at some point, secrets need to be shared, in order to help people." Clearly he had not gotten this far in his own Storytelling training. He needed a better teacher. I wondered if Grandma and Mother would let him share my lessons. "Would that be alright with you? I'll keep your secret but if the time comes to share it..." I looked at him, my question clear.

"Yes, okay, if it will help people, when that time comes, do what you must." He smiled too, feeling good about his decision, no doubt. I felt proud of him for coming to this conclusion on his own.

"Until then, your secret is safe with me." I found that I was touching his arm again.

"You know what? I would like to try it." The dimple was back. It was hard to focus on anything else.

"Try what?"

"I'm going to give you a present." He declared it very matter of factly.

"Oh! Okay?"

"You can go back and wait in the ballroom if you'd like, I'll meet you there." With that he stood, opened the door and hurried off. I followed his instruction and started back towards the ballroom. My stomach growled as I hoped that whatever he gave me was edible. But before I even reached the dark marble doorway of the ballroom, Mother and Grandma appeared, a look of panic on their faces as they silently grabbed my hand and hauled me out of there. We made our way home as quickly as possible.

PART ONE

1

DARBY, TODAY

"Shadows, pay attention!" Miss Hazel calls out to me and the rest of the graduates of Shadow Academy. We are gathered on the training field at the center of the fortress of brutalist stone buildings which make up the Academy grounds. Miss Hazel continues barking orders, her broad frame looming over us. I've never understood her blatant resentment for us. To my knowledge, all Shadows are given missions after completing their training and the three required years where we tutor the younger Shadows. Any additional work for the Academy is optional. If Miss Hazel chose to stay here full time, you would think she could be a little kinder to us. But being *kind* isn't exactly part of our training.

"Sort yourselves by your magic type..." All it takes to become a Shadow is a blood oath and an education. While there are other Shadow training academies on *Gaia*, ours is the only one on this continent. Young women come from near and far to sign away their individuality for the sake of a powerful skillset and a guaranteed career. Any of the three magic types can become Shadows. The profession does not discriminate; in fact at our Shadow Academy they prefer to have one of each magic type on a team, which is why Miss Hazel is attempting to break us into groups at present.

"Solars on the left ..." At Miss Hazel's command, a third of my peers break off to the left. Solars receive their magic from the Sun, so their powers are most potent at midday, when the Sun is at its highest. They are known for their exceptional speed and their connection to fire.

"...Lunars on the right." Following orders, I shuffle over to the right with the rest of the Lunars. We gain our power from the Moon. The height of our strength occurs in the evening, especially when the moon is full. We're connected to water and light.

"...and Stellars here in the middle." We all shift, making space between our two groups for the Stellars to take their place. Stellars draw their power from the Second Star, another sun that appears over our planet twice a year for a month at a time. Stellars are strong healers with the ability to manipulate energy and air. Stellars are incredibly powerful when our planet nears the Second Star in orbit. But because the alignment happens so rarely, Stellars spend most of their lives with limited access to their true power.

All Humans of Gaia have possessed one of the three types ever since the Goddess of The Frequency gifted our planet with magic. In addition to your magic type, if you are born during an Eclipse, the Goddess may bless you with an Eclipse Gift. If you're lucky.

Even though I am Eclipseborn, I've yet to manifest an Eclipse Gift. I doubt I ever will, and that's fine by me. I am a Shadow now. It's us Shadows who have cultivated our Goddess-given power and honed our abilities. As spies, we've been trained to be invisible: neutral, unattached masters of disguise who can adapt and survive in any situation long enough to collect the intel we've been tasked to extract. And given the risks of our job and the potential dangers of our missions, we've even been trained to defend ourselves, to act as weapons, if and when necessary. Our Headmaster would constantly remind us: "Shadows do not stand out, Shadows do not step out."

Miss Hazel clears her throat and continues her announcements.

"All right, ladies. You've completed your training and given your three years as tutors to the younger Shadows. It's now time to set out on your missions, starting today with this sorting. Today we will form the teams you will work with for the rest of your careers." Miss Hazel's posture straightens and we all suck in a collective breath as we notice Headmaster arrive on the field, her signature midnight black cloak swirling silently behind her in the breeze. From where I'm standing, it gives the illusion of *real* shadows dancing around her slender frame, as if she is truly one with the shades. Headmaster nods for Miss Hazel to continue, which she does. "As you know, teams will consist of one Lunar, one Solar and one Stellar. To keep things *balanced*."

It's for the best really, if our teams consisted of all Lunars, we could come up short on power during the day.

It's better for the teams to be mixed so we can take advantage of everyone's strengths and cover for each other's weaknesses. We work together to take full advantage of the three magic types.

This system of forming trios is how we do things here at the Shadow Academy, in our tiny corner of The Border Forest we call home, but every region has their own system.

For example, in the neighboring kingdom of Kadneria, they've implemented a different system for finding balance with the three magic types: Royal Magic, a power sharing system in which you give your magic in exchange for access to the magic of others. Instead of being the strongest of your one kind of magic, you are all equally matched in *every* kind. Or at least you should be, I hear there are still some flaws with Royal Magic, but I've never used it myself. Here in The Border Forest at Shadow Academy, we are out of range of Royal Magic. Headmaster says this was intentional in order to provide for better training. Shadows can be hired for missions all over the world. We must be able to adapt to any and all magic systems. If we joined Royal Magic, it might limit our capabilities.

Nevertheless, some consider Royal Magic to be a revolutionary solution.

I am not one of those people.

Just then, Headmaster's darkened eyes fall to me, the burn of her gaze somehow hotter than the sun, but before I can react, she looks away. It's still so strange to see her like this. I don't even think of her as Mother anymore. How could I when she insists I call her Headmaster, just like the others?

The woman I used to know is completely unrecognizable today. I haven't been within hugging range of Mother in years, but I bet she no longer smells of tomato leaves. Her once flowing rose gold hair, the very same that I learned to braid with, is now cropped short and permanently dyed the signature Shadow color of night black. Eyes that were once the brightest gold-rimmed hazel are magically altered to appear such a dark shade of blue they almost look black as well. She changed the color when we got here so we would look less alike. She wanted to change my eyes too but I cried so loudly she gave up on it. This was after she had already changed my hair, cropping it short and dyeing like all the other Shadows. No, I could not let her change my eyes and give up the final part of me that still looked like Grandma.

"Darby from the Lunars, and Romina from the Solars...." Lost in my own head again, I almost missed my name being called. I look over at the line of Solars to see the smiling face of my best friend in the entire world. Romina. She winks at me as I catch the gaze of her sparkling bright blue eyes. Her most distinct feature. Her perfect posture and upturned chin exude confidence. She knows that she's the smartest one in every room she walks into. My chest swells with excitement to be paired with her for the rest of my career. I may not have a mother anymore, but Romina is my family. She's been by my side ever since we arrived at the Shadow Academy fifteen years ago. The night I took the blood oath and changed my name, it was her who lent me her dagger. Sometimes I feel like our friendship protected us. Shared secrets and stolen moments over the years allowed a spark of our sense of self to be preserved, despite the Academy's best attempts to make us just like everyone else.

My boots squish in the mud as I make my way over to stand with her. She reaches her pinky finger out and I interlace it with mine, sharing a subtle squeeze. I silently thank the Friend that Romina will be by my side for whatever comes next.

"...And Seline from the Stellars." I look up in horror as Seline moves to join us with a wicked gleam in her stormy silver eyes. Romina and Seline can't stand each other. For starters, Seline craves trouble and Romina is one for the rules. Romina is the smartest in our class, with a thirst for knowledge that keeps her nose buried in a book. Seline has never owned a text book, instead she throws herself into compromising situations and figures it out as she goes, relying on her keen intuition and natural abilities. And if that wasn't enough of a reason for them to dislike each other, there's also the fact that I've been seeing Seline on and off for the last three years, and as my best friend, Romina's been my shoulder to cry on every time Seline's played me hot and cold. And now Seline is being paired with us for the *rest of our careers* as Shadows? Foe.

"Hello ladies, we're going to have some fun together, aren't we?" Seline's words melt right off her painted red lips. We're not allowed to wear makeup, but try telling her that.

I look over at Romina who is already rolling her eyes. "Let's get on with our trial mission and see if we can make this work between the three of us." I take a deep breath, remembering that first we will have a trial in these teams and based on how that goes, we will make our trio official. Maybe this won't be so bad. Maybe the three of us can work together as a team.

Seline sticks her leg out so quickly that Romina doesn't see it before flying down into the mud face first, and all hope of us playing nicely together goes out the window.

"Real mature, Seline," Romina says, as I offer her a hand to help her up.

I look around to find the underground cellar in complete darkness. My eyes adjust as I breathe in the musty scent. Being a Shadow isn't always the most glamorous job. At least we will be well compensated once we start getting our real missions, for now I just need to stay focused and prove that Seline, Romina and I can work together. If we can.

I tap my fingers together and summon a light orb using the connection to light my Lunar Magic provides, admiring the warm golden glow for a moment before I signal to the others who are crowded in behind me. Romina approaches first, sniffing the putrid air as she silently steps towards a small stone table at the center of the cramped cellar where a tray containing twelve glass vials sits below a perfect beam of moonlight. The vials are filled with a bubbling purple liquid giving off a slight *hum* that tickles my ears. I close my eyes and listen to it. The gentle *hum* has a pattern to it. Like a melody.

"Dragonstems. And vinegar. And something else..." Romina scrunches her nose as she runs through the encyclopedia that is her brain. Her bright blue eyes close in concentration.

"How can you be sure?" Seline steps forward, cramming in next to Romina as she peers over her to get a good look at the vials.

"I can smell it." Romina opens her eyes again, shooting a glare at Seline.

"They want us to confirm whether or not this lab is producing HelioX." Mischief flashes on Seline's face as she reaches her delicate hand out towards the vials. "Maybe we should try it."

I can't help but notice her intoxicating eyes, the quirk of her lips when she gets a dangerous idea...those lips...

But this is not the time to be thinking about Seline's lips.

Romina glares at me as if she could read my thoughts, which of course she can't, considering she already has her Eclipse Gift: Portal Hopping. It manifested in her early childhood, before we even met, and has come in handy over the years. No, Romina certainly can't read my mind as having two Eclipse Gifts is unheard of, some people never even get *one*.

"Confirmed. I'm certain of it. These vials will ferment overnight and they will jar it and sell it in the morning at the Dark Market." Romina states with little room for debate.

"I've never seen anything like this at the Dark Market." Seline retracts her hand as she says this, stepping around to the other side of the table, her hips swaying in her tight black outfit in a way that always drives me crazy. So crazy I almost miss what she's said. It registers a second later.

"Since when do you go to the Dark Market?" I dare to meet Seline's taunting gaze.

"A good Shadow never reveals her secrets." She turns to face me as she says this, winking.

Is she talking about us?

Romina obviously knows that Seline and I still *see each other* sometimes.

Romina knows all my secrets. Well, most of them.

I inspect the bubbling liquid, wondering if it's dangerous to touch. "The chemist wore gloves," I muse out loud. When we arrived in the outskirts of Kadneria two hours ago, we hid in the darkness and watched as a masked man in a white lab cloak delivered these vials to this cellar. He tended to them while we observed, taking detailed notes on his process from our hiding place. The second he left and sealed the cellar door shut, we emerged and started sniffing around.

"Let's just take it. Sell it ourselves. I bet my contacts at the market would be thrilled to help us out." Seline starts to circle the vials, Romina steps forward.

"They'd kill you for stealing them to begin with." Romina puts a hand out to block Seline from getting too close to the table, catching her arm.

"They'd have to find me first," Seline says, as she removes Romina's hand. The two of them are constantly at each other's throats, it makes things impossibly hard for the three of us considering I'd die for Romina but Seline is well... Seline.

"You're not *that* clever." Romina is still physically

standing between Seline and the vials doing her best to block the way. "Besides, we're supposed to be in and out undetected. Stealing these is not part of our mission." It's clear Romina isn't budging. Seline must realize this too as she offers up in the teasing voice I know too well:

"You just love to follow the rules don't you, Romina?"

Seline is right. Romina loves the rules, but that's why I've always needed her around to keep me in check as I've struggled to stay neutral over the years. Now that we are leaving the Academy behind and venturing off into real world missions, I wonder if the rules have changed. We will no longer be in training. No longer under the watchful eyes of Miss Hazel or Headmaster or any of the other faculty. We will have *real* missions with *real* consequences. Which means our actions could lead to *real* change. Besides, when has following the rules ever led to actually helping people?

All I've ever wanted to do is help people.

"*We help people by collecting information*," Headmaster would always say. "*The work of Shadows is essential for justice.*" But justice for who, I always wondered. Anyone with enough gold can hire a Shadow to do their bidding. Don't we get a say in who deserves to be helped?

Deep down, I can't help but feel that leaving Shadow Academy is going to be the beginning of my story. Depending on where our missions might lead us, I might finally have the chance to do *something*. It's that little spark of hope that gives me an idea.

"Seline is right, if these vials are going to turn into HelioX, we can't leave them here," I say, earning a look from both of them.

Romina mumbles, "What?" as Seline nods for me to go on.

"We've all read the reports. HelioX is destroying families. It's the most highly addictive substance in Kadneria. Even their Royal Magic can't save people from it. I know we're just supposed to get information but, what if this is a test somehow?"

"A test?" Romina's eyes are blown wide. She just loves a test. Preferably the kind she can study for. A fact I've benefited from for 15 years of her helping me in Shadow lessons.

However this is a different kind of test. The unexpected kind. The kind that could *define* us.

"To see what we're capable of. To see what we believe in. We've been given the chance to stop this substance before it fully ferments into HelioX and hurts more people."

"And who is testing us?" Romina asks. Of course she does.

There's a flicker of something across Seline and Romina's faces as they watch me and I have the unmistakable feeling of their full attention, as if my words have somehow tethered to them. It gives me the courage to continue.

"I believe fate is testing us. I believe in doing the right thing." They let my words marinate, so I press on. "We should destroy the vials." As quickly as it appeared, that intangible tether between us is broken.

"We don't believe in anything, Bee. We're just shadows," Seline sighs. Romina glances at Seline and, for the first time in a long time, she agrees with her.

"Maybe that *is* the test, Darbs. Seeing if we can remain neutral."

They are wrong. We can collect intel and still care about helping people. We have to help people. Otherwise what is the point of our training? Of being Shadows?

"We *could* help more people with the money we'd make selling this stuff," Seline offers. But while that might be her idea of helping, I can't agree.

"No. Sel. That's not right. We can't profit from it!" Seline is surprised as I am by my passion. I've never snapped at her before. And then suddenly, the air shifts as an unmistakable smell begins to fill the room.

Smoke.

In an instant, I'm no longer in the cellar with Romina and Seline.

I'm 10 years old wrapped in my mother's arms watching as she carries me away from our home as it goes up in flames. I'm listening as my mother cries out her own mother's name.

The smell of smoke is overwhelming, creeping into my lungs and filling up my throat until I can no longer scream. When did I start screaming?

I see nothing but blue. Three Blue Owls leading us away from the fire. I watch them through the trees as we run through a forest, dirt coating our feet. My heart hurts, my eyes sting. My chest feels like it's going to explode and —

The sound of shattered glass breaks me out of my stupor.

My heart is beating so fast it threatens to leave my chest. The vials have broken, with thick purple liquid splashing onto the floor. I look around for the cause of the wreckage only to realize it's no one's fault but my own.

Foe, I've done it again. Another outburst of power I can't control. It's happening more and more lately. Yes, it's true I wanted to destroy the vials, but not like this, not in a way that may have jeopardized our mission. At least none of it got on —oh, no....

Seline's silver eyes dance up to mine as I take in the coin sized hole burned through the fabric of her sleeve to expose her fair skin, now coated in a bubbling bright purple goo. I meet Seline's gaze and try to hide my panic as she says the words I've never heard her say before.

"Romina, tell me what to do."

I hide my smile because this is no time for laughing, but seriously, I never thought Seline would ask Romina for help!

"So now you want my opinion?" Romina can't help but make light of this too.

"Romina!" Seline sounds frantic, maybe this is worse than we thought.

"Brush it off with your glove, a little skin contact at this stage of fermentation should be totally fine. Strange that it burned through your sleeve though..." Romina sounds reassuring and I feel grateful for her calming presence.

That's when we hear footsteps. Someone must have heard the crash, or could they be running from the smoke? Is there a fire? We have to get out of here. Romina starts using her Eclipse Gift to build a portal for us to leave the cellar, the familiar swirl of glittering magic filling the air before my eyes. I notice Seline hasn't brushed the liquid off yet. I look at her.

"What are you waiting for? Brush it off, we can't take it back with us."

Her eyes float away from mine as she mumbles, "I can't".

"What do you mean?" I ask.

"It... it feels too good." Her eyes flutter in what I can only describe as bliss, not unlike the way she sometimes looks in bed.

I look to Romina for guidance. This isn't good.

"It must be stronger than what I studied. That's not supposed to happen yet. Darbs, you have to do something to help her."

I approach Seline, getting as close as I can without touching her. Smoke is floating in from underneath the cellar door, it must be filling the hallway now.

"Hey, Seline, listen to me. I know it feels good, but it's bad. You have to remember that. Tell yourself that." Romina's portal is open now and the footsteps are getting closer. Seline still isn't responding to me so I'm going to have to touch her, not where the liquid is, of course, but I'll have to make contact.

I reach out and put my hand on her waist. She always likes it when I do that. I lean in closer and try to meet her eyes. If this substance is making her feel good I'll just have to remind her that I can make her feel good too.

"Hey, Seline, remember me?" I lean in closer, tilting up on my toes so my lips graze her ear. "And I'm the real thing, not just a drop of..." I don't even need to finish my sentence as her eyes blow wide open and she uses her gloved hand to swat the drop of purple away just as I nod to Romina and together we grab Seline and jump into the portal.

Darkness consumes us as we get the fuck out of there.

2

"You're back early."

Nice to see you too, Mother, I think to myself, standing perfectly at attention in the Headmaster's office back at Shadow Academy. The walls are coated in a deep green with rich wooden paneling made to blend in with the lush forest that sprawls all around us. I can see the tree tops swaying just outside the large bay windows I stand across from. The wind must be picking up outside, indicating an oncoming storm. The ancient wooden floorboards below me give a small creak as if to remind me to stay grounded in this moment in my mother's office. Luckily, Romina is the first to speak.

"We infiltrated the lab and found a subterranean level. They were mixing Dragonstem, vinegar and something else. They had ten vials of it fermenting in a locked cellar. We intended to stay overnight and observe the process but —"

"We smelled smoke nearby. Then the vials exploded,"

I add. My eyes scan the bookshelves where I find various texts on the other neighboring kingdom: Langha. I wonder if she's actually read any of these. As my vision snags on a cookbook, I realize that I can't remember the last time she cooked anything. Sometimes it's unbearable. My only living relative is right here in front of me, and yet, it's like she's forgotten our connection.

"Exploded?" Headmaster looks right to me as she says this, somehow suspecting I had something to do with it. I hate that she's right. It's not my fault that I keep losing control of my power. Or I guess, maybe it is my fault...

"The substance was stronger than we realized. In the explosion, some of the liquid got on Seline and she found it... hard to remove," I tell her instead of explaining the blip in my control.

Something that looks like worry crosses Headmaster's face before she composes herself and turns to Seline. "Any signs of distress?" she asks.

"I'm alright, Headmaster," Seline offers, as poised as ever.

"Romina, escort Seline to the infirmary for observation. Just in case." Romina offers a polite nod as she and Seline exit the office. I know better than to follow them, since I have not yet been dismissed. Once the others are out of earshot, Headmaster turns to address me. It is rare that we have these private moments together. I take the chance to really look at her. She's thinned out tremendously, though I guess I have, too. It's hard to say, since I was only a child when we got here, but based on my memory of both Mother and Grandma's soft curves, I have a feeling I would have looked different had I stayed and grown up back in our village of Luz. I remember the rocky beaches of Luz. The spray of salt water. Swimming with Mother and Grandma in between my lessons. The fish we would catch and grill over a fire with our neighbors on Eclipse nights. Our eyes, three sets of matching gold rimmed hazel. Two amazing women who cared for me, loved me.

"The vials exploded, did they?" Her words are sharp. I wonder if she still loves me.

"It was an accident," I tell her through gritted teeth.

"A dangerous one. One that compromised your *friend*." There's something about the way she says *friend* that makes me think she knows about me and Seline, but I choose to ignore that for now.

"There was smoke, it distracted me. It made me think of..." She realizes where I'm going with this and a subtle crackle of energy alerts me that she's put up a sound shield. It's an impressive use of her Stellar magic. Mother is probably one of the most powerful Stellars out there. Her ability to control energy has always been useful to us: once to make her an exceptional Storyteller, and now in her new role as a Shadow. Hearing the sound shield lock in place, I continue.

"It made me think of Grandma."

"How many times have we been over this, Darby? You need to forget." She doesn't meet my eyes as she busies herself with a stack of paperwork on her mahogany desk.

"How can I ever forget? That day changed everything. We should have stayed and helped her." My voice breaks before I can even control it. "We didn't help her!"

"She sacrificed herself so we could live. She wanted us

to get out of there, to stay safe". Her tone remains calm, unmoved.

"Stay safe and do nothing? Why are we still hiding?" I slam my fist down on her desk now, demanding her attention. A look of surprise flashes across Mother's face, but I've got too much momentum now, and after years of never standing up to her, I'm about ready to burst.

Why *have* I never stood up to her? It's been bubbling up inside of me for so long and something about smelling that smoke today has made this feeling inescapable. Inevitable even.

"I'm older now, I'm trained, I'm ready to actually DO SOMETHING to help. Almost *all* of the Storytellers were wiped out that day, almost everyone who opposed Royal Magic, multiple villages went up in flames... there's got to be a reason. It's got to be connected somehow and the longer we hide out, the more these secrets will be buried!" My heart is racing and I hear it thumping in my ears so loudly I almost miss what she says next.

"I know."

"What?" The ground beneath my feet feels like it's moving. I must not have heard her correctly.

"We're not *hiding*, Darby. We've been waiting for our moment. And it's almost here."

I turn to look at her and for a second I see a sparkle in her eye, the kind I haven't seen in years.

"Prince Nolan Raines of Kadneria is to find a wife this Season. In a prophecy, a Royal Visionary *saw* that the Prince would acquire exceptional power on his Eclipse wedding night when he marries his Link. King Godwin Raines wants his son to be as powerful as possible, so they are doing whatever it takes to find *her*, even welcoming their rival's daughters to enter into the marriage season."

"Well, that will certainly keep the Kadnerian Court entertained, but why should I care? I don't trust King Godwin and, I've heard his son is nothing more than a philandering puppet to do his bidding."

"You should *care* because the King has grown paranoid, and having *foreigners* roaming around the Palace is a high price to pay for this potential match to be made..."

I shake my head in confusion. "Right, so, why take that risk? Welcoming foreigners, even known rivals, is just inviting chaos into his Kingdom. Is the King really that desperate for his son to gain power?"

"Darby, let me finish," she says in the calm voice of my mother, not the order of my Headmaster. I nod my head for her to go on. "The stakes are high, but he's willing to do whatever it takes to secure this enhanced power for his son. He's even hired *Shadows* to protect the Prince. Young lady Shadows to pose as the Prince's suitors and make sure things go *smoothly* during the marriage season and to keep an eye on the foreigners."

I'm beginning to catch on here.

"More importantly, Shadows whose identities are unknown to those at Court. Now that you've graduated and completed your trial, this will be your mission."

"So we're going undercover into a marriage season? 15 years of training to attend a few balls?"

"You're gaining access to the Winter Palace, Darby."

I swallow once as I process this.

"You are right: we know that something is *wrong* with Royal Magic, that something terrible happened that day, and we've had no way to prove it. You're going in there to find *something* we can use to make our case. Then I will bring the evidence to our allies and together we can finally uncover the truth."

It dawns on me then that Mother really hasn't been in hiding all these years. She's been planning.

"Who are our allies? Do any of the other Shadows know? What about the people from our past? Have you made contact with any of the Storytellers?" My chest expands with the unmistakable feeling of hope, but my mother raises a hand to quiet my endless list of questions.

"I will tell you when the time comes." Of course, she is going to continue to keep me in the dark, just like she has this whole time. Why has she waited this long to tell me that there was *hope* to be had? I could have used it on a few of my more miserable nights over the last 15 years. Nights where I felt so alone that nothing could coax me out of the dark. Nights where my own mind threatened to turn on me until Romina came to my rescue, reminding me that I was cared for. That she was my friend. That she was by my side.

I don't want to keep this from Romina.

"What can the others know?"

"Seline and Romina will learn about the Vision. The rest is not mission imperative." More secrets. I guess I'm not surprised. Maybe I'll tell Romina anyway. Headmaster won't know.

"When the time comes to use Royal Magic, try to avoid it." This thought had not yet occurred to me but of course, Royal Magic is a requirement for all of those at Court in Kadneria who stay longer than one day.

"How do you expect me to do that?" I say in response.

"You should be able to shield against it. Picture the source of your magic and try to cap it off, only releasing the tiniest bit of your magic and accepting a small amount in the exchange, enough to *pass* as using it, but not enough for it to potentially harm you".

I am capable of two types of shields. I can create a small physical shield with my Lunar light magic that is useful in a fight, and I can also shield my mind to block out any Mentalists or Dreamseers... but these are nowhere near as advanced as what she is talking about.

"Shielding is your strength, not mine."

"Then let me give you strength." She pulls a necklace from her pocket that I immediately recognize as Grandma's: a gold heart-shaped medallion on a thin chain. She places it in my hand and before I can protest, she takes out a crystal handled dagger and slices the palm of her hand open before wrapping it around both my hand and the necklace. I breathe in the unmistakable coppery smell as she presses her own blood, her own magic into the medallion and my hand. It feels warm. She winces. Imbibing an object with your magic must be painful. In full honesty, I've never seen someone do it before and I can't help but feel incredibly moved by the gesture. She is bleeding for me. To offer me protection.

When it is over, she unceremoniously wipes the necklace clean on her own black leather pants before handing it to me, then raising her cut hand above her heart to stop the blood flow.

"Thank you," I tell her, as I accept the medallion and clasp it around my neck. It's not only a piece of her, but

Grandma too. She looks up at me with an emotion in her eyes that I don't have time to name before the sound shield drops and the mask of Headmaster returns.

She ushers me out without any further displays of affection.

As if she's once again forgotten I'm her daughter.

3

Seline's fingertips trace up my arm, giving me goosebumps. Her fair skin is in stark contrast to my olive tone. We're so different, and yet somehow we fit together. She's lying next to me in such a way that her short dark hair spikes up in every direction as she drags her eyes up to meet mine, playfully. I love seeing her like this, in a way no one else gets to. This strong, scheming woman whose smile always spells mischief.

With me, she lets her guard down. At least sometimes.

It started around my 22nd Birthday. Right around the time we finished our training and began tutoring the younger Shadows. It was then that we got to explore new privileges: the illusion of freedom. One night, there was a Stellar Eclipse event so the Second Star, the Sun, and the Moon were all in alignment for the first time since I was old enough to feel its more emotional effects. A Stellar Eclipse has the tendency to inspire uninhibited behavior. Especially for twentysomethings.

It was a warm night, and all the girls in my year snuck off the Academy grounds to go swimming under the Eclipse. When the Stellar Eclipse fell into alignment, it didn't go dark like a Solar Eclipse would. Instead, the sky was filled with a soft glowing light which perfectly reflected off the water, giving the illusion that we were swimming in a sparkling pool of milk.

I swam naked amongst my peers and, for the first time, I didn't feel self-conscious in the body that I was still getting used to. It's a funny thing, skinny dipping with a bunch of girls you view as sisters: bodies are just bodies.

But when I looked at Seline that night in the moon-light, I realized that I didn't see her as a sister the way I did the others.

Instead, she made my pulse race.

Seline was stunning, even in our awkward years, but it was her confidence I was drawn to. She has always known *exactly* who she is, even when it went against the norms, even when it got her into trouble. I admired her. And that night when our emotions were all heightened, I *wanted* her.

Everyone else turned back to go inside but Seline caught my eye.

"Race you to the rock!" she called out to me.

Before I could even accept her dare, she dove under the milky surface. I took off after her swimming as fast as I could.

We reached the rock at the same time, putting our hands on its slippery surface to steady ourselves, our hearts racing as we both struggled to catch our breath.

Her mouth hung open and I couldn't help but stare at her parted lips. The Eclipse light. The warm air. Her mouth. It was too much for my senses.

"You're curious." It wasn't a question. My eyes met hers as she continued. "Have you ever kissed someone before?"

My heart was beating so fast I thought it might fall out of my chest.

"I have," I told her.

Romina and I had been sent on a training mission that included living on a farm near the all-boys Agricultural Academy just a couple summers before this. For *educational purposes*. Needless to say, we learned a lot.

"Have you ever kissed a girl?"

My breath hitched as she inched closer. "I have not," I admitted.

Her eyes sparkled at that and she began to close the distance between us, our legs tangling under the water as I steadied my grip on the rock.

"Would you like to?" She pulled me even closer with her legs, her own hand grasping the rock for purchase. The energetic pull of her mixed with the effects of the Eclipse and I found myself unable to speak. I nodded instead.

Her free hand gently moved to my cheek, cupping my face as her lips met mine. Her pillow soft lips gently grazed my own and I instantly felt butterflies in my stomach. I followed her lead and gently pressed into her. Her tongue parted my lips before swirling and exploring my mouth. I couldn't help but smile against her face, causing her to smile too and breaking our kiss.

"We can't keep kissing if you're smiling like that! It pulls your lips away."

"Sorry," I looked up at her, beaming.

"You liked it?"

I nodded again, and with that devilish look of hers she splashed water at me and swam away.

"What are you smiling about?" Seline says, but it is no longer the Seline of the past, instead it is the Seline next to me, lying on an infirmary cot here at Shadow Academy.

Her breath warms my skin due to the proximity of our bodies, my head tucked into the crook of her arm. The memory fades and I'm faced with reality once more: Seline was in danger today.

"I was thinking about our first kiss." I look back at her. She's grown up a lot these last few years, but to me she'll always be that 22 year old in the Eclipse light.

"Feeling all nostalgic because you saved me today?" There is a rare softness on her face when she asks me this. Seline is tough on the outside, but I know deep down she's as sensitive as I am. I cherish the moments she lets her walls slip.

"It was scary, seeing you like that." I wonder if she'll open up to me now, but I know she's more likely to act like it was no big deal. We both know it was.

"It felt weird." She hesitates, turning onto her back, her eyes darting up to the ceiling. "Like I was under some kind of spell, or something. I don't know."

It's not the most descriptive answer but I'm happy she trusted me enough to even share that much. "I'm happy I was there." I inch closer to her, placing my hand on her flat stomach. "I want you to know that I'll always look out for you." I feel her abdominals tighten beneath the weight of my palm as she inhales and exhales deeply.

"You shouldn't."

She closes her eyes as she says this, perhaps avoiding my gaze, but that won't do, so I push up onto my elbows to look down at her.

"Shouldn't? For Foe's sake, Sel, of course I will." Of course I'll always want to protect Seline.

How could I not after everything we've been through together?

Her eyes open now and she looks at me. She reaches across the cot and pulls me closer until my body is flush with her side. One hand reaches for my leg and drapes it over her thigh while the other finds a gentle placement on my rear. Her expression changes to something I'd call sinister, if not for the fact that I've seen this look on her face before. Many times.

"How can I ever repay you for saving me today," she says, her words dripping with promise.

"You don't need to—" Before I can say anymore she cuts me off with a blistering kiss. It's all-consuming sweetness. It's so frustratingly perfect I could scream if not for her mouth on mine.

Seline knows exactly how to kiss me, and she wastes no time parting my lips and taking control. The hand on my backside guides my still parted legs up and down her thigh. The pressure is perfect. The rhythm is steady. But we've had a big day, she should rest. I pull away and try to tell her as much.

"You told me to remember how good you felt, that you were the real thing..." She's talking about earlier when the still fermenting HelioX got on her, the memory of which causes me to shudder. "Well Bee, show me how real you are. Let me see you come for me."

Before I know it, I'm leaning into her body once more, letting her guide me with the most perfect friction building between us. This time it's me kissing her, consuming her.

I'll take as much as she'll give me. I'm just so happy she's okay. That today didn't end badly.

"You're doing so good, Bee. And I haven't even laid a finger on you, yet." She whispers between kisses and crushing me into her upper thigh. Seline likes to play with me, challenging herself to make me come in new ways that tickle her fancy. I'd be lying if I said I didn't enjoy being her plaything, but only in the physical sense. No, I've never enjoyed when she plays with my feelings.

"Maybe it's time," Seline adds, while unlacing my leathers to expose my hip bone. There, she skims her fingers over the familiar ink. My Shadow Mark: The silhouette of two daggers pointed in opposite directions. Her fingers keep moving as she dips down the front of my pants, extending a finger to gently tap at my clit with a practiced rhythm. After three years, she knows exactly what to do to drive me crazy. I release a loud gasp before I remember that we're in the infirmary, anyone could walk in on us at any moment, and the sparkle in her eye tells me she's enjoying that fact.

"Sel!" I manage to say in mock admonishment.

"Better come quickly before someone catches us..." She picks up her pace now, speaking between kisses on the most sensitive part of my neck. "Please Bee, for me?"

she adds, and I'm a goner. I can count on my hand the number of times I've heard Seline say "please", but I have little time to dwell on it as my body explodes into an all-consuming orgasm. She kisses me through it, her hands holding me tight against her until I'm left breathless, folded into her side. We lay like, our heartbeats still racing. I reach up for her, tilting her chin down so I can meet her gaze.

"That was... Thank you."

She gazes back at me and her mouth blooms into a radiant smile. Her beauty steals my breath away. But the smile only lasts a heartbeat before a shadow crosses her face and her eyes harden.

"You should never put me before a mission, Bee, especially since we're on the team together now. For the rest of our careers." The cot squeaks beneath us as she sits upright herself, pulling away from me by inches that feel like miles. My head spins trying to make sense of this shift. Her words don't match the actions of what was just happening. Is she speaking out of fear?

"Sel, I care about you." I reach for her, not with my hands this time, but with my words. I'm hoping to reassure her. Maybe she's just overwhelmed by what is happening between us. We've been on and off for three years and now we will work together for the rest of our careers as Shadows. I could see how that might frighten her.

"You cannot be attached to me. It's a weakness." Her words wash over me and I search her face for clues but find none. No, instead I feel her walls erecting. I may know this song and dance and recognize it for what it is, but still, my temper rises. I hate what she's doing. I hate that she's trying to convince me that caring for someone is a bad thing.

"Then what was this? Why start things up with me again?" I don't know what else to say when I'm pretty sure the next sentence out of her torturous mouth will be an attempt to push me away further.

"We have fun together, we give each other pleasure, that is *natural* and honestly *needed*. But it can't be more than that." She lets out a breath before adding, "It isn't more than that, at least not for me."

And there it is. She is reducing our connection to nothing more than a physical convenience. My chest feels tight and there's definitely salt collecting in my eyes ready to spill out, but I can't let her see me cry. She always does this. Whenever I start to feel comfortable, she puts the walls back up.

Maybe she's right. Maybe caring for someone else will only ever lead to this feeling. To make matters worse, she continues speaking.

"I would never put you above the mission. Don't feel like you should do the same for me. If you can't handle this just being a physical thing, then maybe it would make things easier for us to take some space."

The hurt mixes with anger.

"Okay, Sel. Real nice way to thank the person who saved you today. Next time you're in trouble I'll just *leave you* behind." My words are as sharp as I can manage.

And with that I storm out, giving her the precious *space* she's requested.

❄

I find Romina at her desk in the communal space we share between our bedrooms. We split a room all through our Academy training years, and when it came time to carry out the required three years as tutors, we moved into a two bedroom faculty apartment. It's a modest space made up of bland colors and stone walls, but still, it's our home.

"How's she doing?" Romina asks, without looking up from the various jars of ingredients she appears to be sniffing.

"I — She —It's complicated." How do I even begin to describe the interaction we just had without totally embarrassing myself?

"I meant from the substance," Romina adds. Of course. She wasn't asking about our *relationship*. Get a grip, Darby!

My face must fall because Romina then concludes, "She hurt your feelings again?"

Romina's been there for me when things with Seline have gotten confusing time and time again. It's always the same dance. We grow close then she puts a boundary up, then time passes and I'm drawn to her again thinking this time will be different. It never is.

"We're not supposed to be attached to anyone, let alone another Shadow. I'm an idiot for thinking otherwise. As usual." I fall back on one of our two worn leather chairs. My legs feel like a ton of bricks after the day we've had.

"You're not an idiot. You're a romantic." She stands

from her desk and comes to perch on the twin chair. This is the position we've spent many a night talking through missions in. Sometimes we stay up until sunrise as we walk through all possible outcomes or problems we're facing. I turn to face Romina now. She's the only person who has ever truly stood by my side, willing to chat through anything. "We are shadows. We do not stand out. We do not step out. We do not hook up with other Shadows... even hot silver eyed ones...Why can't I just stay away from her?"

Romina's eyes narrow. She looks down at me in consideration. She's seen me beat myself up over this time and time again. "They take our lives away, Darbs. They strip us of anything that makes us individual, make sure we don't stand out or shine too brightly, and yet against all odds you always find a way to see the best in everyone, to get to know the others for who they really are. You liked Seline for who she really is. Even if it can't go anywhere, it's admirable." Romina exhales a big sigh as she finishes saying this.

While that certainly wasn't what I was expecting her to say, her words have comforted me. I'm so grateful for her.

"I just don't feel like I'll ever fully belong." I can admit this to Romina. I trust her.

"Belong?" The word weighs heavily on her.

"With the Shadows." I release a sigh as the words leave me.

Romina's expression changes slightly but she says nothing. That's when I remember the jars I saw her sniffing.

"What's with the jars?" I nod back towards her desk, noticing the stack of books she's also left piled up besides all the open jars. This breaks her out of her fog. She even perks up a bit.

"Trying to find the other ingredient. The one I couldn't place earlier. It must be what made this batch so strong."

"Any luck?" I ask, sitting up to meet her eyes.

"Not yet, but I'm going to figure it out." She heads back over to her desk, and I have no doubt that she will.

4

There have been days in my lifetime where I felt that perhaps the Goddesses were on my side - The Friend, The Foe, and The Frequency as they are commonly known. The Friend who Protects, The Foe who Confronts and The Frequency who connects us to Magic.

But today was not one of those days.

We'd spent a week traveling on horseback, and the weather had gotten worse each day. Today we were braving a windstorm so strong it stung the skin beneath my leather covered body. The temperature dropped with each mile as we grew closer to Kad, the capital of Kadneria. And if frozen toes and cramped legs weren't enough, Seline rode next to me, the silhouette of her flawless face serving as an everpresent reminder of our conversation the other night.

"I would never put you above the mission. Don't feel like you should do the same for me"

I couldn't bear to face her, not when her words still played over and over in my mind.

"If you can't handle this just being a physical thing, then maybe it would make things easier for us to take some space."

How were we supposed to take space when we were on a mission together?

No, there's no way the Goddesses are still smiling down on me, not when I'm being forced to work alongside my ex in the freezing cold.

"We should stop here and refresh," Romina calls out, her voice competing with both the wind and my memories. She tugs on the reins of her horse, slowing to a stop beneath a group of boulders in the cliffside, their overwhelming mass blocking the wind chill and providing a respite from the cold. We are just one village over from Kad now. Soon we will arrive at the Palace - The Winter Palace, as it is now known.

I hug my thick black cloak tighter around me and follow Romina's lead, directing my horse towards the boulders and casting a glance out over the rough sea down below our path. I hardly recognize this area from my childhood. Once the thriving seaside community of Harville, it is now touched by frost. People can no longer enjoy the rocky beaches or spend hours playing in the sea. Of course, we have read reports of Kadneria growing colder each year, and how it affected the villages, forcing them to rely more and more on Royal Magic to consistently heat their homes and grow their gardens. But to experience it firsthand is different. Luz, where I grew up, is farther south from the capitol. I wonder if the weather has changed this severely in Luz as well. Not that I would dare go back there. Whatever is left of it.

I notice Seline in my peripheral vision as she pulls her horse up next to mine. The two of us haven't directly spoken since our fight. Instead we communicate by way of group announcements about the mission: "This way", "Let's make camp for the night", or my personal favorite, "You're going the wrong way". I feel bad for Romina, having to third wheel this. I also feel bad that my relationship with Seline has now compromised our carefully balanced team dynamic.

Maybe she had a point after all.

Maybe I should just let her go, chalk it up to a formative three-year fling.

I steal a glance as Seline slides off her horse gracefully, landing on the ground before me without a sound. There was no way of knowing, back then, that Seline and I would find ourselves on a three person team being shipped off to the Winter Palace to join the marriage Season and compete for the hand of the Prince while secretly working to protect him from untold danger. For Foe's sake, would I have still kissed her had I known then it would lead to this?

Having fully dismounted, Seline starts to undress and my eyes snag on the delicate bare flesh of her stomach as she strips down.

"W-what are you doing?" I'm stunned.

"We need to wash," Seline says, without looking at me. "We can't arrive like *this*."

"We *have* been on the road for days," Romina adds, using her Solar magic to start a small fire. The warmth immediately works to fend off the frigid air. Glancing down at my own mud soaked leathers, I see she has a point.

I dismount and begin to undress as well. There's no creek nearby but we've done this plenty of times before. I reach for the satchel tied to my horse and unpack a retractable wooden bucket, pulling on a small hidden lever and watching in awe as the carefully constructed contraption springs into its full form. It's not magic, just a piece of fine craftsmanship I picked up on a training mission in the Kingdom of Bouwer, but I've always loved it. Next, I gaze up at the now visible waxing gibbous Moon in the sky, letting its glow wash over me as I reach for the connection to water my Lunar magic allows. The bucket fills instantly and we add our clothes as Romina dips into one of her many velvet pouches. With a quick sniff to confirm it's the one she's looking for, she finds the pouch containing her homemade lavender soap powder we always travel with. A few pinches later and we're washing our clothes in the bucket. I use my magic once more, this time to drain the bucket and extract water from the fabric. Next it's Seline's turn to lend a bit of Stellar magic to blow air into our garments, reinvigorating them. Thankfully, a little goes a long way since Seline has to conserve her power until the Second Star's next visit.

There is a quiet calm as we work together. Romina warms us with her fire while Seline and I wash and dry. It's one of those moments when I feel like it all makes sense. The Goddesses gave us three types of magic so we would have to work together. And here we are, doing just that, living in sync. What more could anyone need?

"This is the meeting spot?" Romina stands before a series of small cobblestone buildings. "We're still in the neighboring village".

It's dark outside, but since I'm at full power thanks to the Moon, I've made light orbs for each of us. Romina uses hers to inspect the path before us.

"You don't believe me? I'm reading it right off the scroll." Seline holds up the missive scroll as evidence. "This is the spot. We're to look for the Royal Crest on the doorway and tap it two times."

I pull my light orb closer and approach one of the buildings, scanning the door for a Royal Crest. Nothing. Moving on to a second building, I stand closer, running my gloved fingers over the jagged stone exterior until I find it. The distinct etchings of The Sun, The Moon and the Second Star connected by a Crown. I tap it two times.

The door opens.

I call back the light orbs I made for Seline and Romina, merging them into my own and and we fall into position. Seline stands at the front with her dagger drawn, I'm in the middle with Romina facing backwards behind me. As a unit we shimmy our way down a long cobblestone hallway until we see light pooling on the ground. I hear the crackling of a fireplace. It's coming from a room just off the hall. Sharing our silent signal, we turn into a windowless room to find two men, smiling, waiting for us before a roaring hearth.

"Welcome, Ladies!" The first man offers us a warm smile. His slicked back bright green hair is unlike anything I've seen before. He's muscular, with a golden brown complexion and eyes in that same shade of bright green. The masculine angles of his square face are adorned with delicate diamond piercings. He wears a long green fur cloak.

"I'm Vesto, I wrote the scroll!" His eyes shine with excitement that feels genuine. The corners of my mouth turn up. His energy is infectious. I glance at Romina and Seline to find them having a similar reaction. Wow, even Seline is smiling. She's stunning when she smiles. I shake my head. Can't think about her *like that* right now.

"Don't worry, I've already *seen* that we will become great friends. I'm the Visionary, you know, the one with the prophecy about the Prince's Eclipse wedding night and all that..." Vesto offers this by way of explanation.

"And who's he?" Seline's eyes dance across the other man's broad chest. He wears deep blue furs and towers over Vesto. His wavy blonde hair is styled back to reveal a handsome face. A single glittering sapphire gemstone protrudes from his left eyebrow. Ethereal sparkles dust the pale skin of his heavy eyelids, and he is struggling to stay awake.

Fashion has certainly changed in the last 15 years since I've been to the Palace. I don't remember the men being dusted in glitter or piercings. And where did they acquire those colorful furs? As ridiculous as their outfits seem to me, I'm also struck by the realization that these two men are undeniably attractive. And they *know* we are Shadows. That's rare. During our training, any field work we did was completely undercover. When duty called for us to flirt and get *acquainted* with someone, it was always an act. Always in character.

I can't remember the last time I encountered someone I found attractive, just as myself, as Darby.

"I'm Cyrus. You can call me Rus," The sleepy blonde offers unhurriedly, as if he's going through the motions, just another day on the job. I suppose for him it might be.

"And what have you seen of our relationship with him? Will we be *great friends* as well?" I turn to the Vesto the Visionary, feeling Romina and Seline's interest piqued.

Vesto blushes, his eyes flit between Seline and I then back to Rus before shrugging.

"With him it's a little more complicated..."

This earns a huff of laughter from Rus, who pulls out a chair and sits down.

"Usually is with me," Rus mumbles.

"Please, come sit! You must be hungry!" Vesto gestures to a table full of plump fruits, fresh bread, and salty dried meats. We move to join them, the wooden legs of our chairs scratching against the stone floor as we find our seats.

"I'll go first so you know it's safe." Vesto picks some dried meat off the platter and downs it in one bite. Rus follows suit, reaching for a basket of bread.

"We are to prepare you for *the Season,* and for *Royal Magic,*" Rus informs us between bites of the flaky roll he carefully selected from the basket. I can't help but notice the strength of his jaw as he chews. The way the bread slides down his throat as he swallows. Seline must notice my gaze because she elbows me, snapping me back to attention. Is that jealousy I see in her eyes?

Maybe I should flirt with this guy, see how *that* makes her feel.

"We have played the part of suitors before," Romina informs them, ever the good student. "Never for a Royal, although we are familiar with the customs." Most women our age would have spent their whole lives preparing for the marriage Season. Instead we were trained in combat, disguise, and seduction and taught to be unfeeling, unbiased extractors of information.

"This Season will be a little different than what you might be familiar with," Vesto chimes in. We look over to him and he takes the cue to go on. "I *saw* the Prince get married during an evening Eclipse, and I also *saw* him super charged with power after bonding to his Link, so for all of this to come to pass, it's imperative that the prince marry his *Link*, his true soul mate, not just a wife."

"So how has that changed the traditional process?" Romina loves history. Nothing excites her more than watching it unfold before her own eyes. It sounds like this season has the makings of a historical event and I feel the weight of realizing we get to be a part of it.

"We've designed everything to help the Prince secure a *true* soul deep connection. For the first time in our kingdom's history we're not just looking to make an arranged marriage for political reasons. It's pretty romantic really..." Vesto trails off before collecting himself. "That's where you come in of course, the Season was open to all eligible ladies, and even though we narrowed it down, there will still be some from *rival* lands in our midst. They will be here in our Court, roaming the Palace. Most importantly, they will have unprecedented access to the Prince. It's a huge risk, but it will be worth it to find his Link."

As I soak in Vesto's words I can't help but wonder: Why on Gaia would the King allow this?

The Royals are incredibly private, it's why we know so little about Royal Magic. However, our intel as Shadows points to the King's paranoia. We know he is distrusting of outsiders. How does he benefit from exposing his own son like this? Even with us joining the suitors to protect him, the Prince will be vulnerable.

"Why take this risk?" Romina asks, clearly sharing my thought process.

"Once the Prince bonds with his Link on his Eclipse wedding night, I've *seen* that the Prince's power will grow immeasurably." Vesto glances at Rus as if he's deciding how much more to share. "That's good for the Kingdom, good for the King, good for everyone! It's worth the risk." Vesto nods his head to underscore this conclusion.

"The *Prince's power*, not the King's," Seline points out.

"The Prince is loyal to the King," Rus clarifies. His jaw clenches and I make a mental note that the Prince very well may be the puppet I accused him of being in Headmaster's office.

"And luckily, we have you three to keep him safe and report any possible threats you observe amongst the other Ladies. We just need to ensure that you all make it through the initial elimination." As Vesto speaks, we all realize something.

"The Prince will not know about us?" I'm the one to ask this time.

The corners of Seline's mouth quirk up. "Oh this will be a fun one!"

She's cruel. Of course Seline would find pleasure in deceiving the Prince.

"But what if he... gets attached to us? That wouldn't be right." Now both Seline and Romina shoot me a warning glance. Rus looks up, meeting my eyes for the first time.

"We've dealt with Shadows before, I thought you were meant to be unbiased?" He runs a hand through his curly blonde hair.

"Why can't the Prince know?" I ask while reaching for a branch of grapes and another piece of cheese so I have something to do with my hands before I continue. "Surely he's aware that there will be increased *protection* given the circumstances."

"The King felt it was better this way. Safer. If the Prince knows you are Shadows he might tell one of the Ladies as he's starting to trust her, and she could betray him, amongst other scenarios the King is fearful of. I've *seen* a world in which the Prince might find out naturally, perhaps it's best we just let it unfold as it's meant to." Vesto sighs. I wonder what it's like to bear the burden of seeing how things *might* turn out but never knowing for sure.

"The Prince is known as quite the ladies' man. Perhaps this is just a ploy to sleep with more women?" Seline asks, and I nearly choke on the grape I had just bitten into. We've all heard about the Prince's exploits, the rumors having even reached the Border Forest where Shadow Academy is located. He is rather notorious actually.

Both men blush as Rus answers Seline. "The Prince favors a *physical* relationship, so the first round will be completely contact free, to ensure he gets to know his suitors properly and not just their um, bodies".

I reach for more grapes from the wooden bowl in the center of the table. And some more cheese. Might as well fill my plate.

"How will that work?" Romina is taking notes now, of course she is.

"You will all meet the Prince for a one on one introduction chat, but he won't be allowed to see or touch you. He'll have to make the first elimination based on your emotional or intellectual connection. I'm rather proud of this idea, I came up with it myself." Vesto is smiling again, I can't help but smile a bit myself.

"Let's change your appearances before we get you going with Royal Magic." Rus is standing from his seat now, stretching as if this conversation bores him. He reaches upwards extending his long arms above his head, his navy blue shirt moves with him, exposing a sliver of his abdominals. "Think about how you'd like to look for the next few months," he says between yawns and I spot what appears to be a massive tattoo on his stomach.

Is that the Second Star?

Seline nudges me back to attention.

"Are you somehow lending us your Shifting ability, or are you an Augmentor?" Romina asks, interest piqued. If he's a Shifter, then he could lend us his Gift by imbuing it into an object, like my mom did with her Stellar power, although that's not common practice in Kadneria. If he's an Augmentor...well I'm not familiar with those. I look at Romina in question.

"If we shift it's like we're wearing a costume. If he's an Augmentor, he can *change* us wholly."

"Permanently?" I ask. The thought terrifies me. It reminds me of how my mother changed her eyes. I wonder if she worked with an Augmentor back then. I don't really remember how she pulled it off, but I know I've never heard of this Eclipse Gift before.

"Until I change you back." Rus is yawning again. Seriously? Doesn't he realize this is important?

"Or another Augmentor," Romina adds casually.

"Good luck finding one. Cyrus Carr is the only Augmentor in Kadneria." Vesto says. I wonder if that's the only reason *Cyrus Carr* is here.

At the sound of *another* yawn I turn to face him.

"Do you need a nap first, *Rus*? Wouldn't want you falling asleep in the middle of *permanently* altering our appearance."

Embarrassment flushes his cheeks, but it seems to have woken him up a bit.

"My apologies. I slept all day so I would have enough strength to do this without Royal Magic, Vesto woke me right before you got here...I'm still adjusting." He rubs his eyes as he says this. I try not to feel bad for snapping at him.

"Royal Magic affects Eclipse Gifts?" Romina is the one to request the clarification, and I'm eager to hear it, this is something we've always wondered about. Vesto chimes in.

"What he means is, all magic performed while using Royal Magic is logged. The King wants us to do this without, as an extra precaution, just in case *someone* were to *check.*"

What. The. Foe.

Royal Magic is logged? All of it? Who has access to that information? Do the people of Kadneria know about this?

"And why is that again?" Romina asks from the end of the table.

"It is for the protection of the people, of course," Vesto offers without hesitation.

"So who wants to go first?" Rus struggles to remove a silver bracelet from his wrist, eventually he succeeds and lays it gently on the table. He then shakes out his shoulders and rolls his head back and forth, getting comfortable.

"The style at court these days is extravagance. The idea is to stand out as much as possible. It's so dreary and gray all the time. We really like to bring color into our lives through our appearance. Have fun with it!"

Seline looks at me over her shoulder. "You hear that? Now they *want us* to stand out." She actually lets out a little laugh and I'm delighted by the sound of it. "I'll go first." Seline steps forward and Rus reaches for her hand.

"Just picture the way you'd like to look and send it through the connection to me."

Seline nods and a second later a swirl of deep blue mist

covers her body. When it clears, there stands a transformed version of the girl whose face I had once memorized. I didn't think it would be possible for her to look any better, but she does. Her short night black hair now falls in long waves down her back, streaked with silver strands of tinsel. Short bangs fall just above her perfectly manicured eyebrows. A permanent cat eye is inked onto her eyelids. Her lips have grown fuller, her body more lean. Her eyes are impossibly more silver, made to match the tinsel of her hair. Her arms are covered in delicate tattoos that I can't quite make out. I want to ask her what each one means. I want to lick them. Maybe I'll find her room later. Maybe she'll let me.

"Oh hello! You look wonderful!" Vesto's facial piercings frame his smile as he gapes at Seline.

"Sel, you look amazing," I echo him, now drooling. I need to get it together. I'm supposed to be giving her *space*. I'm supposed to be moving on.

Romina steps forward next. She takes Rus' hand. With a pulse of his magic, Romina too is transformed. Her black hair grows several inches as it changes to bright blue to match her blue eyes and begins to spiral into perfect curls. I do a double take, actually one of her eyes is light blue while the other is a deep indigo. I've never seen someone with eyes like that before. Her nose looks slightly straightened and a silver nose ring appears at its center. Her lips plump ever so slightly and her flat figure takes on a subtle curve. Her right arm is dipped in rich ink, forming a tree with three owls on it. That's interesting to me, I never knew she was religious. Maybe it's part of the role she wishes to play for this mission.

"For Foe's sake, Mina, you look amazing too!" I know

she will appreciate the compliment, but I really mean it. There's something about seeing Romina this way that feels *right*. As if this is what she was always meant to look like. Maybe if we had grown up differently, she would have.

Seline gives Romina a once over. "You actually look...hot," she says, and Vesto tries to hide his laugh at that. I guess our dynamic amuses him. Good, at least it's fun for someone.

Romina smiles in thanks to Rus and I can tell she feels good. I'm happy for her.

Then it's my turn. I step forward and take Rus' large hand. It's cold. And soft. I'm surprised to find his hands are free of calluses. I guess it's a pretty luxurious life at the Winter Palace. Both Vesto and Rus must hold high positions in Court to be trusted with our true identities. I wonder what their roles are. My train of thought is interrupted by a gentle squeeze from Rus.

"You have to send me your vision. Imagine pushing it towards me." He fights off another yawn.

Right. My vision. How do I wish to look?

Taking inspiration from Romina, I try to imagine what I might have looked like had I not become a Shadow. I think of my Mother and Grandma. They used to wear green velvet bows in their rose gold hair. I think of my childhood body, I was much rounder then. What would that softness have looked like in womanhood?

I solidify my vision and imagine pushing it gently towards Rus. I feel a cool sensation as his deep blue mist curls around me. It feels damp against my skin and smells like eucalyptus. As the mist clears, I look down at my body. My curves are softer, my breasts are fuller, my hair has returned to its true rose gold color. I reach for my ears and find them littered with tiny gold piercings. I always liked the idea of piercings but as Shadows we were never allowed to decorate our bodies in such a way. That reminds me to extend my arm and take in the sight of my new tattoo, a perfect Lunar Eclipse. The source of my power.

Rus is staring straight at me with a fog in his eyes. He must sense my concern, because he finally looks away. "I'm glad you didn't change your eyes. I like them as they are." I realize we're still holding hands as he says this. I slowly step away.

"You look like yourself too, Darbs. You look fantastic." Romina rushes forward to hug me. I can't help but feel that we've just crossed a threshold. We've worn disguises before but they were just temporary. This type of change feels meaningful. This form of expression feels significant. Never before have we been allowed to stand out in this way.

I glance back at Rus, who's seated now, rubbing the sleep from his eyes. I wonder if he has any idea that by using his Gift, he's just given us one.

5

The meeting spot connects to a long underground passageway which winds around the perimeter of Harville before spitting us out directly in Kad, at the side entrance of the Winter Palace. I get my bearings as we emerge from the passageway. Before me stands a massive sculpture of the Royal seal: The Sun, the Moon and the Second Star, connected by a Crown, all carved from thick ice. Glancing over the gates of the Winter Palace, I can make out the sight of manicured cobblestone streets and slate gray houses which blend into the colorless sky. The only hint of color comes from the displays of bustling businesses, their signs pointing toward Kad's Marketplace. I inhale deeply and feel the salt of sea water on the back of my throat before a gust of wind sends small flakes of snow fluttering in the air around me. It's such a curious combination: sea, salt, and snow.

Vesto guides us to the Palace guest quarters where we are each given our own generously-sized room. We haven't seen Rus since he Augmented us. When we left for the Palace, he headed out to secure our horses and relocate them to the stables.

Glancing around my room now, I exhale a big breath. This will be my home for the next few weeks, or however long this takes. First things first, I light the fireplace to warm the room. I don't know if I will ever get used to the cold here.

I drop my bag on the carpeted floor beside an oversized bed. The plush mattress is draped in layers of lavender blankets with delicate silver stitchings. Running my hand over the fabric, I can safely say these are the softest linens I've ever felt. Sleeping here won't be so bad after all. There is a small wooden bedside table with a large wax candle burning on a breathtaking silver candelabra. I take in the finely etched details of the Sun, the Moon and the Second Star. Of course, I could create a light orb whenever needed, but this candle is charming. I'm happy it's here with me.

Moving over to open the doors of a wooden wardrobe, I find it overflowing with bright, colorful clothes and a note from Vesto explaining they have all been fitted into my size. I change into a sheer sparkling olive green matching set that Vesto's note insisted was "casual attire". The top is long-sleeved and fitted with an elegant cowl neck, the pants are loose but well-tailored so that they still flatter my frame. It's an interesting look, I'll have to get used to wearing so much color. And sparkle.

There's a knock on my door. Three quick knocks to be exact. The code Romina and I have used for years.

"Come in, Mina." Her mismatched blue eyes appear a

moment later. Her sheer sparkling butter yellow set is a twin of my olive green one.

"A bit sheer for an ice palace, but you look great," I say as I give her a once over. I wonder if her room looks like mine too.

"It's nice to change things up, let's enjoy it while it lasts," she tells me, as she gets comfortable in my room. She's right. Despite everything feeling so *significant* earlier, I have to remember that this is all just temporary. Just a mission. On the bright side I'll be able to snoop around the Palace as we take our front row seat to watch the Prince find his Link. I try not to think about the fact that we'll have to deceive him in order to stay in the running. I may loath the King and his entire family, but I still have a conscience.

"How are you feeling about Royal Magic?" Her tone is hushed, despite being in my room with the door closed. My fingers fly to my neck and I nervously play with the gold heart-shaped pendant while I consider her question.

"I'm going to shield against it as much as I can. Obviously we have to use Royal Magic to some extent, but I don't trust it fully, not yet." There is more I could say on this, but I choose not to. I've perfected the art of never lying to Romina while also not telling her the full truth. If I could tell her everything, I would. I'd love to actually.

"I will do the same." She probably doesn't even need extra magic to shield like I do. Romina is incredibly powerful. It has always seemed to me that she learned how to harness her magic in ways that I never thought possible. Her devotion to her studies has paid off tremendously. Despite having Solar magic and her Portal

Hopping Eclipse Gift, I've seen Romina bend and wield her magic to do things that Lunars or Solars can as well. It's astonishing really. I'm so impressed by her that I've never addressed it. Clearly she knows that I know, but the implications of what she can do are too massive. It's better left unsaid. What's another unspoken secret to add to our already overflowing trove?

While I may not trust it, I am curious about Royal Magic.

Since each Kingdom has its way of handling magic, we spent our Shadow training learning as much as we could so that we could accept missions all over Gaia. The Academy is located in the Border Forest between Kadneria and Langha, so we received an extensive education on Langhan crystals, but Royal Magic is site specific. Without physically coming here there's only so much we've been able to learn about how it really works. We do know that Royal Magic is a power sharing system in which you give your magic in order to access the magic of others. Instead of being especially powerful with only your Lunar, Solar or Stellar magic, you can have some of everything. In theory, it could create an equal society where all have access to the same amount of power. But what about Eclipse Gifts? They don't seem to be included in Royal Magic. I'd like to learn more about that while I'm here.

Our sources say the King is looking to expand the reach of Royal Magic and offer it to other territories. Maybe one day soon, the Shadow Academy will find itself within range and they'll be able to run experiments.

In the Kingdom of Langha, the people imbue their

magic into crystals. Regardless of what type of magic you are born with, you may challenge another for their crystals to gain more power. It is a system that works for them. Across the sea from Kadneria in the Kingdom of Crichton, all who are born with Stellar magic are seen as weak. They are either ostracized from society or forced into working as Healers. For this reason, most births are timed to avoid the Stellar phases.

Kadneria, Langha and Crichton are just three of the many kingdoms in Gaia, all with their own way of doing things. Ever since the Goddess of The Frequency gifted us with magic, we've been struggling to harness or control more power than we've been given, or to limit the power of others. Sometimes I wonder what the big deal is. Why is no one content with the natural balance the Goddess intended?

Checks and Balances.

The expression haunts my mind, digging up a long forgotten memory of the first time I came to this Palace, many moons ago.

Instantly, my heart hurts for my Grandma. I miss her. I miss our lessons. Lessons that ended when Mother and I became Shadows and she forbade me from ever speaking about our past. There is so much that I never learned, so much of my birthright as a Storyteller that was denied to me because of the King and his Royal Magic–The very same Royal Magic he uses to monitor his own people and for Foe knows what other evil schemes we've yet to uncover!

I think back to that day 15 years ago.

When we got home from the Palace, Mother and Grandma

71

were beside themselves. They explained to me that all of the Storytelling families had been invited to participate in the creation of something called Royal Magic. I didn't know why, but I gleaned that the king needed Storytellers in order to build his new magic system. If we accepted the offer, we were to raise a purple flag above our cottage. If we opposed, a white one.

Mother and I stepped outside to get some air, that's when we saw our neighbors down the hill draw a white flag above their own stone cottage.

"The Royal Guard is coming..." Grandma announced, as she rounded the corner with our overnight bags in hand. Screams sounded from down the hill and we watched in horror as our neighbor's cottage burst into flames. A stone cottage. What type of fire can burn stone? Smoke filled the air but I noticed the silhouette of three owls flying towards our neighbors.

"What's going on?" I cried.

Mother looked down at me, her face unreadable. She turned back to Grandma. "Is it safe for her to hear?"

"We must always tell the truth, Natalie. We have to keep the history and pass it on." Grandma seemed alarmingly calm but my heart was racing.

"As you know darling, the Crown gave us the option to help with Royal Magic. We were told that we had a choice in the matter, but it would appear that we do not." I looked over at the burning house in horror as I realized what she meant: The Crown did this. The King did this.

"We have to go." It was all Mother could say.

"We need to help them!" I reminded her. Clearly, she was in shock and forgetting that our neighbors were in trouble.

"What we need to do is spread the word. If left unchecked

the Crown could take too much power... we can't have another attempt at High King." Grandma's words didn't make sense to me. Why are we still standing here? I felt the need to move, to act, to do something. Mother clearly sensed this because she wrapped her arms around me, holding me in place as she turned to Grandma and for the first time in my life, challenged her logic.

"We need to disappear."

"They will know we fled, they will look for us..." Grandma attempted to reason with Mother.

"They will never find us. We'll follow my plan, I have a Shadow contact..."

"And spend our lives in hiding? No. We have a job to do. People need us, and our work." Yes, exactly, now Grandma was making sense. People need us, we have to help spread the truth of this injustice!

"And what will be left of our work once they burn us?" Mother and Grandma share a look before we notice the Royal Guard's horses appearing in the distance. They begin to circle our neighbor's cottage, checking the damage. I get the feeling they aren't there to put the fire out. Grandma shoves the bags into Mother's hands. "Then take her, go. Disappear."

"You're coming with us." Mother says just as the owls come soaring towards us. Grandma smiles when she sees them.

"I've already made my decision Natalie, follow the Owls, they will get you out of here."

"We can't leave you!" Mother is shouting now, I watch her face crumble. I've never seen her like this. Instantly I find tears in my own eyes.

"You can and you will. This is bigger than us, you two need to survive and to tell this story. Do not let it be forgotten."

Mother pushes me into Grandma and the three of us hold each as Grandma uses her magic to raise a white flag above our cottage. We break the embrace and she urges us along before taking her place in front of our home.

I remember how she stood there proudly. Waiting to greet whatever terror awaited her, as the cottage went up in flames.

Just then, there is another knock on my door, three quick and one slow. I gasp as I return to the present. My room in the Winter Palace. The burning fireplace. Romina is here with me. I am safe.

"Want me to get that?" she asks, smoothing out the creases in her clothes as she stands.

"I've got it!" I cross to the door. I open it to find Rus in the hallway, his midnight blue eyes growing wider at the sight of me as he asks a question I may never be able to answer:

"Ready for Royal Magic?"

6

We collect Seline and find our way to the main part of the Winter Palace. Various members of this colorful Court mill about the Palace corridors in their outlandish fashions. The sound of music can be heard floating through the halls, the smell of roasted meat wafting in from the kitchens. We pass a beautifully detailed portrait of King Godwin and Queen Lydia hanging on the wall and I stop before it, letting Rus, Seline and Romina continue on without me.

The Royals look young, maybe in their early twenties. A dark haired King Godwin stands proudly next to the hauntingly beautiful Queen Lydia. I recognize her from a visit to Kad with Mother and Grandma when I was little. In the painting, the Royals are dressed in formal velvet gowns embroidered with fine details of the Sun, the Moon and the Second Star. Their hands are lovingly clasped between them, hovering over a pair of silver crowns. This must have been their coronation, since, if my memory serves right, they were already married when King Godwin came into power. My eyes scan over to the next painting: another portrait. In this one King Godwin and Queen Lydia look only slightly older, and yet the King's dark hair is now streaked with thick strips of silver. My eyes flash back to the first painting, where the young Royals radiate a hopeful energy, their smiles genuine. In the second painting, there's something different about their energy. The sparkle is gone from the Queen's eyes. She looks bored, or perhaps ambivalent. It is impossible to say. And the King...he looks irritated. They do not touch each other in this portrait. Instead, I notice the delicate detail of the Queen's right hand, perched above her swollen belly. She now wears a ring with a single black pearl. I'm reaching out to graze my fingertips along the finely painted strokes when a cheerful voice startles me into a halt.

"There you are!" Vesto appears at the end of the hallway. "Come with me, the others are waiting." He leads us up to a large sitting room on the third floor. The room is outfitted with plush green velvet sofas and a large roaring fireplace. Through a door in the back, I catch a glimpse of what must be his bedroom, completely decked out in various shades of his signature color.

"Do you ever get used to the cold?" Seline's teeth chatter as she speaks. She's already seated on one of the velvet sofas next to Romina.

"The Royal Magic will keep you warm." Vesto reassures us, and that would certainly explain why no one else appears to be freezing like we are.

Rus is seated to Romina's left on a sofa of his own, his

body so broad he nearly takes up the entire loveseat. He opens a small wooden case that contains three silver bracelets. The thick chains are identical to what we have seen Vesto, Rus and everyone else in Court wearing. He hands one to each of us. The silver is warm to the touch. I notice the delicate etchings of the Royal seal. The Sun, The Moon and the Second Star connect by a crown.

"The Prince knows his suitors will be coming from all over and that some of you are new to Royal Magic, so you don't need to hide that from him. Maybe it will even make for a nice topic of conversation!" Vesto is excited about that.

"So we just put the bracelet on? That's it?" Seline is inspecting hers as if it's her next meal. Vesto starts giggling uncontrollably.

"What's so funny?" Seline turns on Vesto.

"Oh nothing I just had a glimpse of something that you might do."

I watch as Seline holds the bracelet up to her mouth, biting it gently. "Tastes like smoke."

Smoke? I raise the bracelet to my own lips and lick it. The all too familiar taste of smoke creeps onto my tongue. Why does it taste like the smoke we found in the cellar that day? Why does the taste bring me back to that afternoon 15 years ago? Are these events all connected? I fight the urge to fall back into my memory. Not here. Not right now. I need to stay grounded. I breathe in deeply, holding the air in my lungs before exhaling in a long push. That's better. I glance around the room, reminding myself where I am.

"Well you aren't supposed to eat it! You wear it."

Vesto chuckles as if this is amusing. He's constantly amused, isn't he?

"You can really see the future?" Seline eyes Vesto.

"I can see many possible futures. Or like, flashes of them, it's a bit finicky. I'm working on it. Sometimes my visions are clear. Sometimes they are not."

That's when Seline strides up to Vesto and swiftly moves to punch him in the face, he catches her fist at the last second, dodging the blow. He giggles as she meets his gaze.

"Interesting." Seline retreats and Vesto turns to Romina, trying to compose himself. "Lucky guess that time." He winks at us. I'm grateful this interaction has saved me from another panic attack over the memory of smoke. Without ceremony, Seline puts on her bracelet and exhales deeply.

"You'll have to give over your magic in order to receive it, it's a power share," Rus instructs her. Seline nods and closes her eyes. A heartbeat later she opens them, Romina and I study her for any sign of distress but she shows none. All clear. Romina and I exchange a glance and in unison, we put on our bracelets.

I'm immediately hit with a vast sucking sensation. Rus said we'd have to give our magic, but this feels like it's being taken from me. As if I'm falling into a vacuum. That's when I remember my mother's shield. My hands fly to my neck where the gold medallion lays tucked beneath my shirt. I rub the medallion to unlock its magic, a wave of energy slowly beginning to prickle my skin. Soon the vacuum's power decreases. I imagine honing the energy into a tiny channel. As big as a straw. I begin to feed it a tiny drop of my magic. And another. I watch as my power is slurped away, hungrily. I feed it a couple more drops. Then, there's a buzzing sensation. The next thing I know the straw reverses direction and sure enough, power begins to flow *back* to me. It's unfamiliar magic that I've never tasted before. It feels incredible and I've only taken a little bit, I can't imagine what it would feel like to fully bask in this.

No wonder people love Royal Magic.

I glance over at Romina and can tell she's having a similar experience. My mind is racing with the implications of this when suddenly, I realize I'm sweating, and my stomach feels like it's dropping straight out of my body. I don't need to look in a mirror to know the color has left my face. The last thing I see is Romina and Seline exchanging a frantic look before it all goes dark.

7

"Go away! You're not supposed to see any of them before the first round!" I hear Vesto's voice, he sounds close by.

"So I'll keep my eyes closed! I ran over here as soon as I could–" There's another voice, a bit more muffled.

"Just get out of here, she's going to be fine".

My eyes flutter open and I turn towards the sounds I'm hearing. Vesto is by a door, cramming his muscular body to block someone from entering. My mind quickly searches for clues, the last thing I remember was putting on the Royal Magic bracelet and that Seline said the bracelet tasted like smoke. I remember pressing the cool silver to my own tongue. The taste was so similar to the smoke that filled the air when my neighbor's home went up in flames. That's got to be evidence that the King is up to something terrible, right?

Not that I could tell anyone this without giving my history away.

"She's one of my suitors...I need to make sure she's

okay." The mystery man's voice sounds pained. It has an effect on Vesto, who sighs before looking back at me.

"Oh look, you're up!" His eyes sparkle as he takes in the sight of me.

"She's awake?" The voice that I can only assume belongs to Prince Nolan Raines sounds hopeful. Vesto gestures that he needs a moment before gently closing the door. He approaches me, sitting on the bedside. It's then that I realize I'm in bed. Who's bed? I look around at the all green room and assume it must be Vesto's. That would make sense considering that the last thing I remember is being in his study. The blankets smell vaguely of spearmint.

"You had a bad reaction to the Royal Magic, it happens sometimes, we don't really know why. I'm sorry about that. How are you feeling?" He hands me a glass of water that I take down eagerly.

"Mina and Sel?" It's the first thing I can think to ask.

"Both are fine! They were here for a while watching over you but I sent them to get some dinner." He looks over at the door. "Kind of sweet that he wants to check on you, isn't it?" Yes. It *is* sweet that he wants to check on me.

But, it doesn't sit well knowing that the Prince is loyal to the King. The King who destroyed the Storytellers. Destroyed my family. The King who must be using Royal Magic for his own agenda. Therefore, we cannot trust the Prince, no matter how sweet he seems. It's highly likely he's only interested in finding his Link because it is foreseen that it will give him *more power*. The King craves Power. So must the Prince. He was probably raised to blindly follow in his father's footsteps. Actually, I have no way of knowing this. Maybe he's fully aware of his father's schemes. Maybe he has chosen to go along with it and he isn't following *blindly* at all.

But we *are* here to protect him. We need the Prince to trust *us:* so we can stick around the castle and complete the mission, so I can have this unprecedented access to the Winter Palace and the King, so that I can finally discover the truth and *help people.*

Fine. Let him check on me. It will give me an advantage. He will grow warm to me ahead of the Season officially starting. I can get extra information and ensure my place in the first round.

"Let him in," I tell Vesto. My head feels heavy but I try to make myself comfortable. Vesto stands and makes his way back to the door. His feet gently padding across a light pink carpet. It compliments all the green but I'm still surprised to see a different color.

"No peeking." Vesto steps aside to let the Prince in then thinks better of it. "Actually, I know you too well. I'm not giving you the option, your sight will be shielded for an hour." Vesto waves his hands and the Prince exclaims from the other side of the doorway.

"For Foe's sake Vest, I wouldn't have peeked."

Vesto just smiles "You would have, plus now, I can leave you unsupervised, oh and no touching!" Vesto turns back to wink at me before disappearing into the study.

"You think I'm trying to seduce her? I just want to make sure she's okay." His voice sounds sincere, gentle even. "May I enter?" he calls into the doorway.

"You may."

His energy enters the room before he does. I find I'm eager to get a good look at him, but nothing could prepare me for the man that appears before me, his tall frame hunching over to fit through, his dark brown hair falling gently over the most chiseled jawline I've ever seen. He looks sculpted from stone. Everything about him is solid. Steady. Stable. He looks right towards my voice with molten brown eyes that are currently unseeing, I can tell by the way they appear magically glazed over. He takes a small step forward, unsure of what he might find in front of him. I'm glad he can't see me because the sight of him has rendered me speechless and I'm pretty sure my mouth is hanging open. A thick silence spreads between us.

"Would you mind...er, if you could keep speaking I can locate you better... As you may be able to tell, I cannot see." A small dimple forms in his cheek and I swear I've seen that self-conscious smile before. He's wearing loose, dark brown trousers, a thick cream colored linen shirt and a cobalt blue sweater tied across his shoulders. The outfit strikes me as casual, and yet the fine fabrics and perfect tailoring speak of wealth and intention. He must care about his appearance. Even on an off day, Prince Nolan Raines has chosen his clothing carefully.

I need to say something. Anything.

If I sit here in complete silence he will surely eliminate me before the first round and I'll be sent back to the Shadow Academy having failed my first real mission. I'll have let down Romina and Seline. I'll have disappointed Mother. And worse, I'll be no closer to helping expose the

King or finding out what happened to the Storytellers all those years ago...

"Are you still here?" the Prince asks.

I swallow once, finally remembering how to speak.

"Have you been in Vesto's rooms before?" I sit up fully now.

"For poker night, and when we've had one too many and I can't make it all the way home." He takes another step forward, placing his hand against the bookshelf to guide himself towards me. "Foe, I don't know why I just told you that. My rooms are one floor above. What will you think of me?"

"No judgments here. I enjoy a good drink myself. Besides, stairs can be tricky." This earns a smile from him so I continue, still trying to place him. "Since you've been here before, you must remember where his bed is, that's where I'm sitting now. It's very... green." I run my hand up and down the soft linens.

"Vesto's favorite color." He pauses before the bed, his hand reaching for something. "Does he still have a chair somewhere around here?" Okay, so, he's charming. No big deal. That doesn't expunge him from aiding his father in corruption and abusing their Royal power. I have to stay focused.

"He does," I say as the Prince finds the chair and rests his hand atop the worn leather backrest. And yet he does not sit. I look up at him. Scanning his body for clues. I watch as he drums his fingers on the back of the chair as if he's searching for something to do with his hands. I'm at a loss for words again so I sit there quietly, observing his fingers as they patter against the wood. Then, the drumming stops and he begins to fuss with the sleeves of his shirt, rolling them up to reveal his naturally tan arms. That's when I notice the scar. It's hidden amongst three thick black tattooed rings that wrap around his strong forearm, but I recognize that scar as the burn mark it once was. It is stacked just above his Royal Magic bracelet. The scar has grown with him but this *is* him. The little boy from the Palace that day. He wasn't from a wealthy Storytelling family after all. He was the Prince. He is the Prince. And that means... Prince Nolan Raines is a Dreamseer? Why is that not common knowledge?

Suddenly I'm 10 years old again.

"I don't usually give people presents".

"Oh. Why not?"

"Usually people just give me presents".

"Lucky you! Although I do prefer giving presents to receiving them, but receiving them is nice too".

"Maybe my mother would throw me a party, but my father certainly wouldn't. Maybe I shouldn't even tell them".

"Well that's up to you, but it's nothing to be ashamed of, you've gotten a wonderful Eclipse gift."

"If I decide not to tell them, would you keep my secret?"

I look back at the boy in front of me. He's no longer a boy. He is very much a man now. I never told anyone but did *he* truly keep his Eclipse Gift a secret all these years? Or is this just something to do with the King's paranoia?

I could understand why the King would want to keep his son's rare Gift from the general public. Even with our intel as Shadows, there has been much we do not know about the Kadnerian Royals. I wonder who else knows that Prince Nolan Raines is a Dreamseer. I can't be the only one. Immediately, I check that my mental shields are tight in place. Of course they are, we do it by second nature now, part of basic Shadow training.

Finally, he speaks again. "Better if I keep my distance, wouldn't want to break any rules." Despite saying this, he's still standing in front of me, holding onto the chair once more.

I find myself looking at him with new eyes. I can't help but feel warm towards him. Now all I see is that sweet little boy who was scared of his own gift. Who's father wouldn't throw him a party. That detail makes more sense now. Is it possible that he doesn't support the King? Maybe it's more nuanced than I imagined?

I know what a complicated relationship with your only parent can feel like.

"I don't mind, come sit by me." I pat the bed beside me. Without hesitation, he moves towards the bed and takes the spot beside me, his warmth licking my skin. I lean in to get a closer look at his tattoo. It doesn't do much to mask his scar. I wonder if it was supposed to. Maybe it was meant to decorate the blistered part of his flesh and make it more intentional looking. My eyes flick up to his jaw line where it floats above me. Even seated, he's got to be a head taller than me. I note the sharp lines of his face. His skin is smooth and uninterrupted by piercings, unlike Vesto and Rus. Oh wait, is that a tiny gold hoop in his other ear? Yes, yes it is.

"How are you feeling? I'm so sorry about this, I heard you had a bad reaction." He doesn't know where to look, it's cute watching him squirm a bit.

"I'm starting to feel better now," I say.

"You're here early and using Royal Magic for the first time, which must mean that you're not local. Where *are* you from?"

We have practiced a story to tell but I make a last second decision to change it slightly. Something about seeing this ghost from my past makes me want to be as honest as possible.

"I grew up in a small seaside village nearby actually, my parents were touring musicians and we moved to the Border Forest when I was little. My mother always dreamed I would return here to find a partner and start my own family. When this opportunity arrived, I was glad to take it".

"You lived nearby for a time! How close?" I can *feel* the excitement in his voice.

"Very close! In Harville!" Well Luz actually, but close enough, if I told him Luz it would be too risky, Luz was known for its Storytelling community. I wonder who lives there now.

"Musicians for parents, that must have been wonderful. Are they still?" Music is highly respected in Kadneria. A form of magic that is uniquely Human. No Goddesses involved. I figured he'd like this detail and I'm glad this is the question he's chosen instead of the question I feared he'd ask. A question more along the lines of if we've met before.

"My mother is. I lost my father." Not fully a lie, although can you truly lose something you never had to begin with?

"I'm sorry. I know how you feel. I lost my mother when I was 11." Of course I know this. Bells rang out the day Queen Lydia died. But it's different to hear him say it.

"And I am sorry too, for your loss." Before I realize what I've done, I find my hand on his. "Oh!" I quickly move to pull my hand away but the Prince holds on to it. A warm smile spreads on his perfectly symmetrical face and once again, I must admit I'm happy that I've put it there.

"And *he* was worried I'd be the one to touch *you*." The Prince's smile grows impossibly wider as he says this. His fingers gently lace into mine to solidify our connection. His hands are warm. Rough with calluses. I suppose that makes sense as I know the Prince trains with the Royal Guard. It's a stark contrast to Rus' cold smooth palms. I wonder if they are friends, like him and Vesto clearly are. Or "Vest" as he called him. The Prince begins to chuckle.

"I forgot to ask your name, Foe, I'm really blowing this aren't I?"

"You've asked more important questions." I give his hand a gentle squeeze.

"Well I'm Nolan."

"Prince Nolan Raines," I correct him.

"Call me Nolan, please." He squeezes my hand in return. His unseeing eyes flick in my direction, then turn away.

"I'm Darby, some call me Bee or Darbs or..."

"Darby" he says back to me, as if trying my name in his mouth. "Darby, is perfect. I'd prefer to call you by your true name."

I feel myself blushing and I am glad he cannot see me.

I wonder what he makes of this situation. I decide to ask him.

"How are *you* feeling?" The question seems to surprise him.

"How am I feeling? About what? I've had no traumatic events today, not yet at least".

"About the Season starting. About finding your... Link." The dimple is back. It is rather endearing.

"I'm feeling excited. Overwhelmed? But I also feel ready. What about you?" He's so candid. It's refreshing. In my previous experience with Royals or Nobility, I've found them to be rather performative, as if they would rather put on a show instead of exposing any signs of weakness. While masking in such a way is perhaps more strategic, Prince Nolan Ra—*Nolan*, does not appear to be putting on a show for me. At least not right now. I aim to match his cadence.

"Nervous. Overwhelmed. Excited." We sit in a comfortable silence. Our hands still joined. "How will you know that you've found *her*? How do you know what to look for?"

"I suppose *we* will both know. It's different from just seeking a wife, which is wonderful of course, but more about obligation, isn't it? A marriage is a partnership that you enter into with a sense of duty and commitment..."

"Will you not marry your Link?"

"I intend to. But they say that finding your Link is so much more than just a commitment. It's finding your other half. Your soul's mate. One person who undeniably is a part of you as you are a part of them. They say you'll never feel lonely again once you are Linked."

I think of the little boy running through the hallway on his own.

"Do you feel lonely?" I ask the man seated beside me.

I think of my own mother, turning her back to end our last conversation.

"Sometimes," he replies.

I think of the nights I've spent crying myself to sleep.

"I do too, sometimes." My admission hangs in the air as he shifts ever so slightly to face me. Realizing I've been too vulnerable I quickly try to lighten the mood. "And don't they say that being intimate once you are Linked is unlike anything else?"

Nolan blushes. The tiniest bit of color is splashed across his cheeks. "They do."

"Plus finding your Link is known to amplify power." As I add this, his hand twitches in mine.

"Well I suppose *that's* how we will know that we've truly found each other. If it's not obvious already." There's something about the way he says "we", sitting here on the bed next to me, holding my hand, that takes my breath away. Yes, it would appear I am no longer breathing.

But that's ridiculous. I'm not his Link. I'm not even one of his true suitors. I'm here on a mission. And I don't trust him.

The moment is broken by a loud bark and before I realize what's happening, a massive ball of coffee-colored fur is jumping up onto the bed, its dense body nearly knocking me over.

"Buddy! You're not supposed to be over here!" Nolan shouts, as he reaches for the velvet monster I can now see is a bearhound, trying to get him off me. I can't help but giggle to myself as *Buddy's* slimy pink tongue paints a coat of slobber on my face.

"Oh hello there, who is this?" I've never seen a bearhound up close before. His tiny rounded ears and massive head are adorable. His head is as big as my entire torso.

"I'm so sorry, is he attacking you? Please tell me he's not attacking you."

"He is, but I'm enjoying it."

"Buddy! That's enough. Leave Darby alone." Nolan finally succeeds in pulling the bearhound off me, and I watch in pure delight as the furry creature curls up in Nolan's lap. He hardly fits.

"This is Buddy. When I turned 16 my father forced me along on one of his hunting trips. At first I refused, but he told me I'd be King one day, and that Kings went hunting. That it was something I would need to do, plain and simple." Nolan's face falls as he hugs Buddy tighter to his chest, the bearhound's paws curling up as he gets even more comfortable. "We took down two" Nolan nods towards Buddy as if to imply *bearhounds* "and when I went to collect their bodies I saw this little cub all alone, hiding behind a tree. We had killed his parents. *I* had let that happen, and now he was all alone in the world." He hugs Buddy tighter before continuing on. "I couldn't allow it. He came home with me and has been by my side ever since. I vowed to never hunt again."

For Foe's sake, it's getting hard to remember why I don't trust this guy. A small tear has welled in my eye and I can't believe how much the story moved me. I inhale deeply and exhale with a big sigh.

"Darby, are you alright?".

"Yes, but perhaps I should rest a bit more".

"Of course." He takes my hand to his lips and gently presses a kiss on it. It tingles. "It was lovely to meet you Darby, I would say I look forward to seeing you again soon but I am told it will be a short while before I lay my eyes on you." Buddy hops off Nolan's lap as he comes to stand. "Instead I'll say I look forward to *talking* more soon. How's that?"

With one more flash of his dimple, he nods goodbye before swiftly exiting the room with the bearhound in tow. My hand instantly feels cold from the absence of his.

8

"Tell us about the Prince! What do we need to know before tomorrow?" Romina leans over her glass of wine in our cozy corner booth at The Den, the Palace's local tavern that Vesto insisted we frequent in order to be well liked at Court. Not bad for gathering information either. The dimly lit watering hole is packed to the brim with loose-lipped Kadnerian elite, enjoying an adult beverage after a long day of maneuvering Court politics. We've spent the last couple days getting acclimated to life at Court and studying up on the other suitors. Vesto and Rus have kept us so busy that we've hardly had time to catch up on my encounter with Nolan. The Season officially kicks off tomorrow with the contactless "blind dates". After the first elimination, the suitors will be revealed at a ball. The aptly named Grand Reveal Ball.

"And how does he look?" Seline adds. "Just trying to figure out how hard I'll have to try to be attracted to him."

She fluffs her tinsel streaked waves of jet black hair as she says this.

"Are you ever attracted to men?" Romina leans across the wine stained wooden table. I glance around the crowded tavern pretending not to care for her answer. A band has just started playing a cheerful fiddle tune.

"Not in a romantic way, but that doesn't mean I can't have fun with them physically. Plus you know I never get attached to anyone." I avoid her cat eyes. That shot was obviously directed at me and Seline has excellent aim.

"Darbs, report! We need this intel." Romina is right, this is not a gossip session, it's actually part of our mission. I dig through my memory of that afternoon on Vesto's spearmint linens. I can almost feel a phantom hand in mine.

"He's attractive. Very tall. He's also sort of unpolished? But it's charming. Oh, and Nolan has a dimple." I'm not sure why I mentioned his dimple.

"Oh he's *Nolan* now, is he?" Seline's comment causes my cheeks to heat.

"What else?" Romina urges me to go on.

"*Prince Nolan* asked a lot of questions, as if he wanted to get to know me genuinely. He's a bit of a romantic when it comes to finding his Link but it's hard to say if that's his true motive. Could just be the power boost he is after." I sit back now, crossing my arms over the knitted bodice of the bright pink sweater dress I found in the wardrobe this morning.

"Could be both," Romina offers, and maybe she's right. I guess time will tell.

"Shouldn't be too hard to get in his good graces."

Seline finishes her own drink then. "Anyone care for another?" We nod and she stands to fetch our next round.

"It sounds like you like him." Romina has a sparkle in her eyes. She's clearly had too much wine.

"I just met him?" I pour her a glass of water, better she's not hungover tomorrow.

"Oh come on, you're at least attracted to him. And since we have to "court" him anyway, it's more fun if you actually like him!" She finds her water and takes it down in a gulp.

"Is it more fun if *I* like him? What if you like him too, what if Seline does? It's weird we're all going to be *courting* the same guy."

"Courting the same Prince!" Romina adds before leaning back, a look of consideration washing over her. "I'm going to play the friend card. I figure it's my best bet. He'll keep me around until the end as a confidant who can help him figure out how the other Ladies are feeling."

That's a good strategy. Maybe I should do the same, but it's unlikely he'd keep both of us around for that reason. Instead, I *could* just pretend to like him. For the sake of the mission.

"But you're *my* confidant." I poke at her side.

"I am, and that's why I think *you* like him. Your voice got funny when you called him *Nolan*, and you keep bringing him up." She points this out like it's the most obvious thing in the world, but is she right?

Foe. Maybe I've developed a crush. He's handsome and charming and I'm here to court him, technically. But, I can't have a *crush* on Prince Nolan Raines... that would be pointless.

"You asked about him!" I say, my voice rising.

There's no future where anything could actually happen between us. I am a Shadow, blood sworn to never form attachments. He's destined to be eternally *attached* to his Link. Not to mention the fact that he's next in line for the throne of an entire Kingdom. And what if he proves to be just as corrupt as his father? What if he's working with the King? No.

"You've had too much wine," I tell her.

"I've not had nearly enough, this is our last night of freedom before the Season starts."

"I don't *like* him. I don't even trust him. How could we?" Romina knows my distrust of the Kadnerian Royals and Royal magic, even if we can't openly talk about it. At the reminder of this her face turns serious, she leans in to me and lowers her voice as she asks:

"Did you shield?"

"I did, you?" I lower my voice to match hers.

"Of course, I plan to study it. We've never had access to Royal Magic before, I can't imagine all that we'll learn..." We notice Vesto and Rus approaching and quickly I give her the signal to change the subject. "At least I'm finally warm again!" she adds, raising her voice. We both start to laugh a bit too loudly as they arrive at our table with drinks in hand and elegant swords strapped around their shoulders.

"Ladies! We saw Seline and she said to give you these." Vesto places the glasses of wine down in front of us. "She scares me," he adds with a shudder.

"Is she not returning?" I scan the room for Seline but she is nowhere to be found.

"Said something about wanting to rest before everything starts up tomorrow," Rus supplies.

"A pretty blonde may have been involved," Vesto adds, blushing.

A pretty blonde huh? I guess that didn't take her long. Surprisingly, the knowledge that Seline is moving on doesn't sting as much as I thought it would. Instead my mind flashes to the memory of a certain pair of molten chocolate eyes. The way they twinkled in amusement as we sat holding hands... Oh no. I'm going to need to stop this crush from blossoming into anything more substantial. I need to turn my attention elsewhere.

"Mind if we join?" Vesto asks from where he's still standing before our table. Romina nods in approval, then he and Rus slide into the booth, the worn leather seat cushions crunching below their weight. Vesto grabs what would have been Seline's drink and downs it.

"None for you?" Romina asks Rus.

"Work tomorrow," he shrugs his broad shoulders.

"And what is it that you do exactly?" Romina's blue hair is tied up in twin buns atop her head. A few perfect curls hang loosely in front of her glitter dusted face. Her lips are tinted a deep plum color, which is perfectly accentuated by the cool undertone of her rich complexion. I've rarely seen her with makeup on and yet, it's hard to remember a time when she didn't look like this, it's just so *her*.

"With your deduction skills I'm surprised you don't already know." He phrases that like a challenge and we love a challenge. Romina and I each take one of Rus' hands in our own. I notice he's painted his nails dark blue since the last time we saw him.

"We always start with the hands," I offer.

"Why is that?" Vesto asks, curiously.

"No calluses. That eliminates manual labor. And combat." I turn his hand to show Vesto. Feeling the familiar coolness of Rus' palm. "Is the sword for show?" I ask, glancing over at the gemstone hilt of his weapon.

"Jewelry, essentially," Rus offers, and Vesto smirks.

"Maybe you're an academic." Romina guesses, searching Rus' face for a reaction.

"No he's far too handsome to be locked away in the archives." I notice how Rus' expression changes with the compliment. He can't be that surprised, he must realize he is attractive. I'm sure everyone at Court does too. "Maybe you use your body but in a different way. Brothel?"

"Brothel!?" Vesto sounds scandalized, and as usual, amused.

"Royal Brothel," I correct. Rus must sense that I'm teasing him.

"Only the finest," he adds. Good sport.

"You work together, no?" Romina questions them. They nod in confirmation. "You carry weapons but don't use them, and you see to matters involving the Prince. You were trusted with *delicate* information... You must be members of the Prince's Council," she concludes. "Is that a full time job?"

"More than full time!" Vesto beams. "But we enjoy it, don't we, Russy?".

"Most of the time." For every bit that Vesto exudes joy, Rus has a heaviness to him. They make quite the pair.

"So if you have the same job, why is he drinking if you're not?" Romina clinks her glass with Vesto as she says this.

"Rus can't handle his liquor like I can," Vesto is quick to supply. Rus looks at him in apparent thanks. It's a curious interaction that I'd dwell on if not for Romina slapping her hands down on the table and declaring it time for another round. Both her and Vesto rise to fetch us more wine. I get the feeling they will make for dangerous drinking companions as the night goes on. Left alone with Rus at the table, I decide to make small talk.

"No shame in not drinking."

"I know." He fidgets with the fabric of his indigo sweater. As usual he's dressed in shades of blue.

"And you don't mind if we do?"

"Be my guest." He gestures towards the nearly empty glass in front of me. "How are you feeling, by the way?"

"I'm alright, thanks."

"Royal Magic can be a little...overwhelming at first." He looks up at me again and I have to blink to focus on his stunning sea blue eyes. Wow. He really is attractive.

Maybe he could help me take my mind off Prince Nolan before this crush grows any bigger...

"Has anyone ever told you that you are distractingly handsome?" Okay maybe it's me who has had too much wine. Have I totally forgotten how to flirt?

"Thank you?" Of course he has no idea how to react to what I've just said. How could anyone? To make matters worse, I hear myself continue speaking.

"You didn't...did you do this on purpose?"

"Do what on purpose?" The corners of his mouth turn down in the slightest of frowns.

"Did you change your own appearance? I can imagine how useful it would be to look the way you do. It disarms people really, it's a weapon of its own." He shifts in his seat then.

"It's exceptionally hard to Augment yourself. Maybe one day I'll be strong enough, but not quite there yet." He's looking at me now with something like concern and yup, I'm totally blowing this.

"More naps, maybe." Okay bad plan. I shouldn't try to use him to take my mind off *Prince Nolan.*

I wish Seline hadn't left already.

Not that I should be getting involved with Seline again.

"I'm sorry about that," Rus mumbles.

"About what?" I can't imagine what he might apologize for.

"You thought I was sleeping on the job the other day, I should have explained myself sooner." He actually looks sincere as he says this.

"Oh no, that was fine. You were perfect." Now he averts my gaze. It's clear that he's uncomfortable with flattery. So why do I keep complimenting him?

When he finally looks back at me his expression has softened. There really is something alluring about him. Maybe I just feel a special sort of way towards him because of the gift he gave us? The freedom of choosing our own appearances, of expressing ourselves in a way we never have before. That must be it.

Vesto and Romina return with more wine. It's clear from their laughter that their friendship has been solidified by their journey to the bar and back to our table.

We spend the rest of the night sharing stories. Vesto and Rus both know who we are, and what we are meant to be doing here, and yet they want to hang out with us anyway. It's not lost on me that they must like us for *us*. Maybe we can all truly be friends. Real friends. So long as none of us do something to mess it up.

9

"Just one more round!" Romina cries out with residual tears of laughter in her eyes from the story Vesto just shared about a vision he once interpreted all wrong.

"I'll stay with you! I've got no one waiting for me and nowhere else to be," Vesto is happy to offer.

"You two enjoy, I'm ready for bed. Big day tomorrow," I move to slide out of the booth.

"I'll walk you back." Rus stands as well.

We walk in silence down a cobblestone path. The cold night air makes our breath visible. That's when I notice it. The full Moon. Foe. I must have lost track of it over the past few days, no wonder my hormones have been so... active. No wonder everyone has seemed so *attractive*.

"With Royal Magic, do people still feel the effects?" I glance up at the shining white orb in the endless night sky and Rus follows my eyeline, catching my meaning.

"I wouldn't know, I'm not a Lunar, plus that's not

really a thing here." His sharp profile is illuminated by moonlight as he walks beside me.

"What do you mean?" I'm eager to learn more.

"Since everyone has all the magic types, most people don't share what they were born with, it's not really part of our culture here at Court." That's interesting to me, maybe people even hide the tells? Find any Lunar at the Academy on a full Moon and you'd probably know right away. While everyone experiences a general loss of inhibition during an Eclipse, all of the Lunars are overwhelmed by lust when it comes to the full Moon.

Maybe Royal Magic tones this down? Otherwise I'm pretty sure the people at Court would have noticed. No, I'm certain they would. If keeping your magic type hidden is normal, I wonder if hiding your Eclipse Gift is too. My mind briefly dips to Prince Nolan and his seemingly absent gift.

"What about Eclipse gifts? Do people talk about those?" I ask to steer my thoughts away from the Prince.

"That is personal really, everyone is different. I don't mind people knowing about mine, so that I can be helpful." Rus offers this with a gentle shrug of his shoulders. I'm starting to notice how he's always turned inwards, his posture slumped over despite his impressive height.

"*Cyrus Carr is the only Augmentor in Kadneria.*" Vesto told us this earlier. It's a powerful Gift and one he can use for many different reasons.

"Helpful to who?" I wonder out loud.

"People who need...help." He nods towards me. Of course, I needed his help just days ago. But I suspect there's more to this. Who else is he helping? The idea of him helping *anyone* is incredibly exciting to me. A spark of joy shoots through me and I'm speaking before I even realize it.

"Rus! Are you secretly a good guy!?" I've practically yelled this for all to hear. I immediately want to take back what I've said. The implications are wild.

ARE YOU SECRETLY A GOOD GUY!? Why did I say that? That means I had thought of him as a bad guy...that I had an opinion of him at all... oh Foe. Foe. Foe. I'm losing my touch. It's like ever since we got here, my Shadow training is going straight down the drain. Not that I was ever as good of a Shadow as Romina or Seline, but still.

"No Darby. I'm not a good guy." His mask of darkness remains in place and that heaviness I felt earlier has returned. Alright then. I guess, we're in the clear? Maybe he didn't even register how deeply inappropriate my last comment was.

"Seems like you enjoy helping people, that's all," I say, but he's too lost in own mind to process my words. There must be something troubling him. "I enjoy it too," I add.

"Despite the fact that you are meant to be unbiased." He's bringing this up again.

"Despite that, yes." I hug a rose-colored fur around my body, finding comfort in the warmth. Even with the sweater dress on, I've been cold all evening. I might need to use a little more Royal Magic so I can keep myself heated at all times, like everyone else does. In the distance I can still hear a mix of laughter and fiddle tunes coming from the noisy tavern, but one glance around tells me we are alone on the path back to the Palace's guest quarters. We continue to walk in silence as we head up the path to the regal apartment building which resembles the Palace, only smaller.

Prince Nolan lives in the Palace, somewhere. He said his rooms were right above Vesto's. I wonder where he is tonight. I wonder what would happen if I ran into him...

No. Don't think about him.

A couple of Royal Guards dip their heads to Rus as we enter the main gate and approach the doors to the apartment building.

"Do you live here too?" I ask, desperate to end this silence and with it, my thoughts of the Prince.

"No, I have my own place closer to the water." He nods toward the beach.

"Oh, that's nice."

"It is."

Another beat of silence passes between us as we come to a stop.

"Thanks for walking me, I hope it wasn't out of your way." We remain paused by the entranceway, the guards no longer in our line of sight. I have to get away from this Moon, especially considering how much wine I had. My brain feels like mush. All I can think about is what it would be like to seek out the Prince and take his hand in mine again. He was so *warm*. And he smelled so *good*. I wonder what he would feel like. Taste like.

"What are the effects?" asks the blue eyed man before me, his voice a bit deeper than before.

"What do you mean?" I manage to respond.

"The Moon. What does it do to you?" He's curious, I can see it in his eyes. I wonder how I look to him right now, standing here pining for the Prince like this. I must look ridiculous. I blame the Moon.

"It heightens my senses. It makes my power stronger. Which is great when I need to use a lot of power." I notice the dryness of my mouth and I swallow to try and bring some moisture back. I don't know why I'm finding this whole situation so embarrassing, it's perfectly natural, and yet, I'm barely able to get the words out. "But if I'm *not* making use of that power boost, the Moon super-charges my...um... desire."

"So, you're horny?" The corners of his mouth actually turn upwards in his version of a smile.

"Horny!?" My cheeks grow hot.

"The Moon makes you horny." He provides this as a statement. Not a question.

"That is such an uncivilized way to put it." I need to get inside *now*. I turn to leave.He stops me by placing one of his large hands on my shoulder.

"I'm not judging you... there's no shame in it." His tone is sincere but I do feel shame. It's creeping up my spine in hot prickles that warm me more than any fur could. This is all wrong. Just a few days ago I was still hung up on Seline and now my head is filled with visions of running my hands through Prince Nolan's soft hair. The Prince who I'm meant to be both *protecting* and *spying on*. The Prince who's marriage season gives me access to the corrupt King. The Prince who I most inconveniently have developed a crush on. And because of this Foe Forsaken Moon all I can think about is finding him and kissing him and...

"That's why you were hitting on me earlier." Rus takes a step toward me.

"I wasn't hitting on you!" I respond instantly. I mean I sort of *was* but it was just to take my mind of Prince Nolan, and Seline and...

"You told me I was disarmingly attractive?" His mouth twists, it's not a full smile but it's working for him.

"Distractingly handsome." I have to avert my gaze, as if proving my own point.

"Either way, it was quite the compliment." I watch the breath leave his flawless mouth. It forms a cloud between us in the cold night air. "Would it help if I kissed you?" His blue eyes meet mine. My chest rises and falls. He takes another step forward so we're pressed up against the stone of the building, his arms moving to cage me in. He's much larger than me and almost as tall as the Prince, maybe taller if he ever stood up straight.

"So you *do* like helping people!" I say, still processing this turn of events.

"I never said I didn't."

"But, you said you weren't a good guy..." This time I dare to look up at him. I have to crane my neck to hold his eye contact.

"I'm not," he says, our gazes locked.

There's no one around right now but it doesn't mean someone couldn't walk out of that door and catch us like this. To the untrained eye it would look like a member of the Prince's council is seducing one of the Prince's suitors. That wouldn't be good. Not good at all. Romina could be heading back from The Den. I wonder what she'd think of this. His head dips down. He's going to kiss me? He's going to kiss me!

Before I can decide how to feel about his advance, the front door of the building swings open and a blonde woman sprints past us, tying up her undone dress as she goes, giggling to herself.

I think of earlier.

"A pretty blonde may have been involved".

So Seline *is* seeing other people. Of course she is. But wasn't I just lusting for the Prince? And what about Rus? Was I really about to let him kiss me?

Only because of the Moon. And the wine.

Rus doesn't deserve that. Besides, he just wants to help. He probably doesn't really want to kiss me anyway. Why would he want to kiss someone who's about to start courting the Prince. And, he knows I'm a Shadow, so he knows how complicated this all would be.

I put my hands on his chest and look up at him. I feel the urge to touch the gemstone that pierces through his left eyebrow, but I resist the temptation, shaking my head.

"You've helped enough. I appreciate the offer but... you don't need to do this too." The moonlight falls on my skin and I know that if I don't head back inside right this second I won't be able to at all. Luckily, Rus senses the energy shift between us and gives me a quick nod before he turns to leave.

I enter the building and head straight up to my room on the top floor. Once the door is closed I splash some water on my face and wash up for the night. My heart is still racing and the moonlight has followed me home. It's now pooling in through the large bay window.

I feel the all too familiar stirring inside of me.

An itch that must be scratched.

Usually this is when I'd go knock on Seline's door, but I can't do that tonight.

I could touch myself.

That's one solution, but the truth is, I've never mastered it. I'm embarrassed that at 25 years of age I can't give myself a proper orgasm. Perhaps I could learn, but I've never taken the time to figure out exactly *how*. I haven't really needed to. We were always busy training. It was rare to ever have a night alone, and when I felt an urge, Seline was always around to seek pleasure together. It's probably time I figure this out. Especially since Seline is clearly moving on. I *should* be able to make myself feel good, on my own.

Alternatively, I could just use a bunch of magic to blow off steam. But such an outpour feels frivolous. It would be better if I used my magic more intentionally, especially if all magic use is being logged.

The moonlight grows impossibly brighter. Orgasm it is.

I hang my fur and am about to slip off my dress when there's a knock at my door.

Three quick knocks. Romina? Why is she knocking so late?

Then there's a fourth knock. A slow one.

Rus!

Quickly I open the door and pull him inside, if anyone sees him standing out there this late I'll have some explaining to do. His hair looks like he's been running his hands through it. He smells like eucalyptus. I make the mistake of sniffing him. If he doesn't leave soon, I'm going to kiss him.

"Yes?" It's all I can think to say.

"Maybe I like that you'll have excuses." His words are no more than a rasp.

"Excuses for what?"

His eyes bounce back and forth between mine. I can feel his pulse racing.

"For doing this." His soft hands find the nape of my neck and he tilts my face up to meet his.

His lips land on mine with a hunger I'm surprised by. I can't believe we are kissing. I know I flirted with him earlier, but I never imagined it would actually lead to this. He wasn't interested in me... But the kiss feels good. In fact, I can already sense the tension of my coiled up power beginning to dissipate. I lean into him and he takes it as permission to slide his tongue into my mouth.

While I find Rus to be generally lethargic, there's nothing sleepy about the way he kisses. I wrap my arms around his neck as he slides his hands behind my legs and lifts me up, turning to press my back against the wall. His tongue is just as soft as his hands and I realize how strong he must be to hold me in place like this. I'm shocked by the combination. Soft and Strong. It's been a while since I kissed a man like this. I want more. I press my body forward, locking my legs around his waist, sending my sweater dress inching up the top of my thighs as we continue to devour each other's mouths. It is right then that I discover his tongue is also pierced. The chill of smooth metal makes me gasp against his mouth. He pulls away to look at me.

"Is this helping?" he asks breathlessly, before starting to kiss my neck. I lean forward to grind up against him. I can feel how hard he's getting beneath his finely tailored trousers.

"Yes but..." I'm embarrassed to say it. Maybe I'll just make out with him for a bit then touch myself after he leaves, that will be fine. Totally fine.

"But what?" He breaks the kiss again and turns us around to gently place me down on the bed. I sit there catching my breath before looking up at him. His shirt is unbuttoned and there's a bulge in his pants. He looks even better like this, and now that he's here, standing in the moonlight of my bedroom, it's time I find some courage.

"I'm going to need to come." Better to just say it now and put it out there.

"Okay," he says without an ounce of hesitation as he starts to take off his shirt. With each button another inch of his incredibly muscular body is revealed. As his shirt falls to the ground, I notice that I was right about the tattoo which covers his sculpted abs. It's a massive rendering of the Second Star. I wonder if he is a Stellar, but I'm far too distracted to ask.

"You don't need to... I mean I can take care of it after you..." I watch as he makes his way to join me on the bed. He reaches around me, inspecting my dress, trying to figure out how to take it off. There's no tie, the whole thing has to go over my head. I start to tug at the thick fabric and he catches on.

"I want to," he mumbles as he helps me peel it off over my head leaving me in nothing more than a silk bralette and matching bottoms, my heavy breasts now spilling over the former. I skim my hand over my hip bone, admiring the smooth flesh no longer inked with the Shadow Mark, thanks to Rus' Augmenting. While the blood oath remains intact, at least I've escaped the physical manifestation of my commitment. He tosses the dress somewhere on the floor and I realize I've totally lost the thread of whatever conversation we were having.

"Want to what?"

"I want to make you come." Oh right. That.

Before I can say something stupid, we're kissing again. We fall back onto my bed. Rus places me beside him and tucks me under his arm, with one hand tenderly holding my jaw as we kiss, his other hand begins to travel down between my legs. He lightly traces the edges of my undergarments before gently skimming his fingers across my center.

"Darby." He breaks away from our kiss, his voice a whisper. "You're soaked." My face flushes and I burrow into his neck. "Are you embarrassed by that?" he asks.

"Yes! This whole situation is mortifying!"

"The Moon made you horny, there's nothing wrong with that." He continues to caress me. "Besides, I find it incredibly attractive."

"You do?"

"I find *you* incredibly attractive. Some might even say, disarmingly so." With one hand between my legs, the other hand begins to trace the edge of my bralette, my eyes fixate on how my swollen flesh threatens to break free of the thin silk. He's teasing me in more ways than one.

"Oh, shut up." I kiss him again to end the conversation as his fingers slip below my underwear and gently rub the bud of nerves between my legs. I gasp and he takes that as his cue to keep exploring, kissing my neck as he changes up the pace.

"Yes," I offer, as I arch into him. He can definitely tell that I'm enjoying this and he takes my encouragement as permission to slide a finger up inside of me. It feels good. Really good. "More." He listens, adding a second finger. The next thing I know I'm moving my hips to match his rhythm as his fingers pump in and out of me.

"Can you come like this?" Maybe in the past I would have said yes just to be low maintenance. But this interaction is about me. The goal is my release, and he signed up for it willingly. Best to be honest, so I shake my head. No.

"You need me to rub your little clit again, don't you, *Goldie?*" I nod yes. Yes. He keeps kissing my neck as his fingers travel back to my clit, alternating between slow and fast circles. The pressure is building quickly now.

"I'm close." I was close before we even started. My eyes flutter up to him and I take in the look of focus on his face as he hovers above me. I can't believe I'm kissing someone so attractive. He's gorgeous. The thought of this beautiful man touching me makes me even wetter. Based on the glint in his eyes, he can tell.

"It's time." He's right. He's totally right. And before I can overthink it, the most incredible rush of electricity courses through me. My whole body begins to shake. He plunges his two fingers back inside me to gently coax out the rest of my orgasm. Holding me against his chest as I completely unravel.

"Thank you," is all I can manage to say. He's still cradling me in his strong arms.

"Is it always like that? With the full Moon?" He shifts slightly to look down at me.

"Usually I plan better, I think since I have Royal Magic now I didn't use up enough power ahead of time...Maybe once I'm more acclimated it won't be an issue at all." I allow myself to burrow deeper into his chest. This feels nice.

"You were incredible." His praise washes over me. It feels good. I wonder if this is just a physical thing for him, or could it be that he's actually into me? He's still here, holding me.

"You were pretty great too." I meet his gaze and start searching for clues.

"Happy to be of service." He brings his face close to mine now, our noses touch but we do not kiss again. I wonder what he makes of all of this. It all happened so quickly, one moment he was being nice walking me home, the next, he was as hungry for my touch as I suddenly was for his. And the way he talked to me while touching me? It sends a flash of heat to my cheeks just thinking about it.

"Did you call me... Goldie?" I feel like I remember him saying that.

"The gold rings in your eyes. I'm happy you kept them." That's right, he did mention it the other day. I'm happy I kept them too. I feel grateful to Rus. Not just for helping me out with the uncontrollable lust of the full

Moon but for the other day as well. I want to show him how grateful I am. I reach over to him, my hand finding him still hard.

"No, that's okay." He moves my hand away and I can't help but feel rejected.

"Are you sure? It's only fair." But it's not just that, I want to give him pleasure. Just like he did for me. I want him to want it from me. Why doesn't he?

"Don't worry about it, I should get going." He gently turns me over and scoots out from under me, moving to gather his shirt before slipping out. My eyes are growing heavy and I find that I don't have the energy to protest as I drift off to sleep.

10

I tell Romina about it first thing the next morning as she helps lace up my dress in preparation for our contact free "blind" dates with the Prince. The back of my ensemble features a complicated web of pink satin ribbons that took us ages to figure out, while the front consists of pleated fabric in a matching petal pink cut to perfectly flatter my shape and tease a bit of cleavage. My hair is pulled into a high ponytail with an oversized pink ribbon.

"Did it feel romantic?" As usual, Romina isn't judging me at all.

"It sort of felt like he was doing me a favor?" I rub my temples. This morning I am feeling the effects of last night's wine and full Moon combo.

I finish helping Romina into her delicately beaded light blue gown which gives the illusion of ice crystals falling softly from her curves. We place matching beads along her cheekbones using a pinch of magic to secure them. She looks beautiful. The Prince won't see us today but the rest of the Court certainly will. It's important we make a good impression.

"I'm just happy you stayed away from Seline. I think it's good you two are taking space from your relationship. It complicates our team dynamic. Plus, she always hurts your feelings."

"I know." I hate that Romina is always right. Maybe Seline did us both a favor by leaving The Den early with someone else. I could have easily found my way to her room last night if not.

Romina offers me a spray of her perfume. It's so rare that we get to wear fragrance since our missions often require us to be completely undetectable. When the opportunity does present itself, we love to indulge. I hold the glass bottle to my nose and inhale the familiar scent of birch trees and lavender. Romina always smells like an untamed forest. Full of life. After getting a good whiff, I decline to spray myself with it. This is her scent. Not mine. Instead I opt for my favorite honey vanilla sandalwood fragrance. The sweetness reminds me of home. A place that no longer exists.

After putting on the finishing touches of our attire, we join Seline and the other suitors in one of the Palace's smaller ballrooms. Seline looks flawless in a shimmering black gown that is draped around her body leaving key features exposed. Her delicate shoulders and a slice of her hip tempt my eyes, but I force myself to look away. Instead I focus on the ballroom itself, finding endless dark marble walls with delicate silver decorations leading up to the high ceilings. Candles burn around us, providing light, in addition to a scattering of light orbs which bob around freely.

There are much fewer children running around this time, but I remember this ballroom as the room Mother and Grandma left me to wait in on that fateful day 15 years ago. I shudder just thinking about it, but the tension is broken by a tray of sweets and sparkling wine in delicate silver stemmed glasses, which magically floats by on its own. I reach for a cookie, thinking of my dedication to sweets back then and how a trip to the kitchens resulted in my collision with the young Prince.

Vesto flutters about greeting the Ladies as they arrive, but there's no sign of Rus yet. This is where all the suitors will be held while the contactless dates take place in the adjoining room. I'm told that the initial search for Prince Nolan's suitors consisted of *hundreds*, as every eligible maiden was to be considered. After a series of interviews and an extensive screening process, it was narrowed down to the 14 who are now here at the Winter Palace, including three of us. We plan to spend today getting to know the other women and pinpoint any possible threats to the Prince. Romina, Seline and I decide to divide and conquer and a couple hours later I find myself in a conversation with Princess Amarie of Langha, the neighboring territory to Kadneria, known for its use of magical crystals.

"I'm excited to get away from my Kingdom for a bit. Things at home have gotten incredibly boring since my sister became Queen." She speaks in a monotone. Her bluntness is exhilarating. There is something immediately likeable about her.

"Not here to make friends then?" I ask in response, my eyes trailing over her voluptuous curves. She's striking, with soft waves in her golden hair and bronze complexion.

"You want to be friends?" She gives me a once over too. I notice that her leaf green eyes are decorated in silver glitter.

"Better than enemies." I bring my wineglass to my lips. It's my second glass but what she doesn't know is that I used my magic to take out the alcohol. Today, I need to stay focused.

"I don't mind enemies, to be honest, I'm looking forward to a bit of drama. Keeps things interesting." Amarie would be a good political match for the Prince. As the sister of the Queen, it's unlikely she will ever be given the chance to rule. The crown will be passed on to her sister's children. If Amarie were to marry the Prince, it would form an alliance between the neighboring territories of Langha and Kadneria. Territories that have struggled to see eye to eye on how to balance power and regulate magic.

Could Amarie pose a threat to the Prince? In coming here and joining the Season, she was required to use Royal Magic for the first time. Having the Princess agree to forsake her Crystals was undoubtedly seen as a political act, the first step in a possible alliance, but a gamble for the Langhan Royals. They really must want her to be chosen. But what if things don't work out between Amarie and the Prince? Would Langha retaliate?

"What do you make of Royal Magic?" I glance down at her silver bracelet.

"It's rather fun isn't it?" Her eyes float to my matching bracelet. "A small price to pay for finding my Link." Her link. I note her phrasing. She says this as if we aren't but two of his many suitors sipping sparkling wine in the ballroom.

"You think you're a match then?" If I were actually in the running to be his Link, I would be offended by her use of words. I better play the part. I find it's not that hard.

"I was the first one to officially speak with him, you know. The King arranged for it himself." She's making my job easy. I file away this information. Perhaps the King is hoping for the Langha alliance. An alliance that involves Amarie using Royal Magic. Could it tip the scales of their disagreement on power regulation in his favor?

"Plus, Nolan and I go way back. Being eligible young Royals and all..." I note her casual use of his first name as Vesto appears to let me know I'm up next. I say goodbye to Amarie and wonder if she brought any crystals with her to the Palace.

11

"Mind if we walk and talk? The last few were seated and it's time to stretch my legs, if you don't mind." The Prince is standing in front of me as a magical one-way glass separates us. I can see him, but he can't see me. He started speaking just as I entered the room, he must have heard me come in. It's charming how informal he is.

"It's a small room to stroll in, but whatever you prefer." I say it plainly. His face lights up as he recognizes my voice.

"Darby!"

"Hello, Prince."

"Nolan, remember?" he says, as if I could forget. As if I haven't been making an effort not to address him so informally... "I've been wondering when you'd turn up."

"It's nice to see you again," I tell him.

"That's right, you've seen me twice now, but I've yet to lay my eyes on you."

If only he knew that he had. Not that he'd recognize

me now. I have no scars to tie me to the little girl he met that day 15 years ago - well, no scars that are visible. But it's for the best, because Nolan can never find out that we've met before. That I belong to a Storytelling family.

"So how will this work?" My eyes dart around the small room we're in. It's been set up for tea with plush velvet couches on either side of the one-way glass.

"Easy." He taps his fingers together and the room is changed into a garden. The Palace Garden from what I can tell. It's lovely and covered in snow. Nolan looks around admiring his work before an idea occurs to him. "Oh wait actually, since it's you, let me show you something even better." And then it's no longer winter. I feel the warmth of the Sun on my face for the first time since arriving here. There's not a gray winter cloud in the sky. I'm floored by it.

"Nolan! This is... how is this possible?"

"It's like shielding but with imagery. If you combine a shield with a memory, it can look and feel real. You could do this too, Royal Magic is amazing."

"I'll have to try it sometime." I think about what he said. "So this is one of your memories then?"

"It's one of my favorites actually, the weird thing is, I have no idea where it's from. I don't have any other memories of the Sun shining like this. I must have been really little. The Palace has always been dreary and gray, I guess that's why everyone calls it the Winter Palace, huh?" He runs a self-conscious hand through his hair before adding, "But it's home so I'm not complaining."

I take a look around, basking in the warmth of the illusion's Sun. I can't deny that this is charming, but the fact that he can't place this memory is raising major red flags. Perhaps once I get to know him more and earn his trust, I can ask about that.

"This memory is special then. Thank you for sharing it with me."

"You are special, Darby, there's no one I'd rather share it with." Suddenly my cheeks are hot. That's really sweet. "And Buddy sends his best, by the way," he adds with a sly smile.

"Please give him my regards as well." I'm smiling too as I remember the velvet monster who slobbered all over me.

But we don't trust him!

I have to keep reminding myself.

Time to stop flirting and start getting information.

"So how have the conversations been going so far?" I hope he doesn't think it's weird that I'm asking this. It is important for the mission that I know how his other options are looking.

"They've been interesting. It's strange not to see what everyone looks like. I find myself making up ideas in my head. Like you for example... I feel like you are golden." He puts his hands out as he says this, as if painting me on an invisible canvas of his own making.

"You need me to rub your little clit again, don't you, Goldie?"

Oh Foe.

The rumble of Rus' voice is in my head before I can even swat it away. I've been trying not to think about him all day, and I was succeeding. Until now.

"Golden?" I swallow hard, forcing myself to stay present.

"Your voice feels warm, like the sunshine." He points up at the sky. "There's a golden quality to it, and you smell like honey...and whiskey? Which are both golden in color are they not?" There's a hop in his step as he weaves through the magic garden.

"Indeed they are." There's a small bounce in my own step as I try to keep up with him. It feels playful moving like this, like we're kids again.

"What color is your hair?"

Rose gold, but I'm not telling him that.

"If I tell you what I look like, won't that defeat the purpose of the blind date?"

He turns to look towards my voice and I use the opportunity to admire the beautiful blue suit he's wearing. It's covered in tiny gemstones. The light catches on the stones and the Prince truly sparkles.

"Can't blame me for trying." He smiles and the dimple is back. We both begin walking again. "Plus, I think the true purpose of all this is to keep me from touching you. But you've already touched me, haven't you?" His smile grows impossibly wider as he begins to fiddle with a flower sprouting on a nearby tree.

"Are you like this with everyone?" I'd really love to know.

"Not everyone. Are you?" There's a soft snapping sound as he gently breaks the flower off its branch and twirls it absentmindedly between his thumb and index finger.

"Not everyone, no." I'm staring at his fingers now,

wondering if he's going to give that flower to me? How can he with the barrier between us?

"There's something about you that feels reassuring, like I can just be myself." He pauses again, turning to me. "I *can* be myself around you, can't I?"

"I'd prefer it that way." We continue walking as he tucks the flower into his breast pocket.

"Good. Now what more should I know about you, Darby?"

A lot. But what can I actually tell him?

"I've been enjoying being back in this part of Kadneria" Maybe enjoying it a little too much, actually.

"That's right. Vesto told me he had quite the night with you and Romina at The Den."

Vesto told him that? I wonder if Vesto left out the fact that Rus was there too, or if it's the Prince who's failing to mention him. Either way I decide not to bring it up.

"We did."

"I'm incredibly jealous. That's one of our favorite places."

It never occurred to me that the Prince might have been at The Den with us. Is he allowed there?

"Are you sequestered?" I try to keep my voice casual as I ask.

"I'm afraid I am. Until after the *Grand Reveal Ball*," he responds easily.

"Well that's not too long from now, perhaps we can all go to the Den together afterwards."

"I'd very much enjoy that. If it were up to me, I'd find my Link just like that, living my normal life."

"You're a Prince, nothing about your life is normal," I say too quickly. He slows, as if considering.

"I suppose that's true." We continue to stroll through his memory garden, our conversation flowing freely without any effort at all. It's refreshing, being able to talk to him like this. Again I'm amazed by how candid he is. Eventually there's a knock on the door to let us know our time is ending. The Prince taps his fingers and the garden disappears.

"Our little secret." He winks at me, lifting the flower from his pocket and blowing magic on it. The flower floats through the air, passing through the magical barrier between us and landing directly in the palm of my hand. My fingers twirl around the bright green stem as I pull the soft pink petals to my nose, inhaling the sweet floral scent. I look up to find Nolan easing down into one of the velvet sofas as if he had been sitting there the whole time.

When Vesto walks in a moment later, he looks over at the Prince.

"Getting bored of this room yet?"

Nolan just smiles. "At least I had good company this time."

I tuck the flower into the base of my ponytail, securing it against the pink ribbons.

On my way out, Vesto hands me a silver charm. A tiny heart with a crown on it.

"For your bracelet, they'll be returned at the point of elimination," he explains to me. "I designed them myself, it's the Prince's heart."

I clip the charm onto my Royal Magic bracelet and hurry off to find the others.

"You'll never believe this." Romina grabs my arm and pulls me towards a redheaded woman in a silky bright orange gown, who is currently chatting up Seline. We pause a couple feet away and I recognize her from our intel as a wealthy Kadnerian who goes by Ingrid. Her family has long since hoped to get in good graces with the King, but it appears their wealth alone has failed to earn them an invite to Court. Having their eldest daughter Linked to the Prince would certainly guarantee their social status.

"Oh it was just lovely, the Prince is soooo lovely? Don't you think?" Ingrid is cooing more than speaking. Her words are no louder than a whisper as they slip out of her mouth. Her eyes flutter closed. It reminds me of the way Seline looked when the HelioX got on her arm, but more extreme.

"And get a whiff of her," Romina says, as I lean in and find she reeks of that all too familiar purple substance.

"We've got to help her!" I say immediately, earning a glare from Seline, who apparently was aware of my presence. Her eyes lock on mine, and Romina pulls me off towards the beverage table.

"We need to be discreet." Romina picks up one of the delicate wine glasses and waves at Ruby and Sidney, two of the Prince's suitors that seem more interested in each other than they do him, before lowering her voice to continue. "Ingrid invited Seline to a *gathering* tonight."

"A gathering?" I press, not catching on.

"We'll go with her and see what we can find out. Clearly this new batch of HelioX has made its way to the Palace. Maybe we can determine what that ingredient is, and who's supplying it."

"So you've got a whole plan sorted and everything." I can't take my eyes off Ingrid. I wonder if anyone else noticed. Maybe they just credited her behavior to drinking too much.

HelioX is dangerous. What was once considered a recreational drug has turned into something much darker. We've seen too many innocent lives taken by the highly addictive substance which provides extreme pleasure while it slowly deteriorates your mind and body.

"Of course, how else would I have spent the afternoon? You were gone for a while by the way, one of the longest dates so far. And yes, I've been timing them." Romina pulls a stunning gold pocket watch from her beaded purse, tapping it with her long ice blue painted nails.

"It wasn't that long, was it?" I open my own tiny beaded purse in search of my lip salve, then dip my finger into the small pot of honey butter and spread it onto my lips.

"Must have gone well," she says with a knowing smile.

"When is your turn?" I'm eager to deflect.

"I'm up next actually. Any advice?" Finally, I look up at

her. She needs to do well too. We have to make it through the first elimination.

"Just be yourself."

"Which version?" Romina's eyes narrow as she says this. As if she's trying to remind me that the two of us will never get to be our true selves with anyone. Not even each other. "I'll see you later for the *gathering*." She gives my arm a gentle squeeze as she prances off towards her date with the Prince.

There's warmth at my back and I turn to find Seline has slid up behind me. We stand there in silence. We haven't been alone since our fight and I refuse to speak first. Instead, I grab a new glass of sparkling wine from a floating tray, and this time, I don't remove the alcohol.

"Your date went well." She must have been keeping time as well. She and Romina are really upstaging me these days, that or I'm losing my touch as a Shadow. Keeping track of how long he's spent with each suitor is a brilliant way to figure out who our front runners are and most likely who we need to keep a closer eye on.

"It did."

"Was *Nolan* as charming as your previous encounter?" Seline's posture is as straight as I've ever seen it. She stands so still that she may as well be a statue.

"Even more so," I offer without turning.

"I'm looking forward to meeting him myself, as you know, I'm planning to enjoy our time here." It is when saying this that she finally turns to face me, and I feel the attention of her silver eyes hone in on my newly glossed lips.

"I thought you were already *enjoying* your time here."

My implication is clear. I know about the blonde last night. Seline leans closer so she can whisper in my ear. She smells like jasmine and mint. It's a lovely combination.

"Don't tell me you're jealous, Bee." I can hear the smile on her voice.

"I'm just as jealous as you are."

"So not at all." She says this so close to my ear that she's practically licking it. My body betrays me as it recognizes Seline. My hands ache to reach out and touch her. This person who has brought me pleasure for the last three years. I have to tell my body no. I have to remind my hands that this person has also pushed us away time and time again.

"Exactly." As the word leaves my mouth, I fear it failed to convey the confidence I intended. We remain there, unmoving, until finally, sensing that I'm not budging, she pulls away.

"Suppose it's for the best that we ended things then," Seline says as she storms off, and I can't help but feel that she was somehow actually upset.

12

It's completely dark in the underground tunnel where *the gathering* is meant to take place. We follow the sounds of laughter and strange thumping music. Our light orbs are dimmed low, giving us the faintest glow to help navigate the stretch of tunnel in front of us. It used to only be me who could summon a light orb, but now thanks to Royal Magic, Seline and Romina can too. We're about to turn into a main clearing where a circle of people are seated on the floor, when Seline stops us.

"When the time comes to try it, allow me." She stands before us unflinching.

"No one needs to try it," Romina reminds her.

"But they'll trust us more if we're here to take part." Seline pulls a solid black spoon from the inside of her cloak.

"Where'd you get that?" Romina looks it over. We've seen spoons like this before, usually clutched in the hands of someone who's overdosed. I shake my head to clear the morbid thought from my mind.

"Ingrid," Seline answers quickly.

"How about this, you take the smallest amount and then we get you out of here. We'll stay with you the whole time and monitor the effects, it will be like a study." Romina looks excited by this. Too excited.

"She's a person, not an experiment." I find myself worried for Seline's well being.

"Relax Bee, I've touched it before and I was fine. Remember?"

Of course I remember. It was the same night we ended things.

"Fine," I acquiesce. I'd still prefer it if she didn't ingest any, but when Seline sets her mind on something, there is no stopping her.

We enter the room and find seats on the floor in a circle of people. We're all wearing hooded cloaks to conceal our faces. Despite this, it's easy to recognize Ingrid with her long red curls poking out from under her hood. I take a look around the room, memorizing as many details as I can. Romina and Seline are doing the same.

A hooded person passes a jar of purple sparkling liquid to Romina. She lifts it to her nose and inhales deeply. She's mentally cataloguing each ingredient. I can tell.

"You don't sniff it, you eat it," the hooded figure croaks, their voice barely there.

"Forgot my spoon," Romina shrugs, passing the jar to Seline who is ready with her own utensil. I watch as Seline dips the solid black spoon into the jar, fills it to the brim, then downs the purple gooey substance without flinching. That's a lot more than I thought she'd take.

For Foe's sake. I guess we're really doing this.

"Goldie."

The sharp sound of my new nickname stops me in my tracks. I turn to face the hooded person in the circle next to me. It can't be him? Can it?

I lean in and inhale his scent. Eucalyptus. Just like I remember from last night.

"What are you doing here?" My mind immediately goes to the worst case scenario. Rus is already addicted to HelioX. We need to help him before the substance damages his internal organs and brain function. My mind flashes to the reports we've read, the scouts we've been on...

"What are *you* doing here?" The anger in his voice tells me all I need to know. He's upset that I've figured out his secret. Before I can say anything else, a swarm of red light orbs fly into the room, illuminating everything in an eerie glow. Rus jumps to his feat, dropping his cloak and drawing his sword. The same sword he insisted he never used. Just a piece of jewelry, isn't that what he said?

"Everybody freeze!" Vesto comes running in with a few Royal Guards. People start to scramble, most of them too out of it to get very far. Romina and I grab Seline, hoisting her up.

"He said we wouldn't get caught...." Ingrid's sing-song voice fails to match her concern but I'm happy to learn she is aware enough to know something is not right here.

"Let's take Ingrid too." I look at Romina, but she

shakes her head no. I hate this. We're back in Shadow mode.

"Come on," Romina insists, and I join her in ushering Seline down the tunnel as quickly as we can.

"Wait!" Rus is racing after us with a sober expression on his face that tells me he wasn't there to indulge in HelioX for himself. Romina and I exchange a glance and then slow our pace. There's no one else around and we don't need to hide our motives from him.

"What was that about?" Romina asks bluntly.

"We've been planning this raid for weeks, didn't know the exact location but luckily one of the Ladies couldn't keep her mouth shut about it, nearly invited the Prince himself." Rus notices Seline. "I'm guessing this was her first time?"

"She took one for the team." I wrap my arm around Seline's waist to hold her up properly and she reaches out to touch my face tenderly.

"Bee, you're so pretty..." She nuzzles into me and Romina and I lock eyes. Clearly Seline is feeling the effects if she's treating me so differently from earlier.

"We've been collecting intel on HelioX for a while now, are *gatherings* like this one common?" I ask, as Seline burrows into me.

"They are popping up more and more, we can't stop them from happening but we have been able to develop an antidote. It's not perfect yet, but it's good enough."

"An antidote?" Romina's interest is piqued, I must admit mine is too.

"Come on, let's get her some." Rus takes off down the tunnel and we follow behind.

❄

A little later we find ourselves in Rus' small cottage by the sea. It's a short walk from the Palace but feels much more private. The quaint space features a small sitting room and a screened in front porch. I notice two large wooden boards leaning against the wall by the door.

"You surf?" It was common for people to haul large boards out into the water and ride the waves when I was younger and Kadneria was warmer. I can't imagine going out there now in the cold, although I suppose they can use Royal Magic to warm themselves.

"The Prince and I do it together." Rus looks out towards the water, his strong jaw relaxing for a second before tension gathers again. "We haven't had much time for it recently..." He trails off as I try to picture Rus and Nolan surfing together. I try to imagine them doing *anything* together but try as I might, I just can't picture them as friends. Maybe this was the missing piece, a shared interest which unites them: Surfing. If only they knew they also had a shared interest in *me*. Not that Nolan would actually like me if he knew who I really was. Does he even like me now?

Our conversations have been going well enough so far, from what I can tell. And what of Rus? Does he like me? Or was he just caught up in the moment last night?

"Vesto will be here soon." Rus's gruff voice steals my attention back. We're here at his house to debrief. Seline is passed out on the sofa with the antidote pumping through her system, while Rus is pouring tea for Romina and I from a copper kettle.

"Where did Vesto go?" The window is cracked and I can hear the waves crashing against the shore. It must be nice to wake up here. I wonder if I ever will. Maybe things between Rus and I will continue to develop. Maybe we'll start spending more time together.

"He went to update the Prince. Ending the HelioX crisis is one of his main initiatives. The antidote is the work of the Prince's council," Rus tells us with the authority of a diplomat. Romina and I exchange a look. This is news to us but I'm glad to hear it. Perhaps Prince Nolan is more altruistic than we realized.

"Why haven't we heard of this before?" Romina blows on her tea, it's still too hot to drink.

"We're putting together a briefing for the King's council, once we present our plan to them, the King will decide how to move forward." Rus's whole demeanor is that of a professional. There is no hint of the man who stuck his pierced tongue down my throat last night, the memory of which now causes me to shiver. I wonder what that little piece of jewelry would feel like on other parts of me...

I need to get a grip. We're in the middle of a serious conversation and my mind is wandering down a dangerous path. I clear my throat. Time for me to act like a professional as well.

"The antidote should be made widely available. Even if someone can't break the addiction, they could still avoid the dangerous effects." It is easy to fall back into work mode. It's easy to take something so serious seriously.

"You would think that's the obvious choice, but it's

complicated." Rus looks down now, his eyes buried in his own steaming tea cup. I glance at Romina, trying to make sense of his mixed emotions. Perhaps he agrees with us but is frustrated by the progress they are making?

"The King doesn't support the distribution of the Antidote? Wasn't he a renowned Alchemist? If I remember correctly, his first act as King was to make all sorts of tonics and medicines widely accessible to the people..."

"We don't know what the King supports yet, we're still working on our presentation. It's more complicated than you might think." Yes, that's it, he is frustrated. It brings me back to our conversation last night.

"Rus! Are you secretly a good guy!?"

"No Darby. I'm not a good guy."

I decide then that I don't care what he tries to tell me. Rus is definitely a good guy.

"So the Prince must really care about this, then?" Romina yawns a little bit, it's been a long day.

"He does. We all do." I turn this information over in my head. The Prince cares about helping with the HelioX crisis. That's good. Maybe he's not all bad either.

"What will happen to Ingrid?" I think of her sing-song voice during the raid.

"Oh no! He said we wouldn't get caught...." Who was she talking about?

"After she detoxes, we'll bring her in for questioning, see what we can learn," Rus offers.

"Well hello there!" Vesto appears in the doorway dropping his own sword straight on to the floor and plopping down in a chair next to Romina. "It's just the ladies I was talking about!"

"You told the Prince we were at the *gathering?*" Romina perks up as his weapon clatters into the spot next to her.

"Of course not, but I did help him review the notes from his dates today. I do believe we have an elimination coming up and a certain three Shadows need to stay in the running." Of course Vesto is helping the Prince choose. He's his friend and council member. I wonder why Rus wasn't included? I look at him with a question in my eyes.

"Moving forward we'll all meet and discuss with him. Tonight, I was preoccupied." He nods towards Seline who is still sound asleep.

"The elimination, what will that be like?" I ask the room.

"It will all take place at the Grand Reveal Ball, first the Prince will have a blind speed dating round to chat with everyone once more. Then he'll cast his final votes and the remaining Ladies will be welcomed into the ballroom and we'll drink and dance until sunrise!" Vesto is all smiles as he reaches forward to pour a cup of tea from the still steaming pot.

"And that will be the end of the Prince's containment?" I think of the brown eyed Prince, all alone in his Palace. Sequestered for the duration of the blind dates.

"Only if he behaves himself." Vesto for once does not seem amused by this. We all know the Prince has a reputation for sleeping around. It's funny to think about now that I've met him. He is far too sweet to be the philanderer his reputation spoke of. And yet he is comforted by physical touch. Perhaps for him, it's more about seeking comfort.

"Should he not sleep with his suitors before committing to someone?" Romina chimes in. She has a point, he isn't just looking for a wife after all. Maybe being intimate is a necessary step in trying to determine if someone is your soulmate. Since we're Shadows, the option of marriage has never been in the cards for us. Instead, Shadows value pleasure over companionship. When life is dangerous and you never know where your next mission will take you, moments of release become valuable. Needed. We have no stigma against intimacy. At least that's how Shadows are supposed to feel. Obviously I've struggled with this concept - the pleasure over companionship part that is. Time and time again I've confused my *relations* for real relationships. It's like every time I've been told not to be attached, it's made me crave that attachment even more. The idea of a Link intrigues me. The thought that someone would be a part of me, and I a part of them. That there would be someone on this planet who knows me fully, who I know fully in return. That we could trust each other. I wonder what that would be like.

And yet, being Linked will never be an option for me.

"Trust me, it's been a topic of conversation." Vesto glances at Rus, who huffs a tired laugh. "The King actually had an idea that maybe the Prince could sleep with the final three – not that he must sleep with them but that he should be given the option to. We would have a series of overnight dates leading up to the Royal Wedding. At that point the families of the final three will be invited to court and remain here until the ceremony." Vesto looks between me and Romina as he says this. "Obviously it can't be the three of you, we're going to need to have a *real* option in the running by that point, but we can cross that bridge once we get there."

We are going to have to tell him we are Shadows before it gets that far.

"Maybe we should tell him that we're Shadows right now, before the first elimination." I run my hands across the smooth marble surface of Rus' table. It dawns on me that the more I get to know the Prince, the worse I will feel about deceiving him.

Vesto exhales a big breath, sitting back in his chair as he considers what I've suggested. He runs his tired hands through a crop of bright green hair. One of his diamond facial piercings captures the light in a way that makes his face sparkle. "It's been a long night, there's enough going on with the HelioX, we don't need to tell him yet."

An unruly snore escapes Seline and we all turn to face her on the sofa.

"We should probably get her to bed," Romina suggests.

"I can help." Rus stands.

"That's not necessary, you shouldn't have to leave your own place." I motion for him to sit down.

"I can carry her easily, it's not a big deal." I think of how effortlessly he picked me up and pressed me against the wall. I think of how strong he felt. Strong arms and a soft tongue. I think of his hands roaming all over my body. He clears his throat and I realize I'm staring at him.

"Fine by me. Thanks Rus!" Romina downs the rest of her tea and heads to the door.

13

The halls are empty when we return to the guest quarters and we don't run into anyone while making our way up to the top floor where Romina, Seline and I occupy the only three rooms. After successfully escorting Seline and tucking her into bed, Romina and I say goodnight to Rus in the hallway. Romina turns left to her own room, and I turn right for mine.

"Can we talk?" Rus asks, before I round the corner. I look back at him and nod my head, indicating for him to follow. Once we reach my room, I close the door behind us.

"I don't want things to be weird between us." He's standing in the same spot as last night but with none of the heat. It doesn't take a trained Shadow to know that the vibe is different from the last time we were alone together.

That's *fine*. Just fine.

Last night was just physical. He was doing me a favor.

Clearly he isn't interested in something real developing between us. Now that I think of it, he did turn me down when I tried to touch him. Heat colors my cheeks as I realize how foolish I was to entertain the idea of something more happening between us.

I exhale a sigh, why do I always do this? My imagination always jumps ahead, it's like I'm inventing a relationship where there isn't anything more than a physical attraction. And I didn't even want *him* initially, I was just trying to get my mind off Nolan, and Seline. But then he had to go and kiss me...

Why did he come all the way over here tonight? Could it be that he just wanted to clear the air between us?

If that's the case, we might as well get this conversation over with.

"Does it seem weird?" I start to go through the motions of getting ready for bed. It's late and if he's looking to reject me then I'd rather it be over with as soon as possible.

"It's weird that you're courting my friend now." Rus shuffles his weight between his feet, lurking by my doorway as if he isn't sure what to do with himself.

"I didn't realize you and the Prince were friends." I don't give him the courtesy of a glance as I continue my nighttime routine. Instead, my eyes flit over to the single flower which stands at alert in a glass vase on my nightstand, the one Prince Nolan gave me on our blind date. I wonder what the flower makes of our visitor.

"We are." He raises his voice a level, as if trying to win back my attention.

"And we're not actually courting. As you know." I turn

my back to him and shimmy out of the matching pants and tunic set I had put on before we left for the *gathering*, slipping into a nightgown instead. I don't bother stepping behind the dressing screen, he saw me in less clothing than this last night anyway.

"But *he* doesn't know that. And we're both tasked to protect him. It wouldn't be right to get involved..." I turn around to find that Rus' eyes are on me. He's been watching closely as I changed. There's the unmistakable look of lust in his eyes. So he finds me attractive, that is confirmed. But he doesn't want things to continue between us? Why not?

I think about our interaction last night. He was hard to read. While what he said confused me, I didn't stop to question him. Perhaps now it's time to ask.

"What did you mean by *excuses*?" I cross my arms over my nightgown, covering my chest that would otherwise be visible through the thin fabric.

"What?" He clears his throat.

"Last night. You said that you liked that I'd have *excuses*." My eyes meet his. He swallows once before responding.

"In case you woke up today and found that you regret what happened between us." He takes a step closer to me.

"I don't." But maybe he regrets it? I gaze up at him and take a long look into his deep blue eyes. Maybe he's just as confused by our attraction as I am. If anything, this is more of a compromising position for him than it is for me. Pursuing one of the Prince's suitors can't be a good look for someone on the Prince's council. A person who claims that they are friends. He runs a hand through his curly blonde hair and I watch his bicep flex.

"Neither do I," he mumbles.

Relief washes over me.

But if he doesn't regret it, then why is he acting like this? And why didn't he want me to touch him? And why aren't we kissing now?

He's still got his sword strapped to him. I glance at it. Then I remember his hands. Uncrossing my arms, I reach for them and gently rub my thumbs over his palms. Scanning over the fronts and backs for any imperfections. There are none. His hands remain as flawless and as cool to the touch as I remembered them.

"You lied." My implication is clear as I look up at him once more.

He lets my words sit there before responding.

"You assumed." His fingers curl around mine.

"No, I clearly asked if you Augmented yourself." I hold his own hands up to face him. "These hands have had some work done, *Rus.*"

"It wasn't a full lie, it *is* hard to do it on yourself. And I haven't touched my face." He doesn't take his hands back, instead he lets me hold them.

"Sure you haven't." I release his hands and glance back up at his stunning face. There's no way he hasn't altered some element of his own appearance. Plus he already lied once, so I know I can't fully trust him.

"I'm surprised you expected me to be fully truthful. Every time I deal with Shadows I am humbly reminded that you are the masters of secrets." He leans into my door frame now, crossing one leg over the other, finally finding a comfortable position. I drink in the sight of him, his broad frame swallowing up space in my entryway, his tilted posture sending his gaze piercing through me. I consider his words. Rus must have some history with Shadows. I wonder who he dealt with and under what circumstances. We're not all the same. Our methods at the Academy are unlike most of the others. We have my mother to thank for that.

"Keeping secrets is different than lying," I tell him. And now we're just standing here, looking at each other. Did he come here to kiss me again? Why has he plastered himself to my door frame? I might as well just ask him. It's late, and I'm done guessing.

"Why are you here Rus?"

His eyes alternate between my own before dipping down to my mouth.

"I don't know." He takes a step forward, and I do the same. He raises his left hand and brings it to my face, using his knuckles to graze the side of my cheek until he reaches the corner of my mouth. He's hardly even touching me and yet my breath hitches. His eyes hone in on my lips. I think he's going to kiss me, but heartbeat later he steps away. With a quick nod of his head, he sees himself out. The door gently closes behind him, and with it, I feel a part of me closing off as well.

14

"Today is going to be a terrible day," Seline grumbles, as she takes in the sight of Romina and I standing over her with tea we've commandeered from the kitchen staff. She's still wearing last night's clothes and her hair is a mess, but as usual, she looks beautiful.

We coax her out of bed and into the washroom, filling the tub for her.

"I can do it on my own." She rolls her eyes and we retreat back into the bedroom area to wait by her fireplace. Once she's cleaned up, we head out to explore town. The antidote may have protected her body and mind from HelioX's harmful effects, but the substance is still highly addictive. Rus and Vesto think that based on her dosage, if we can keep her away from it for the next twenty-four hours, she should be in the clear from further cravings. That means Romina and I are going to spend the day babysitting Seline. Fantastic.

With our colorful fur cloaks pulled tight around us,

we make our way out into the crisp morning air. Today we are exploring Kad. I'm particularly excited about checking out the yearlong indoor marketplace known as The Halls where various vendors have set up booths with a range of products. Some sell meats and cheese while others showcase fruits and vegetables that they've been able to grow despite the perpetual winter. I have no doubt the farmers have relied on the help of Royal Magic for that.

We move through the booths with a comfortable silence. The three of us have spent so much time together by now that we can communicate without speaking. When we stumble upon an alleyway of more exotic goods, we share a look of excitement, nodding in agreement to follow the trail of our curiosity.

"Finally, something interesting." Seline turns to lead us toward this new section of vendor booths.

"Don't stray too far." Romina's voice is stern.

"I'm not a child, Romina." Seline hurries off and we agree to give her some distance, at least we can still see her up ahead of us. She's not leaving our peripheral vision.

We poke around a booth which sells enchanted objects. Romina picks up a small trinket, it looks like a bell. She turns it over in her hands before putting it down. Next she picks up a glass jar of pink liquid.

"What does this do?" She asks the seller who's name plate reads Urma: a green scaled female with pink rosy cheeks. I realize she's a Sprite, a non-human magical being whose limited power can only be used on natural materials, like water or stone. In a kingdom like Kadneria,

Sprites do not pose much of a threat, especially in comparison to Royal Magic. I check her wrist, no bracelet. I pinch Romina's arm and indicate towards Urma. She gives her a quick scan and looks back to me with a nod, understanding. We'll have to look into this later. It is strange that Sprites living in the kingdom would be exempt from the mandatory use of Royal Magic. Come to think of it, no Sprites are in the running for the Prince's hand this Season.

"Two sips each night will make you even more beautiful!" Urma beams. "Not that you two need it." She nods towards a different jar, this one has green liquid. "Or, you could use that one to take away someone else's beauty, perhaps a competitor, someone else vying for the Prince!" She's smart to assume that we are two of the Prince's Suitors. Everyone knows about the Marriage Season. No doubt there are extra vendors here today looking to sell their goods to the foreigners who have gathered to participate in the Season or simply bear witness to it. The people of Kadneria love to be entertained by the drama of Court, and an unprecedented marriage Season like this is quite the spectacle. People have come from all over to try and catch a glimpse of it. Hence why we are here, keeping tabs.

"And what of the bell?" Romina picks it up again. She gives it a little jingle.

"Just a bell, but I could enchant it for you, for a price," Urma shrugs.

"I'll take it as is!" Romina exclaims, handing over a couple coins.

"Mina, what for?" It's a nice bell but I have no idea what use she would have for it.

"A trinket for the Prince. I think it will endear him to me." It's a good idea. Maybe I should look for something to give him as well.

"If your goal is endearment... how about one of these?" Urma pulls out a wooden box and opens it to reveal an assortment of polished blue stones. Their smooth surface looks like silk. Some are rounded, no bigger than the palm of my hand, while others are ring shaped as if the middles have been carved out then smoothed over.

"What are they for?" I look up at Urma as her rosy cheeks spread into a wicked smile.

"They are enchanted for pleasure," she proclaims.

Of course they are. I should have guessed. Romina giggles. She looks over her shoulder to check on Seline then back to the wooden box.

"Maybe we should get one for Seline," she whispers to me, her eyes flickering in the way they do when she suggests an uncharacteristically risky idea.

Get one for Seline? Why would we do that? Seline certainly knows how to pleasure herself.

"You can use them on yourself or with a partner, they are enchanted after all," Urma offers, eager to make a sale.

"Darbs, maybe *you* could use this to help *distract her*." Romina gives me a gentle nudge and I can't believe she is suggesting this.

"I thought you were happy I was staying away from her."

"I am, that's why I think this would work," she says by

way of explanation, as if any of this makes sense. "You don't need to be anywhere near her but could still give her something to take her mind off *you know what.*"

"Then why don't you do it?" I cross my arms, glancing back at Seline. If only she knew what we were talking about. I'm sure she'd get a kick out of this.

"You know what she likes." Romina has a point. "Plus this way maybe you can get the best of both worlds, enjoy Seline without getting emotionally attached. Pleasure with boundaries in place, right?" Romina nudges me again and I look back towards the wooden box. Am I actually considering this?

As soon as we are properly distracted, our focus trained on Urma's enchanted items, Seline makes a run for it, disappearing into a tunnel. Romina releases a small gasp before sprinting off after her, cursing under her breath. I quickly purchase two of the stones and then race after them.

After corralling Seline back to her room in the guest quarters we all start to get ready for the ball. There's a firm single knock on the door. We open it to find Vesto with three garment bags draped over his arm. He marches straight into the room with the confidence of a life long companion of ours. As if we haven't just met. As if we aren't just a few days into working together.

"How's she doing?" Vesto asks, his bright green eyes never dulling.

"*She's* doing just fine," Seline answers for herself.

"You're my favorite Shadow, you know that?" Vesto's usual amusement dances across his handsome face.

"What are those?!" Romina takes in the garment bags that Vesto now bears across both arms, as if carrying a maiden to her bedchamber.

"The Prince has been so bored in his confinement he decided to design gowns for everyone based on what he thinks would suit you." No sooner has Vesto finished explaining this than we're peeling the garment bags open to discover Prince Nolan's creations. We find Romina's gown first. The beautiful lavender silk garment has an empire waist with a cascading floor length skirt covered in thousands of tiny sparkling flowers. A delicate lace collar sits at her neck. The light purple hue brings out the brightness of her eyes. The cut is modest, but beautiful, perfect for twirling around a dance floor or rolling in a bed of wild forest flowers.

"Well done, Prince!" She smiles, hugging the garment against her chest.

For every bit that Romina's gown was modest, Seline's gown drips sex. The gown is made up of bright red lace coated in a some sort of lacquered red fabric that looks like melted sugar. While the lace hugs her chest and torso, the shiny fabric dips and folds, draping over her breasts and thighs before cascading to the floor. She looks like candy. I swallow hard. I wonder how Seline's date with the Prince went if he walked away thinking *this* would suit her.

"He's quite talented isn't he!?" Vesto marvels at Seline's gown before handing me the final bag. "Let's see what he made for you, Darby."

I take the bag and I dip behind the changing screen. A sea of sheer pink tulle flows out from the garment bag in the most perfect pale shade as soon as I pry the bag open. Gently, I remove the dress and begin to find my way into it. There's a tight bodice that secures around my middle with three bows. One right above my full breasts, then two more below that serve to cinch in my waist and accentuate my curves. The bodice fabric is pure gold and it continues down my legs into little shorts. I step into it, realizing it's all one piece. A full tulle skirt surrounds the shorts, sheer pink cascades to the floor covering my legs and as it catches the light I realize it's covered in tiny sparkling gemstones. The gold of the bodice subtly blends into the pink tulle which puffs up over my arms, leaving my shoulders bare. It's the most ethereal dress I've ever worn. I step out from behind the screen and Vesto's jaw drops.

"Wow, you look stunning, Darbs!" Romina races to my side, handing me a pair of gold stilettos. "Let's make the most of this, shall we?" she says, and I squeeze her hands in response. After providing more intel, Vesto excuses himself to finish getting ready and we go back to doing our makeup for the ball. Seline is positioned before me on the edge of her bed as I lean over to dust glitter onto her sharp cheekbones. She's having trouble sitting still and has barely eaten all day.

"You should really eat something before we go," I tell her between brush strokes.

"I'm not hungry," she mumbles.

"It might help take your mind off..."

"Getting my hands on the substance? Dipping in for

another spoonful?" Seline's voice takes on an unexpected burst of enthusiasm as she continues. "Aren't you curious what it was like? How good it felt?" Her fingers are wrapped up in the tulle of my skirt, playing with the delicate fabric as she says this. I wonder if she realizes.

"No, actually, I'm not." I look down at her and she tilts her head up to meet my gaze as if noticing me for the first time.

"You look pretty in this dress." She's quieter now, more reserved.

"Could say the same thing about you," I tell her.

"I was going for hot, not pretty," she declares in response.

"Then you look hot, not pretty," I reply, earning a hard won smile from Seline.

"Bee... will you help me get through this?" Seline only asks for help when she's desperate. She must really be fighting against her urges right now. I place my hand on her shoulder, gently.

"If you find yourself struggling once we get there, just give me the signal."

She nods in reply and I make sure to pack the stones in my purse when we leave.

15

Ingrid is notably absent from the night's activities.

"I heard she entered the Season without her family's consent, and when they found out, they stole her back to their farmlands!" Princess Brianna of Crichton sips her sparkling wine while dishing out this obviously false tale. Her short brown hair is streaked with ruby red and decorated with red gemstones. Her deep blue eyes match the midnight blue gown that drapes over her shoulders elegantly. The top of the gown is in stark contrast to the impossibly short skirt which shows off her tan, toned legs and extremely high heels. She looks regal and seductive at the same time, and her accent becomes more prevalent the more she drinks.

"Really? I heard she wasn't impressed with the Prince and packed her bags all on her own," Amarie offers in her familiar monotone. Her buttery golden hair is decorated with pearls, her white gown shares an equally pearlescent quality. She looks rather *bridal*.

"Either way, one down, 13 more to go." Brianna makes a good point. There were 14 Ladies in the running for the Prince's hand. After tonight's elimination, there will only be 10.

We're all gathered in a small holding room while the Prince completes his final blind dates. He's got two minutes with each of us before he makes his first elimination and gets to see us for the first time at the *Grand Reveal Ball.*

I notice Rus is stationed in the corner watching over the festivities. He meets my gaze for a moment then looks away. I don't have time for whatever games he's playing. Romina has just returned from her chat when I pull her aside. It's imperative that all three of us make it past this first elimination since the Prince doesn't yet know we are Shadows.

"How'd it go?" I study her face for clues.

"Good I think, he enjoyed the trinket." I'm glad that the Prince likes Romina. With her brains and beauty I wouldn't be surprised if he fell for her for *real.* Romina is a catch. That being said, she's much better at the whole don't-get-attached thing than I am. I've never seen her get her feelings hurt over the years. She always guards her heart. She's never let anyone break it. As per usual, I admire her.

Seline marches up to me and Romina with a look of panic in her eyes. She's sweating.

"I need to get out of here," she says through gritted teeth.

"You haven't chatted with the Prince yet, you have to

stay." Romina's voice is a heavy whisper, her face a mask of calm.

"Then you've got to give me *something*." Seline means HelioX, which we obviously do not have.

"We don't *have* anything to give you Seline," Romina reminds her. I can't believe how strong this substance must be to have such a profound effect on Seline after just one use. I watch the beads of sweat building on her forehead. We have to do something to help distract her.

"I have something to take your mind off it." I think of the stones in my purse.

Romina gives me a knowing glance. "Take her to the washroom, I'll cover for you."

I take Seline's hand and pull her along behind me. Once we reach the washroom I shut the door behind us and pull out the two silky blue stones. Seline looks down at them, then back up at me.

"They are enchanted," I tell her. She frowns in confusion. "For pleasure," I add. At that, her face quirks up into that all too familiar mischievous smile. "Just give it a light squeeze and think about sending your magic to it."

Seline takes one of the pebbles and presses it firmly in her hand, it starts to vibrate. She gives it another squeeze and it stops. She then holds it flat in her palm and blinks her eyes. It begins to vibrate again, she blinks once more and it stops. I do the same with the other stone. We practice binding our magic with the enchanted stone a couple more times until we don't even need to blink to control the vibrations and can do it by thought alone. Then, I hand her my stone and she hands me hers. I slide the smooth stone under my dress, under the little shorts, and fit it firmly in place against me. Seline does the same with hers. All it takes is one single thought of that stone pressing against the apex of her thighs, and it begins to vibrate. Seline's expression changes. She whimpers, putting her hands on the wall to brace herself. She closes her eyes and I watch her in that candy red lace dress as her pleasure begins to rear its head. But I can't give it to her all at once. We've got a long night ahead of us. With another thought, I stop the vibrations. Her eyes fly open immediately.

"First one to finish loses," she dares me.

"Don't you mean wins?" I say back to her.

"I guess we win either way." With that she pivots and makes her way back out into the ballroom.

I send a couple small flutters of vibration to Seline later when I see that she is being called in to chat with the Prince. I resist the urge to send anything during her actual conversation with him, she is already distracted and if she blows this and gets eliminated it will make our job even more complicated. She hasn't sent anything to me yet. It's possible she never will, yet, the knowledge of this possibility alone has had an effect on me. I feel my pulse quickening.

The two minutes pass, and Seline floats back into the room without looking at me. I fiddle with my wineglass, barely able to concentrate on the conversation Amarie is having with Lucci the Sea Nymph, despite the fact that I find Sea Nymph culture incredibly interesting and am desperate to get to know Lucci better. I make a mental note to chat with Romina about why the non-human Sea Nymphs can use Royal Magic but Sprites can't. Most likely because Sea Nymphs are more powerful, but I'm curious to hear what she thinks.

Maybe I should just take my stone out. Seline probably won't even use it on me. I send her another small flutter. And another. I watch in delight as she nearly knocks over a tray of cheeses. And yet, she sends me nothing back.

Why would she?

We're doing this to help her, why would pleasuring me benefit her at this point?

The dates are almost over and I'm the last one called in. I make my way into a sitting room where Prince Nolan is seated on a plush velvet sofa behind the same one-way glass as yesterday's date.

"And so we meet again, *Nolan*." I make sure to use his first name this time.

"Darby, Darby, Darby, they saved the best for last." His voice greets me like a warm hug.

"It's too soon to be picking favorites." This earns a smile from him.

"It's never too early, Darby." He crosses his legs and I take note of the absolutely gorgeous beading of his trousers. They are covered in deep green sparkling stones. His shirt is a woven net of the same color with stones sewn intermittently. His chiseled abs and silky smooth skin are visible through the netting. He looks divine.

"Did you design your own outfit as well?" I can't take my eyes off him.

"Not this one, but some of my others." He shifts in his seat self-consciously, as if he knows I'm drooling over him. "Were you pleased with your own gown? I had this idea that..."

He continues talking but I can't hear him because the most thrilling, piercing, delicious vibration I've ever felt is taking my body by storm.

I gasp. Audibly.

"Darby?" The prince sounds concerned. Which makes sense, considering the noise he just heard me make. I quickly try to collect myself.

"Oh sorry, I thought I saw another bearhound!" Good thing he can't see me. The vibration stops and I fan my face. Seline isn't playing nice. I need to do my best to remain composed no matter what else she sends my way.

"Sadly, Buddy is confined to my room tonight." Nolan buys my excuse, or maybe he's just amused by my outburst.

"That's too bad. However, the gown is breathtaking, thank you." I ensure that my words are even keeled as they leave my mouth.

"I can't wait to see you in it!" he exclaims.

"I can't wait for you to *see me* in it!" The vibration is back and this time it has taken on a steady rhythm. Is she going to sustain this for my entire conversation with the Prince?

Seline is evil. Pure Evil.

"You will save me a dance tonight, won't you?" he asks, and I force myself to concentrate on him, on his sparkling suit, on his elated expression.

"If I'm not eliminated!" I find myself rocking forward

in my seat so the stone can touch me at a better angle and wow, does that feel good. I spread my legs ever so slightly. Thank the Friend for this one-way glass so that he cannot see me.

"You're not getting eliminated. I really meant it when I said that I think you're special Darby, I feel so at ease with you already. Like we could talk to each other forever." His verbal affirmations are making me feel warm inside. That, in combination with the stone's unrelenting vibrations, and I'm about ready to burst.

"I like it when... you say things like that." My voice quivers, giving me away.

His expression changes.

Can he tell how turned on I am?

I fear that he might.

"What kind of *things?*" The corners of his mouth quirk up in a type of smile I haven't seen from him yet. A hungry smile.

"I like it when you speak with so much assurance. When you say how you're feeling about me. How I make you feel..." His pupils are dilating now, like he can tell from my voice alone that I'm aroused at present.

"I can say some more if you like." He uncrosses his legs now, leaning forward in his seat.

"Please do." I spread my legs even wider.

"Even though I haven't seen you yet, I find myself lying awake at night trying to picture you. Your golden glow. Your honey scent. Your warm hand interlaced with mine again..."

Oh, yes.

Yes, this is fantastic.

The vibrations are getting *faster* now, and his voice is so deep. So steady. This unlikely turn of events is really working for me and I feel myself getting closer just as...

"Times up!" It isn't Vesto who calls out from the doorway this time.

It's Rus.

The vibration immediately stops and my legs lock together tightly. Nolan clears his throat. He sits up straighter. As do I.

"See you on the dance floor, Nolan!" I squeak out, collecting my skirt and exiting without looking at Rus. Out of the corner of my eye I can't help but notice the Prince adjusting himself before standing. It would seem we both were enjoying ourselves.

16

Silence falls over the waiting room where I'm now crowded amongst the other ladies. Some tap their feet nervously while others fan their faces. We were told that Prince Nolan would be delivering his decision to Vesto and Rus, who would then share the news with us. Any moment now, the first elimination will take place.

Amarie doesn't look bothered in the slightest as Vesto finally joins us with a scroll in his hands. He steps forward and calls out the names of three Ladies I've hardly spoken to. The women step forward.

"I'm sorry Ladies, you will not be moving forward with the Season. Thank you for your time. May The Friend, The Foe and The Frequency watch over you. Please return your charms."

One of the women throws her silver charm then runs out crying, the other two hand theirs over and exit gracefully. Their time with the Prince is over, and so their piece of his heart must be returned.

It's no surprise that Amarie, Lucci, and Brianna all remain, as do Ruby, Gabrielle, Nicole and Sidney. Including the three of us Shadows, that means it's down to 10. My mind briefly goes to Ingrid, I wonder how she's doing.

"Now let's get this party started!" Vesto leads us to the top of a staircase where we will be announced as we each enter the ball. One by one, he calls out our formal titles.

"Lady Seline LeStray!"

Seline steps forward and I hold off on sending any more vibrations. I'd like to give her a taste of what the anticipation did for me. Now she'll have to wait as well.

"How come Seline got to be a Lady? You and I are both just *Miss* this time," Romina huffs from behind me. The two of them can be so competitive, even over fictional identities. As Shadows, we are given a new first name upon enrollment into the Academy. This name becomes our primary alias, the same first name with a revolving door of fictional surnames.

"Miss Darby Contess!"

I reach my pinky out to Romina, interlocking with hers as we share a final look. Then, I step forward onto the stairs to enter the ballroom.

The grand ballroom is filled with hundreds of glowing lavender and gold orbs. They float between silver pillars, drifting up towards the ceiling like stars. The dance floor is a perfect checkerboard of gold and silver tiles. I take in the smiling faces of the Royal Court. They're all dressed in their finest and most outlandish suits and gowns, which unlike the gray skies outside, are bursting with color. A band strikes up a romantic ballad. This would all be perfect, if not for the man who stands in front of me at the bottom of the stairs. Not Prince Nolan, but King Godwin.

He wears silver sparkling furs. In fact, he's the only one here who isn't doused in a rich color. His now wispy, fully silver hair flops casually atop his head around a silver crown I recognize from the painting. His jaw line is coated in a salt and pepper beard. There is a clear resemblance between him and Nolan. I suppose that should make him handsome, but there is something deeply unsettling about his smile. He extends a leathery hand toward me and I realize with horror that I am meant to take it. My hand lands in his and he begins to guide me from the base of the stairs over to where Prince Nolan is beaming at me. But I can't focus on Nolan. Not when I am holding hands with the King. The King who called all the Storytelling families to the Winter Palace and gave them the option to help with Royal Magic. The King who told us to choose a flag but set our homes aflame if he did not agree with the decision we made. The King who is using Royal Magic for his own agenda, even if I don't yet know *how*. This King is a monster.

"Darby! You are even better than I imagined." My thoughts are interrupted by Prince Nolan as he swoops in, wrapping his arms around me and earning a few gasps from the other Ladies.

"You flatter me." I politely pull away, smiling at him. He's just as handsome as he was through the one-way glass but now I can *feel* him too. There's a warmth to him, an energy that makes my skin tingle.

"Remember, you promised me a dance." He takes my

hand and presses it to his lips again, just like he did in Vesto's room that day. My eyes linger on the King and he stares straight back at me. It sends a chill down my spine, immediately cooling the warmth that Nolan's presence had created.

"I could never forget," I offer, as I make my way to wait with the others while the announcements continue.

Amarie is the first to dance with the Prince. And the Second.

I'm standing as close to them as I can without making it obvious that I'm eavesdropping.

"You didn't like the dress I sent you?" Prince Nolan asks, while twirling her.

"I loved it, I just felt this one was better for the grand reveal. I want all of Court to see me for what I truly am," she responds with confidence.

"And what is that?" The Prince looks flustered as she steps back into his embrace, even closer this time.

"Your future bride," she says, with complete conviction.

So her bridal look was on purpose then. Well played, Amarie.

"Care to dance?" I turn to find Vesto before me, looking as handsome as ever in a deep green suit similar to the Prince's. His hair has been styled into a mohawk. It looks good on him. I smile and offer him my hand. We find a spot on the other side of the ballroom.

We're out of earshot of Prince Nolan and Princess

Amarie now, but they remain in our line of sight. I watch as she attempts to keep him for a third dance.

"So we have just a teeny tiny problem on our hands." Vesto's eyes never leave the Prince as he clasps my hand in his and we begin to step in time to the music.

"And what is that, my darling Vesto?" In my high heels, Vesto and I are about eyeline. For the first time, I notice the intense hue of his naturally green eyes. How fitting.

"I spoke to the Prince. You're his favorite," Vesto informs me.

"I thought he was just flirting." Heat colors my cheeks, I don't know why this information has caused me to blush.

"He was, but also, he meant it." Vesto's amused smirk drops as his tone turns chastising. "Do you think you could tone it down a little?"

I shrug my shoulders in response. Clearly I understand why being Nolan's favorite presents an issue since he doesn't yet know I'm not actually an option. And yet, part of me feels proud that I've earned his notice without him even seeing me until now. The most Nolan and I have done is hold hands, and yet, he favors me. Meanwhile both Seline and Rus were only ever interested in something physical with me. It feels nice to be on the receiving end of this more innocent type of affection. I'm flattered.

"I'm just being myself." Vesto spins me out now and I use the opportunity to gaze over at the Prince who has successfully excused himself from Princess Amarie and is now dancing with Princess Brianna.

"Maybe you need to play more of a character instead,

could you take on a new role? One less similar to your true self?" Vesto asks as I return to face him.

"So my entire personality just changes overnight? That would be jarring don't you think?" We sway and watch as Nolan rolls his eyes playfully, earning a laugh from Brianna. They are comfortable with each other. I wonder if they've met before. Most likely the Prince has encountered both of the young Princesses over the years. I remember Amarie mentioning something about a history with Nolan. He really should marry a Princess.

"Why don't we just tell him we are Shadows, then he will know I'm not truly one of his options." The words have only just left my lips when Vesto's expression goes blank. His eyes glaze over.

"Are you alright?" I give his hand a squeeze, picking up our dance again. He collects himself and joins me.

"I just had a vision," his voice drops as he whispers to me.

"Tell me more."

"You need to remember that my visions aren't set in stone, they are things that *might* happen, especially if they are faint, the more faint they are the less likely I find they are actually going to happen. Like for example, my vision about the Prince finding his Link and getting more powerful? That one was solid. It was as real as a memory, I know it will happen, and sure I didn't see *who* she was but I know for certain that she exists..."

"Vesto, stay focused, what did you see?" I adjust my hand on his shoulder, calling him back to attention.

"I saw a world in which you *were* a real option." He gives my side a squeeze as he says this. I almost laugh.

Sure, of course there's a world in which that would happen considering I am here as part of the marriage Season, technically I am an *option*. It would seem that at this point, I'm even the favorite. But it would never actually pan out that it is me he is looking for.

"Even if I'm his favorite so far, don't forget it's not fully up to him. His Link is his fated mate. You don't get to choose your soulmate, the Goddesses have chosen for us, and there's no way they've chosen me." Vesto looks a little sad as he listens to me, but I continue. "I hear your concern about me distracting him from finding *her*, whoever she is. I'll adjust my behavior."

I feel a sense of relief when Vesto's signature amused smile returns.

"It's a nice thought that there is someone out there for each of us, isn't it?" His eyes scan the room. I wonder if there is anyone here he likes.

"Except for Shadows," I say, as he holds his arm out for me to turn about him. I take my time circling.

"You think Shadows are exempt from fated mates!?" he exclaims.

"Shadows swear a blood oath not to form attachments," I inform him.

"And you think that's yours to decide? I don't think anyone gets to choose who they feel attached to. Especially if the Goddesses have a say in it," he challenges, and so I allow my thoughts to travel to an unknown world in which Nolan and I could actually be right for each other. A world in which I wasn't a Shadow. A world without Royal Magic. A world in which we were just two kids who met in the hallway of the Palace.

"May I cut in?" There's a tap on Vesto's shoulder and as if I had conjured him with my thoughts, we look up to see Prince Nolan smiling down at us. He is much taller than Vesto. It's funny seeing them side by side.

"Of course." Vesto gives Nolan a knowing smile. "Behave yourselves!" he says, before heading off to check in on the other Ladies.

Prince Nolan places one hand on the small of my waist, collecting my own hand in his other. The band slows their pace and we inch closer to sway to the new rhythm. I press in against his solid chest. He is warm and smells like chocolate. My favorite.

"The dress suits you perfectly," he murmurs in my ear.

"You're very intuitive. I'm impressed that you could nail us all so perfectly."

Nail us all so perfectly!? Why did I have to phrase it that way!

"I mean, you just got us all so well– you know what I mean." I correct myself, rolling my eyes at my own eloquence. Or lack thereof.

He laughs in my ear and it's the best sound in the world.

"I know what you mean." He pulls me impossibly closer to his chest. His wet lips are now touching my ear. My first thought is that I want to get a tattoo of the imprint, my second thought is that I've clearly lost my mind. "Maybe I got you a little too excited earlier, now you're inadvertently making innuendos..." he continues. Maybe he did get me too excited.

Well, him plus the stone.

Plus Seline.

Although right now, it's him who is making my heart flutter.

I need to cool it. I've gotten completely carried away in a fantasy that was meant to only last a moment. I need to bring this conversation back to safe territory.

Back to *reality*.

"So that's your Father, huh?" Yes. This will do. Hearing him talk about his loyalty to the King will be the cold shower I need.

"That's him. It's traditional that the King should offer the Prince a bride, so we thought the way he passed you all off was a nice nod to that, since I'm choosing my own bride this Season." I would bet money that the King is less than thrilled about this arrangement. It must be really worth it for him to have Nolan grow more powerful. I wonder why.

"How progressive. Do you find that he is a kind Monarch?" I mask my contempt behind a sugarcoated smile.

"Kind? Why, yes, don't you think? Royal Magic ensures there is equality amongst the three magic types. It brings peace to our land. I would consider that a kindness."

This plan is working, I feel that my anger is growing to a soft boil below the surface of my skin. I think of my neighbor's home going up in flames. I think of my Grandma.

"Funny, I don't remember a lack of peace *before* Royal Magic was introduced," I say through gritted teeth.

Prince Nolan laughs again, but this time it doesn't give me goosebumps.

"How could you possibly remember a time before Royal Magic?" He shakes his head as I snag on the meaning of his words.

"What do you mean?" I look at him in disbelief.

"My father brought Royal Magic to the Kingdom years before we were born. You are one year younger than me, are you not?" I search Nolan's face for any sign of jest but I find no evidence. In fact, he thinks *I'm* the one being playful. He truly believes this. Something is seriously wrong with the Prince, but I've got a part to play.

I hide any trace of the surprise I feel.

"You're totally right, I must have forgotten. Perhaps you really did get me too excited earlier," I say without meaning it, itching for this song to end. Before I can escape his clutches all on my own, Seline appears. She taps the Prince's shoulder.

"Mind if I cut in? I'm growing tired of waiting." She looks at me as she says this and I catch her meaning.

"We weren't quite finished yet." Nolan says this as kindly as possible but I'm done dancing with him, so I pause our movements.

"Please, go ahead, I would hate to make you wait any longer." I step aside to allow Seline to take my place as the band picks up their pace. Nolan accepts his fate of dancing with her as I head off without looking back at them. I send a subtle round of vibrations Seline's way and can only imagine the smile that must spread across her face.

I need to find Romina immediately.

17

Romina and I step outside the ballroom to get some air and I fill her in on my discoveries. We come up with a list of events in recent history and for the rest of the evening, we find ways to weave them into conversation with other members of Court at the ball. To our amazement, no one can remember a time before Royal Magic, and in some cases, people are blurry on the details of their own lives before they started using it.

We also discover that no one can remember how Queen Lydia died.

The details of the Queen's death has long since been a Royal secret. If the only people who know about it are here at Court amongst the Royals, then I fear we will never learn how it truly happened. I wonder if Nolan knows. He was so young when it happened.

He was young when Royal Magic came to be. He was young when he got his Eclipse Gift too. Is it possible that he has forgotten his gift?

"Mina." I grab her arm and pull her away from the handsome nobleman she's now flirting with for information.

"Yes, Darbs?" She bats her lashes as she speaks.

"Do you think it's possible to forget your own Eclipse Gift?"

She looks up then, her mismatched blue eyes turned towards the sky as if scanning her own brain for information, then responds.

"It's possible. Depending on what it is."

"Let's say you had a Gift that manifested before Royal Magic and in the wiping of memories, it was swept away."

"Well I'm beginning to think that the missing memories are things that had to do with the Royal Magic, or the lack thereof, so when altering their minds to forget a time without it, certain events wouldn't make sense anymore, so the memories were wiped to avoid confusion," she says, and I find that I agree with her line of thinking.

"So let's say that before Royal Magic, you manifested Dreamseeing-" I begin to say when Romina cuts me off abruptly.

"Darby, have you met a Dreamseer?" Her face turns serious.

"I have." She knows that if I could tell her more I would. But I can't. This isn't my secret to share, at least not yet.

"Yet, they no longer seem to be aware that they *are* a Dreamseer. How is that possible? Even if they forgot, wouldn't the Gift still present itself?"

"Maybe they don't realize what is happening. Perhaps

the memory of what it *is* that's going on has left them. In the case of a Dreamseer, they may just think they are experiencing an overactive imagination, or increased intuition." Her excitement grows with each word, as if she's just made a scientific discovery. "Even when not using their Gift, Dreamseers would be highly sensitive to how others are feeling and what they desire or fear."

Holy Foe. *The Gowns.*

He knew what would please us. Even with my shielding. Nolan is incredibly intuitive.

"Why would the King want people to forget a time before Royal Magic?" Romina wonders out loud and I begin to follow her down the rabbit hole.

"Hard to rebel against something that's been around forever," I suggest.

"And if the people can't remember a time without it, they can't argue that life was better beforehand," she adds on.

"It's just another way to control them." I turn to scan the ballroom, thinking of all of these innocent people at Court who are required to use the Royal Magic. Sure, most people in Kadneria praise the power-sharing system. Most people choose to live within its range of use. But do they know that their minds are being tampered with? Would they still opt in if they knew?

"To alter their memories... that's such an invasion," Romina shudders, clearly on my same train of thought.

"Mina, we have to do something about this." I turn back to her now.

"Darbs, that's not our mission." We've reached a stalemate once again, but I will no longer stand for it.

"Maybe it's not *your* mission." My fist clenches at my side as I say this.

"Are you saying you have your own orders?" She leans closer, her eyes scanning me.

"I am." It is true. My mother sent me here for a reason. She said it was time to stop hiding. It's time to tell Romina more than I've ever told her before. I trust her. If I let her in, I know she will agree with me because what's happening here is wrong. We need to help people.

"Ladies." We look up to see Rus standing in front of us.

"Hi Rus, are you enjoying the ball?" Romina smiles warmly at him, the tension between us dissipating as if we were not just in the middle of a heated discussion.

"I would enjoy it more if I were dancing. Would either of you care to join me?" he asks us both, as if he couldn't care less which one of us he danced with this evening. As if this wasn't the first time we are interacting since he almost kissed me last night then left without another word. That won't do. Not at all.

"Can't decide between the two of us?" Romina puts her hand on her hip. She knows what I'm thinking.

"Well it is Darby I wished to ask originally, but I didn't want to offend you, Romina."

So he's just being polite. Okay, that's fine, Rus.

Romina must be on the same page as me, because without missing a beat, she bows her head to him and says, "Not offended at all, enjoy yourselves." She nudges me towards Rus and I follow him to the dance floor. Once we reach the edge of the silver and gold checkerboard tiles, he offers me one of his large, cold hands and pulls me in. Not too close. We begin to glide along the dance floor in time to the music. His moves are elegant. I follow his lead but my mind is still racing from the conversion with Romina.

"Are we no longer speaking?" Rus asks, glancing down at me. I find it interesting that he thinks I might be upset with him. But if I'm being honest, I'm not. He came to my room last night to end things, he left without kissing me. Based on these facts, I can only assume that what happened between us was a one time thing. A physical connection and nothing more. It's time I started paying attention to the facts instead of my own ideas. Ideas have only ever led me to getting my feelings hurt. Besides, between Nolan, Royal Magic, HelioX, and Seline, there's too much going on right now to think about whatever is or isn't happening between the two of us.

"No, it's just, there's a lot on my mind," I tell him, and I mean it.

"The same for me." We continue our silent steps. I notice Seline gossiping with Amarie in the corner. They start to laugh over something and I send a round of vibration her way. She looks up. Her eyes lock on mine immediately. She smiles and sends a vibration straight back to me, the first one she's sent my way in hours. It takes me by surprise and I let out a tiny whimper. The vibrations have an entirely different effect when she's looking directly at me. Even from across the room, it's so much more intimate this way. It makes the stone between my legs no longer feel like a phantom source of pleasure, instead it connects this feeling to *her*. To Seline.

"You okay?" Rus looks down again, this time with concern.

"Oh yes, I'm good. It's nice, just dancing like this." I try to hide the change in my heart rate.

"It is." The music slows and he settles his head against mine, pulling me closer. "I'm glad things are okay between us, after last night, and the night before." He mumbles, his broad shoulders tipping forward to surround me as the unmistakable smell of eucalyptus fills my lungs. There's so much of *Rus* surrounding me right now, but I look over his shoulder at Seline. I make contact with her beautiful silver eyes and send a series of vibrations her way. Without hesitation, she sends them right back at me and I know I'm in trouble. This call and response feels good. Too good. She's been teasing me all night and while I'd love to stick around this ball and continue to do research with Romina, my body has other ideas.

Seline cocks her head towards the exit, signaling that she wants to get out of here. I tilt my head towards Rus as if to say *I need a minute*, but it's clear she's done waiting. She sends a massive jolt to the stone between my legs and it nearly takes me over the edge. Before I realize what I'm doing I lean in to Rus, pressing myself against him in an attempt to quell the ache.

"Oh Foe." I look up at him in horror, and he is equally as surprised. Glancing behind him I see Seline is already making her way to the exit. "Sorry I... I need to go," I say without thinking. And with that, I break away from his hold and quickly leave the ballroom, exiting just a few paces behind Seline.

18

"You haven't come yet," Seline breaks our kiss long enough to declare.

"Neither have you," I respond, before taking her lips in mine again.

All plans of using the enchanted stones to ensure boundaries with Seline have gone out the window as I toss her down on my bed. She starts to remove her dress and I will not allow it.

"No. Keep it on," I demand. This red dress is the hottest thing I've ever seen her wear, and I refuse to think of the man who designed it for her. In fact, I'm banishing all thoughts of *him* for the rest of the evening.

I tap my fingers to kill the light orb I used to lead us here then glance over at my nightstand where the unlit candelabra sits next to the flower Nolan gave me. Nope. Not thinking about him.

Seline must have followed my gaze because it's her who magically sends a small spark of flame to light the candelabra, casting a warm glow over the room. Now the room is illuminated by only the fireplace and the bedside candle. Seline smiles in approval over the shift in energy. It's much more intimate.

I climb back on top of her. Kissing her deeply. I missed this so much. I missed the way our bodies fit together. I missed her smooth skin. Her hands are tugging through my hair as her red stained lips crush against mine. I pull away and begin to undo my own dress. Unfortunately two gowns are just too many gowns and I need more skin contact with her candy-coated body. There's a knock on my door. More specifically, it's three quick knocks followed by one slow one.

What is he doing here?

I pull away and Seline rolls her eyes in annoyance. I gesture that I'll be right back before opening the door half way, covering my body as my gown hangs off me halfway undone.

"Are you alright? You left so abruptly." Rus stands there in the hallway before my door, panting.

"Yes. I'm fine, goodnight, Rus." I try to close the door in his face but he stops it.

"Are you sure? You sound frazzled." He sounds concerned. The door swings open as Seline comes up behind me, she uses her arm to hold my dress up, wrapping herself tightly around my breasts.

"I'm afraid that's my fault. I needed a distraction to help with the come down. Bee here stepped up to the challenge." She gives one of my breasts a light squeeze.

Rus' jaw drops. He takes in the sight of us. What a sight it must be.

"What are you really doing here, Cyrus?" Seline looks him over as we both note his slightly disheveled state. Did he run here? I find it interesting that he would be so concerned about me that he would chase me out of the ballroom. He didn't care much last night.

Was that just last night? It feels like a lifetime ago now.

But he did come to my rescue during the full Moon. If you could call it a rescue. Maybe he likes it when I'm in distress. Maybe that's his thing.

"As I said, I wanted to check on her." Rus clears his throat.

"He helped me out the other night," I don't know why I feel the need to share this with Seline, but now that it's out there, I can't take it back.

"Which night?" Seline looks down at me, her lips now skimming against my cheek bone.

"During the full Moon, Goldie was in need of some assistance," Rus offers, and I turn as red as her dress. Of course Seline knows exactly what type of assistance I was in need of considering it's been her who *assisted* me for the better part of the last three years.

"Goldie?" Seline's lips form a tight smile. I have no idea how she is going to react to this.

Will she be jealous? Is she ever jealous?

Her posture relaxes. "I suppose I should thank you for *taking care* of our girl." Of all the ways she might have responded, I never could have imagined that. "Want to come in?"

I watch in slow motion as Seline welcomes Rus into my room and closes the door behind him. She takes his hand and guides him to the foot of my bed. She then gently nudges me to sit down next to him. He seems just as bewildered as I am.

"I'm in need of some assistance of my own. These urges are driving me wild and the only thing stopping me from running out of here and tearing up all of Kadneria until I find more HelioX is the promise of an exceptional orgasm. Preferably more than one," Seline explains this to us, her voice unfaltering, as cool and calm as ever.

There's no way her heart is beating as fast as mine is.

She perches on my lap. My eyes dip to the red lace covering her cleavage. The lacquered fabric looks like melted sugar. I hold myself back from licking it. It occurs to me that her desire must have been to look good enough to eat. Nolan really came through for her.

Don't think about Nolan!

"Bee's been getting me worked up all night. She's a big tease, did you know that?" Seline steals my attention back easily as she traces a fingertip through my hair.

Rus looks over at me, then to Seline.

"Are you two...?" His Adam's apple bobs up the length of his throat as he swallows, unable to find the words to finish that sentence.

"Sometimes, but it's nothing serious," Seline answers for us casually. I try to school my features so as not to look upset. As if you could call three years nothing serious.

Seline shifts over to Rus' lap, and I'm stunned by the sight of them together. These two gorgeous creatures. I wonder what it would be like to watch them kiss. I've never seen Seline kiss a man before. My memory floats back to the discovery of Rus' tongue piercing. I wonder what Seline would think of it.

"Dicks aren't usually my thing, but this is an extraordinary circumstance and I find the idea amusing." She brings her face close to his, their mouths nearly touching before she pulls away and stands up in front of us. I nearly gasp. I wonder if she can hear my heart beating. I wonder if she knows what the sight of their mouths so close together just did to me. Based on the way her eyes just flicked up to meet mine, I have a feeling she knows exactly what she's doing right now.

"So what do you say Cyrus? Care to join us this evening?" She's blunt, but it's effective.

I've always loved how straightforward she is. Even when it hurts me.

Rus turns to face me. There is no way this is what he thought he was walking into tonight.

"Whatever Goldie wants." Now they're both looking at me.

What do I want?

Honestly, it's hard to argue against this since it will help Seline.

But beyond that, maybe this is what I need to do to disentangle myself from her. It's clear this experience is about pleasure, not feelings. I know that going in. I'm being given the chance to sign up for it. And with Rus, he's made it clear it's just physical between us as well. For once I won't be expecting more and then find myself disappointed.

It feels empowering to choose this for myself. Yes. This feels good, freeing.

"I'm in," I tell them, and I mean it.

"Okay," Rus says in agreement.

"Good, now show me what you did the other night." Seline looms over us. She licks her lips.

"You want to watch?" I look at Seline and she nods. It's dark enough in here that I don't feel self-conscious, so I stand up and let my already undone dress fall completely off. Shimming out of the tulle skirt and the built-in gold shorts, I subtly slide out my stone. I know Seline is still wearing hers. Rus puts a gentle hand on the bare skin of my hip to guide me back down next to him on the bed. His hand is cold, as usual, but I find it grounding. Without his cool touch I may burn straight out of my own skin. I'm so worked up right now.

Without hesitation, I lean in and kiss him. One of his hands floats across my chest and begins to slowly tease my exposed nipples while the other travels between my legs. I send a round of pulsing vibrations to Seline's stone and she audibly gasps. I imagine that she's watching us and the thought of that excites me. Rus gently slides an exploratory finger inside of me and he gasps as well, breaking our kiss.

"You're already so wet." He sounds surprised by this.

"Did I mention I've been teasing her too?" Seline coos from in front of us.

Rus turns to Seline with hooded eyes. "And how wet are you?"

He's piqued Seline's interest, I can tell by the way she approaches him. "You'll find out soon, darling." She runs a hand through his blonde waves, tilting his head back to meet her eyes. "Now tell me, did you lick her last time?"

Rus shakes his head no. Seline pouts her candy red lips. "That's too bad, it's her favorite."

Rus frowns like he's just gotten in trouble. Maybe he has.

"Bee, would you like to be licked tonight?" Seline asks me.

I nod yes and Seline turns her attention back to him. "Well, you heard her, Cyrus." She encourages him and he springs into action. I fall back on the bed and he lifts me up to scoot me towards the top. It's an impressive movement. Next he shimmies himself down my body between my legs. I send another round of vibrations to Seline who giggles as she stands over Rus and watches him dive in. His tongue presses flat against my clit and I cry out as the cold metal of his tongue piercing touches my most sensitive area.

"Oh, you like being told what to do, don't you Cyrus?" Seline leans over his shoulder and there's a spark of something in his eyes. Maybe he does like it.

"Be a good boy and make her come. Won't you?" The order must really do something for him because he moans deeply into my folds and it nearly destroys me. I reach my hand out for Seline and pull her up towards me. She slips off her undergarment removing the stone with it, then makes to take off her dress *again*.

"No!" I demand, spreading her skirts and pulling her up to sit on my face.

"So bossy, Bee!" She finds her spot against my lips as I slip my tongue into her tender center, finding her soaked already. I begin to make out with her throbbing clit, emulating the swirling motions Rus is performing on me.

Seline faces forward, her fingertips caressing both of my breasts as she watches Rus' head bob between my legs.

It's so hot. I'm obsessed with this feeling. The three of us are forming a train of pleasure. He gives it to me and I give it to her. My mind is free of all thoughts except for soft wet tongues and the candy red skirt that splays around my face. Rus's tongue dances around my clit in the most perfect way and it causes me to moan involuntarily. He then brings his fingers back into the mix, pressing down on the exact same spot that took me over the edge last time. As if he's memorized it. Seline chooses this exact moment to flick the peaked bud of my hard nipple and the combination of it all is too much for me to handle. The biggest orgasm of my short, insignificant life comes crashing over me. Watching me come on his face is Seline's undoing and in an instant she's pulsing against my tongue. She tastes incredible.

When she slides off my face, we are both breathless. Rus sits up smiling at the two of us. My pleasure is shining on his wet lips, he lazily wipes his mouth with the back of his hand just as Seline and I notice the tent of his pants.

"Take them off," she demands, in that tone we now know he likes. He does so without hesitation and we are greeted by the sight of his smooth, stoic manhood. It stands perfectly, flawlessly erect.

"It's been a while since I rode one of those," Seline muses out loud. I do not voice the fact that I have *never* ridden one because this is neither the time nor place for that.

"Would you like to?" Rus smiles at her.

And to my absolute surprise, Seline responds, "I would."

I've had sex with women. And I've had my fair share of intimate experiences with men, but I've never taken that final step with a man before. We haven't had many opportunities to be with men outside of missions and it was never something I wanted to do while pretending to be someone else. When I do take that step, I want it to be with someone who's interested in me, the real me. And sure, Rus knows I'm a Shadow. But we don't really know each other.

Would I even want it to be like this? With him *and* Seline?

No, I don't think so. And after waiting this long, I might as well hold out for a night that isn't just about the physical act of seeking pleasure. I want my first time with a man inside of me to mean something. Besides, tonight is about helping Seline, so if she wants to ride Rus, then I'm going to help make that happen.

"How?" Rus has been reduced to one syllable words, I don't blame him.

"I want to fuck you while I kiss her," Seline says without a second thought.

Rus lays down on the bed and Seline moves to straddle him, taking his hard dick in her hand. I decide it's finally time to say goodbye to the dress and I lean forward to pull it over her head and gently toss it to the floor. This dress is a work of art, it should hang in a museum, or at least on the back of a chair, but for now the floor is the best we can do.

She starts to kiss me while stroking him up and down a couple of times. She breaks away to address him.

"We both take a tonic, just so you know, Cyrus darling," Seline tells him, referring to the contraceptive tonic we've been taking since puberty.

"I do too," he grunts.

"Good." She lifts herself up and starts to guide his length inside of her. I watch closely as Seline works her way down, taking an inch of him at a time and kissing me intermittently. It's during the break between kisses that I catch a glimpse of familiar ink on her left hip bone: the silhouette of two daggers pointed in opposite directions. The Shadow Mark. How does Seline still have hers if mine was Augmented away?

"Oh, Foe," Rus mutters under his breath, his head rolling back. I break away from Seline and scoot back on the bed, I'm going to have to ask Romina about this later. For now I level myself with Rus. He looks as beautiful as ever. He is such a pretty man. I run my fingers over his lips while Seline continues to ride him. He's all the way inside her now but his hands are on me. He cups my jaw and brings my lips to his. He kisses me deeply while Seline picks up the pace of her thrusts. She is grinding against him to seek her own pleasure atop his toned body. I run my hands over his Second Star tattoo. His stomach is firm beneath dark blue ink.

"Sit on *my* face," Rus mumbles into my mouth, and I like the idea. I shift back and find my position atop him, facing Seline. I'm still ultra sensitive from the last orgasm and this time he licks me lazily. Seline grabs for me, but we can hardly reach each other since he's so tall. Rus puts his hands on my thighs, holding me in place so I can lean forward towards Seline, placing my hands on her face and tugging to close the distance between us, her soft lips at odds with the fury of her tongue as it explores every inch of my mouth.

It occurs to me that this may be the last time we ever kiss. After this unusual circumstance, we may never be physical with each other again. The feeling makes my chest ache, and she must feel it too because I swear she pulls me in tighter, kissing me impossibly harder as if trying to soak up every last drop of this. Of us. For a relationship that she only saw as physical, I can think of no better send off. Maybe later I'll allow myself to mourn the loss of our connection. The connection she must have felt but never would admit to.

It's then that Rus moans loudly and I'm reminded of where we are, of what we are currently doing. What I chose to do. Yes. The idea of *her* riding *him* while I kiss her and he licks me becomes simply too much for me to bear. I come within seconds. Followed by Rus, then finally Seline.

We are an explosion of pleasure. Burning hotter than any star in the sky.

I find it absolutely stunning.

19

Seline must have left in the night because when I wake up it's just Rus in my bed. Staring at me.

"Hi," he mumbles sleepily.

"Hi," I say right back.

"That was a first for me." He rubs his eyes.

"Me too," I admit. I've never shared Seline before.

"I guess hooking up with one of the Prince's potential wives wasn't enough, I had to go and sleep with two of them." His comment earns a frown from me. What a strange thing for him to say this early in the morning.

"Rus. I'll remind you one last time, he's not marrying either of us." I pull the soft blankets up around my naked body, suddenly self-conscious in the light of day.

"But he likes you. He told me." Guilt washes over Rus' face.

So is that what this is all about?

"He won't like me once he learns I'm a Shadow. I plan

to tell him as soon as I get the chance." I rub the sleep out of my eyes as I speak.

"You do?" His gemstone piercing catches the morning light.

"Yes, it's time. We can't distract him from finding his actual Link."

"So, does that mean you don't have feelings for him?" Rus sits up now, stretching out his toned body. His wavy blond hair is the most untamed I've ever seen it. But he still looks good. He always does.

"Of course not," I say quickly.

"Of course not, as in, you do?"

"Of course I *don't* have feelings for him. I'm a Shadow, this is my mission. Whatever he's experiencing of me is just part of that," I say with nearly enough enthusiasm to convince myself.

"The Prince said he felt like you two had a real connection." Rus fluffs the pillows behind him and leans back again, turning to face me. "It can't all have been an act, I've watched you with him, you're being yourself."

"You don't know the first thing about me." I sit up as well, keeping the blankets over my body.

"I know how to make you come." There's a trace of seduction in his voice and I must admit has a point there. It's more than I can say about myself, but I'm going to have to remedy that soon.

"You don't know anything *else*."

Must we talk about Nolan while we are here together? Naked.

And why is Rus so confusing? I take a deep breath, alerting him to my frustration.

"Hey, come here." He shifts onto his back and pulls me flush against his side. I rest my head on his chest. I can hear his heart beating. Fast.

"Why do you keep coming to my room?" I speak straight to his pectorals, not bothering to glance up at his face. He avoids my gaze as well, looking up at the ceiling.

"I don't know." He pauses and I hold my breath, waiting for whatever comes next. When nothing comes I press further.

"Seriously? We just slept together and still you can't be honest with me?" I'm on the verge of being angry with him. He must sense it because he's quick to respond.

"I can't explain it, but I feel drawn to you. And I know I shouldn't." This admission takes me by surprise. Is he saying that this is more than just a physical attraction for him?

"Why?" I dare to ask.

"Why do I feel drawn to you?" There's actually a smile in his voice as he says this.

"Why shouldn't you?" I notice he is absentmindedly playing with a strand of my hair as he holds me against his chest.

"Let's see... It's a rather long list, but the highlights? You're in the running to marry the Prince. The Prince is my friend. You are an elite spy. Shadow. Whatever. My friend, the Prince, doesn't know that you are a Shadow." He continues and I listen eagerly, suddenly aware that this is the most forthcoming he's ever been with me. "Not to mention that I'm completely emotionally unavailable. I'm just getting out of a serious relationship."

Now that is news to me. I push up from his chest so I can see his face.

"You are?"

"Yeah...but I don't like to talk about it." His shoulders curve in once more.

"Tell me what you can." I lay down again, but this time, next to him, not on top of him. So that we can see each other.

"You know I'm not from here, right?" he says with a sigh, and no, I didn't know that. Unlike more homogenous lands, Kadneria is very diverse, so you can't tell an outsider just by looking at them. Being a seaside Kingdom with major port access, it was once a land of immigrants, and thus their descendants became one people. Not that you'd know that today when the King is so distrusting of *foreigners*.

"Where are you from?"

"Wow, you're a terrible Shadow, aren't you?" He smiles, only slightly.

"These days I have to agree with you, but go on..." I urge him.

He takes a big breath before speaking again.

"We left Crichton when I was really little." At the mention of the cruel kingdom of Crichton, I have a feeling I know where this is going. I won't rush him. If he needs to take his time with this, I'll let him. "I was born with Stellar magic and that's pretty taboo, as you probably know. Stellars are essentially outcast from society in Crichton, and the only jobs we can get are as healers. You would think people would have respect for the ones who can save their lives, but no, it isn't like that. Do you know why?"

I shake my head no.

"It's the geographical position of Crichton. The Second Star doesn't reach as easily as she does the rest of Gaia. We only see her once a year. And Crichton values power above all else, so without the Second Star, the Stellars are the least powerful." I glance down at his tattoo again as he keeps speaking. "Most people time births to avoid their children being Stellars, but I was an accident, as my mother likes to say. Shortly after I was born, my father was invited here to Kadneria to join the King's council as a foreign relations advisor. My parents jumped at the opportunity to move. Here in Kadneria, it didn't matter that I was born Stellar." There is gratitude in his voice. It sounds like he has good parents, even if his father worked for the King.

I wonder if he still does?

"They gave up their whole lives back in Crichton for me to have a future here." I can hear the weight of the world on his shoulders as he tells me this. It makes sense. There's always a dark cloud hanging over Rus and I wonder if part of it has to do with feeling responsible for his parents uprooting their lives for him. I want to tell him that it isn't his fault. I want to remind him that Crichton is a cruel place. That the discrimination against Stellars is wrong.

"Your parents gave up their lives in Crichton because they love you. There's nothing wrong with that. In fact, you're lucky to have that," I tell him.

"It doesn't feel lucky," he says back, and there's a

million different ways this conversation could go from here, but we were talking about his romantic relationship, so I decide to steer us back to that.

"So when did you fall in love?" He never said that he *had* been in love, just that he'd been in a serious relationship. I figure his response will be telling.

"A couple years ago, some young Crichton royals were sent to spend the summer in Kadneria and learn Royal Magic. The idea was that they would bring it back to their parents and make a case for it overseas. It was my idea actually."

Okay, so he didn't deny having been in love. Good to know.

"It's horrible what they do to the Stellarborns, and for no reason. If everyone had access to the same magic, like we do here, it wouldn't happen." He's making a passionate case for Royal Magic and I get where he is coming from. I really do.

"There was a Princess..." he continues.

"Brianna!?" I'm shocked by this. Were Brianna and Rus lovers? Brianna is a Crichton Princess but I've never even seen them interact with each other. My mind immediately jumps back to her elegant blue dress, the impossibly short one that made her look regal and sexy at the same time.

"No, not Brianna, her sister Cleo," he corrects me.

Cleo. Princess Cleo of Crichton. I close my eyes and scan through the archives of my mind and all the research we did before coming here.

Cleo is two years older than Brianna, making her twenty seven. She is set to inherit the throne once she marries; if she hasn't found a match of her choosing by the time she turns thirty, a political match will be made on her behalf.

Unlike most Kingdoms, where the crown is passed after the death of the current monarch, Crichton passes the crown while the heir is considered to be in their prime. Most say this is in order to allow the reigning monarchs to retire while they still have years left to enjoy their Royal status free of responsibility, but I've always thought it was to prevent regicide amongst such brutal people.

So Rus wasn't *just* in a relationship with the Princess of Crichton. He was tied to the heir apparent who only has three years left to find her own consort before a political match is made on her behalf. Interesting. There's more to this story, and I'm eager to hear it.

"Why isn't *she* here for The Prince's season? You could sleep with a *third* of his potential wives!" I swat at him playfully, but he doesn't find it funny.

No of course Cleo isn't participating in Nolan's marriage season, why would she when she has a crown of her own within reach?

"It isn't pleasant." Rus puts his hand on mine to slow my enthusiasm. I give it a gentle squeeze as if to say sorry for getting carried away. I'm listening. He continues.

"Cleo and I spent that summer here together and it went by too fast. She petitioned to stay longer, and was approved, so we stole a couple more seasons together. Eventually her time ran out and she had to go back. I started making trips to visit her, as often as I could using my position in the Kadnerian Court to gain access. But it turns out, once I was out of range of the Royal Magic, it became more and more obvious that I was a Stellar. And the Crichton Royals weren't thrilled about that, not when Cleo would become Queen as soon as she married and, I mean, if she wanted to marry me, a Stellar? That couldn't possibly happen. And even though I knew there was no future for us, I still fell for her. I fell hard. Being with her was...." He appears to be searching for the right words. "When the current King and Queen realized that Cleo and I were romantic, they retaliated. They cut her off from society. Banished her to a tower." He swallows a lump in his throat. "We never even got to say goodbye."

"Rus, that's awful, I'm so sorry." I tuck a loose blonde wave behind his ear.

"I guess, I feel bad that I'm drawn to you because Cleo and I really never had any closure. So I can't exactly move on, even though I keep finding myself at your door." His blue eyes begin to well over with tears, making them impossibly more blue. "And Cleo was punished because of me. Because of the way I was born. And that isn't fair. I should have helped her...I couldn't help her." Now he's speaking directly to my soul. When Rus's tears begin to fall uncontrollably, I pull him into my chest. I hold him tightly, letting him cry it out for as long as he needs.

20

"Shadows! Report!"

I adjust the belt slung across my hips, admiring the sparkling clasp that compliments my matching gold sweater and pant set. The thick fabric is soft against my skin. We all opted for less sheer outfits for our audience with the King. While I don't know if I'll ever be used to the outlandish style of dress here in the court of Kad, I do prefer this to my leather Shadow uniform.

The King is midway through his lunch, a chicken leg held to his lips as his council flanks him, they sit with plates before them but it is only him who eats. I study the weathered looking man to the King's left. With deep blue eyes and blonde hair dusted in gray, he must be Rus' father. I can't help but assume that the green haired woman to the King's right is related to Vesto. It would make sense if these roles were generational. Their parents serve the King, Vesto and Rus serve the Prince.

Romina confidently steps forward to address the King.

"What would you like to know, your Majesty?" She stands before him in a deep purple version of the gold set I'm wearing. Seline remains poised on my left, although I do my best not to look at her. I've decided not to bring up our night with Rus, not unless she does first.

"Let's start with any threats or possible motives." His gravely voice carries through the chamber. We fill him in on our observations so far. The eliminations. The Ball.

"Amarie of Langha has shown no signs of crystal use. She's acclimating to Royal Magic well. She danced with the Prince more than anyone else at the Ball," I offer, thinking back to their conversation last night.

"You didn't like the dress I sent you?"

"Oh I loved it, I just felt this one was better for the grand reveal. I want all of Court to see me for what I truly am."

"And what is that?"

"Your future bride."

The King seems pleased with my report on Amarie. He sinks his bleached white teeth into another bite of chicken, talking while he chews.

"How's the Sea Nymph doing?" He doesn't use her name. I wonder if he views her as any more than just an unfamiliar species. The thought doesn't sit well with me.

"Lucci had a bad reaction at first but is feeling better about Royal Magic each day. She's attracted to the Prince but feels they haven't spent enough time together yet." Romina reports. She has spoken to Lucci the most so far.

"Is she in contact with her people?"

Lucci's *people* reside on an island between Kadneria and Crichton. They live both above and below the water. If the Prince were to marry her, it would be a powerful alliance and most certainly guarantee favorable conditions for Kadnerian ships in both trade and battle. Not that we are at war with anyone. At the moment.

"She has not contacted them since her arrival," Romina supplies.

"Good girl," the King croons, and I hate the way he says this. I hate that Lucci had to agree to cut herself off from her family during her stay here. I hate that the King is so distrustful. I hate that he calls us all *girls.*

Tensions have been high between Humans and Sea Nymphs for a long time. Humans are wary of Sea Nymphs because their magic comes from the sea and not the sky. And yet, other than that one detail, we are not that different. I think of Rus being looked down upon in Crichton simply because he was born a Stellar. Just like my mother. If she had been born in Crichton her life would have been alarmingly different. I might not even exist. The injustices of this world threaten to overwhelm me and I taste bile in my throat.

"Who are his favorites?" The King leans forward in his seat, looking down at where we stand before his lunch table. The smell of his overcooked meat prickles my nose and I focus back on the task at hand.

Who *are* his favorites?

"I spoke to the Prince. You're his favorite."

I clear Vesto's voice from my head and meet the King's gaze.

"Amarie is the front runner. He was partial to Ingrid too until she had to *step away.*" I actually have no idea how the Prince feels about Ingrid but I use this opportunity to watch the King for a reaction. I wonder what he knows of the *gathering*.

"Oh yes, Miss Ingrid, I heard she was unwell. I hope she makes a quick recovery." There is nothing empathetic in his tone. I look to the faces of his council members but they remain unreadable.

"Has the Crichton Princess been snooping around again?" Brianna is a Crichton Royal. She must have spent the summer here with her sister, like Rus mentioned. He said they were invited to learn about Royal Magic, and yet the King called it snooping. The man I assume to be Rus' father leans forward to whisper in the King's ear.

"Oh, that was her sister? Alright then." The King resumes chewing.

So Brianna wasn't the one *snooping*. Cleo was?

"Well if she's anything like her sister, watch her closely."

That's not very unique, considering the King doesn't trust anyone, but I find it interesting that he should have any opinion of Cleo. Rus' father clears his throat and the King throws a glance his way. They exchange a look I can't read before the King adds to his original thought.

"That being said, Crichton would be a powerful ally for our Kingdom, perhaps it's worth guiding the Prince in her direction."

Now he wants us to play matchmaker?

I catch Seline rolling her eyes as if she's come to a similar conclusion. Luckily the King doesn't notice because he's busy looking at a scroll spread out in front of him.

"So Shadows, tell me, why is it that you've barely

participated in the great power exchange? Is my Royal Magic not good enough for you?" His voice is ice cold. I freeze, and so does Romina, as the realization dawns on us that he knows we didn't fully onboard ourselves to the Royal Magic. Seline's smile doesn't reach her eyes as she looks over at us. This must be news to her. She probably went all in, as she does with most things. Seline has never had any restraint. Seline is reckless. Romina is careful. I fall somewhere in between. I feel grateful for the two of them. I am glad we are here together. That we are a team. No matter what happens, I know that we can handle it together.

"We felt it was better for the mission if we didn't change our methods, so we can fully support your goals, your Majesty," Romina offers on our behalf, she speaks with an unfaltering confidence. "We can do a better job for the Prince that way." The King seems to buy it.

"Very well. But once you really try it, you'll find that the Royal Magic will only increase your abilities." He smiles brightly and his council members follow suit, emulating his enthusiasm. "After all, who wouldn't want more power!"

"We will take that into consideration." Romina bows her head and I count the seconds until this painful meeting is over.

"We need to tell him." I've been waiting all day to speak with Romina and Seline alone. Finally, we are huddled in our now regular booth at The Den. The Prince and his suitors are spending the day on group dates. We planned this so that he would not notice our absence. As a result, Seline, Romina and I will have our own group date with him tomorrow.

"Already? I haven't had much fun with him yet." Seline pouts into her whiskey and it makes me think of the way she pouted last night. I take a big sip of my own drink before I can get lost in the thought of our tangled limbs and her candy red dress.

I am proud of myself that it's just the physical details my thoughts keep going back to. No trace of hurt feelings. At least, not from last night. Yes, so far I have managed to remain unemotional about our evening together.

"Darbs is right, we need to make sure the Prince finds his Link and he can't fall for one of us." Romina is lost in thought. She's forming a plan. I can tell.

"Fine. Let's tell him on our group date tomorrow," Seline relents.

I am glad that for once, we're all on the same page.

"How are you feeling today, Seline? Any lasting effects?" Romina takes out a notebook.

"I'm feeling much better now," she says, deflecting as she often does, "I do need to catch up on sleep though. If you'll excuse me." She shimmies out of the booth and I can tell Romina is disappointed she didn't provide more details on her HelioX experience.

"She needs time. We can ask her more later." I put a comforting hand on Romina's shoulder.

"Time won't help, Seline never cares to share her feelings with us." Romina releases a sigh. "I'll just have to help her understand how important this is. We need to learn more about that substance." She pockets the notebook.

"So. About the mission." I attempt to change the subject. Romina taps her fingers and I feel the unmistakable sensation of a magical sound shield spreading around us. She must have done this when we were talking at the Grand Reveal Ball last night. I hadn't even noticed. I guess I really was distracted. There was a lot *going on*. Romina turns to face me. It's time to tell her what I'm really doing here.

"Headmaster wants me to figure out the truth behind Royal Magic." I scan her face for signs of alarm but she's listening calmly, so I continue. "Perhaps you've heard of the Storytellers? They disappeared about 15 years ago, around the same time Royal Magic started. We believe that it's connected."

Now it's Romina's turn to take a deep breath.

"I know," she says.

She knows? My eyes dance between her light blue eye and her dark one. How does she know? What does she know?

"I know that Headmaster is your mother." My heart is pounding as Romina keeps speaking. "And I know who you really are."

Her words crash into me and I'm left with one question. "How?"

At that she just smiles as if to say, *come on, really?* As if I could possibly doubt her powers of perception. We *have* shared lodgings since we were kids. Maybe I wasn't as subtle as I thought. Maybe deep down I always suspected that she knew there was something more going on with me. Maybe I was happy about the prospect of not having to bear the burden of this secret completely alone. Either way, it's a huge relief. I find myself releasing a breath I didn't realize I was holding.

"You can trust me." She holds out her pinky to inter-lock it with mine, like we always do, and I know she means it. I know I can trust her.

"We didn't ask anyone about the Storytellers, but I bet they've been wiped from memory too." The thought sends a shiver down my spine. If the demise of the Story-tellers is connected to the creation of Royal Magic then there is no way people remember this happening.

"There were some who survived, right?" Romina asks.

"If they agreed to help the King with the creation of Royal Magic, they were spared." I think of the white flags. I think of the flames. What happened to them?

"They must still be here somewhere, at the Palace." Her gaze falls beyond the tavern walls, as if looking right into the Winter Palace. "We need to find them, talk to them," she reasons.

"How will we manage that?" I wonder out loud.

"After we tell the Prince who we really are, we can request more information, for the sake of his *protection*," she suggests.

"That just might work." I agree with her, but I'm worried about how Nolan will react when we tell him. "As long as we manage to earn his trust back after revealing we are Shadows," I voice my concern. Romina gives me a reassuring look before tilting her wine glass to mine in a silent salute. And for the first time since arriving at the

Winter Palace, I feel that we're finally making progress with our mission.

Alone in my room later, I wonder if Rus will appear at my door again as he has for the last three nights. As I wash up and prepare for bed, I find myself pausing every now and then to listen for sounds in the hallway, but it is completely quiet. After last night, and the truths he shared this morning, it's clear that Rus' love life is complicated enough without allowing our connection to turn into something more than it already is. I decide there's no way Rus is showing up at my door again. No, it looks like I'll be alone tonight.

Besides, why would I want to get attached to yet another person who's keeping me at arm's length? All he can offer me is something physical. Just like Seline.

Seline, who's back to only speaking with me if it involves the mission.

I don't understand. Why is it that no one is ever interested in something more than just a physical relationship with me?

I can only conclude that it must somehow be my fault.

There must be something deeply unlovable about me.

Realizing this, I can't bear to look at my own reflection. I finish washing up and dive straight under my covers, pulling the blankets tight around me and shutting my eyes tightly.

Will anyone ever love me?

The thought hangs in the air above my bed, weighing down on me.

But the tiniest little idea pokes out from the corner of my mind: There *is* one person who's interested in more. The Prince likes me, and he's only laid eyes on me once. We've done nothing more than hold hands, and he wants a real relationship. He thinks I could be his Link. Of course. How ironic is that?

Finally, someone wants more with me, and it could never be. Tomorrow we will tell him we are Shadows. There's no way he's still going to like me after that. He will no longer trust me after learning that we deceived him, that this connection he feels with me has been based on a false pretense. I have to remind myself that it's fine. That I could never have a serious relationship anyway. Being attached to someone like that, it would only hold me back from being a Shadow. From my missions. That's *why* we swore the blood oath.

But it wasn't my choice to become a Shadow. No, Mother was the one who decided we would commit our lives to being untethered. But still, I sliced my hand, changed my name and gave my vow to the Shadows. She told me that as Shadows, we could still help people.

All I've ever wanted to do is help people.

I toss and turn, unable to calm my mind. Usually making a mental list helps me quiet the racing thoughts, so I force myself to list all the reasons that remaining unattached to others is for the best.

I fall asleep before I can convince myself of any of it.

21

There's a snow storm on the day of our group date, so we're having warm drinks with the Prince in his personal library. It is located in a wing of the Palace that I've never been to before. The library is cozy, with plush velvet sofas in rich shades of teal and indigo, silver-trimmed walls and a beautiful stained glass mural of the royal seal, which causes colorful light to streak in against the wood floors. For every bit that the weather remains gray and dreary here, the Winter Palace is always filled with color.

The Prince is looking as handsome as ever in a cozy cream suit. It looks soft. I wish I could bury my face in his chest and wrap his arms around me like a blanket. That would be preferable to sitting here across from him, dreading the conversation we're about to have.

At least the Prince's bearhound Buddy is with us today, curled up tightly in a furry ball at my feet as if he wasn't born to live outside in the forest.

I'm wearing my favorite outfit yet. A light pink netted

top that's woven into a high necked collar. The entire thing is held together by a golden crescent moon clasp at the center of my back, which is otherwise bare. I paired it with matching light pink tailored pants and my fur sits on the back of a nearby chair in case I should need it. It is warm in here with the fireplace or perhaps the Prince's heating magic. Maybe a bit of both.

When I spotted this outfit in the wardrobe it felt like it had been made just for me. I chose it for today so I could feel confident. Anything to help with the nerves I'm experiencing.

Today we will tell Prince Nolan that we are Shadows.

"How were your group dates yesterday?" Romina is easing us into this. Thank the Friend for her.

"Had a bit of fun out in the snow, but I must admit I'm happy to be inside today," the Prince offers easily. He is so diplomatic, answering her question but never dwelling on the other women in a way that might offend us. I wonder if he will speak more candidly about them with us in the future, once he knows we are not options for the marriage season. Once he knows that none of us could be his Link.

"We're happy to be inside." Seline tugs her own fur tighter around her shoulders, she's never liked the cold. Beneath the fur, she's wearing a shimmering slate gray turtleneck dress that hugs her figure tightly. It's modest and yet somehow incredibly sexy.

"I don't know, there's always been something sort of enchanting about fresh snow." Romina looks longingly out the window as she says this. Then, as if remembering where we are, she adds, "But perpetual winter must get pretty boring after a while. I guess it takes the sense of wonder out of it all?"

"Well, it's home," the Prince shrugs. He is all too used to making excuses for the way things work around here. I wonder why he never questions the status quo.

And I can't believe we are talking about the weather!

We need to tell him *now*.

"Nolan, there is something that the three of us would like to tell you." I hear my own voice leave my lips.

My heart is racing.

Why is this so difficult?

"Oh?" The Prince looks right at me then, brushing a hand through his chocolate brown hair in the most adorable way that makes my heart flutter. I open my mouth to continue when suddenly, there's a loud crash in the hallway just outside the library.

Buddy jumps from my feet and begins growling at the door.

We all stand and my hand slips to the dagger I've tucked into the hidden pocket of my pants. I note that Seline has done the same with her own dagger and I don't have time to consider where she stored the weapon in such a form fitting dress. We have several plans in place to protect the Prince should it come to it. Luckily we have not had to use them, yet.

But that might be about to change.

Tension ripples through the room as we all turn to face the door, ready for whatever is about to walk through it.

"No! I must see him now! This isn't fair!" A woman's voice calls out.

Perhaps it's just a disgruntled suitor.

"You can't go in there!" Someone else shouts as the door bursts open and we see Vesto blocking Ingrid's path of fury as she forces past him. We watch in horror as she clocks Vesto straight in the face. Vesto falls to the ground gripping his once perfect nose in pain.

Foe. Maybe we will need the daggers?

"He said I wouldn't be eliminated! I made a deal with him! So you can't eliminate me!" She's screaming now and charging straight towards the Prince, Buddy is growling with so much rigor his mouth begins to foam as he stands protectively in front of the Prince. The bearhound is twice Ingirid's weight, there's no way she's going up against him, is she?

"She's having a bad reaction to her antidote!" Vesto calls out, his words muffled as he tries to stop the bleeding of his nose. Romina gives me and Seline a signal and I immediately know which plan we're going with.

Before Ingrid can take another step, Seline tackles her to the ground. The Prince watches in horror, but he has no time to react before Romina opens a portal and I grab him by his collar, pulling him securely against my body and falling back into the black abyss.

22

"Darby. What's going on?"

We land with a thud on the forest floor. The Prince's weight is bearing down on top of me. He feels so solid. I don't even mind that my outfit is probably a mess of grass stains. He stands quickly and offers a hand to help me up. "Where are we?"

I look up to find the small cottage that Romina and I have used as a safe house for years. It's tucked beneath a canopy of trees within the Border Forest that separates Kadneria and Langha. Just outside the grounds of our Shadow Academy.

"Follow me," I say without hesitation.

"Wait." His hand wraps around my arm. He's touching my bare skin. Luckily it's warmer here as the Sun hasn't set yet and we're far enough away from the Winter Palace that it's actually early summer. I didn't have time to grab my fur on our way out, hopefully I won't need it.

"Tell me what is going on first," the Prince demands.

I turn to face him. Here goes nothing.

"This is what we wanted to tell you." I look straight into his eyes, watching their molten brown glow almost gold in the Sun.

"Then tell me," he says, uneasily.

"Seline, Romina and I were hired to protect you. We are Shadows." A heaviness falls over him. His usual sparkle dims down completely.

"Who *hired* you?" His jaw tightens as the words leave his lips.

"The King."

"What is your exact mission?" He speaks through gritted teeth.

"To monitor your suitors and make sure no one is taking advantage of the opportunity to get close to you. To ensure that everyone is here for the right reasons."

"Then you have already failed." His shoulders tense as he turns away from me.

The unmistakable sound of an animal growling fills the air. The leaves rustle nearby. Unfortunately, Buddy didn't join us in the portal hop, so we have no wild animal of our own to protect us in the forest. We need to get inside.

"Come with me and I'll tell you whatever you want to know." I hope he hears the urgency in my voice, we need to *move*. I turn towards the cottage, it's just a few short steps away but the growling is getting louder. I draw my dagger once more, holding it out in front of me when suddenly, a blur of bright orange streaks by us before vanishing into the forest. The Prince yelps in surprise as I lunge in front of him. I'd know that bright orange color anywhere. It's a Treeshark. A large reptilian bird known to hunt in this area.

"What the Foe was—" Before he can finish his sentence the Treeshark appears again, its massive orange wings spread wide, saliva dripping from its oversized beak as steely gray eyes seek out its prey: Us.

The Treeshark lunges forward, a single talon lashing out in our direction. I watch in horror as it clips the Prince's arm with its razor sharp claw. He cries out in pain and it causes something deep in my chest to snap.

Nolan!

I move without thinking, reaching deep into my magic and drawing upon light. I blast a ball of light out in front of us, blinding the monster and forcing it back.

"Come on!" I tug on Nolan's sleeve and we make a run for it, reaching the door and slamming it shut behind us. "It's shielded so only Romina and I can see it from outside," I explain as we catch our breath with our backs pressed against the door. Nolan looks around the small space; it's cozy but in need of some love. There's a small washroom and a fireplace but most of the cottage is taken up by one large bed. That's never been an issue before and I'm curious how Nolan and I will manage it later, but there's no time for worrying about that now. Not when I look down at his arm to find his sleeve is ripped and he's bleeding.

I did this. I put him in danger. The idea makes me sick.

"You're hurt," I announce, before setting into motion opening drawers. We have medical supplies here, some-where. Nolan remains quiet, a look of anguish on his handsome face. I can't tell if he's in pain or just trying to make sense of this situation. I find some gauze and a bandage and bring it back over towards him. "May I?" I ask gently, reaching for his cut arm. He nods once and I set to work cleaning and dressing his wound, to his credit, he doesn't flinch. In some ways I'm grateful that I don't have healing magic like Stellars do, it forced me to undergo first aid training. This way even if Humans had no magic, I'd still be able to treat myself or those I love.

"Why not Seline?" Nolan asks me.

"Why not Seline what?" I'm so distracted by tending to his injury I have no idea what he's talking about.

"You said it's only shielded for you and Romina. Why not include Seline in that?" he clarifies. Oh right. Of course. That's a logical question to ask.

I look up at him and get the feeling he will be skeptical of everything I tell him from this point forward. Maybe I should flood him with truths to make up for the deception. We're going to need his trust back if we want to learn anything about Royal Magic and those Storytellers. Not to mention any other truths about the King that Nolan might know.

"Romina and I have been friends since we were children at the Shadow Academy, Seline is our team member, we were all recently assigned to work together. To protect you."

"So you didn't trust her enough to add her to the shielding?" He glances around nervously. Considering he trained with the Royal Guard, I can only assume he's counting the exits and forming an escape plan.

"We're trained not to trust anyone."

I keep my face neutral, I want him to know he is safe here.

"But you trust Romina," he says steadily.

"I do." I finish off the bandage as I say this. "You're all set," I add as I release him from my grasp and remember a bottle of whiskey tucked away in the cupboard. I start to search for it, happy to have another distraction for my hands.

"Who else knows?" He sits on the edge of the bed and I can hear the defeat in his voice. I find the whiskey and pour some into two tin cups then hand him one.

"The King's council, plus Vesto and Rus."

I force myself to hold his gaze as he takes this in.

"So all my closest companions have been lying to me."

He's angry. No, not angry. He's upset.

"I did my best to avoid lying to you." I was as truthful as I could have been in every one of our conversations. I am sure of it.

"Well your best wasn't good enough." Okay no, he's definitely angry.

I understand. I would be too. We should have told him from the start.

"I wanted to tell you sooner, but they felt it was better this way. As soon as I heard you were starting to favor me, I demanded we come clean. That was the purpose of our group date today." I take a seat in front of him now, pulling up a chair to the bedside.

Hurt, then embarrassment flash across his face.

I realize I've just told him that I know he has feelings for me. Or that I'm his favorite, or whatever. He opens his mouth. Then closes it. I watch as he takes down his whiskey in one gulp then holds the tin cup out to me. I refill it.

"I am sorry for deceiving you, Nolan." I press my sincerity into each word, inching my chair closer so that our knees nearly touch.

"Aren't Shadows supposed to be chameleons? Were you just putting on a show so that I'd keep you in the running? What was the plan anyway? Were you planning to wait for me to completely fall for you before..."

His anger is bubbling over now. I put my hand on his leg to steady him.

"Nolan, take a deep breath."

He does.

"I have always felt that you should know the truth. About everything." I lean forward to make sure his eyes are on mine. I need him to know that I mean this.

"Everything?" He looks at me with those molten chocolate brown eyes and finally I see that little boy again. The one who I've always felt a fondness for.

I really do wish to tell him everything.

My pulse is quickening again but I do my best to calm down. I want to be the steady one this time. He looks about ready to crumble and I want to show him he can lean on me. I can support him through this turbulent moment where the rug has been swept out from under him.

"Ask me what you wish to know." My hand is still on his leg and I let my thumb begin to trace a small soothing circle on his thigh. He shifts his body to settle into a more comfortable position but does not push my hand away. Good. I know he is comforted by physical touch. It worked back when we were kids and it seems to be working again now. His mind is clearly overflowing with questions. Finally, he picks one.

"Was any of it real between us?" His voice falters slightly as he asks.

I close my eyes and think of all the times I've lost myself in the idea of being with him. I think of the impossible circumstances stacked against us. I think of the smile on his younger face when he first realized what his Eclipse Gift was. That it wasn't so scary. That it was something he could be proud of. I loved helping him then. I loved teaching him something, I wanted to teach him more, to explore more, and to learn things together too. He was going to give me a gift. I wonder what it was.

Opening my eyes, instinctively I know that I will always want to be the reason for his smile. That I will always want to take care of him just like I am now.

Just like I did then.

"Yes," I say.

The tiniest bit of sparkle has returned to his eyes. He sets his tin cup down.

"Yes?"

"It was real." My voice is but a whisper.

"Which parts?" He takes my own cup and places it beside his on the floor, freeing my other hand so he can lace it into his own. As he gently rubs against the back of my hand I feel the almost imperceptible shift of my walls coming down. The reasons to stay away from Nolan are becoming impossible to remember the longer my hands remain entwined with his. He has this effect on me.

He calms my heart.

He calms my mind.

Maybe he could take care of me too. Maybe together we could fight off the darkness that threatens to break through on the nights when we both feel most alone in the world. The air between us grows heavy with an electricity that could scorch my skin as I scoot my chair closer and our knees interlock with one another. I inhale deeply. I've always thought he smelled like chocolate but for the first time I realize his scent is so much more than just that. It's rich and smoky. Like a campfire after a thunderstorm. Dangerous. Decadent. All consuming.

"Perhaps you did not know the truth of where I came from or how I came to be here, but every moment between us was real." I give his leg a gentle squeeze. "The way you feel. I feel it too."

His hands are on my face a second later as he pulls my lips in to collide with his. I swear I see sparks fly as our hungry mouths meet and we attempt to devour each other. His tongue parts my lips and I tilt my head to give him a better angle. He pulls me forward onto his lap and my legs land on either side of his, straddling him. I can finally run my hands up and down the soft fabric of his cream suit jacket I've been dreaming about touching all day. I'm overwhelmed by the smell of him, the taste of him. Beyond that, I'm drowning in the sudden realization of how much I care about this human in front of me. How much I always have, ever since our first meeting when we were kids.

This gives me an idea.

I lower my mental shields the tiniest inch and send him a vision of how badly I want him. How deeply I care for him. Perhaps I'm emboldened by the fact that he won't know that it's coming from me but I do hope that the thought will comfort him.

A moan escapes his throat as he pulls me in closer. Our bodies flushed. His hand strokes gently up and down my bare back. I smile to myself, thinking I picked the right top.

Our kiss is endless. Unbreaking. But this kiss is not about pleasure. This kiss is about feeling. As if we are using our mouths to show each other how deeply we have yearned for this. How full our hearts are. It's the complete opposite of what I've experienced before. It's what I've always wanted, and the inconceivable reality of it sends my skin aflame as my whole body ignites in feeling.

He must be having a similar experience because I'm suddenly aware that Nolan is hard beneath me. My body goes into autopilot, rocking gently in his lap to rub against him.

It feels so good.

We feel so *connected*.

He pulls away and looks up at me. His hands on my face.

"Darby." He is breathless.

"Nolan." As am I.

"I've never felt anything like that," he tells me. *Me neither*, I want to say but I don't since I want to get back to kissing him. I lean forward again, aiming for his lips but instead of meeting my mouth with his, Nolan frowns slightly. He gently picks me up off his lap and places me next to him. He does this easily, as if I'm light as a feather.

But the break in our kiss has me concerned. Did I do something wrong?

I turn to him, a look of confusion undoubtedly on my face.

"Would you ever consider abandoning your position and rejoining the Season just as...yourself?" he asks.

What did he just say?

I must look as puzzled as I feel because he continues on to explain.

"I'm just thinking out loud here, but Vesto's vision was of me finding my Link on my Eclipse wedding night, so that means my Link is someone I could marry, and I can't marry a Shadow. But I could marry you, just as a normal citizen of Kadneria. I mean I don't really remember a time when a Royal married a civilian but, maybe that is the beauty of all this..." He turns back to face me, collecting my hands in his. "What if you turn out to be my Link, Darby?" He touches his lip, as if remembering our kiss. "I've already explored a physical connection with some of the others and it didn't feel like *that*. What just happened between us, that was more than just physical."

I'm lightheaded now. I lay back on the bed to steady myself. He's confirming that he felt what I felt. Hearing him say that is incredibly validating. I need to ignore the part where he's already been physical with some of the others and focus on the offer he's just laid out.

Could I give up being a Shadow? So that I could *potentially* – not certainly – marry Prince Nolan? It wasn't a proposal by any means, but it was a significant ask.

I never wanted to be a Shadow.

I wanted to be a Storyteller like my Grandma.

And for the first time ever, we have a plan in place to unearth the secrets of Royal Magic. What if we actually succeed in solving this mystery? What if we have a chance to right the wrongs of the past? What if we can bring back Storytelling?

And what about my oath? If there even *was* a way to leave the Shadows, I wouldn't want to do it for *him*, I would want to do it to become a Storyteller. Like I was born to be.

And while I'm now trying to be as truthful as possible with him, I can't tell him about my past. There's no way he is prepared to hear what his father did to my family, especially not while he is still clearly under the influence of the lies the Royal Magic has been feeding him. Until we figure out how Royal Magic has been affecting him, there is no way I can trust him with the secret of who I really am. I mean, what if it got back to the King somehow? What if the King can pluck secrets from Nolan's brain as easily as he can place lies there?

And we could never build a real relationship atop this mountain of secrets.

Shadow or not, I'm on a mission that is much larger than the marriage Season. I'm here to find out the truth about Royal Magic. I'm here to help people. I can't throw it all away for him. No matter how much I already care for him. No matter how amazing that kiss was.

He lays down beside me, turning to meet my gaze.

"I have a duty Nolan, I'm not just a Shadow, I'm working to protect people. To help them. I can't give up on it now." It's as honest as I've ever been with anyone.

"I can understand what that's like." I think of his work with the HelioX antidote. I think of the burden of being a Prince, how it must weigh on his shoulders. I think of his scheming father who very well might be manipulating his own son's mind.

"Thank you for asking me, but I must decline." I struggle to say this, but it's the right thing to do. Besides, I can't throw it all away for the sheer possibility of being his Link. It's not like he told me he was sure about me. I'm not even sure I could have a Link myself.

Even if I have feelings for him, we're still just getting to know each other. He reaches out to touch my Lunar Eclipse tattoo. Tracing slow circles around it with his fingers. I am tremendously comforted by the feeling of his hands on me.

"Where do we go from here?" he asks me.

It's a good question. I consider.

"I will help you find your Link. You deserve to be happy, to never feel alone again." I think of his words from earlier. Perhaps he really does want to find his person. Perhaps for Nolan it isn't just about power. He's never given me a reason to doubt his intentions.

"And what of your happiness?" With our faces this close together his eyes are so much more than just choco-late brown, they have those tiny gold flakes in them too. That's probably why they turned gold in the direct sunlight. His eyes are captivating.

"Shadows don't have attachments. It is what I signed up for." I don't need to tell him that I never actually signed up to be a shadow. No, now is not the time to tell him that I never had a choice in the matter. That it was his father's actions against the Storytellers that forced me and Mother into hiding.

We stay like that in silence until our stomachs start to growl and I break away from him, rising off the bed. I rummage through the cupboards and manage to put together some dinner for us from the supplies Romina and I keep here. It's not lost on me that it's our first time having a meal together, just the two of us. I never imagined it would be under these circumstances. Later, we fall asleep holding each other, exhausted by the day's turn of events. I dream of chocolate cakes and sunny gardens.

When I wake up, birds are chirping and his arms are wrapped tight around me from behind. His lips press against my neck and I feel the unmistakable presence of hardness between his legs. I allow myself to daydream about a world where we could wake up like this every morning. Where we lay awake in bed kissing and touching each other without a care in the world beyond our care for each other. I allow that thought to pass over to him.

Taking inspiration from the vision he did not know I sent him, Nolan gently turns me over and I gaze up at him. His brown hair is charmingly messy. The day's worth of scruff coating his sharp jawline makes him look softer. Sleepy. I smile at him. He smiles back at me then dips down to kiss me. I press my body against his, wanting more of him. More of this. His hands find my back again and he undoes the golden clasp. I can't believe we fell asleep in our clothes.

We work together to remove my top and his hands begin to tenderly roam my breasts. Gently squeezing and then kissing. And it's not just my breasts, he's exploring my stomach as well, the soft areas of flesh that I often feel self-conscious over are now fully on display for him. The only way I can think to describe what he is doing is: Worshiping. He's worshiping my body. Slowly. Tenderly. It feels fantastic.

I close my eyes and savor every second of his early morning exploration. I wonder how far this will go. As badly as I want him, it wouldn't be right to have sex with him knowing that there are still secrets between us. Especially not for my first time with a man.

Before I can get ahead of myself, the familiar scent of birch trees and lavender fills the room. Romina's scent. We look around in surprise, but she isn't here, just her portal. It waits for us on the other side of the room.

It's time to go back to the Winter Palace. Time to face reality.

I reach for my top and he helps me back into it, kissing my shoulder as he clasps me in.

"Can I keep you around until it proves impossible?" He holds me against his chest one last time.

"It's already impossible." I slide out of bed and tidy up the cottage before heading to the portal and escorting the Prince back to his Palace.

PART TWO

23

CYRUS, LAST NIGHT

"I'm sorry it's taken me so long to meet, things have been a bit *busy* for the Prince's Council." I'm sitting on the edge of a steep cliff overlooking the water. The night sky is littered with stars and only a slice of the Moon is visible. I try not to think of that night, not too long ago, when it was full and I found myself unable to avoid a certain pink haired Shadow with gold rings in her ever searching eyes. We hardly even know each other. And yet, Darby understands me. I wept in her arms that morning like the complete embarrassment I am, but she did not judge me. Being with her is straightforward. There are no odds stacked against us. It's not like my relationship with Cleo at all. And then I think of the sounds Darby made as I brought her pleasure. Twice. No, three times.

It felt amazing to feel her explode like that, knowing that I was the reason. Well, part of the reason. Finally, it felt like I had done something right. Something good. And when Seline told me exactly what to do, it was like for the first time in a long time, I forgot all about the constant aching in my chest. My mind was focused on nothing more than the job at hand and following the instructions of a simple task. A deeply Human task that I knew I could deliver on. It was liberating.

But as soon as I left her room, both times, reality sunk in that I had been with someone else, someone who was decidedly *not Cleo*. It sent me into an even deeper pit of despair than I started in. I can only conclude that love is like a hole in the ground - you fall in without trying, but climbing out takes every ounce of strength you have. And I fear that I am weak.

Tonight it is Brianna who sits by my side on the cliff's edge. She is draped in a dark cloak so as not to be noticed out here with me. The other Ladies are out on the town tonight while Darby, Seline and Romina have their group date with Prince Nolan. Tonight they will tell him that they are Shadows who were hired by the King to keep a watchful eye during the marriage Season. I wonder how Prince Nolan will take it. Hopefully he isn't mad at me and Vesto for keeping the secret. We really didn't have much say in the matter. It was for his own good. Sometimes my position as his friend is at odds with my position as his council member. But to me, he will always be Prince first, and friend second. How could I ever feel differently when I know that my family's place at Court is never guaranteed? The King's behavior has changed over the years. He's grown more paranoid and fearful of foreigners. Should my father ever stop proving himself useful, I have no doubt the King would try to send us back to Crichton.

I kick my heels against the cliff, sending a parade of

pebbles sputtering down below into the sea. Brianna wraps her cloak tighter around her shoulders. I wonder what people would think if they saw us here together. They'd have no idea she's just a kid I'm offering advice to. At least that's how I feel about *her*.

"I've always been patient." Bri looks at me with a glimmer in her eye that lets me know she isn't over her crush yet. I'm surprised she hasn't outgrown it. It's been a little over two years since we first met. That summer, she and Cleo first came to stay at the Winter Palace. Summer for them at least, it was freezing here. Her crush on me makes no sense, not when she knows how her family treated Cleo. And that it was my fault. I cannot fathom how she could look at me with anything other than contempt. Or at the very least, resentment. Glancing over at her, I'm struck by the realization that out here in the dark, with her hood up, Bri looks exactly like Cleo. Only two years apart in age, they could be twins. Luckily, Bri wears her hair short with red streaks. One of their key differences in appearance. Seeing her like this right now, it's like I'm looking at a ghost of the woman I loved. The woman I never got to say goodbye to. What would she think if she knew what I'd been up to with Darby. Or worse, with Darby *and* Seline. The thought of Bri looking at me with any trace of *longing* is simply unacceptable.

"Bri, don't look at me like that." I turn towards the night sky, distracting myself by counting the bright gold stars which make up the constellation of Emirold, the God of Weather. People don't talk about him much here in Kad where there is only one season, but back in Crichton they throw festivals in his honor. While there's plenty I don't miss about Crichton, the summer festival was always my favorite. What I wouldn't give for a cold glass of Sun-brewed tea on a hot day.

"Like what?" Bri kicks her feet against the stone, calling me back to attention. I glance over at her, the faintest hint of mischief in her eyes. She knows what I'm talking about even if she plays innocent. Personality wise, Bri is far more quiet and calculated than Cleo. She's always been careful with her words and I find she often speaks in double meaning. She's very clever. Cleo told me Bri was shy growing up, apparently she spent a lot of time on her own, reading. She actually has that in common with the Prince. I should tell her that, maybe they can bond over it.

"How's it going with the Prince?" I change the subject.

"He took us snowshoeing on the group date, I remember what you said, about how he favors physical touch, so I made sure to get him alone and I kissed him." Bri seems pleased with herself and I feel proud of her for going for it. Maybe she isn't so shy anymore.

"And how was it?" I nudge her, playfully. Is it weird that I'm her wingman? No, I don't think so. I'm her older sister's former lover. Who better for the job than me.

"My kiss with the Prince?" she responds, leaning into my nudge.

"Yes, do you think he liked it? Did you feel a connection?" I watch the swell of a wave crash on the shore and part of me aches to run home and grab my board. The water is the only other place I can clear my mind. And I feel far less guilty afterwards.

"*I don't like talking about this with you.*" It takes me a

moment to realize she is speaking Scalzi, the noble language of Crichton. While I'm still fluent, I'd prefer to stick to the common tongue.

"Just trying to help you make the final three," I respond in the common language. Bri looks at me as if she can see right through my act. She knows that if she makes the final three her family will be invited to Kadneria for the remainder of the Season leading up to the wedding. She also knows I'm desperate to see Cleo again.

"They won't bring her, you know." She slips into the sharp sounds of Scalzi again.

Did I mention that Bri is clever?

I wonder if she's just saying this to hurt me, or if it could be true that the King and Queen of Crichton would leave Cleo at home on their journey across the sea. If there is even the slightest chance that Cleo could come with them, I must ensure that Bri makes the final three. It's been half a year since they punished Cleo for nothing more than falling in love with someone she wasn't supposed to. They can't keep her locked away forever. While I have no real intel, I can only assume her parents banished her because it was the only way to break us up. Since they succeeded in doing that, there should be no reason to keep her locked away. No reason why Cleo should be kept from attending her only sister's wedding. My chest hurts at the realization that, even if Cleo were to return to Kadneria, there is no hope of a future for us together, not when her family would go to such lengths to keep us apart. Not when she will become Queen as soon as she marries, and her chosen partner will rule by her side. There is no way they would allow a Stellar to be in a position of power in Crichton.

No. There is no future for me and Cleo. And I care for Bri, even if not romantically, so I guess I'll help her anyway.

"This isn't about Cleo, I want to help you." I hold my palms up in the universal sign for surrender. No more games, I want her to know I'm being honest. She lets the silence stretch between us before responding.

"Do you think the Prince really cares to be Linked?" She pulls her knees up to her chest, hugging them tightly. *"Or is this all a power play disguised as some fairytale?"*

She's right to question it. I have myself, at times. But I know that Prince Nolan is a romantic. He truly wants to find his *person*. His Link. I glance over at Bri's wrist where the heart shaped charm dangles from her Royal Magic bracelet. Without thinking, I reach for it, pressing the warm metal between my thumb and pointer finger. I notice the heart charm is wearing a crown. In doing this, my fingers graze her hand. Bri's breath catches at our proximity and the sound surprises me, I glance up to meet her eyes.

"I believe that for the Prince, it is genuine," I tell her, again in the common language.

"So then why is it that you keep trying to tell me what he likes, what he's into, instead of learning more about me? Doesn't he care to know how to win my heart?" Bri takes her hand back. This close to her, I can see the reflection of the stars above shining bright in her classically Crichton blue eyes. She has matured since I first met her, there's a confi-

dence in her now and I find myself impressed by it. Maybe she's not just a kid anymore.

"I'm sure he does, but that's for you to discuss with him."

"Do you not wish to know me better yourself?"

It would seem I've fallen into one of her traps. Clever, clever Bri. If we were indeed flirting, this back and forth would be delightful. Had I any more space in my heart, perhaps I could fall for a cunning girl like her. But unfortunately, there is no room left. And I could never be interested in Cleo's sister.

"I know you well enough." I say it as gently as I can and I pray to the Gods and Goddesses that she understands as I inch away from her. We shouldn't be getting comfortable with each other.

"You're not as charming as you used to be." This isn't news to me but I am glad she is finally catching on. I watch as she stands, dusting off her cloak as she switches back to the common tongue. "Tell the prince I like lemons."

I stay on the cliff's edge for a while longer, gazing at the sky. I notice the Second Star has begun to appear above us, marking the start of its month-long visit. At some point this month, The Second Star will fall into an Eclipse with the Moon and the Sun. Perhaps this will mark the Prince's wedding night. Vesto's vision wasn't clear on the exact time line, but at the rate this Season is going, I am hopeful it will happen soon.

And so I say hello to an old friend:

The source of my power, and the cause of my heartbreak.

24

SELINE, LAST NIGHT

I toss another log in the fire and plant myself back in the plush red velvet chair I've come to favor in the corner of my room. It's my thinking chair. A place where I can get lost in the maze of my own mind and turn over the strange series of events that have unfolded ever since we arrived at the Winter Palace. Never in my years of dabbling in HelioX have I experienced anything like what I felt at the *gathering* that night.

"You've been dabbling for years!?" I can just picture Darby's reaction, the pupils of her hazel eyes blowing wide in shock that I've kept this secret. It's obviously why I'm never going to tell her. Besides, I'm off it now. Ever since our night with Cyrus. There is something different about this new version, and I'm smart enough to know to keep my distance. That, and the comedown was hell on Gaia. The Goddesses must have had it out for me because I truly didn't think I'd survive it. It's safe to say that if I resorted to having sex with a man again, I really must have been in trouble. I haven't done *that* since I was a curious little teenager trying to figure out what all the fuss was about. No, men have never really done it for me. I had fun with Cyrus, but I suspect the look on Darby's face as she watched me use his body to seek my own pleasure had more to do with it than he did. I know her expressions well. And true, I was never much of a star student, but when it comes to Darby's body, I've certainly done my homework. I could tell how turned on she was and I leaned right into it, kissing her and pushing her out of her comfort zone, but still making sure she felt taken care of as I guided Cyrus to do the things I know she likes. When pleasure finally found her, it was unlike anything I've seen before, and over the last three years with Darby, I've seen a lot. She should really try new things more often. I've always found it rather rewarding. With the exception of trying this new version of HelioX, that is.

The good news is that after making it to the other side of those brutal 24 hours, my urges to take more subsided completely. I wonder how many people make it this far. I bet it's not many. The redhead must have had more in her system, considering the state I'm finding her in now. It's been three nights since the *gathering,* so her urges to find more have passed, but her mood remains wretched.

After Darby relocated the Prince, Romina helped me wrangle Ingrid to my room. I've been monitoring her ever since. I don't know what type of questioning the Royal Guard was doing, but I know she's safer here with me. I don't trust any of these Royals.

Romina insisted she stay and help but I told her I could handle it on my own. Usually she'd challenge me, but this time she didn't. Strange. She must be up to something.

Romina is an overachiever. She loves to boss me around and insert her own opinion. I've never known her to step away from an opportunity to prove how much smarter than me she is.

She has always been a little closed off. "She prefers books to people," Darby would joke when we would make good use of the nights Romina spent off in the library. Yes, I was grateful for Romina's commitment to her studies back then when I was sleeping with her roommate. But they aren't roommates anymore.

Being here at the Winter Palace has afforded us a level of freedom we've never had before. Not just in our living arrangements, but in our appearances and daily routines as well. I'm enjoying this freedom. I wonder if it will continue in our future missions. We've got a long road ahead of us as Shadows. This is only our first real mission together as a team. Being on a team is strange. I much prefer working on my own. Actually, it's not just working. I prefer doing everything on my own. Other people slow you down. It's better not to have any attachments.

I think back on that day at Shadow Academy where I was assigned to work with Darby and Romina. Obviously I had my own hesitations about how the three of us would collaborate. If Darby would get over me once and for all, it would make things so much easier.

I do lead her on. Of course I do. I can't be expected to completely resist her. Especially now that we're working together and I am forced to see her every day in those outrageously sexy little outfits. I had no idea ribbons and bows would have such an effect on me.

It's like she's a present I'm meant to unwrap. With my teeth.

Try as I might to avoid her, she always draws me back in.

Sure, I can feel a little possessive sometimes, like when we first arrived and she started drooling over the Prince. She spent one afternoon with him and the next thing you know she couldn't stop talking about his *dimple*. That infuriating dimple. Darby has always liked both men and women, and it's never bothered me before to hear her talk about the others who catch her eye. But with the Prince it's different. She is more smitten than I've seen her before.

Maybe I should just let her fall for him and get over me completely.

Maybe.

But, she is my escape. When I'm with her, I believe that I can be a better version of myself. I want to keep her in my pocket and call upon her magic as it pleases me. I want to claim her as my own so no one else can know the sparkle of her touch.

But I can't feel this way. I need to stop it. I have to push her away because the truth is, I'll never be a better version of me. Darby has no idea what I've been up to.

What I've been involved in.

Who I've been with.

And she never should. Darby is inherently good. She knows right from wrong. She always wants to help people, she always wants to do the right thing. I forgot what the right thing was a long time ago. Instead, I go for the hot thing. Or the dangerous one. Or the one that will pay the most.

I think of my guys at the Dark Market who first introduced me to HelioX, the old kind. The old kind was delicious, you could take the tiniest bit and feel totally numb in the best possible way. I used to slip a single drop in my tea at the Academy. No one even knew.

I think of the deals I've organized right beneath their noses.

Headmaster never suspected me.

But then I think of that mission we had in that creepy cellar. That night when the new version of the substance got on me, I could immediately tell something was different. It freaked me out. None of my guys knew anything about it. I even tasted some of their supply, it was the old kind. No, there's something going on here and I'm eager to find out what the deal is. Especially since this more potent version has found its way to the Winter Palace.

"So, will I be eliminated, then?" Ingrid's soft voice pulls me from my mind maze. I sit up straighter in my chair, taking her in. She's curled up in a ball by the window. Her fiery red hair is a mess of curls and she looks exhausted. I can only imagine what she has been going through.

"That isn't my decision," I tell her.

Ingrid gives me a once over, taking me in for what might be the first time despite the hours that have passed since we relocated here.

"And who are you really?" She recrosses her arms over her silk robe, her glossy coral-colored lips pouted.

"We were hired to protect the Prince." I stand from my chair and stalk towards her. There's no use in hiding who we are now, not when she's already seen us in action. "And you attacked him, so it's a good thing we were there. Isn't it?"

"So, you're not in the running? None of you are?" This excites her. "That means he's down three options. He needs me to stay. I could be his *Link!*"

For Foe's sake, she's obsessed with him!

I almost feel bad for her. I doubt the Prince is going to get over the sight of her punching the Visionary in the face. Well, maybe he's into that. I don't know. He does strike me as the type to like it a little more *rough*. No judgments there.

I simply shrug my shoulders.

"I don't care either way." It's time for a drink. It's been a long day and I can tell it's also going to be a long night. I reach for a crystal tumbler and pour myself some whiskey, then conjure up an ice cube or two with my Royal Magic. It's so fun to finally be able to do that. I think I'm going to miss all this power when our mission is over.

Maybe there's a way I can keep using it.

"What do you want with me?" Ingrid sits up straighter now. My nonchalance worked to disarm her. She's grown curious about me, about what I might be able to do for her.

"Tell me what really happened. HelioX, *the gathering*, whatever deal you made. Tell me all of it." I ease back into my chair slowly, as if to remind her how patient I can be. We have all the time in the world for this. I've nowhere to be until the next ball tomorrow night. The *Anything But Clothes Ball*, whatever that entails.

"Why?" She makes a face like she's just bitten into something sour.

"I need to know what's going on so I can protect the Prince," I explain.

"What's in it for me?" She leans forward now, ready to play.

"You want to stay in the Season? Fine. You tell me everything and I'll speak with the Prince myself. Trust me, I can be very convincing." At that, Ingrid's lips quirk up into a genuine smile. Teeth and everything. It transforms her face. She actually looks quite attractive when she's smiling.

And then she starts talking.

25

ROMINA, LAST NIGHT

From up here, the trees look no bigger than pebbles on the shoreline and that is exactly how I like it. I've gone way too long without flying. Nature was calling to me so loudly that I thought everyone could hear it. I was nearly caught staring out the window earlier. Usually, I'm able to sneak off and stretch my wings while the others are preoccupied.

"I'm headed to the library!" I'd tell Darby and Seline when we were still at Shadow Academy. They never studied anyway. Never even set foot in the library to check if I was really there.

Ever since we arrived at the Winter Palace, there's been too much going on for me to sneak away. While I craved a flight around the snowy Palace grounds, there has been so much to do in our quickly lapsing time. *Time.* This meeting is most certainly going to be about how we are running out of time. Taking a breath, I push forward, flapping my wings harder and picking up speed as the wind rushes over my feathers. Eventually I reach the glowing gates which welcome me home to the land of Gods and Goddesses.

The Forest In The Sky. The air smells of lavender up here and the sweetest sound of birdsong tickles my ears. Landing softly on the cloud surface, I change back into my female form and break into a sprint for the trees. Tarajian hates to be kept waiting and I'm already late.

I find her beneath her usual willow tree, tending to some pesky weeds in a small lagoon that begins at the tree's base and spreads widely through the enchanted forest ahead of us. Tarajian, or Tara as she insists I call her, wears her typical coveralls and galoshes, her long white hair flowing freely to her waist. She is quite the sight to behold, this all-powerful Goddess who prefers to do her own weed work, knee deep in the mucky magical water.

"Sorry I'm late, it took a while to get out of there unnoticed," I offer by way of greeting. Tara looks over to me, her nearly white irises as alarming as ever, even after centuries of knowing her. I lean into the trunk of the nearest tree, catching my breath. The familiar sound of singing birds filling the silence like gentle music. She gives me a once over, then steps up and out of the lagoon.

"So Arabella hasn't manifested her Eclipse Gift yet? Is that right?" I've always loved how informal she is. She might be my favorite Goddess.

"No, it has not fully manifested. But she has had some magical outbursts," I reply. I've spent the better part of my immortal life studying humans, and still they surprise me. Arabella, or Darby as we call her now, should have manifested her Gift ages ago. Instead, she is having an emotional blockage.

"We are running out of time." Tara joins me now. She takes my hand in her own, and I find it surprisingly soft, like a lovingly worn leather coat. I glance down at her deeply freckled skin. There is history written across the top of this hand which now holds mine. She gently begins to lead me on a stroll through the willows. Yes, I had a feeling that *time* would be the topic of conversation today. I'm only ever summoned here to see Tara, the Goddess of The Frequency, in person when it is a matter of urgency; otherwise, we have alternative ways of communicating.

"King Godwin Raines is seeking too much power. I'm afraid I've been busy, my attention turned elsewhere, and I let this get too far out of control. He has plans in place, Romina. Terrible plans. An abuse of the power I have given them. We need Arabella, she is able to help stop it, but she must first manifest her Gift, among other things." We reach a fork in the forest's path and I move to head towards Tara's treehouse, finding myself thirsty for a glass of her homemade lavender mint lemonade while I'm up here. But she shakes her head and nods towards the other road, the one which leads to our formal receiving rooms in the Temple of All. We continue on as she speaks. "He wasn't always like this, you know. As an Alchemist, Godwin used to do a great deal of good. Then he became King and something changed. These Humans, they always keep us on our toes don't they?" Her eyes crinkle as a concerned smile spreads on her face. "Speaking of Humans, we have a visitor." It is nearly unheard of for Humans to visit The Forest in The Sky.

Usually they are only allowed access as part of their Service Agreement. They come here to study or train with the Gods and Goddesses and commit their lives to working with us. And even then, only a select few are actually allowed. But I'd never call them *visitors*. No, this must be someone else, someone related to Darby. I have a feeling I know who. I follow Tara down the path until we reach the familiar stained glass door of the temple, which I hold open for her. As she steps into the more formal setting, her attire changes. I now find her wearing a long blue silk robe with delicate crystal detailing. Her long white hair is woven in an elegant braid that cascades down the perfect posture of her back. Despite being hundreds of years my senior, she doesn't look a day over 50 human years. Glancing down at my own shimmering blue ensemble, a draped neck top with a matching skirt slung low on my hips and black leather boots, I decide it's good enough. It's what I wore for our group date with Prince Nolan Raines, after all.

We enter the formal receiving chamber and I try to school my features as I find Natalie seated stiffly on one of the many wooden chairs set up around a large table. Warm, colorful light streams in through the stained glass windows, but it doesn't hide the way her face contorts when she sees me. Needless to say, we've never really seen eye to eye.

"Hello, Natalie. Or should I say, "Headmaster." She can feel the contempt in my words, I'm sure of it. Regardless, she stands, bowing to us in a sign of respect for the immortal Queens we are. As she should.

"Hello, Romina."

I flinch at her use of the pedestrian version of my name. It's what I go by most of the time, but not here inside the sacred Temple of All.

"Rominanna actually, it's my formal name. And this is a formal setting," I respond.

"We don't have time for pleasantries, we need to help Arabella manifest her Gift as quickly as possible. It's taking too long." Tara plops down into a chair unceremoniously. So much for formalities. Natalie and I both follow suit, finding our chairs and joining her at the table. Then to my absolute joy, Tara summons a pitcher of her lemonade. It appears before us in a beautiful crystal decanter alongside three crystal glasses. I reach forward to pour a glass for Tara, then for myself.

"Maybe if she hadn't had such a traumatic childhood, she would have manifested it already." I mumble under my breath while filling our glasses to the brim, or maybe I say it loudly, either way I've been waiting years to have this out with the dark eyed woman in front of me.

I set Tara's glass in front of her and bring my own to my lips. I *missed* this delicate taste of home. I give Tara a nod of my gratitude and recline in my chair. Natalie can tend to her own beverage.

"You say that as if I could have prevented what happened to us? It was the King's fault..." There is hurt in Natalie's tone as she responds to my comment, as if I've offended her. This angers me of course, and I hear the heat in my own voice as I respond.

"I'm not talking about that. What you've done to her over the years was far worse. She needed you, she was so scared, so lonely in those early years at the Academy..."

"That is what *you* were there for, to be her *friend*," she tells me.

"A friend does not replace a family," I do not hesitate to respond.

Tara puts her hands up to silence us and I am glad for it. Natalie gets me so worked up sometimes. I can't believe the way she's treated Darby. I pour myself another glass of lemonade.

"The past is the past, we are here now. Please, offer me ideas, we need to work together to find a solution."

Natalie takes a deep breath, her nails anxiously tapping against the empty crystal glass she has yet to fill with liquid. Strange. I've never seen her nervous before.

"Is something the matter, Natalie?" I ask.

"I think my mother could help. Arabella needs her Grandma, and I would like to see her again too." She looks up at us with hope in her eyes before adding, "Is that possible?"

"As you know, your mother signed a Service Agreement." Tara takes a slow sip of her beverage before continuing. There's no trace of emotion in her tone. "She committed her life to work with us. She did it in exchange for your daughter's protection."

And of course, Darby thinks her Grandma died in a fire. And Natalie has allowed her to think that. Surely there was some other path we could have taken, one that didn't involve so much deceit. Unfortunately, I was never allowed to tell her the truth.

"Can you not break the Service Agreement? I thought Goddesses could alter any oath?" Does Natalie want this for Darby's sake? Or is it just out of a selfish desire to be reunited with her own mother?

"Even if we could break the agreement, that would mean *our* end of the arrangement is broken as well. Are you sure you want Rominanna to abandon her position at Arabella's side? Especially now in your own daughter's time of need?" Tara's voice is so calm. I wonder how she has this much patience for humans. I've already lost my temper once in this meeting.

"Perhaps our goals are all aligned. You said the King is growing too powerful, that Arabella has a part to play in restoring the balance. Maybe you could send my mother to help us, as one of your own servants," Natalie urges us. I wonder what she's planning.

Tara looks at me but I can't tell what she's really thinking. It doesn't make a difference to us if Natalie's mother helps or not, all we care about is getting Darby's Gift to manifest as soon as possible.

"Your mother is currently on the other side of Gaia, seeing to a different matter, but I will take this into consideration," Tara says, definitively.

This answer pleases Natalie.

"Thank you. Now, what do you need from me?" She relaxes her hands and smiles faintly.

"Tell us more about the woman she has grown up to be, what might trigger her Gift to finally manifest?" Tara leans forward as if eager to hear Natalie's answers and my anger boils up once again. What does *she* know about the woman Darby has grown up to be?

What a waste of time bringing Natalie up here for this!

"I'm afraid I've pushed her too far away. I hardly know her anymore." Natalie's voice is hollow as she admits this. At least she is self aware, but still I huff a laugh and Tara's eyes turn to me.

"Well you've missed out. Darby - Arabella - is a wonderful person," I start to explain. "She is brave, she is charming, she always looks to see the best in people and she cares deeply about helping others." I find myself beaming with pride as I tell Natalie this. Of all the Humans I've ever been stuck with, Darby is one of my favorites. Natalie looks right at me now, her eyes unreadable. An impossibly dark set of onyx marbles.

"I hope you know that I only pushed her away to protect her." She pauses as if finding the courage to continue. "If I was ever discovered as one of the missing Storytellers, and if she was connected to me...I couldn't begin to imagine what the King might do to her. I just knew it would be safer for us to be unattached from each other." Natalie exhales a big breath, as if this has been weighing on her for years. Maybe it has. "I have to admit it also made things easier for me to deal with; every time I look at *her* I am reminded of how much we lost that day. My life's work as a Storyteller, my community, my family... It was too much to bear. Being a Shadow, pushing our feelings away... it was the only way I could think to cope with it all. I had to distance myself from her, from the reminder." Natalie dabs at the corner of her eyes—is she crying? "But you have protected her, Rominanna. Thank you for taking such good care of her." I'm stunned by her admission. That was actually nice? Maybe she's not as bad as I think?

"Well, clearly the care was not good enough, considering the issue at hand." Tara says. and it does not offend me. No, she is totally right.

But I've done all I can for Darby, I'm not sure what else to try. Unless...

Unless I've done too much?

Maybe all of those times I found her on the brink of letting her own fears and self doubts consume her, those nights I pulled her from the depths of her own loneliness and helped her back to the light...maybe I should have let her fall?

Maybe her only way out of her own darkness is *through*.

"I have an idea actually, but it won't be pleasant."

They both look at me now, so I continue.

"Well, as you may know, Dar–Arabella, struggles sometimes. It can get very dark in her mind and I have seen her nearly drown in it. Usually I come to her rescue, offer her some perspective and words of encouragement, sometimes I just sit there and keep her company while she cries...but what if I didn't? What if she needs to try getting through it on her own? Perhaps her enlightenment is waiting on the other side."

"I never knew that she was struggling..." Natalie's gaze turns towards the window as if trying to scan the heavens for the daughter she closed herself off to many moons ago.

"There's a lot you don't know about her, as we've established." My words are clipped as I find that my momentary softening to Natalie was just that, momentary. Tara rubs her temples like I've seen her do so many times when she is thinking. Eventually she makes her own announcement. "Next time she is lost to that darkness, we could send her to see Candacesetta."

Candacesetta.

Even her name sends goosebumps down my arm. It's no wonder the humans call her The Foe. Even though I'm one of the few who gets to call her Candace, she still scares me. But Tara has a point, if anyone could guide Darby through the darkness, it would be Candace.

"Unfortunately we can't wait for this to happen on its own, Rominanna, you have to push her towards this, what usually triggers her?" Tara turns to me now.

"It's when she feels most alone," I tell them.

The reality hangs in the air between us. Natalie clearly didn't know this either, I'm starting to understand that perhaps Natalie has no idea how much her own daughter has been hurting over the years and how pushing Darby away was not serving to protect her much at all.

Tara stands now, taking up a slow pace around the table.

"She hasn't found her Link yet, right?"

I understand where Tara's train of thought is going now, so I offer the details she's asked of me.

"She hasn't found them yet, no, but they are circling each other."

"Well they cannot be Linked yet, we need her to feel alone so she can manifest her Gift," Tara orders. Natalie's face falls as she catches on.

"You mean to tell me the plan is to keep her from her *Link*?" Natalie looks between the two of us as she processes this. "Hasn't she dealt with enough? Arabella shouldn't have to suffer anymore." She sounds angry, and I admire Natalie's passion here, really I do, but why has she chosen this pivotal moment for her change of heart?

"So now you wish to end her suffering?" I glance back at my former Headmaster.

"I never.... I was trying to..." Natalie struggles to explain again but she doesn't need to. I hold up my hand to stop her.

"I want nothing but the best for Darby, but as you well know, there are bigger forces at play here. The balance of power depends on this. Darby must go on a journey into her own darkness, she must work through it. She will never come into her full power if not. She will never be able to fully accept herself. And if she does not accept herself, then she may never be able to *Link* with another anyway." My words engulf the room, leaving Natalie silent.

This must happen. And we must help her get there.

"Rominanna is right," Tara nods.

"I will do whatever it takes," I add, vowing to Tara with my hand over my chest.

"Good, then you better get going," she nods back at me. And without another word, I excuse myself from the receiving room, pushing through the stained glass doors of the temple once more.

As the fresh air kisses my cheeks once more, I close my eyes and breathe it all in. The Forest In The Sky is my true home, and after I help Darby restore the balance of power, perhaps it will be time to return. Opening my eyes once more, I'm drinking in the sight of pastel clouds and rich green leaves when movement in my peripheral snags my attention. Suddenly, I feel *him*. His energy is foreign and familiar at the same time.

"Emirold." I'm so surprised to see him that his true name escapes my lips. The word is no more than a whisper, and yet, with my mention of it, a forgotten spell breaks.

"Finally." His rumbling voice strikes my ears like lightning, instantly causing my blood to boil. And just when I thought I had calmed down!

He's leaning against a willow tree. His shoulder length hair is as white as his mother's, his long muscular honey glazed arms folded casually over his broad chest. He is the picture of health, and yet I immediately scan his body for any signs of injury, it's been years since I've seen him. Who knows how many brawls he's been in since then. Not that he can't heal himself but old habits die hard, what can I say. I'll always worry about him.

"You thought a spell could keep me away, Ro? Really?" He pushes off the tree gracefully and approaches me. His strides are long and even. Every tree leaf and blade of grass turns its attention towards him as he makes his way to greet me. He comes close. Too close. Before I can think better of it I'm breathing in the scent of him. He smells like rainwater. Like a summer storm. His giant hand is on my face now, grazing my cheek bone with a feather light touch.

"No one calls me Ro anymore." I refuse to meet the gaze of his pale gray eyes.

"Well, I still do," he says, commanding my attention. Despite his gentle touch, I can feel the waves of anger emanating off him. "I've been searching for years. You were hiding all along? What was the spell, Ro? Why?" Finally I look up and find anguish in his face that matches his tone. Unfortunately, fury looks good on him. Before I can think better of it, I give in to the demand of my aching heart and lean in to kiss him. His massive hands encircle my waist immediately, pulling me in tight against his solid chest. My hands find their way into his cloud soft hair, gripping his face to get better access to his spring blossom lips. His tongue finds mine as he lifts me up and carries me back to the tree trunk, pressing me against it. He tastes like a hurricane. I hate to admit how much I missed him. But I also hate him for what he did. The memory of which comes crashing back now.

I pull away, breaking the very kiss that I initiated.

"Emirold... Put me down." He does a heartbeat later, taking a step back to collect himself.

"My name was the key then, wasn't it? You really haven't said it out loud this whole time?" There's a tiny smirk on his stupidly handsome face. "So you didn't miss me?"

This God of mine. What am I going to do with him?

"Of course I missed you, but I'm still—"

"Ro, stop hiding." He steps forward again, placing his hands firmly on the tree trunk on either side of my head, effectively caging me in. He levels his eyes to mine.

"I'm not *hiding*, I'm upset," I hug my hands to my chest to avoid groping him further.

"Then talk to me. Whatever it is I've done, let me spend the rest of our very long lives making it up to you."

"You don't even know what you've done!?" A flock of birds vacate the tree, sensing the tension between us.

"I have an idea. Certainly have had some time to run through the possibilities..." His jaw clenches and I incline my head for him to go on. "But the past is the past. Tell me what I can do to earn your forgiveness?" He asks and I'm prepared to see him beg, really I am, but when he's this close to me it's hard to concentrate. All I can think about is the smell of him. The taste of him. It's why I used a spell to keep him away all these years. I needed to teach him a lesson, and when we're together I lose all sense of reason.

"You could start by saying sorry." My hands find his chest and I savor the warmth of his skin. I am weak. Clearly I've been spending too much time with Humans.

"I am sorry. Of course I am sorry. Ro," he clears his throat."Rominanna, Immortal Goddess, my truest Friend and Queen of my heart, I am beyond sorry for any pain I have caused, let me erase all memory of it and replace it with pleasure." His hands are at my waist again and he is pulling me back in for another kiss. I press my lips to his slowly, tenderly even, but we don't have time for this. I pull away.

"I have to go. I'm in the middle of something important." This he understands, he takes his own work as seriously as I do. It's something we have always seen eye to eye on. I wonder if he's up here on business. I might as well just ask him. "Are you here to meet with Tara?"

"Yes, my mother and I have a situation to discuss." His

face hardens. "An abuse of power that is altering the weather. Should be a fun one for us to figure out together."

This sets my mind racing. He can't be talking about the Winter Palace, can he? Is the perpetual winter somehow connected to whatever King Godwin Raines is doing with Royal Magic? Why didn't Tara tell me about that? She's always so cryptic, keeping us all in the dark until the last moment.

"The Winter Palace?" I take his hand, offering a final squeeze before I step away from him, I really must be going.

"Indeed." He steps away as well, his eyes floating to the colorful glass doors of the Temple Of All where he is headed for his meeting.

"Keep me posted on what you find, it could be helpful to me as well."

He nods his approval of my request and we hold each other's gaze. There's so much more for us to say to each other, but there's no time now. Our troubles will need to be talked through on another day, perhaps even in another year. Although now that we've kissed again, I find it would be hard to go even another *hour* without him being in my life again, let alone years. Even if that time-frame is but a drop in the bucket of our immortal lives. That's probably why, when he turns back to say, "I finally have permission to find you? No more spells?"

I smile and tell him that yes, he finally does.

26

After stepping through the portal which appeared within the walls of the forest cottage, Darby and I were transported back to my library at the Palace. Portal hopping is something I'll never get used to. Why even call it *hopping*. It's more like falling. Flailing even, as I slipped through an endless void, my stomach twisting and pulling from somewhere unnaturally positioned, as if my legs were above my head. Truly, I'd be happy to never portal hop again.

Now we're back. I inhale the familiar scent of wood burning in my fireplace. The Sun has just begun to rise, and as I look around the room in this early morning lavender light, I find last night's half-drunk silver tumbler of whiskey still sitting on the side table, next to the book on Langhan Crystals I was planning to share with my dates. Last night, I figured we'd have a couple cocktails and some entertaining conversation. Turns out I was very wrong about how the night would play out. I never could have expected to wind up in a forest cottage with Darby, confessing our feelings for one another while also acknowledging that there's no future for the two of us.

I don't know what I'm more disappointed about. The fact that everyone lied to me about the Shadows, or the fact that Darby isn't truly one of my suitors.

Romina and Seline are already here waiting for us. They've changed their clothes since I last saw them. What will they think of my own day-old appearance? It's not like I had a chance to bring a change of clothes when I was thrown into the portal last night.

It is strange to think that the four of us were here in this same spot only 12 hours ago and yet, everything feels different now. They are Shadows. Elite spies hired by my father to *protect* me during my own marriage Season.

"Darby has gotten me up to speed." I announce to the room. We might as well get this part over with. Romina looks at me, her mismatched blue eyes are as alluring as always. She has a windswept quality to her this morning, as if she's been flying through the forest on a run. Seeing as the Sun is just now rising, she must have woken very early. I admire her for that.

"I hope we can still be friends." She says this as if she's breaking up with me, I suppose in a way, she is. I really like Romina, she's smart and outgoing. If there's any chance that the woman I got to know was the real her, then I'd find it hard not to be her friend as the Shadows continue to stick around and *protect me*.

My father must have forgotten that I train with the

Royal Guard. He must doubt my ability to protect myself. He's always kept a close eye on me, but Shadows? Why Shadows? Unless they are here more for spying than protecting. My father wouldn't spy on my suitors... would he?

"Sorry we didn't get to play together more, Princey," Seline purrs from her side of the room. I think it's for the best that she and I didn't get any closer. I was never sure if she wanted to kiss me or eat me alive.

Maybe Seline and Romina will be useful. If they know what's going on with the other Ladies then perhaps they can help move the marriage Season along faster. Maybe it's better if we just get this over with. No matter how it ends, I'm having trouble seeing how this whole process won't involve some level of heartbreak.

"Well, it sounds like we're working together now, right?" I think of what Darby said.

She offered to help me find my Link.

I only wish it could have been her. If she was my Link, it would make sense why I feel this way about her. There's no other logical reason for feeling so attached to someone you basically just met. With Darby, I felt a connection right away. Even before I laid eyes on her. Like the sound of her voice was a song that had been stuck in my head but I could never place. When I met her, it just felt right. Like I'd found something I'd been searching for. But she has insisted that there's no way we could be together. That she can't be my Link. That we could never marry.

It doesn't mean I'm ready to give her up yet. No, if I must court several women at once then I'll keep her in the mix for as long as I can. I would do anything just to spend a little more time together. Foe, or will that only make things worse when we eventually do have to part ways?

"We need to debrief, want us to find you later, your Highness?" Romina places a gentle hand on my arm as she gets ready to escort me out of my own library. I should leave them to do their Shadow business. I could head over to my room and collect Buddy, I'm sure he missed me last night. Maybe I'll take him for a walk in the forest, or along the beach. Usually I have to keep him off the sand because he digs too many holes but today I might welcome a distraction.

"No, he should stay." Darby stands blocking the exit with her body, judging by the way her head reaches my collar bone, I'd say it's all five feet two inches of her. "From now on, he hears everything," she says, and I can't help but smile as we lock eyes.

"Really? Everything?" Romina seems surprised.

"It's the only way we can earn his trust back. As you know, we need to *work together*." She turns her gaze to Romina, inclining her head as if her words are meant to jog Romina's memory of something. Perhaps they've discussed this before. Maybe I'll ask her about it later. Test out how honest she's really feeling.

"Alright then, stay, make yourself comfortable." Romina gestures for me to take a seat on my own sofa.

"Very well then. Please begin." I return to the library and settle in. The Shadows find their own seats as well. I guess we are having a group date after all.

"Ingrid would like to be allowed back into the

Season," Seline says, as she inspects her manicure. The very picture of nonchalance.

"Is she feeling better?" I can sense the worry in Darby's voice as she asks this. I'm reminded of the way Ingrid stormed in here, how out of control she seemed. She punched Vesto in the face for Foe's sake.

"And how's Vest?"

"He's fine," Romina chimes in. "I saw him on the walk over here, he seemed good as new, maybe Rus helped him out with a new nose." The corners of her mouth quirk up, maybe she's amused by the thought of this. I know I certainly am.

"Ingrid is doing much better now. I spent the night monitoring her. I was also able to question her." Seline stands now and she has our full attention.

"What was that deal she was talking about? Who told her she wouldn't be eliminated?" Darby sits on the edge of her seat, desperate for answers.

Seline nods to Romina who takes the cue to place a sound shield over us.

"Ready to hear some uncomfortable truths, Prince?" Seline's silver eyes meet my own.

I'm as ready as I'll ever be. I nod to her to go on.

"Ingrid insisted that *the King* offered her a place in the top six if she could create a distraction involving HelioX." Her words hit me like a ton of bricks.

The King.

My Father.

That can't be right.

He wouldn't guarantee her placement when it's my

decision who gets picked. My father can be stubborn and close-minded, and sure we have our disagreements about how to run the Kingdom from time to time, but he wouldn't meddle like that.

And HelioX? My Father made medicine available for all. He was my inspiration in pursuing an *antidote* for HelioX. There's no way he'd be supporting something so harmful. Especially when he knows how much I care about ridding our Kingdom of it.

Maybe Ingrid is misremembering. Maybe she was under the influence of HelioX when she said this.

"That does not sound right at all." I cross my arms tightly around my chest; I'm going to need evidence.

"Apparently she had only ever had HelioX *once* before, on a dare with some friends here in Kad. She got caught by the Royal Guard who recognized her as one of the potential candidates for your Season. They pulled her aside and offered her free reign to indulge, as well as the placement, by order of the King, if she could get the Prince's Council to turn their eyes."

"Turn our eyes from what?" I ask her to clarify, this makes absolutely zero sense. My temper is boiling over, there is no way this is true. Ingrid must be lying. She *is* the daughter of that wealthy vegetable farmer with the front booth at the Halls. If memory serves me right, they've been trying to scheme their way into Court for years. This could just be another ploy to up their social status.

Oh Foe, now I do sound like my father. His gut reaction is always to be wary of others, paranoid even. I know he does it to try and protect our Kingdom, but it's where he and I differ. I want to give the benefit of the doubt. I take a deep breath and remind myself that Ingrid must have her reasons for doing what she did. We need to try and figure out what's really going on here.

"Did something happen four nights ago, your Highness?" Romina leans in closer, her voice is steady, emotionless even.

I bury my face in my hands as if I'd find the answer there. Darby puts her hand on my lap, it's reassuring.

"Nolan, was there something going on that your father wouldn't want you and your council paying attention to?" She asks as my own hand takes hold of hers before my head can tell it not to. I glance up at her big beautiful eyes. Her gaze steadies me enough to find my focus.

Four nights ago...

Four nights ago I was preparing to make the first elimination.

"Four nights ago I was sequestered in my rooms after the blind dates, designing ball gowns," I tell them.

It's embarrassing actually, the amount of effort I put into creating something unique for each of the Ladies. But I found I couldn't help myself. It was as if the visions of what they'd all dreamed of wearing were flooding through my mind uncontrollably, the images threatening to overwhelm me until I released the ideas into my sketch book and sent them down to the palace seamstress to make them real. And, it was a good way to keep my mind off the anniversary of my mother's passing. It's always hard when that fateful night rolls around each year. Father knows it plagues me— oh. *That* is why he wanted to distract me.

But why not just ask me to have a meal together for once like a normal father?

Instead he left me sequestered, alone in my rooms until Vest barged in to tell me about raiding the *gathering*. And after that, I was most certainly distracted. Figures he'd have such a roundabout way of comforting me.

"Four nights ago was also the anniversary of my mother's passing." I release a sigh as the words tumble out of me. Romina and Darby exchange worried looks. Nice of them to worry for me.

"Excuse me?" Seline looks like she's seen a ghost. Talking about my mother certainly is haunting. "That's a pretty significant detail, Princey." She places her hand on her hip in a way that should be seductive if I wasn't somewhat afraid of the silver-eyed Shadow.

"Nolan, it can't be a coincidence." Darby gives my hand a gentle squeeze as she says this, my eyes traveling back to her for comfort, for every bit that Seline is sharp and biting, Darby is soft and welcoming.

"Of course, my father, in his own fucked up way, was trying to distract me from feeling sorry on the anniversary of losing her. *That's* why he wanted there to be a distraction. It worked, after the raid, Vest paid me a visit to tell me about what went down, kept my mind off my mother, that's for sure." I'm embarrassed to admit this to them, to reveal the dysfunction of my own family.

"I fear that there may be more to it than that." Romina now chimes in. She nods to Darby who scoots closer to me and I immediately pick up on her trepidation.

"Nolan, we think there may be some connection between the passing of your mother and the creation of

Royal Magic. We've been doing some *research* on it." I look at her now, realizing that what she means is, they've been spying. Spying on my family. At my Palace. Darby is a Shadow. I'll never get used to this. But how could anything involving my mother be connected to the creation of Royal Magic? That's impossible.

"Royal Magic was already around for years before—" I begin to explain, but Darby cuts me off with another gentle squeeze of her hand.

"I know that is what you believe but Romina and I remember it differently," she says, earning an eyebrow raise from Seline. I assume I'm not the only one in the dark here, as Seline looks surprised by this news. I think back to what Darby told me, Romina is the only one she actually trusts. The two of them must be keeping secrets from their own teammate. Darby continues on and Seline seems just as eager as me to hear what she's about to say.

"When we got to the Palace, Romina and I both shielded ourselves from fully joining the Royal Magic. We started to notice that when people fully use it, it can have an effect on their memory."

"What do you remember differently?" I ask her, my curiosity getting the better of me.

"I remember a time before Royal Magic. When it came to be, you would have been about 11."

"That's when my mother..." I've never said the D word and I refuse to do so now.

"Exactly," she supplies before I have to finish my sentence. My head begins throbbing with the influx of information. There is simply no way any of it makes sense.

"Even if I did believe you, I don't understand how these two things are possibly connected." I snatch my hand away from Darby. What if this is all some elaborate plan to further mislead me? Can I even trust her? What if they're all just playing me? First, my father and my own council deceived me, and they are the people who are closest to me. Why wouldn't Darby, Seline and Romina deceive me too?

I need to move my legs. I rise from the sofa and pace over towards the window, cracking it open to get some air in my lungs. I breathe in the taste of winter. Fresh snow is covering the Palace lawn. Craning my neck down below, I see Buddy is already out running around in circles, his massive paws sinking into the fresh powder. I'll have to thank my staff for taking such good care of him in my absence. Sometimes it feels like he's my only real friend. The only one I can trust. He always protects me, and he's an excellent judge of character. And he loves Darby. Every time he sees her, his tail wags uncontrollably and he attempts to permanently cement himself to her side.

I glance back at her over my shoulder, the Shadows remain seated, giving me some space. If Buddy trusts Darby, maybe I can too. Maybe I can even work with them to make sense of all this. Exhaling again, I try to think of any details I might have missed. Any information that can help us connect the dots here.

"Usually, my father spends the anniversary hunting, but once every few years he locks himself below the Palace to do maintenance on the Royal Magic. Says that it helps to clear his mind to work with his hands again, like in his Alchemist days," I tell them without turning around, although I can feel their attention on my back.

"What do you mean by maintenance?" Seline asks.

"Well, confidentially of course, every few years the system that powers Royal Magic—we call it the Eye, needs a tune up, or it will overheat. So much power and all that. I don't really know, I try to stay out of it." I fiddle with a loose thread on my jacket. The truth is, sometimes I think my father loves Royal Magic more than he loves me. I don't have a sibling, but when it comes to earning his affection I often feel like the second child. And that's saying a lot, considering I'm his only *heir*. So when it comes time to deal with his *favorite* child, I tend to tune out. It's a bit of a coping mechanism I suppose, but so far it has worked for me.

"What does the process involve?" Romina asks this time.

"I know it involves going down to tend to the Eye. Other than that I'm not sure...I've never taken part in it. Neither have Vesto or Rus." The more I share with them, the more obvious it becomes that something isn't right here.

"Let me guess, because your attention is always *turned elsewhere*." Seline supplies this conclusion and her meaning lingers in the air. Could it be that my father wanted us to turn a blind eye on Royal Magic four nights ago? What does the maintenance entail? Why have I never cared to ask?

I've spent years looking for the best in my father. Even as he's grown colder and more paranoid each year since my mother's passing, I've worked to present a united front and make sure all at Court know I still believe in him. That I look up to him, not just as a father but as my King. But what has he ever done to deserve my trust in him? My loyalty?

The thought reverberates through my skull. Unlocking something.

Now Darby stands and crosses over to the window to join me.

"Vesto can see the future, but can he also see the past?" she asks as she grows nearer.

"He can hardly see the future." It's my instinct to tease Vest. But I remind myself this is no time for joking. I try to think more seriously about her question. I can't remember Vest ever mentioning visions of the past.

"I don't think so, but even if he could see the past, the use of magic would be logged, my father would question it," I explain.

Darby gently taps her fingers against the frozen window pane as she begins to think through a plan. She looks good like this. I like seeing her in *action*, doing what she does best, and getting to be a part of it. I'd much rather be in on the secret than be the person it is kept from. My hand flexes at my side, wanting to reach out and touch her but knowing I shouldn't right now.

"Remember when Rus took off his bracelet?" she says, turning back to the other Shadows. "Why can't Vesto do the same? Then it wouldn't be logged right?" Darby seems excited about this idea but I almost have to laugh. Doesn't she know?

When her hopeful eyes meet mine I realize that she

must not. Since she's new to the power sharing system, I'll have to tell her.

"It's incredibly uncomfortable to remove your Royal Magic bracelet, it uses a great deal of energy. Plus, well I don't really know how to describe it but....it's almost as if Royal Magic doesn't *want* you to remove it." What I don't share is that Rus taking off his bracelet is news to me, and I can't imagine it was a pleasant experience. Immediately, all three Shadows look down to try and remove their bracelets. One by one they start to understand what I mean. Even Darby and Romina seem to experience great difficulty, and they are apparently shielding from most of its influence. It's fascinating actually. "Beyond that, if you stopped using Royal Magic, it would appear in the logs and raise questions. Since my father sent Rus to greet you, he must have had permission," I add on as they half listen.

"If we can't get Vesto to remove the Royal Magic, what if we take him out of range?" Romina's eyes light up with a new plan. "Darby, did you and the Prince feel anything at the cottage? You were outside of Kadneria in The Border Forest. You should have been out of range then." She turns to Darby, hopeful.

"Oh um, well, we were a bit busy talking things out. I didn't get the chance to test anything." Darby turns bright red as she responds. Romina and Seline both seem interested in exploring what we must have been *talking* about to have caused Darby's cheeks to flush like that, but luckily we don't have time to share with them. There's something going on here and it feels important.

"If there's a way to take Vesto out of range, I think you

should try it." I jump in before they can press Darby further. "If you see something that can confirm your claims about my father, then I am willing to help you figure this out, however I can." I declare this in my most authoritative tone, the one normally reserved for meetings with my council. Romina nods gratefully. They didn't need my support, but if they can prove that my father is up to something, they'll have it nonetheless.

Ever since losing my mother, my father is the only real family I have. And yet, he often puts me second to Royal Magic, or his own agenda. It's pushed me to work harder. To be a noble Prince, to form my own council and begin work on my own agenda, like our work to help those affected by HelioX. And yes, maybe I hoped that by finding an antidote I'd be following in his footsteps. Maybe I did *all of* this to try and win his approval. But the more I learn about him, the more I fear he may not truly be the peaceful monarch I have claimed him to be. So, if they can show me evidence, then perhaps I can figure out what's really going on with him.

"I'll take Vesto to the cottage," Romina offers.

"I'll go with you" Darby is quick to volunteer and I worry she's trying to put distance between us. Maybe I should let her.

"I should probably feed Ingrid," Seline muses, as if Ingrid were her pet.

All three Shadows are heading for the door now and I can't stand the thought of being left alone here to deal with everything that they've just told me.

"What should I do?" I call after these three intriguing women who I'm now seeing in a new light.

"Try to find out more about your mother. We need to know what really happened to her." Darby offers one last smile as she suggests this, and then she turns, disappearing down the hall with the others. I find that her smile stays with me, even after she is gone, as if her words have inspired something new in me, or perhaps dusted off the cobwebs of a long forgotten memory.

What really happened to her...

Yes. It's time I paid a visit to my mother's rooms.

The door isn't locked. I press my weight against it, urging it open with a creek. Anyone could have come in here at any time, and yet taking a look around at the thick layer of dust coating the floor, it's clear no one ever has. No one has even thought to look in here for clues.

Why is that?

And why did I never think to come here?

There were nights when I was younger where I would have done anything to curl up in the blankets of her bed, blankets that may have still smelled like her. Why did I never just venture to her rooms?

The thought of this nearly paralyzes me but I take a big breath and push on. The door creaks closed behind me as I step carefully into the room. I reach for her bed first, finding the silky sheets stiff from years of neglect. I don't think the Palace staff even come here.

Grabbing one of the deflated lavender pillows, I bring it to my nose, inhaling deeply. Cinnamon. My mother always smelled like cinnamon, her scent still lingers here, just barely.

I hug the pillow to my chest. I wish she were still here. I wish I could hear her voice, or at the very least, I wish that I could remember what happened to her.

Could my father have truly taken away my memories of her?

Why would he do something so cruel?

Perhaps it was a misguided attempt at protecting me from the pain of losing her.

Or is that just me trying to see the best in him again?

My own reflection catches my eye in the mirror of my mother's vanity. I drift towards it, taking a seat on the wooden bench carefully as I am unsure if the dainty piece of furniture will hold me. Like many of the decorations in this room, the antique wooden bench is painted with symbols of The Friend, The Foe and The Frequency. My mother was religious, I remember that much. So much so that in her absence my father banned the minor holidays because they reminded him too much of her. He didn't tell me this directly, but Vesto did, after hearing it from his own mother who sits on my Father's council. We still celebrate the major holidays though, I can only guess it's for fear that the Goddess of The Frequency would revoke our power if we stopped worshiping her, or that The Foe might strike our people.

The bench creaks below my weight and I realize I'm much bigger than I was the last time I visited this room. Sitting carefully, I reach for the mirror and dust it off, meeting my own gaze. I look more like my mother than my father. My eyes match hers exactly, or at least, from what I can remember. I wonder what she would think if she could see me now. Gone are my rounded cheeks, pudgy frame and awkward posture. Somewhere over the course of the last 15 years I've turned into a man I hardly recognize. Looking around the vanity, my heart nearly stops when I spot my mother's ring. Her favorite ring, the silver band with a single black pearl. My father made it for her when they found out she was pregnant. She wore it everyday, but I remember her promising to give me the ring once I found a love of my own. Is that why it's here now? Did someone place it here after she...Foe. There's something *else* about this ring, and I can't remember. It feels like a carrot dangling just out of my grasp.

Hmmm. I reach for the ring, collecting the delicate silver band in my hands.

What else? What am I forgetting?

As soon as the ring is in my hand, it snaps me with a jolt of magic.

"Ouch!" I say out loud, to no one in particular.

And then I hear something. The desk is vibrating.

A trap drawer shoots out from below the vanity, hitting me in the knee.

"Ow," I say again, and the desk responds by retreating the drawer back in slightly. "Thank you," I tell it, realizing I'm now conversing with a piece of furniture. The drawer wiggles in response and I suppose we are friends now. I reach inside of it, peering in to find a stack of letters.

That's weird.

Pulling the stack out, it takes me no longer than a heartbeat to recognize my mothers handwriting. These are *her* letters.

"Dear Nolan....." My eyes go wide as I read a note pinned to the top of the stack.

My heart nearly plummets into my stomach.

These letters are for me. My mother wrote them *to me*.

I'm overwhelmed, completely glowing, and it's with a huge smile that I grab the letters and inch out of the room back towards the hallway.

I need to get back to my room where I can read these in private.

"Don't you look excited?" coos a familiar voice. I turn to find Seline strolling down the hallway, her usual mischief filled smile painted on her decorated face. "All over some mail? What sort of naughty fan letters are they sending you, Prince?"

"I thought you were tending to Ingrid." I say, colder than I mean to.

"On my way there now, I just got a little side tracked by this gorgeous art collection." She tips her head to the side, indicating a large oil painting. It's a portrait of my parents. I note the black pearl ring is pictured, so it must have been around the time she was pregnant with me.

"Beautiful ring," she says with a chilling flourish to her words. I clear my throat, how strange that Seline should bring up the very ring I just rediscovered.

The one I now hold clenched in my hand, within my left pocket.

"Yes, it's a family heirloom," I say, as my fingers tense.

"Do you plan to offer it to your betrothed? Once you choose her, that is?" I consider Seline's words carefully. There's something about this question that is raising my suspicions.

"I'd love to, but that ring was lost with my mother," I tell her with as much conviction as I can manage. It's not a total lie, the ring *was lost*, until today. She seems to buy it though, and I watch as she releases a sigh.

"That's too bad then, sure is pretty," is all she says before she slinks off, and I make a run for my room, locking the door behind me and instructing Buddy to sit at full alert, so that I can safely uncover whatever truths my mother has left for me in her letters.

27

VESTO, TODAY

Normally, I spend the morning before a ball finalizing the arrangements. There's something deeply satisfying about checking off those items on my to-do list. It elicits a feeling of pride in the work I have accomplished to provide beauty and merriment for the Kingdom. What was once a seemingly endless scroll of menus to arrange, invites to send, and decorations to choose becomes no more than a series of lines drawn in rich ink as each task is completed.

But this morning, I shall have no such closure.

Yes, right now, while I should be taste-testing with the chef or walking through the venue with the florist, I am otherwise engaged. Instead, I find myself sitting on the splintered floor of a tiny cottage in the middle of the forest, holding a baby Treeshark. A live one. A live baby Treeshark who's monstrous parents have not yet realized they are missing and hopefully never will.

"Is the Treeshark really necessary?" I ask Romina,

while swatting the storm of salt from my eyes–why is she pouring it all over me? "If I didn't know better, I'd think you were preparing us for roast, Mina!"

"That would require even more seasoning," she winks, pocketing the small velvet pouch of coarse sea salt. I just adore her sense of humor.

"You really think this will work?" I gaze up at her mismatched blue eyes. I treasure the friendship we've formed these past couple weeks. I can't believe it's only been that long, I feel I've known these women all my life.

Darby emerges from the washroom with a large wooden bucket of water. She places it down in front of me without even breaking a sweat. She's strong for her small size. My eyes snag on the bucket, the fine craftsmanship reminds me of the wooden contraptions common to the people of my homeland. Curiosity gets the better of me as I reach out to touch it.

"Is this from Bouwer?" I ask while pressing my hand against the familiar soft wood.

"I picked it up on one of our training missions, years ago," Darby offers, "Have you been?"

"I was born there," I tell her as memories of the floating city of innovation cloud my head. The wet wooden smell of the boats which float in the murky canals fill my nose as if I were really there.

"So you're not Kadnerian by birth?" Darby asks.

"We moved here when I was little. As I'm sure you know, Bouwer is prized for its innovations and crafts. The Visionaries are the heart of society. They *see* how to build the future. And I come from a long line of those Visionaries..."

"Your mother is a Visionary too. Is that how she ended up in Kadneria serving on the King's council? She is there to advise on innovation?" Romina asks now with an unusual intensity.

"Yes, among other reasons." My throat feels tight as I attempt to swallow.

"What other reasons?" Darby takes a seat beside me on the floor, placing a gentle hand on my shoulder.

"Well let's just say that, when my Eclipse Gift manifested, I wasn't exactly *celebrated* back home." I clutch my feathered friend tighter. She gives a little squawk in response.

"Why not? You're a Visionary! Just like your mother." Darby's face lights up in an encouraging smile and I feel bad that I'm about to disappoint her.

"I'm a Visionary, yes, but I'm not like my mother. She, and the many generations in our family before her, have visions of future innovations. Technology. They help improve water irrigation, weaponry, magic-capturing machinery! My ancestor invented forks for Foe's sake." Darby and Romina exchange a look I can't read. "All I see are people's love lives, and usually I don't even get it right!" Romina takes a seat next to us as I continue on.

"Vesto, you are a gifted Visionary. You're doing wonderful work. Without you, we wouldn't even be here," Romina says sweetly. I glance over at her and continue my tale.

"When my mother was offered a place on the King's council, she accepted, so that I would have a chance to start fresh in a new Kingdom and not grow up to be the laughing stock of our family." Shame colors my cheeks red.

"You're not a laughing stock." Romina's eyes find mine.

"I hope you don't mind me asking, but why would the King offer your mother a seat on his council?" Darby chimes in.

"Because she's amazing?" I don't even hesitate before replying.

"Of course, but, isn't it interesting that the King who is so weary of foreigners would invite so many foreigners to join his council?" I should be offended that she's questioning my mother's aptitude but there's something about her words that set loose a long-forgotten memory, like dust clearing off a book in an old library.

"My mother had a vision of the Eye! The one that controls Royal Magic!" I announce as the memory comes back into focus. This causes Darby and Mina to snap to attention.

"When—"

"What—"

They say at the same time.

"That's why he offered her a seat on his Council. She *saw* the machine that captures magic and harnesses it into the power sharing system. She had a Vision of the King of Kadneria and used it to get us out of Bouwer...I don't know when. I was really little....why have I never remembered this before?" I gaze down at the baby tree-shark who looks as confused as I am. My heart is racing now and an uneasy feeling spreads in my stomach.

"Perhaps you've never been asked about the past

while outside the range of Royal Magic like we are now..."
Romina considers.

"Is there anything else you remember about the King?" Darby urges me on. I close my eyes and try to lean into my own newly accessible memory. It's almost like using my Gift. Unfortunately, I come up short and no new information surfaces. I reopen my eyes and look at my Shadow friends hoping I haven't let them down.

"No other memories yet...I'm sorry."

"Oh don't be sorry! This information is incredibly helpful. We really appreciate you sharing your story." Darby's words send a shiver up my spine, in a good way. It feels nice to be seen like this. "If I ever find myself back in Bouwer I'll let them know I'm proud to be friends with the one and only Vesto– Vesto forgive me, what is your full name?" Her brow scunches in concern.

Apparently I've hidden my full name too well if even the Shadows don't know it.

"Vesto Toekomstige Bouwer" I say, earning an immediate look of surprise from Darby and a poorly concealed smile from Romina. "I don't use it, for obvious reasons." I add quickly. No, it's better that no one at Court knows that I'm part of the reigning family of another Kingdom.

"Just Vesto then." She gives me arm a gentle squeeze

"Just Vesto," I say, covering her hand with my own to squeeze back.

"Maybe all of this remembering will help you *see* the past as well?" Romina gestures back to the bucket of water which started this conversation. "Do you feel ready to try?"

"Oh right. Of course." I shake away the gnawing

feeling in my stomach and try to focus on the task at hand. My Shadow friends are helping me attempt to *see* into the past. "And we think this will work?"

"Mina read it in an old scroll, there was a Visionary in another Kingdom who had success *seeing* into the past this way," Darby steps in to explain. "We don't have enough information to know what exactly about the setup actually helped, but we figured it was worth trying to replicate his exact conditions. Treeshark and all." She sounds confident and I find it reassuring.

"Treeshark it is then." I nod in agreement.

"There's something terrible going on with Royal Magic and we need to figure it out," Darby adds, her tone turning serious. "If you can share a vision of the past with us, it will bring us one step closer".

When the Shadows filled me in earlier, I was admittedly horrified by the details of their discoveries. The evidence does make it seem like the King is up to no good. And it would make sense. You can never trust a man whose teeth are shinier than his hair. Everyone knows that.

"My mother and I, we don't have evidence, but we've always felt something was off with the King. It's hard to explain, but we both know there's a reason we don't trust him, even if we can't put our finger on exactly why or what it may be." It feels good to finally tell someone this, and I know I can trust the Shadows. My mother has been on the King's council for years, so we have closely guarded our concerns. When they offered me a role at Nolan's side, I knew it was the best way to protect him should the King ever prove to be as unsavory as we suspected.

"Then let's do this, for Nolan," Darby says, and we share a nod in agreement.

The Prince is my best friend. So, if attempting to see the past will help him, then there is nothing I wouldn't try. No salt I wouldn't coat myself in. No baby Treeshark I wouldn't hold. No ball I wouldn't.... Well no, I'm not missing the ball!

"My only requirement is that you get us back in time for the ABC Ball."

"What does that stand for again?" Darby dares to ask, prompting my temper to rise.

"Anything But Clothes! Darby, I've told you this a thousand times!" Darby and Romina start to giggle and I realize they are messing with me. Very funny.

"Don't worry Vesty, you won't miss your ball." Romina gives my hand a gentle pat and I relax again. "It shouldn't take long to get dressed either." She laughs again, so I know she's just teasing me. We've already been over the attire. It's Anything But Clothes, not a Naked Ball! We tried a Naked Ball for the holidays last year and let's just say, things got messy.

Their teasing helped me calm down and now I'm ready to get started. The only problem is, I have no idea where to begin. Sometimes I can barely see the future, how am I supposed to see the past?

I've told Romina and Darby as much.

"We can start with something easy... something that took place right here," Romina gestures around the small cottage. It's humble but charming. There's a nice fireplace and a large cozy bed. I can imagine snuggling up here on a chilly night with a good book. Romina waves her hand over the bucket of water and it begins to bubble. Next, she puts her palm out, gesturing for me to give her one of my hands, preferably the one that isn't holding the bright orange baby bird monster. My left hand. I offer it to her, and she guides it to the bucket's side, which I am surprised to find is now warm. She mumbles an enchantment I'm not familiar with.

"Close your eyes and reach for the past. Think about this space, I've already given you some magical assistance," she instructs me. There's a tingling sensation from the enchanted salts around me. I focus on this cottage in my mind's eyes, and then I see a flash of light.

A Vision!

Yes!

I reach for it. Imagining that I'm grabbing hold of it with my own hands.

"Perhaps you did not know the truth of where I came from or how I came to be here..."

I hear Darby's voice but it sounds muffled. I open my eyes to see that the bubbles have settled in the bucket and the water is now working as a reflective surface.

There's a memory projected across it! Holy Foe! I did it!

The three of us lean forward to get a better look as Past Darby continues her conversation with... is that Nolan! It must have been last night. When they were here together.

"...but every moment between us was real. The way you feel. I feel it too."

We watch in absolute shock and delight as Darby and Nolan start kissing!

"Darby! You and Nolan?" I hear myself exclaim.

"Oh Foe." Darby covers her face, clearly embarrassed. I don't see what she has to be embarrassed about, I mean they've been *courting* this whole time. I'd be surprised if they hadn't kissed! Plus I know they like each other. It's rather obvious.

Romina puts a hand on Darby as if to say, "it's alright," and then the vision ends. I look up at them and await further instructions.

"Well done Vesty, you saw the past! Now that we know you can do it, shall we try something a little harder?" She pours more salt around me as she says this. I nod eagerly, that was fun actually. I'd like to try something more challenging. I never knew I could use my Eclipse Gift like this. I wonder what else I can do.

"How are you feeling energy wise?" Darby's eyes shine bright with concern, she's thinking about how much energy it took for Cyrus to Augment them, no doubt. But I'm doing okay. At least so far. I smile in response.

"Let's try finding a Nolan memory, something at the Winter Palace. I'm going to use more salt this time, see if we can keep it going longer. Hopefully it's helping to siphon your magic so you don't get as drained." We repeat the entire process and after a couple false starts, I finally have a vision of Nolan's past.

Leaning forward to look into the water bucket, we find Nolan in his room, late at night. Based on what he is wearing, that gorgeous green suit with jewel encrusted netted top, I can contextualize that this was right after the

Grand Reveal Ball. Nolan looks surprised, as if someone has shown up unexpectedly, and that's when we see *her*.

Amarie.

I hold my breath as we watch the memory unfold.

"I wanted you to get a chance to see me in it," she says as she stands before him in a dark violet ball gown with a deep ruffled V neck that shows off her ample cleavage. Fluffing her perfectly curled hair, she turns her body to reveal that the halter neck line is tied in an absolutely stunning chiffon bow of the same rich purple color, it trails down her bare back onto the floor. The dress is elegant, and sexy, and not at all like what I remember her wearing to the ball that night.

"You changed. That's the dress I designed for you," Nolan says back to her, his voice sounds gruff as he tries not to stare at that tempting neck line. But let's be honest, we're all looking at it. Her boobs are pressed together so tightly they could hold a wine glass without spilling.

"Figured it would be better for doing this," Amarie says as she ever so slowly pulls on that delicate trail of fabric until the bow unties and the entire dress falls to the floor in a flourish of purple. Nolan stands speechless as Amarie giggles, her flawless naked body bared completely to him. And us, because we can see this now too.

"Oh my!" Darby gasps.

Romina leans forward. "This feels a little intrusive, Vesty, can you skip ahead?"

I find that I cannot. There is nothing I can do to stop this memory from playing out. I tell them as much and we look on in horror as Nolan tries and fails to avoid Amarie's seduction.

"I'm not supposed to sleep with anyone until the final three," he says, and I've got to give him credit for trying to resist her allure.

"So I won't stay overnight. No sleeping," Amarie replies, before she begins kissing his neck. Nolan loses the battle with his self control as his hands grip her plump ass, causing her to moan in celebration of her victory. Their mouths find each other and they kiss their way over to Nolan's bed.

"We can't watch this." Darby puts her hands over the bucket, blocking our view. I think she means *she* can't watch this. Me? I'm having a blast. Even if this is a breach of Nolan's trust, even if calling it intrusive doesn't begin to describe it, I cannot look away!

"Vesty, try again, jump ahead," Romina pleads.

"Why ahead and not just ending it?" Darby demands of Romina.

"Oh Nolan!" Amarie screams from inside of the bucket.

"Because I want Darby to see what happened after..." Romina gives me a look of encouragement and I try once more, focusing on pushing the memory along in time. I see another flash of light and I think I've done it!

We look back into the wooden bucket. There stands Nolan at the door, kissing Amarie's cheek as she leaves. He closes the door behind her and his face completely melts. He doesn't look like a Prince who just got laid. No, he looks unhappy. Empty even. He appears to be spiraling, like every negative thought he could possibly think of is crashing down on him all at once. He looks terrible.

"I wanted you to see that he's not fulfilled by her. She

doesn't make him happy. There is no way she is his Link."
Romina pulls Darby closer, forcing her to look.

"Why would I care if she was?" Darby's face is free of
all emotion but her voice gives her away. She's hurt,
maybe jealous. Poor Darbs. But doesn't she see what a
wreck he is?

There are three quick knocks on Nolan's door in the
memory and the sound of it pulls our attention back to
the bucket. When Past Nolan opens the door, Past Mina is
standing there with a tray of tea and cookies. A smile
spreads on my face. She went there to cheer him up,
didn't she?

But that can't be right, how would she have known he
was upset to begin with...

"You didn't fuck him too did you?" Darby's tone is
pure ice.

"Darbs, of course I didn't! I just thought he might
need a friend." We return our focus to the memory where
Past Mina and Past Nolan settle in for their late night
snack and slowly, the color of life returns to Nolan's
handsome face.

"You were right Mina. He did." I don't know how she
knew he needed help, but Romina was there for him. I
wonder where I was then? Why didn't I think to check on
him that night?

Darby must come to the same conclusion because she
turns to Romina and says, "You're good at that Mina, it's
like what you always do for me." And she sounds like she
means it. I think that's Darby's version of an apology for
being rude to her friend. The dynamics of these Shadows
always entertain me. The vision ends, and I let the baby

treeshark escape my arms. She hops right into the bucket and begins splashing around. Darby produces a snack tray for us and I gorge myself on cheese and dried meat. Using my Gift like this has left me famished.

The afternoon drags on in a series of failed attempts at seeing deeper into the past. Just when I'm starting to feel like a disappointment, Darby suggests we take a walk around to stretch our legs. We stroll in a comfortable silence for a while and I find it tremendously relaxing. Darby mentioned something about staying alert in case we run into any of the adult Treesharks, but my eyelids are heavy after using so much magic and I allow myself to zone out. The forest surrounding the cottage is different from what I'm used to. Instead of towering pine trees, this forest has lush flowering Dogwoods, their fragrant blooms gently floating on the breeze. Here the air is humid. A warm wet breeze kisses the backs of my arms as I remove my overcoat and toss it over my shoulder. Enjoying the squelch of my boots in the wet grass, I watch in delight as a pair of butterflies meld their bodies together and land on a blossoming flower as one.

They are Linked. I wonder who Nolan's Link will turn out to be. It's so wonderful that he has a Link. I wonder if I ever will. I've never seen any visions of my own life. Only the lives of others. Maybe if I had some insight into my own love life, I could actually *find* someone to date. It's not that I'm not interested, really, it's just that it's so hard to get close to someone romantically when I'm constantly being hit with visions of their future. Often a future that doesn't involve me. I know that the relationship will end before it's even started. It's better just to keep to myself. Focus on my friends. I would do anything for them.

Darby and Romina are up ahead now, laughing as they absentmindedly wander the clearing between the trees. There is an unmistakable comfort between them as they walk along, undeterred by the sounds of this unfamiliar forest. I guess for them it isn't so unfamiliar. I find myself wondering how many hours they've spent together out here. And just as I'm flirting with the idea of reaching for a vision of Darby and Romina's past at the Shadow Academy, a flash of light appears before my eyes and a vision begins.

A vision of the King.

"Mina!! Get the bucket!" I shout and they both turn, their eyes wide as they run back towards me. I'm afraid to move so I just stand still, bracing my hands out on a tree.

"Forget the bucket, tell us what you see." Darby comes to my side, her hands pressing into me for support.

"I see the King!" I tell them. He looks as he does now, it's hard to say when this was exactly. "He's underground I think? He's talking to these people... they look frail, and they are...he's getting them to do something to the Eye of the Royal Magic, it's like, the center of it, where all the magic comes from!" I'm struggling to pay attention to the past while also describing it to them. And then I realize.

"Oh my Foe, I'm having a vision of the Eye! It's not someone's love life!!"

"Congratulations Vesty! But who are the frail people? What are they doing to the Eye?" Romina prompts me.

"What does the Eye look like? Where is it kept?" Darby asks.

"They are talking to it…. and their words are fueling it?" I do the best I can to share the details of the memory with them and when it is finished, Darby's hand drops from my side and she pulls away.

"Mina, it has to be the missing Storytellers right? They were telling it something and it *fueled it?*" Darby's eyes blow wide as she continues, "The King must be using the Storytellers to feed the Royal Magic. He's using them to create a false history. To spread lies right into people's heads!" Darby looks incredibly upset over this, I can't say I fully understand what she is talking about. Who are the Storytellers? I've never heard of them.

"It makes sense." Romina bobs her head solemnly.

"That's why he asked the Storytellers for help in creating Royal Magic. *That's* what became of those who agreed. A life in a dungeon somewhere, but that is no life at all! He said they looked frail!" Darby exclaims.

"Who are the Storytellers?" I ask gently. Darby turns back to me, collecting herself.

"Storytelling was a highly respected tradition. There were families, many of them, they raised generations of honorable, knowledgeable people to keep the secrets and the history of all, so that nothing would ever be forgotten. So that we could always learn from our past, our mistakes and our successes. So that we would never lose sight of the truth." Her voice quivers with emotion as she speaks. "It was a gift. It was a magic of its own. And thanks to the King, it all went up in flames." A dark shadow crosses over

Darby's face as she shares this with me. I can't help but shudder.

"Not all, it would seem." Romina steps in, trying to calm us both. "We have to go back and tell the others. And we need to find a way to search the dungeons. The Storytellers must be in the Winter Palace somewhere. We will find them, Darbs." Romina offers me her arm to lean on and I take it, since I'm now totally drained.

And I hate to admit it, but I can't even imagine going to a party tonight...

"Wow, what a buzzkill, how are we supposed to enjoy the ball now knowing what evil the King is up to?" I say, as I lean on Romina as we make our way back to the cottage to collect our things before returning to the Palace.

"Oh Vesty, of course we still have to enjoy the ball. If we don't, then he wins," she assures me.

"What do you mean?"

"Sometimes having fun, living your life, *that* can in itself be an act of rebellion." Her words sit with me, marinating. She continues, "And if that doesn't cheer you up, think of all the scheming we will do right under the King's nose. All of Court will be at the ball tonight, we can gather more information."

Maybe she has a point there. And despite the horror we just unearthed, I feel proud of myself for accomplishing all this. I had a vision of the past! I had a vision that wasn't just someone's interpersonal relationships! I guess I didn't need that Treeshark after all.

❄

Back at the Palace, I part ways with the Shadows to meet Nolan and Rus to get ready for the ABC Ball. But upon arriving in the Prince's rooms as planned, I find that neither Nolan nor Rus are present.

Where could they be?

Don't they know we have a ball to attend tonight? Don't they know that everything is going to shit and this ball is the only good thing we have to hold on to?

I run to the window, throwing it open to stick my head out into the freezing winter air and scan all of Kad for those traitorous friends of mine. This must be some kind of joke.

And that's when I spot them, their equally tall and broad bodies totally drenched in sea water, their giant wooden boards tucked under their strong arms as they leisurely stroll back up the snow covered path from the beach to the Palace without a care in the world.

Surfing?! Who has time for surfing when we have problems to figure out and a ball to attend?! By the time they reach the study I am livid. But as soon as they enter and I see the look on their faces, it's hard to stay mad.

Nolan is beaming, now half naked, a towel tightly wrapped around his lower half as he and Rus clean themselves off, leaving a trail of wet clothes behind as they make their way towards me. His smile is the biggest one I've seen in ages as he runs a hand through his mess of chestnut hair.

"What's going on?" I ask.

"My mother is alive!" Nolan lifts me into a hug as he says this. Crushing my entire body against the wet warmth of his. Thank the Friend for the Royal Magic he's using to heat himself or else he'd be an icicle.

"You're getting sea water on me!" I try to break free of his hold, but I'm trapped - and what did he just say?

"Your mother is alive?" I echo, my brain still catching up. Rus pats him on the back, then joins our embrace. I'm not sure we've ever hugged like this.

"The Shadows told Nolan to look for more information on the Queen, so he went searching in her olds rooms and..." Rus is just as excited as Nolan.

"She's not dead, Vest!" Nolan finally breaks his hold on me and I nearly tumble to the ground. I take a step back, collecting myself.

"Then where is she?" I ask.

Nolan crosses to his desk and pulls a stack of letters out from inside his drawers. Before he says anymore, he glances at the door then nods to Rus to throw a silencing shield around us all. Once the shield clicks into place, he continues.

"She knew my father was up to something and apparently, in the early days of Royal Magic, which by the way, were more recent than we think, my father hurt me, somehow...something happened and my mother saw that I was no longer safe. I don't remember what happened, it's like... all my memories of these events have been wiped from my mind..." He clutches the letters tighter. "But she references it all here in these letters. They were hidden *for me* to find, and she explains how she..." Now he's tearing up a little bit. I take a seat on the sofa, I'm not going to rush him through this. However much time he needs. "She committed her life to serve the Goddess of

The Frequency in exchange for the Goddesses' protection of me. That the Goddesses would help me when the time came to stop my father, if he ever went too far."

Holy Foe. The Queen isn't dead? But she committed her life?

"So *where is she?*" My eyes threaten to fall out of my head as my brain scrambles to keep up with all that I'm learning today.

"She's with them, I guess, the Goddesses...I don't really know how it works." Nolan looks to Rus to elaborate.

"But she's alive. That is what we are focusing on. And Nolan filled me in on his conversation with the Shadows this morning. They were right, Vest, the King is up to something, and Royal Magic is altering our memories. The Queen's letters prove it," Rus finishes for Nolan. It's all a bit overwhelming, but I realize now it's my turn to fill them in.

"So yeah, about that, I was able to look into the past–"

"No way! Vest! You did it!?" Now Nolan is hugging me again, his arms nearly squashing me. I don't think we've hugged this much since we were kids. When he puts me down I continue.

"We saw that the King is using these people...Darby called them Storytellers...I don't know much about them, but they looked ragged, their clothes were *old*, like they'd been down there for decades..."

"Down where? What were they doing?" Nolan's forehead is scrunched in worry.

"The King was using them to feed us false histories, well that's what Darby called it. They were working on the Eye of Royal Magic...it looked like they were under-ground somewhere." Rus' expression must match mine. It's a lot to take in. We've been living here at the Winter Palace for years, our whole lives almost. How could we have never known about this? And how many of our own memories have been altered?

"It's all so crazy, can you believe my father would do this?" Nolan looks white as a ghost now, but Rus and I just exchange a look and shrug. I mean, I sort of can believe it? Nolan's father has always been unsavory. He's power hungry. He's paranoid. Could I believe that he's doing all of this without us knowing?

I find that I can. In fact, it's more alarming how surprised Nolan is.

"Well I..." I begin to speak but Rus puts his hand on me, pulling me back with a look that says *"let's not get into this right now."* I suppose he's right. Nolan is on cloud nine with this news about his mother, no point in telling him we all think his father is a world class asshole and that he'd have to be brainwashed not to have noticed. Maybe they've brainwashed the Prince more than others?

I'm about to nod back to Rus when I get hit with a vision.

I see Rus... he's standing with Brianna and a girl who could be her twin.

It's Cleo! His long lost love Cleo!

Yes, I know that is Cleo. They're all standing in a hallway that looks like the Winter Palace. Cleo is laughing!

The Vision leaves me as quickly as it appears. Nolan and Rus are looking at me expectantly, they know the look on my face by now, that unmistakable indicator that my Gift has reared its spontaneous head.

"What was it, Vest? What did you see?" Nolan is at my side in an instant but it's Rus I turn to, studying him for comparison to the version of him I had just seen in my mind's eye.

"I saw you Rus... you were here at the Winter Palace with Brianna and Cleo."

"Was it the past or the future?" Nolan asks.

"It must have been the past. There's no future where Cleo will be returning here." Rus deflates as he speaks. My heart aches for him. It is truly awful what happened between them. Rus hasn't been the same since. Nolan and I have done what we can to help cheer him up, I've even joined them in the freezing water for a surf morning or two, but it's never seemed to help. Could my vision have been of the past? Now that I can see both, I guess I'll have to pay more attention... but wait. I reach my hand up to touch Rus' piercing. A striking blue gemstone puncturing his handsome brow.

"When did you get this?" I ask.

"After everything that happened with Cleo, I wanted a change..." He shifts uncomfortably. I realize I'm still touching his face and drop my hand back to my side.

"So you didn't have it when Cleo was here at the Winter Palace last time," I conclude.

"I did not."

"You had the piercing in my vision. She was here, with you, and she was laughing. It was in the future! It must be in the future!" I say this as I place my hands on his broad shoulders, feeling a warmth spread through my heart again.

Maybe the King is up to no good. Maybe he's using Storytellers to brainwash us all and manipulate our magic for the sake of his own agenda. Maybe all of that is true. But... Nolan's mother is alive. And Rus' long lost love is coming back to the Palace. We have to hold onto these small wins.

"That's incredible!" Nolan cheers, patting a rather shocked looking Rus on the back. "We must celebrate!" Nolan's quick to magically summon a perfectly chilled bottle of sparkling wine. And so against all odds, I find myself sharing a smile with Rus and Nolan and finally understanding what Mina meant. In spite of what is happening here, we have stolen some joy, and that in itself feels like a rebellion. With happiness in our hearts, we finally start to get ready for the ABC ball.

28

DARBY

I never thought I'd be painting my naked body in a thick layer of magenta glitter for the sake of a mission, but here we are. The Anything But Clothes Ball is tonight, and as three of the final seven Ladies in the running for Prince Nolan's marriage Season, we are doing our best to look the part. The sparkling, nearly nude part.

Romina helped me magically seal the glitter onto my skin. All of my more private parts are covered by sparkling layers of bright pink, but there's little of my body left to the imagination.

"You look incredible." Seline gives me a smile of approval, and I note the seductive look in her eyes. I think of the last time we attended a ball together, and where that led the two of us. The memory of our night together still makes my pulse spike, and yet, I don't feel like going home with Seline again tonight. There's someone else I want now, someone else I know I can't fully have.

Seline got us up to speed as she decorated herself in

strands of silver tinsel. While we were gone with Vesto earlier today, Ruby, Gabrielle, Nicole and Sidney were all eliminated. And as promised, Ingrid was welcomed back into the official running.

Seven of us remain. Only four are real options. Prince Nolan will find his Link amongst those four women. And then, he will marry one of them. So I can't keep doing whatever it is that I'm doing with him. It will only end badly for me when he picks someone else. And no matter how many times today my mind floats back to last night; the way he kissed me, the way his fingers traced up and down my back, the way we both *felt* so much; I have to get over it. As soon as possible.

So maybe flirting with Seline isn't the worst idea? What's the point in working with your ex if a little shameless flirting is off the table anyway?

I eye her outfit again. The reflective silver strands are wrapped around her body in a detailed design that reminds me of a meteor shower. She's left strategic pockets of her delicate flesh visible while covering enough to keep me curious. Her hair is tied back in a bun with glittering silver stones both in her hairline and dripping down from her ears. She looks mesmerizing.

"You don't look so bad yourself, Sel." Her eyes meet mine and we drink in the sight of one another. It's a look we've shared a thousand times. There's so much history with Seline. It makes it all too easy to fall right back in with her. "Going for hot or pretty this time?" I say.

"Hot, always," she replies without hesitation, her ruby red lips twisting into a smile.

"Well, your plan is working," I reply, my face flushing.

"They tend to. Or did you forget that I'm very good with plans?" She shifts her weight forward slightly and I get the feeling that she isn't talking about any of our missions. Instantly my mind is flooded with memories of Seline and the plans she's made for us in the past. Most recently, how she organized our night with Rus. I picture her sitting on my lap that night, the spill of her cleavage at my eye level as I ate up the sight of her in that candy red dress. The dress we later discarded to the floor as she kissed me while riding Rus. "I'm also good at giving orders, taking charge," she adds, and now I *know* she's talking about our night with Rus. The way she bossed him around. The way she told him exactly what to do to me to make me–

"Come on, ladies! We have a ball to attend!" Romina announces, as she re-emerges from the washroom and breaks the tension. I follow Seline's gaze, turning to find Romina, whose body has been completely covered in striking blue feathers. She looks good.

"Unless you two need a moment?" Romina quirks a brow in question, clearly aware of the energy in this room.

"Nope! We're good!" I say, my voice a little too high as I ready myself to make our way towards the Palace.

"Welcome to the second ball of the Season. This evening, we'll be taking a ride together," the King's voice booms over the crowd, amplified by magic. He raises his glass high above the crowd of guests who fill out the newly placed black and white checkered dance floor, which now sits on the front lawn of the Palace. "And until my son has danced with all his beautiful lady suitors, no one's getting off!" The King finishes with a flourish. There are murmurs all around us as he downs his first glass of wine. Then the dance floor below us begins to shake before it starts to *rise from the ground.* The entire platform rumbles up into the air, held aloft by four silver pillars which swirl upwards from straight out of the ground. Lords and Ladies dressed in outlandish interpretations of the theme all grasp on to one another to keep from toppling over as the dance floor continues its ascent. I squeeze Romina's hand as we lurch into our final position, towering over the Palace, and all of Kad. We steady ourselves before glancing out in wonder at the completely unobstructed view of the stars that paint the night sky above our heads. It's more clear than usual, the frost-inducing clouds are nowhere in sight. The clear sky is breathtakingly beautiful. Below us, the familiar buildings of Kad are no bigger than pins on a map. Romina and I exchange a look as we both realize our plan of sneaking off to look for the Storyteller's dungeon is no longer possible. No, no one is sneaking anywhere tonight. Instead we will all be forced to remain here and observe each other in our nearly naked outfits. Everything is on display tonight.

The King finds his way to a perch which has been set up for him in one of the corners, his Royal Council and cronies crowding around, their hands filled with the Winter Palace's signature silver wine glasses. I notice how the man who I believe to be Rus' father sits closest to the King with a solid silver thermos in his hands. I watch him refill the King's glass from it. I tap Romina's arm to get her attention, then gesture to the King very subtly. Her eyes hone in on the thermos and I can tell she's forming a plan.

"Vesto, Darling..." Romina says casually, stopping Vesto as he strolls by in a finely tailored suit made entirely of tangerine colored flower petals. He looks more at ease than when we last saw him.

"Hello Shad– I mean, Ladies!" We pull him in between us, interlacing our arms so I can dip down to whisper in his ear.

"What's with Rus' father playing bartender to the King?" I nod my chin in their direction and Vesto follows my gaze.

"Oh it's nothing, the King is weird about what he drinks. He'll only sip from his personal stash of elixirs. Sometimes we all have to drink it at Court events, but I made sure we'd be pouring the good wine tonight. The very best for Prince Nolan's Marriage Season!" Vesto offers easily, as upbeat music fills the crisp night air courtesy of a live band. I take in the sight of banquet tables of roasted meats and vegetables which line the perimeter. There are also a series of nearly private tents for more intimate seating.

"You've done a wonderful job planning this," I tell him.

"Thank you! Now, Mina, may I have this dance?" Vesto turns to Romina, who smiles widely in return. We unhook arms and she offers me a nod before skipping across the dance floor with him. They begin to twirl into a blur of blue feathers and tangerine petals. It's a sight to behold, until Rus crosses my eyeline and my smile disappears. Much like my own outfit, he's covered in bright blue glitter. We're matching, but in different colors. We'd look perfect together, and the idea of that upsets me as the memory of our last conversation comes flooding back.

"I feel bad that I'm drawn to you because Cleo and I really never had any closure. So I can't exactly move on, even though I keep finding myself at your door."

He's in love with someone else. Or at least, he was.

And he has a list of reasons to stay away from me.

So why should I throw myself at him?

Do I even like him?

I've always found him attractive, that's for sure, but I've never felt connected to him in the way I do with Nolan.

Ugh. Why do I keep thinking about Nolan?

Rus was headed towards me but seeing my smile falter he must have thought better of it. I watch him pivot and change his course. He finds Brianna and asks her to dance, her own dress crafted from what appears to be slices of citrus. I can smell her zest from all the way over here on the other side of the quickly crowding floor.

There's movement beside me and I turn to find Lucci, covered in beautiful iridescent scales. Her own scales.

"You look lovely," I offer by way of greeting. She nods her head slightly, scanning the dance floor in front of us.

"My people don't wear clothes in the same way to begin with, this is more normal for us." Her accented voice is silky smooth. I've noticed that she always speaks with an intoxicating passion, no matter what it is she's saying. I imagine even her weather reports are inspiring to hear.

"A taste of home then... Do you miss it?" Out of all the

suitors, Lucci is the only one who had to agree to cut off communication with her homeland in order to participate.

"I do." She finally looks at me, I can see the heaviness in her eyes, I can feel her honesty. It's this honesty that empowers me to push for a more personal question.

"If you married the Prince, would you ever be allowed back?" A tray of sparkling wine floats by and I'm sure she's happy for the distraction as she grabs two glasses, handing one to me. She takes a small sip before answering.

"The goal of our union would be to unite our people, so even if that were the case, it would be worth it for the greater good," she says confidently.

"Spoken like someone who is clearly smitten with the Prince," I reply before I can think better of it, stealing a sip of my own beverage as I hope my sarcasm hasn't offended her. But I don't think it has because she responds immediately, her bravado never breaking.

"My people are relying on me. It doesn't matter if I have feelings for him or not."

As if we summoned him with our conversation, Nolan sweeps by on the dance floor with Ingrid in his arms, he twirls her, putting her revealing dress of what appears to be sweets wrappers on impressive display as her bright red hair flows down her otherwise exposed back, it appears as though she added tinsel streaks to it, like Seline's. Nolan and Ingrid look to be having fun and I feel grateful he was open to letting her back in the Season. Everyone deserves a second chance.

Nolan's outfit is made up of blue and green

gemstones magically adhered to his skin. He looks somewhat ridiculous and yet, I can't take my eyes off his sparkling body and his muscles which are on display for all to see. But it's not just his body that takes my breath away. He's smiling bigger than I've ever seen before.

Perhaps that was the point of all of this *Anything But Clothes* business, to encourage us to be silly, to let our walls down. To have fun.

Fun looks good on Nolan.

Nolan pivots, sending Ingrid back out into another spin, and as he turns, his eyes catch mine. It's like time freezes as our gazes lock. For no longer than a heartbeat, the music fades away and an electric pulse takes over. I feel it throbbing between us, like a current. His smile grows impossibly wider, and I smile back in return. But the moment is broken by Ingrid, who twirls back into him, blocking our eyeline once more. And the sounds of the ball return.

"I don't really get the appeal." Lucci is looking at the same handsome gemstone-adorned human that I am, right?

What's there not to get?

He's kind, smart, caring, and attractive. He's the whole package. I wonder if he acts the same around the other Ladies as he does with me. Maybe she has not seen his soft side yet. Maybe they just need to get to know each other better.

"You might want to try to get to know him more." Maybe Nolan hasn't let his walls down with Lucci yet. Maybe she hasn't with him either.

She turns to face me, her aquamarine eyes squinting as she considers this, so I take that as a sign to continue.

"He's looking for his Link, not just a wife, remember? He wants to feel a connection. Try opening up to him more, maybe he'll do the same. I'm sure there is something you could find attractive about him." Her squint turns into more of a scowl.

"You're helping me?" she says.

There's a question mark practically painted across her flawless face, and yeah, I'd probably be suspicious too if one of the other Ladies tried to help me, but I want Nolan to be happy and that means leaving no stone unturned.

I think of Lucci, willing to never return to her homeland if it meant helping unite the Humans and Sea Nymphs. That's the kind of heroic woman Nolan deserves to be with. Someone good. Someone selfless. She would make for the perfect Queen. A Queen Kadneria deserves.

"I understand what it's like to have people relying on you. I'm happy to help you help *them*." I offer her this with sincerity in my tone that I hope she can feel.

"I'll try it," she says, finally. We clink our glasses in salute before she glides towards the dance floor to tap Ingrid on the shoulder, ready to claim her own dance with the Prince.

It's not long before Romina and Seline pull me into one of the nearly private tents that have been erected at the side of the dance floor. I'm surprised we found an open one. All the other tents are in use by lords and ladies exploring each other's barely covered bodies. Why is it that outfits made of *anything but clothes* all turned out to be so revealing?

Romina throws a sound shield up as soon as we're inside.

"Vesto filled me in while we were dancing and you're NOT going to believe this."

Seline and I brace ourselves for what is to come, as Romina shares Nolan's revelation about his mother.

The Queen lives. His mother *lives.*

And she committed her life to work for the Goddess of The Frequency?

I didn't know that was even possible. But what kind of life is that if it means turning your back on your only child. Suddenly I'm angry with a woman I've never met.

How could she leave Nolan behind?

Romina must sense my anger because she holds my arm gently, turning to meet my eyes,

"Nolan is happy about this Darbs, he thought she was dead, but she isn't!" she tries to explain.

"No wonder he's been smiling like that all night, I just assumed he'd gotten laid before the ball, or possibly during, have you *seen* these outfits?" Seline mumbles into her wine but I hardly hear her, still stuck on my own train of thought.

"The Queen might as well be dead if she agreed to give her life up!" I say with a surprising amount of passion. Romina looks as though I've offended her somehow.

"It's a very noble thing to dedicate your life to the Goddesses, plus she did it to earn his protection. That's a wildly selfless act. Wouldn't you have done the same for someone you love?" she says, and I let her words sink in and really think about them.

Nolan's mother loved him so much she risked it all to protect him. And yet it has resulted in him living his whole life feeling lonely. But knowing now, that it was all done in the name of love, that must offer him some comfort. I peer my head out of the tent and see him dancing with Brianna. The red streaks in her hair seem brighter under the starlight. As usual she's giggling with him, and it would seem tonight the smile plastered on his face is unfaltering, it's the same smile I saw on his face earlier when he was dancing with Ingrid, then Lucci. He really is happy about the news of his mother.

If it pleases him then I will try to let it do the same for me.

Who am I to judge anyway? My mother didn't dedicate her life to the Goddesses in order to protect me. Instead, she stole my future from me, took away all reminders of our past, and turned us into shadows of our former selves, all in the name of protection. Along the way I think she forgot why she had done it all in the first place. I think she forgot she loved me. And thus, I still feel alone. I have no sense of comfort, no revelation as to *why* this all happened.

Maybe that is why Romina's report bothers me so much.

Noticing the change in my mood, Romina tugs at my elbow.

"Come, let's dance."

We make our way out of the tent and Nolan immediately looks towards us, meeting my eyes again in that same electric way.

"I guess I'll take one for the team and go next." Seline steps in front of me to make her way towards the Prince, breaking our eye contact in the process.

The night pulses forward in a blur of colorful bodies and endless glasses of sparkling wine. The music picks up and Romina and I find ourselves sandwiched between Lords and Ladies in various states of dress as we twirl and twist to the ever changing rhythm of the live music. My troubles have vacated my mind and I'm finally having fun.

Out of the corner of my eye, I can see Nolan dancing with Amarie. Well, I guess you could call it dancing, but from here it looks more like grinding. Her voluptuous pearl encrusted body is pressed up against his and if I didn't know better I'd think she was rubbing her hips up and down his leg with the goal of bringing herself to orgasm. Right here on the dance floor.

Or maybe it's just the vision of them together in the memory that I can't get out of my mind. I shake the thought from my head and look back at them.

Okay, so they are dancing rather close but it's not nearly as inappropriate as I had originally imagined. My mind is getting the better of me.

Am I jealous?

I can't be jealous.

That isn't fair. To me or him.

Nolan's eyes float my way again and he catches me

staring. For the first time all night, his smile falters. I quickly look away but it's too late, he's leaving Amarie behind and coming towards me, closing the distance between us quickly with his long elegant steps.

"What's wrong?" He dips down to speak right into my ear, it's loud enough here at the center of the dance floor that there's no other way I could hear him. I tell myself that's the only reason he's standing this close to me. Still I find myself inhaling his rich and smoky chocolate scent deeply as his warm breath tickles the ridge of my ear.

"I saw you with Amarie." I shout up at him to compete with the music.

"Dancing? I'm supposed to dance with everyone, trying to get through it as quickly as I can so we can get out of here..." I pretend not to hear the way he said "we".

"When Vesto was looking into the Past. I saw you *with* her." I make my meaning more clear this time. His face fully falls into a frown now.

"Which time?" he responds flatly.

"Which time!?" I hear myself say this and immediately feel embarrassed. I have no right to respond this way, and yet I cannot help it.

My stomach flips. He and Amarie have been *together* more than once. Probably several times. I wonder what people will think of the sight of us standing here arguing in the middle of the dance floor.

I steady my tone and continue.

"After the Grand Reveal Ball," I say, avoiding his gaze and crossing my arms.

He glances over his shoulder where Amarie is still dancing, but she's no longer alone, she's enjoying the company of a couple of handsome young Lords now, both sets of their hands exploring her pearl-coated body.

"We've known each other for a long time, we see each other at balls and such and..." he turns back to me now, "...our relationship has always been physical. But nothing more," he admits with some difficulty.

"You don't need to explain." He really doesn't, I'm being a total hypocrite, I was also with someone else after the Grand Reveal Ball. Two people actually.

Nolan's hand finds the small of my waist. He pulls me closer.

"But I want to explain. I want you to know, there's never been a deeper connection between Amarie and me. And I'm sorry you had to see it."

His apology helps, but still, I need to get over myself, I'm being cruel. He needs to focus on finding his Link.

Could Amarie be his Link? Since they already have a physical connection, maybe the two of them could work towards something deeper.

"Maybe it could be more," I pull back slightly so I can see his face. "Have you ever tried?" I ask him in earnest.

"Tried? With her?" Hurt flashes across his handsome face.

"You already have the physical part, maybe she could be your Link?" I look over at Amarie and find she remains happily tangled between those two handsome men, their bodies swaying to the rhythm of the music. Nolan doesn't turn to look. His eyes are solely fixed on my face as if he's searching for something.

"You want me to try?" I notice the way his throat bobs as he swallows.

"Yes, I do." I steal my eyes away from his throat, finally glancing back up at his face.

"Fine. I'll try." His expression has morphed into something I can't read. Or maybe I don't want to. He tugs me closer and I feel his thumb gently tracing small circles on my back. "After tonight," he adds.

"Why after tonight?" The contact of his fingers on my back is grounding me, I feel more at ease than I have all evening.

"Because I want to spend tonight with you." His admission steals the breath right out of my lungs. I have no idea how to respond to that. Luckily I don't have to, because he continues. "I've got two more dances, then we can go." He gives my waist a quick squeeze before stepping to my right and offering his hand to Romina, who I forgot was still dancing by my side as we simply stood here, having this conversation. Nolan signals to the band. They immediately switch to a classic tune and the crowd reverts to a more civilized style of dancing.

I watch as Nolan twirls Romina around the floor a couple of times with the most charming smiles plastered across their faces. There's no jealousy this time from me, just the familiar warm feeling of knowing two people you care for are getting along nicely. I find my way to the edge of the dance floor to get some water, trying to cool down for once.

"I'm surprised to see the redhead back in the running, Ingrid wasn't it?" The King's acidic voice fills my ears and I'm alarmed to find him standing next to me in his chain mail suit. Luckily, he's pretty covered up by the cold metal. "It's true she attacked him, no?" he asks me.

"We handled the situation. There was no harm done." I keep my eyes fixed on the dance floor as I respond. His reply is a soft hum as he joins me in watching Nolan dip Romina in time to the music.

"Well she won't be in the top three, that's for sure. And neither will any of you." There is an unmistakable order being given here. Of course we won't be in the top three, but hearing him say it makes it sound real. The weight of it all sinking in.

"The two Princesses and The Sea Nymph. That's who I pick for him," he tells me casually while sipping from his drink.

"It's his choice in the end, isn't it?" I match his casualness. And so as to avoid any confusion over my understanding of the situation, I add, "What if he likes Ingrid?"

"He won't," the King says in a definitive way. I can't help but wonder what mind control he would use if Nolan's own selection isn't to his liking. I'm surprised when the King continues speaking. "And if you make sure of it, I'll consider hiring you again for something else." The King punctuates his question with a sip of his wine.

So he's offering me another job, is he? That I'd like to hear.

"Something else?" I school my features as I press for more.

"I've got plans brewing, I could use someone around Court who I can trust for valuable information. Especially someone my son favors."

As a master manipulator, I'm not surprised he has more than one way of attempting to control Nolan. Why waste the power of Royal Magic if he can do things the old fashioned way and bribe *me* into bending the Prince's ear. The King turns to me now, reaching out to gently stroke the backs of his fingers against my glitter-coated arm as I freeze in place, my breath catching as he purrs, "I may disagree with most of his choices, but my son has always had excellent taste in beautiful things."

I flinch my arm away without turning to face him, yet his pearly white teeth and shimmering gray hair overwhelm my peripheral vision. He doesn't react to my movement, but he does keep speaking. "He does favor you, doesn't he?"

I simply nod. I'd never betray Nolan's trust again, but the King doesn't need to know that. Besides, getting more access to information will only help my cause.

"I'll speak to him about the top three," I promise, because I was planning to discuss it with Nolan anyway.

"Good," the King says, before revealing a strap across his chest. He tugs it lightly and a parachute begins to inflate behind him as if it is being magically filled with air. "I've had enough of all this."

Before I realize what he's doing, he takes a step back and dives straight off the suspended platform as his parachute expands in a silver flourish.

And he's gone.

"And that's one way to exit." I'm momentarily stunned by the King's departure until Nolan approaches and finds me with my jaw agape.

"Good riddance," he says, teetering over the edge to watch his father land safely down below. I turn to Nolan now, his brown hair messy from a night of dancing. A smile is back on his lips, his whole face illuminated by it. He's glowing from a mixture of sweat and starlight.

"Care to join me, for the last dance of the night?" His question hangs in the air.

I'm glad the King is gone because I know the rumors at Court will spread the second everyone realizes Nolan saved me for last. Because *he does* favor me. Everyone will think I am going to be in his final three. Imagine how surprised they'll be when I'm eliminated within the next few days.

Might as well put on a good show for now, while I still can.

"It's been torturing me." Nolan takes my hand and leads us back to the center of the floor.

"What has?" I grip his hand tighter, strengthening our connection.

"Waiting all night to dance with you." We find our spot and he turns to face me now, his eyes like planets in the night sky as I gaze up at him.

"Why didn't you sooner?" I'm smiling too.

"So you couldn't give me any excuses to cut it short, couldn't tell me I had to go explore my other options." His hands close around my waist again and I snake my arms around his neck. We sway to the music, now a slow and steady rhythm. "I've already explored the other options, Darby. It's you I want, at least, while I can still have you."

I find myself leaning in closer. It's impossible to resist him. We're kissing before I even realize it, so deep and passionate that we forget we're dancing in the center of the floor, we forget anyone else is here around us until the song finishes.

I break away and embarrassment colors my cheeks. All of Court is watching. Nolan barely registers the attention of every set of eyes around us. "Leave with me?" he asks into my ear. A subtle nod of my head is all the confirmation he needs before grabbing my hand and leading us towards the edge of the now slowly descending dance floor. He begins to tug on a strap similar to what the King had.

"Leave now? What about the ball..." It's all I can manage to say before he folds me in close against his chest.

"I've officially danced with everyone now, it's about to be over anyway." He wraps a strap around my middle, securing me to him. "Hang on."

With a loud snap, he releases his own parachute and sends us off the edge, soaring out over the lip of the suspended dance floor. At first I'm stunned. But then, once my mind has caught up with what he's done, I settle into the safety of his arms around me and actually look around. We're drifting slowly through the night sky as the parachute elongates our fall. I feel the glow of the Moon on my face. I feel the crisp night air on my skin. I feel weightless. I feel free. I swing myself around to face Nolan, our bodies pressed together as we leisurely sail through the cool breeze. His hands graze my jaw and he tips my chin up towards his. Our lips meet in the slowest of kisses and we glide gently back down to the ground, but not fully back to reality. Not yet, at least.

29

CYRUS

Abandoned seashells, mounds of glitter, and a few pairs of shoes. The typical aftermath of one of Vesto's elaborate themed balls sits in a neat pile at the center of the now grounded black and white checkered dance floor. Tomorrow morning, the Palace staff will place it all in the lost and found. Well, maybe not the glitter. I kneel down to inspect the pile once more. My fingers find a scalloped seashell. I wonder if this was part of someone's outfit tonight. Must have been. I hold it up higher, inspecting the silver rimmed purple ridges further in the rays of the Second Star's light. The massive star now joins the half Moon in filling the sky. My fingers gently brush against the shell's delicate edges. I trace a deep crack through the center that threatens, but does not yet succeed in severing the shell in two. The shell is broken, but it remains in one piece, hanging on by a thread. I can relate.

"Sir, we've finished our sweep. All clear." Harland, one of the few Royal Guards who I actually trust, looms over me. I've just finished my own security sweep of the tents, so I nod in approval, letting him know that he and the others can disband for the night. "See you in the ring later?" Harland asks as he signals for his crew to retreat towards the Palace. Occasionally, I do join him for an afterhours boxing match on the outskirts of Kad. I find that physical exertion helps when I need to take the edge off. But, tonight isn't one of those nights.

"Some other time," I tell him as I stand, letting the shell fall back into the pile of forgotten items. Tonight I'd rather be alone. I can't risk running into anyone. Can't risk running into *her*. The ball was brutal enough. It seemed everywhere I looked there was Darby, her glitter-coated body a sparkling reminder of how I've been unfaithful to the woman I supposedly love. And Vesto said he *saw* that Cleo would be returning. What would I tell her if she did show up?

I could never deny that I'm attracted to Darby, but it's different from the explosion of passion I had with Cleo. I think that's okay. Cleo and I burned hot like a star falling from the Sky. Cleo set me on fire, and thus, I got burnt to a crisp. I don't think I could survive another love like the one I had with Cleo.

Darby is calming, *cooling* even. It's easy to talk to her, be with her. I feel like she really understands me. Maybe it's companionship–that's what it is. Darby is comforting. And is it so wrong of me to seek comfort after what I've been through?

The guards have turned in now and most of Court has wandered off into the night, either to seek their own beds or someone else's. I notice a small circle of Ladies still lurking by the dance floor, unsure of their next move, looking for an afterparty, perhaps. I spot Vesto's signature green mohawked head amongst them.

He *saw* me with Cleo. Here at the Winter Palace. He saw her laughing. When I close my eyes I can still picture her perfectly. Her sea blue eyes, her heart-shaped face, but her laugh I've lost track of. Guilt washes over me. How could I forget something so precious? It hasn't been *that long* since I've seen her. Since I held her in my arms.

"Hey Russy! Come with us!" Vesto calls, beckoning me over to join the crowd of stragglers. I approach slowly, taking in their various states of intoxication. It's a stark contrast to my own sobriety.

"Oh, hello Cyrus, darling." Seline's familiar coo meets my ears as she unlinks her arms from Ingrid's and slides a tinsel-wrapped arm around me instead, tilting her head up to speak in my ear. "Where's our girl?" she asks.

Her words send a shiver down my spine and I dip my head to meet her seductive silver eyes. She looks at me like we're conspirators, and I suppose we are. Being with Seline was unlike any experience I've had in the bedroom before. We were teammates. Collaborating towards the common goal of bringing Darby pleasure. My eyes dip down briefly to her tinsel-coated body. There is no denying her beauty, and yet, I know that what exists between us isn't romantic. Still, I find I feel more comfortable with her than I was before we slept together.

"You didn't see her run off into the sunset with the Prince?" How could Seline have missed the way Darby and Prince Nolan literally jumped off the platform and sailed off into the sky? I guess her eyes weren't glued to Darby all night like mine were.

Seline's face falls into a frown of disappointment. "We can still have fun without her, come with us, Amarie promised an afterparty." Seline tugs on my arm now, but I'm firmly planted as I take in the crowd. There's no sign of Lucci or Romina; of course the two most responsible ladies have already seen themselves home. Amarie now holds court amongst the more mischievous bunch, her pearl-covered body is impossible to ignore, she's always known how to get attention. Beside Amarie, Ingrid and Vesto chat excitedly while Brianna idles nearby, wobbling uncomfortably in her high heels, eyes glazed over from too much wine. My protective instincts kick into high alert.

"Oh yes! You must come!" Vesto adds enthusiastically, apparently hearing what Seline has been purring into my ear.

"No thanks," I unhook her arm from mine.

"Suit yourself! Let's go, Ladies!" Vesto pivots, marching towards wherever the afterparty will take place. "Bye, bye, Russy!"

"Next time." Seline uses her now free hand to gently pat my cheek and then slinks away with the others who all mumble their goodnights as they peel off.

Bri hesitates, looking back at me.

"You're going with them?" I ask her plainly but it's clear I don't approve.

"Why should you care?" She looks over her shoulder as the crowd disperses, slurring her words in Scalzi, clearly she's in no state for an afterparty.

"It's late, I'll walk you home." I move to her side, placing my hand at her back to guide her.

"*I'm not a child, Cyrus!*" She moves away, practically yelling at me. I place my hands on her arms protectively, in an attempt to calm her down.

"*Bri, I'm just looking out for you,*" I say back in her preferred language, which seems to calm her. She glances up at me, her big blue eyes glowing in the Second Star's light. Again. Just like that night on the cliff side.

She takes note of my hands on her bare arms and I follow her gaze.

"*I'd take a walk. But I'm not ready to go home yet,*" she says. My hands fall away as she folds her arms across her delicate dress made entirely of citrus peels. The frock looks about ready to disintegrate. Maybe if I play along she'll get tired and allow me to escort her home. I'd feel better knowing she made it back safely.

"*Fine. Let's take a walk.*" I offer her my arm. She hesitates, then wraps her hands around my bicep. If I'm not mistaken, she even gives my muscles a small squeeze, the corners of her mouth quirking up at the discovery of my strength. I've been working out more these past few months, not to mention the extra hours I've put in with the Royal Guard in an effort to distract myself.

She leads us down toward the water and I let her. Our uncomfortable silence underscored by the crashing of waves.

"*Did you have fun tonight?*" I ask, as we wind our way down a cobblestone path that opens up to the beachfront. My tongue feels heavy as it works to create the harsh Scalzi sounds I'd nearly forgotten how to form in my mouth. Like everything in Crichton, the language is both brutal and beautiful.

"More fun than you did. You didn't smile once all evening." The words slip from her lips and I can't imagine she meant for them to. She's given away how closely she must have been watching me. But is she right? I must have smiled at least once? It wasn't a bad night. I just had a lot on my mind. As usual.

"I'm sure that's not true," I offer.

"You never smile anymore." We make our way down onto the sand now and she bends to remove her shoes, leaning on me as she frees them from her feet. I reach down to collect them, dangling the strappy sandals in my hand. Luckily the ball was heated tonight, but after such a night of dancing I don't think anyone minds the cool breeze that kisses our exposed skin. She watches me collecting her shoes and takes a step back before continuing to speak.

"You used to smile, you used to take risks, you used to drink! And your name! What's with 'Rus'? Sounds like 'Rust'. It's terrible." She goes as far as to give me a small shove. As if trying to shake me from the paralyzed state I now live in. *"What happened to the guy I met two years ago?"*

I wonder why she even bothers to ask this question. She must know that everything was easier when there was no blame on my shoulders. Now I overthink my every move. I'm terrified of how my actions may lead to the suffering of others. I cannot stand the blame. I must be careful so that no one else is punished because of me like Cleo was. But, before I can even begin to form a sentence that might express this, Bri takes off into a sprint towards the water.

"Bri! No! It's not safe there." I call out to her immediately, too panicked to speak Scalzi. She's heading for the worst part of the break, the part us surfers know to avoid when paddling out.

"I don't want to be safe! Safe is boring!" She yells back at me, switching to the common tongue as she dives under a small wave and begins wading out even further. My heart rate skyrockets.

"Bri, come back here!" I shout as my feet move to follow her, kicking off my own leather boots and reaching to remove my shirt, only to remember I'm not wearing one, I'm wearing nothing but a thick layer of glitter and a concealed pair of undershorts.

"You're going to have to come and get me!" She turns back to look at me then with a huge smile on her face, her eyes glimmering with delight. It's as if time freezes and there's nothing else but Brianna and the sparkling sea that glows in the light of the night sky. Her eyes are fixed on me, and it's a perfect sight. And it's then, when she's looking at me, her back turned to the ocean, as we are taught to never do, that a surprisingly rough wave comes out of nowhere and crashes right atop her, knocking her over and sending her limbs flying out in all directions before she disappears into the rough white water.

I move without thinking, years of experience in this rough break guiding me on autopilot. I'm in the water before I can register its cold kiss. There is no time to hesitate. If something were to happen to her, I could never forgive myself.

If she were hurt because of me? No.

No. No.

I dive under and seek her out from the rough white water, scooping Bri up in my arms and lifting her above the surface. Her gown has completely washed away and I'm relieved to see she was also wearing a small pair of silk undershorts, minuscule as they may be. My own ensemble made solely of glitter has vanished as well. But I barely register our near nakedness as I wade through the water and bring her over to the safety of a sandbar, the water only waist deep. I clutch her in my arms, cupping her face in my hand.

"Bri! Are you okay?!" I demand, while checking to make sure she is breathing.

"Well that's one way to sober up." She coughs a little in my arms as she glances up at me with a lazy smile. She's totally fine. But I am shaking.

"For Foe's sake Bri, you scared me!" I'm overwhelmed. It's too much, my lungs feel tight and my vision blurs. I clutch her tighter to my chest, one arm around her back, the other tucked under her legs. I wonder if she can feel how badly I'm trembling. She must because she pushes back from me, guiding herself down to stand.

"It's okay... I'm okay." She finds her footing in front of me, the water reaches just below her breasts, leaving their perfectly rounded peaks exposed, and I do my best to avoid looking.

"Bri if something had happened to you..." My voice cracks and I'm a goner. The possibility of adding more guilt to my already overflowing pile completely ruins me. A tear escapes my eye. This is mortifying. But Bri doesn't falter, instead she reaches forward to touch me, one hand gently drifting to my face to wipe the tear away, while the other finds the tattoo on my stomach.

"It's not your fault. My parents are to blame for Cleo. Not you. And I'm okay, nothing bad happened." We stand there in silence until my breathing slows to a normal rhythm. I realize she's still tracing small circles over my tattoo, or perhaps my abdominals beneath it.

"When did you get this?" She presses the palm of her hand against my ink.

"After Cleo," is all I can think to say.

"Thank you for speaking Scalzi with me. I know you don't enjoy it, but it helps me feel less alone," she says. I nod, understanding. Then she tugs on my hand and continues. "Come on, it's getting cold, let me walk *you* home. Actually, I'll race you there!"

We wade our way out of the water and back to the sand. Luckily we're close enough to my cottage that we make it there in a few short bursts. As soon as we're inside, I offer Bri a towel to wrap herself in and I do the same.

"You can sleep in my room. I'll take the couch." As embarrassed as I am about my outburst of emotion, our playful race home has certainly lifted my mood. I feel grateful for Bri's company tonight.

"No that's okay, I can head back to mine." She does sound more sober than before. I take in the sight of her pacing by the door in nothing but a towel, her hair dripping water on the floor. She shouldn't go back out there wet in the cold.

"It's late Bri. You should stay." I place a hand on the

small of her back and guide her towards my room, following her in. Once we've crossed the threshold she pauses and turns to face me.

"Can I ask you something?" Her voice comes out as no more than a whisper.

"Of course." I'm surprised to find my own voice is an equal rasp to hers.

"Have you ever seen me like that?" She's looking up at me now, her hands clasped at her chest, securing the towel tight around her.

"Like what?" I lean forward to get a better look at her as water drips from my own wet waves of hair. I use my hand to smooth it back away from my face.

"Like how you see her." Bri's eyes never leave mine. With her hair slicked back with water it's impossible to see the red streaks or the short styling. Dark as it is like this, I'm struck by how much she looks like Cleo. And she's here, alone in my room late at night, the swells of her breasts rising and falling rapidly against the lip of the towel that is wrapped around her.

When did she start breathing so quickly? When did I?

"Bri." I don't know what else to say. Her name is all I can manage. As if I need to remind myself who it is that I am talking to. Which sister is standing here before me. She takes a step closer to me, reaching out to place a hand on my jaw, her head tilted back to meet my gaze.

"Loving her has changed you. You aren't who you used to be." She takes a deep breath, dropping her hand from my face to my collarbone. "I miss that guy. For the last two years I've thought about him. Constantly. And coming back here, part of me was excited about the

Prince, yes but part of me just wanted to see *him* again... to see you. Part of me has been dying to know if you ever think of me too. If you could ever see me as more than just..." My own hand floats to where her fingers brush my clavicle, swallowing her hand in mine as I gently remove it, cutting her off.

She's confirmed it. The crush I always suspected. Despite the fact that I have always been aware that she might have feelings for me, it is different to hear her voice them. I owe her some response.

"I don't know, I've never tried." I hold her hand in place between us.

"Could you try?" She stands before me with expectation in her eyes. This shy girl has somehow found the courage to bear her heart to me. I do not want to take that courage for granted. I also do not want to hurt her, because, based on the vulnerable look on her face right now, I can't help but feel that she is on the brink of heartbreak. I think of the purple scalloped sea shell cracking through its center, threatening to fracture in half. I think of my own cracked surface. I refuse to be the source of her pain. To inflict upon her what I myself have struggled to deal with. But is that reason enough to lead her on? To give her false hope?

It is false hope, isn't it?

Bri is from Crichton just like Cleo. It would be another long distance relationship, it would be another case of her family not accepting me as a Stellar, it would be another instance of *her* parents going to unimaginable lengths to keep us apart. But Bri is the younger sister and therefore not the heir to the throne, so maybe it wouldn't be as big of a deal for her to be romantic with an outsider like me. I'd still never be welcomed back to Crichton. Not by her family. No, I will not let another Crichton Princess be banished from society because of me.

And why am I entertaining that thought process anyway?

This is Cleo's little sister.

What would Cleo think when she found out? Not if. When.

If I were with Bri, Cleo and I would no longer be a possibility. I allow myself to follow the thread. If I were with Bri, it may preclude me from ever being with Cleo again, but at least it would have been my own choice. Unlike now, where Cleo and I are not a possibility but I had no say in the matter. No choice. Would that make me feel better?

Maybe it would.

Yet, I do not think any of this would be fair to Bri.

"Bri, it's too complicated." I release her hands and her face falls as she lets my words sink in.

"Of course. I shouldn't have." She steps back and I can see the pain that is crashing down on her now. The disappointment. Because of me. I can see the crack forming. I can see her heart breaking. For two years she has pined over me. I know what that feels like all too well. For two years I loved someone too, and within seconds, it was all over. It kills me to think I'd send her into the darkness that I have hardly been able to manage myself. Her lip quivers and her shoulders turn in and I cannot bear to see this beautiful woman crumble. All thoughts vacate my mind, everything except for making this right, making her feel better again. My hands find her jaw as I pull her face towards mine, all she manages is a gasp as our bodies collide, my towel falling to the floor as our foreheads press together, our lips threatening to touch.

"It's too much to see you upset, Bri. I can't take it." The words are mostly air upon my lips but she is close enough to hear them as I lean in to kiss her and–

"No, wait." She stops me with a hand to my chest and I'm stunned into silence. *"Not like this."* She continues in our mother language before reaching down to pick up my towel and handing it back to me.

As she sits down on my bed I clear my throat, trying to wrap my head around the huge mistake I almost just made. I almost kissed Cleo's sister.

Unable to face her, I turn towards the door as the mortification sets in. "Stay, take my bed, I'll be on the couch if you need me." I'm nearly out of the room when she speaks again.

"I'm sorry."

I halt in the door frame, angling back without meeting her gaze.

"Bri, you have nothing to apologize for. It's me who is sorry."

"Okay," she mumbles, her voice no louder than the waves crashing in the distance.

"Goodnight, Bri," I tell her as I make my way back to the main room, closing the door on whatever what-if's remain between me and the Princess of Crichton.

30

DARBY

I'm standing before a large marble tub at the center of Nolan's generously sized washroom. The moonlight streaks in through his stained glass windows, painting the room in iridescent hues, as flickering pastels dance along the tile floor. Candles burn on either side of the tub. I watch as wax drips in thick, slow bursts. Nolan submerges his hand into the now bubble-filled tub to test the temperature of the water. Finding it to his liking, he turns back to face me where I wait on a soft woven mat.

"May I?" he asks, his voice rich with desire as he looks down at me, taking in the sight of my glitter-coated body, my outfit from the *Anything But Clothes Ball* still magically adhered to my skin. I'm not entirely sure what he's asking permission for, but still I nod yes.

He wraps his arms around me and lifts me up to swing me over the tub's ledge. He gently places me inside, the warm water greeting me like a hug. I take a deep breath, inhaling the soapy mix of lavender and leather. It smells good. It feels even better.

With a splash, Nolan finds his spot in the tub next to me, his long, toned legs bending to fit. Luckily, it's a large tub. I take in the sight of ink on his legs, discovering for the first time that he's covered in tattoos from ankle to thigh. I want to get a better look at them but my attention is stolen as Nolan pours more of that leathery scented soap across a round natural sponge. I watch his muscles work as he dispenses the soap and lathers the coarse sponge, then reaches for me, gently pressing the porous pouf to my chest. He begins to scrub with a tender rough-ness until the pink glitter breaks its magical hold. Realiza-tion dawns on me that he's cleaning my outfit off.

"We could just use magic, it's how I got dressed," I offer, looking up at him. There's no need for him to scrub me clean by hand. But he continues anyway, working determinedly with that same firm gentleness.

"No more magic tonight," he declares, as the sponge makes its way across my chest leaving my breasts exposed to him. It's an innocent bubble bath, and yet there's nothing sweet about the way his eyes shimmer in concentration as he scrubs over my nipples, leaving them peaked and raw. The tiny gold specks in his brown eyes glow in the candle light as he continues speaking. "I want to do this myself, with my own hands, so that this night is just for us. So that this is all ours."

It occurs to me that Nolan has only ever known life with Royal Magic. Magic that belongs to the Crown. Magic that is controlled. His every movement has been logged and most likely monitored. My heart swells as I realize what he is really saying: He wants this moment to be untainted by Royal Magic and the limitations it presents. He wants to protect whatever is happening between us.

He wants it to be ours. Just ours.

The thought makes me feel cherished. Cared for, even.

"You're so beautiful, Darby." His voice is nearly a whisper as he turns me so my back is to him, wrapping his arms around me as he continues to scrub the glitter away. I think it might be the first time anyone has ever said that to me. Of course, I've had my appearance praised before, but never like this, never those words used in such an intimate setting. I feel the vibration of his voice wash over me like a warm embrace. I want to offer the same level of comfort and care to him as well. I turn around to face him and the gemstones still magically adhered to his skin.

"My turn," I tell him. He smiles as I take the sponge from his hand, applying more of the luxurious liquid soap and then lathering slow circles on his chest, his muscles flexing gently beneath my touch.

"You are too." I glance up at him.

"I am too?" he says, his eyelids falling closed as he enjoys the feeling of me scrubbing him down.

"Beautiful. You are too. Everything about you," I tell him. He's blushing now and it's adorable. He leans forward to press his lips to my forehead, as if to say thank you for the compliment. I continue to wash away his gemstones, tenderly scrubbing every inch of his skin until I reach the three tattooed rings that wrap around his forearm, and his scar.

"What do they mean?" I run my hands over the thick black ink, washing away bubbles with warm water.

"My other tattoos have meaning, but those....I just thought it looked cool."

I examine them more closely, the way the lines draw attention away from his charred skin.

"Were you trying to hide it?" I don't need to say what.

"It's not that I'm ashamed of my scar." He looks down at his own arm, considering it before continuing. "It's just that, people always asked about it, and I can't remember what it's from. It frustrated me always having to answer, so getting this tattoo helped cover it up. But, now that I know my memories have been taken from me, I feel so angry that I can't bear to look at it." He puts his hand on mine to slow my scrubbing of his arm. I motion for him to turn now, giving me his back and exposing a canvas of stunning tattoos I've never even seen before. Tonight I am discovering so many new parts of him that have been hiding below the surface.

The center of his back depicts a giant wave crashing over a forest. I trace the rich ink with my fingers, spotting the point where the forest leaves blend into the unmistakable image of bearhound paws in the snow.

"Today, when I read my mother's letters, I was just so happy she was alive, I didn't give myself a chance to think about the rest of it. But her letters, Darby, she implied that my father has been up to something. That he did something to me when I was younger... What if this scar is part of that? And what if he took the memory of it away from me?" I can't see his face since he's turned away from me, but his tone turns serious.

I let the sponge float away and pull his back flush against my chest, pressing our bodies together as I wrap my arms around him from behind. Holding him tight against me. Letting him know I've got him. Giving him the strength to go on.

"It looks like a bracelet doesn't it? What if he used Royal Magic on me somehow and... *that* was my mother's final straw. *That* was why she gave up a life with me, in order to protect me from harm."

"We will figure this out, Nolan. Together. I'm here to help you." I do my best to reassure him.

"The vision said I'd grow more powerful once I'm Linked. I can't help but feel my father only wants this for me so he can abuse that power. It almost makes me not even want to be Linked." He leans forward, turning around to face me, his eyes slowly dragging over my exposed clavicle, the rest of me now hidden below the surface of the bubbles. I'm aware of my chest rising and falling. My heart is racing. "I don't want to let him control me anymore... I don't want him to have any more access to me," Nolan says with the steady voice of a Prince.

"He won't. We will put an end to this," I promise him, because we must. That has become abundantly clear. The King has hurt too many people, and learning that he's also done something to Nolan is *my* final straw as well, just as it must have been his mother's.

The King must be stopped, and I will do whatever it takes.

Now it isn't just the Storytellers I need to protect, it's Nolan too. I will always protect Nolan.

I can't believe we're here. I think of those two children

running through the hallway. They had no idea what the Goddesses had in store for them. What their fate would become. Perhaps this is the reason I met Nolan, the reason I was destined to care for him. Perhaps it was all leading to this moment where I finally have the tools at my disposal to seek my revenge on the King. Nolan will be my ally. He will help us learn what we need to learn and do what needs to be done. It's sad to think the end of our story won't be marriage and a lifetime of companionship, but I try to tell myself that this is enough. Working together to bring down the King, that will be our happy ending. Yes. That *must* be why our paths have crossed again. That must be why we feel so much for each other.

Marriage was never an option for me anyway.

This is better. This is good.

We will always have this night in our hearts.

"What's wrong?" he asks then. My face must have fallen because he leans forward, pulling me in towards him. I shake my head, clearing my thoughts away.

"I wish this was the beginning of us. Instead, it feels like the end," I tell him, honestly. Then my hands are on his face, and his hands are on mine as we share a deep breath. The warmth of the soapy water soothes the aching of our hearts.

"Come, it's time for bed," Nolan says before standing up. My eyes go wide as his fully exposed naked body meets my eyeline. My mouth is instantly dry as I tilt my head up to absorb the sight of him in front of me. He's stunning. He's all cut muscles and the deepest V leading straight down to the most perfect extension of him, a long straight rod of masculinity which points right at me. He offers me a hand and I take it, dragging my eyes away from his erection. Nolan didn't seem embarrassed by it, so why should I?

Standing up, water cascades down from me. Without any doubt, I know he's drinking in the sight of me naked here before him, just like I did for him. He reaches for a soft towel, then wraps it around me before doing the same for himself. He scoops me in his arms again and carries me out of the tub, out of the washroom, and back into his sleeping suite. I can't stop thinking about how hard he was.

What would it feel like to touch him?

To let him put himself inside me the way no man has before.

To join our bodies until they mold into one.

He deposits me down on his oversized, plush bed and I try to ground my thoughts back in the present. He pulls the covers back and ushers me into the soft, warm, sheets before taking his own place beside me. I glance around his room. It's all soft whites and plush fabrics. It's incredibly warm and welcoming, just like him.

And then we just lay there, next to each other, the blankets trapping the warmth of our bodies. I roll onto my side to face him and he does the same for me. Our fingers find each other and interlace.

"How do you feel?" Nolan asks, softly.

How *do* I feel?

If only it were a simple question. Part of me feels charged. Determined. Ready to finally do something to right the wrongs of the past.

Another part of me feels heartbroken, knowing that

the connection I'm experiencing tonight will need to be severed. Knowing that my life beyond this mission will never again consist of bubble baths and balls.

But then there's a part of me that feels at ease. A part that's calmed by the presence of him and the care that he's showing me beneath these blankets.

"Relaxed," is how I choose to answer.

"Good," he responds, his own eyelids seeming to grow heavy. He begins to trace his fingers up and down my arms, building a steady rhythm. Then his hand moves to the tops of my legs. He begins teasing at the hem of the plush towel I'm still wrapped in below our blankets. His unhurried movements are hypnotizing. My mind becomes free of all worry, all thoughts escaping me except for the feeling of his fingertips skimming closer and closer to the place I am now aching.

"Nolan." His name escapes my lips, taking him by surprise. His eyes open again and he looks down at me.

"Darby," he responds, as I decide my name has never sounded better than it does on his lips. Those lips. Those dangerous lips.

We've only ever kissed but I know that he is experienced. It's not only his reputation, but the fact that I've now actually seen him *with* Amarie. He's been intimate with many women. Has he bathed with them before too? Is this one of his moves? Does he expect that we will have sex now?

Suddenly, I don't know if I'm ready for that with him.

How would it feel to take that step just to then end things between us?

I sit up a little bit, the thought unsettling. He senses

the shift, and being intuitive as he is, he starts to piece it all together.

"You saw me with Amarie, yes, but I want you to know, it was nothing like this," he tells me as his fingers drift up my arm. "And I'm aware of my reputation." There's no hint of embarrassment in his voice. "But I can't deny that I enjoy being physical. The hard part is just..." He pauses, possibly to collect his thoughts as his eyes drift down to where his fingers tease my skin. "It's a lot easier to find a willing bedfellow than a real connection. So yes I enjoy being intimate but, I always think it's going to be *more*." His eyes flick up to meet mine again, and I can tell he is being honest with me, so I should be honest with him too.

"I've been *intimate* with women too, you know." I glance up at him, wrapping my fingers around his own again. "I've had sex with women, and I've been with men but, technically I've never gone *all the way* with a man." I let my truth sit there between us for a beat before I continue. "I think it's the same for me, I crave that deeper connection, and I haven't found it with a man before, so I haven't given up that final piece of me yet."

"Was there a woman you connected with?" he asks, genuinely.

"I thought there was, but it turns out she didn't reciprocate my feelings, for her it was only physical." It's weird to talk about Seline in the past tense, but I finally feel like I can. "I wanted more too. I always want more."

He scoots impossibly closer to me. So close that I feel his eyelashes flutter against my forehead.

"You deserve more," he tells me.

ROYAL MAGIC

"So do you," I say right back.

"You know I didn't just bring you home from the ball with me to have sex, right?" The scruff of his beard prickles my nose as he speaks this close up. I don't know what I thought, but I certainly feel better hearing him say that. He continues. "Of course, we can do whatever you'd like, but I'd be happy with just this, laying next to each other, touching, talking. This is far more intimate to me."

Nolan's admission sends butterflies fluttering in my stomach and I'm overwhelmed by the desire to touch him and be touched in return. All of this vulnerability is proving to be a huge turn on. I wonder if it is for him too?

I let my hand wander down below the covers and find him still completely hard.

I guess it is.

"Talking and touching huh? Getting you all worked up?" I gently trace my hands over his smooth shaft. He huffs out a breath.

"Is it not for you?" He barely manages the words.

"Why don't you see for yourself?" I gaze into his eyes. At some point his hands returned to exploring the hem of my towel, and I now dare him to go further. One of his hands slides under the towel's edge, ever so slightly, until his fingertips float up my thighs. I spread my legs, giving him better access and he keeps roaming until his fingers kiss my center. He must discover how wet I am because he releases a small breath, followed by a single word.

"*Baby.*"

It slips from his mouth and the term of endearment alarms us both, but I find I don't mind it. He slips a single finger inside me, following the trail of wetness, his rough

337

calloused hands calling all my attention to the point of contact between us. He then removes his finger, pulling his whole hand away from me and I ache at the absence of him. I watch in slow motion as he drags that finger back up to his mouth and licks it clean. He brings a second finger to his mouth and wets both of them thoroughly, his perfectly pink tongue wrapping around his tanned skin.

I gasp.

"Perfect," he says.

I'm honestly speechless as I watch him bring those now wet fingers back down to that throbbing spot between my legs. He begins to gently massage my apex. Slow circles and perfect pressure. He knows exactly what I need, exactly where to rub and pull, how firm to press, some combination of his Dreamseer Eclipse Gift and his experience has made him a master of my body. As if he's studied it his whole life. As if he was made to bring me pleasure.

Maybe he was.

Remembering that my own fingers are still absent-mindedly teasing the long length of his hardness, I take inspiration from him and bring my own hand to my mouth to spit in it. I place it back on him then, using the wetness of my own saliva to glide up and down him.

He moans in approval.

That's how we find ourselves in a game of wills, teasing and rubbing each other in our own natural lubricant with our eyes fighting to remain open as the push and pull of pleasure threatens to take over. But I never want this to end.

"You first," he tells me. But I shake my head no, feeling

him get impossibly harder in my hand. It makes me melt, I know that a flood is building between my legs and I want to experience this with him.

"Together," I rasp out and the demand in my voice makes his eyes flare.

"Together," he agrees. And then it's time, and I can't take my eyes off him, this man is the most gorgeous creature I've ever seen; the way his face contorts in pleasure, the sounds he makes, I'm fighting to keep my eyelids from fluttering shut so I can memorize how he looks as he loses all sense of control. And I'm wrapping around him, pulsing against his fingers as he never relents, despite his own release. I start to come and he slips two fingers inside me to make sure I can ride out every last wave of this incredible release.

When it's over, we lay there breathless. He uses one of our forgotten towels to clean us off and then he turns us on our sides, pulling my behind into his lap as he wraps his arms around me, so tight that I could never leave. Not that I want to.

My eyes scan his room. It's rather tidy, except for a pile of papers on his desk, and a colorful collection of what look to be oil based crayons.

"You draw?" I don't know why I'm surprised by this, but I am.

"Not here usually but, it helped when I was sequestered." His now gravely voice tickles the back of my neck as he speaks. I want to ask where he prefers to draw. I want to see his creations. There is so much more I want to know. That I'm desperate to learn about him.

But my eyes are heavy and his breathing is slowing.

And just as I'm about to fall asleep I realize something.

"I don't have any clothes! What will I wear home?"

"Tomorrow's problem." He fights off sleep to respond.

"And tomorrow you'll choose your final three. You have to try to make it work with one of them," I add on.

"Tomorrow's problem as well." He hugs me tighter, smoothing my hair down my back and away from his face. This feels so nice. I lean into his touch, which he takes note of. He always notices when I like something. He notices everything about me, doesn't he?

31

NOLAN

The warm water gently laps at my torso. It's so warm I
don't need to use magic to heat my body as I guide her
out past the break. She smiles at me from atop my board,
her face as bright as the Sun which looms behind her, and
Foe, does it do something to me to see her happy in the
water. Noticing the perfect wave coming our way, I turn
her and the board into position and launch us forward,
hopping on beside her. I paddle quickly, making sure we
catch the wave. As soon as we gain enough momentum,
we pop up in synchrony, finding our balance as we begin
to dance atop its surface together. A slowly unfolding
wave rolls out beneath us until the board disappears
beyond our feet and we are left dancing in the air. Darby
looks at me and smiles, and I lean in to kiss her.

But then there's nothing there.

She vanishes just as another wave comes crashing
over me.

The water is no longer clear. It's a deep, dark, charcoal

color. And I'm drowning in it. Water fills my lungs and I look up to see my father. He's out on his own silver board, the board I have not seen him touch in years.

"Stand up, Nolan," he tells me. "It's time you stood up," he says again, but I can hardly make out the words over my own coughing.

I wake up then, gasping for breath. My face is wet and soon I discover Buddy on my bed, licking my face. That's weird, considering I locked him out last night so he would let me and Darby have some alone time.

Darby. Where is she?

Leaning over, I find she's gone from my room. I glance around and notice that my closet is open; she must have borrowed something to wear seeing as I washed her glittering outfit away in my tub last night, the memory of which puts a smile on my face. Maybe she let Buddy in on her way out. I'm disappointed that she left without saying goodbye. But perhaps it was for the best that she snuck out, had I been awake, I wouldn't have been able to let her leave.

Laying back on my pillow, I inhale deeply. My bed still smells like her. Buddy must notice this too because he curls up in the spot where her head once rested. My thoughts return to last night. It was so easy to discuss everything with her. She made difficult conversations feel manageable. Yes, my problems are overwhelming, but with her by my side, I didn't feel afraid. I believe that together, her and I can figure this out. All of it.

As I lay here now, the feeling solidifies: it's not my father I fear anymore, nor is it the dangers of his scheming. The only thing I'm afraid of now is that I've fallen for *her*. That I can no longer seriously consider marrying anyone but her. And most of all, I'm afraid that she really believes that there is no way we could figure this out between us. I'm afraid that she is too scared to even try.

"But I'm not a real option." That's what she would say if she were here.

But should I believe her?

When I'm with her, I feel my chest expand. I feel a warm glow that paints the insides of my skin. It's so much more than just the pulse-racing thrill of lust or attraction. It's a deep, steady rhythm that parades through my senses. She's all I think about. Dream about. I don't feel this way about any of my other options. Sure, some of my current suitors would be a good choice for a politically arranged marriage. But I've been given the opportunity to find more than that. I've been given the chance to find my Link.

Why couldn't a Shadow be my Link?

She's an elite spy, surely that is an admirable profession for a future Queen.

I have never had a Link before, obviously, but the way I feel about Darby can only point in that direction.

But then why aren't I 100% sure about this?

Maybe because she keeps pushing me away.

That's probably it.

She keeps sowing doubt in my mind.

But I think the feelings between us are starting to speak louder than her words of caution. We need more nights like last night. We need more time together to see what this really is between us. I want to explore our connection further. Last night couldn't have been good-bye. What was it she said in the tub?

"I wish this was the beginning of us. Instead, it feels like the end,"

No. It isn't the end. I wish I had told her that last night. I wish I had put a stop to her constant attempts to create space between us. Now I'll have to convince her otherwise. I'll have to show her that we can make this work somehow. She's going to have to open her mind to me the same way she has opened her heart. That's the only way we will figure out once and for all if we are each other's missing Link.

Buddy raises his eyebrows at me and I give him a small pat between his rounded ears. Maybe as Darby and I continue to work together, she'll come around to the idea of us. I'm going to need her help as I come up with a plan to expose my father, steal back my memories, right the wrongs he's committed, and eventually track down my mother. My mother, who is very much alive. We should oust my father as King and lock him in the dungeons. I'll need my mother's support for that. She will need to come back and rule this kingdom, be the Queen the people of Kadneria deserve.

I wonder how long I can put off choosing a bride who isn't Darby.

Vesto foresaw that I had an Eclipse wedding night, not that it had to be *this* coming Eclipse. Yes, all I need to do is drag this whole process on until she realizes that there is hope for us. That she truly could be my Link.

❄

Vesto, Cyrus and I are seated across from our parents in the formal dining room. Apparently we've had this breakfast meeting scheduled for a while, although I just learned about it. My father and his council wish to present me with their ideas on who my Link might be.

"This Season has provided some much needed entertainment for all at Court, but it's time you made your choice for the final three. Enough games," my father states casually as he fills his plate with colorful fruits. As if finding a soulmate were as easy as finding a wife. But what would he know about soul mates? He and my mother married for political reasons. I wonder if he even loved her. My hand clenches into a fist as I watch him raise an oversized berry to his lips, bright red juice streaming down his chin and staining his silver beard as he bites in. I feel so foolish for trusting him. Now that my eyes have been opened to the truth about him, it's impossible to ignore the ill intent behind each and every one of his actions. The way he seeks to control me and every facet of my life.

Vesto nudges me beneath the table, reminding me to stay calm. I unclench my fist. The time for taking down my father will come; for now, we need more information. For now, we need to play along.

"Of course, I would like to do a round of solo dates before the next ball, after that, I'll be able to announce the final three." I drum my fingers on the wooden table as I lean back in my chair, sipping a warm cup of coffee. I need to appear unbothered, despite my racing heart.

"Another round of dates and a ball? That's rather a lot, isn't it?" My father leans back in his own chair, matching my leisurely appearance. "If you're having trouble decid-ing, perhaps you'd consider our selection." He nods to his aide Tilda, Vesto's mom. Her long green hair and matching bright green eyes are striking, but it's her soothing voice that I've always admired. Whenever there is bad news to share, I prefer to hear it from her.

"Nolan dear, this is a big decision, and our council, along with your father, the King, have simply put together some ideas for you to *consider*." Tilda unravels a long scroll and begins to read off it. "Seeing as you are a Prince, we feel it would be best for you to marry a Princess." She glances over at my father before continu-ing. "Princess Amarie of Langha would be a formidable partner, we would also be pleased with Princess Brianna of Crichton, as for the third position in the finals, we ask that you include Lucci the Sea Nymph. She does not hold an official royal title, but she is the daughter of her people's leader, thus she is essentially a Princess." Tilda drops the scroll and looks at me with a smile on her face, a genuine one. I wonder how much she knows of my fathers corruption. Tilda has always seemed to have good intentions, but now I fear I don't know who to trust.

"Are you truly asking me to name them the final three? Or are you telling me to?" I say with a snide smile.

"Of course it is ultimately your decision who you choose," she quickly supplies.

"What if I wanted to choose someone else? Someone without a Royal title?" I don't even look up at them as I move some toast around my plate. I hear Vesto curse under his breath to my right. Tilda looks to my father then, he simply smiles, wiping his chin with a cloth napkin before he speaks again.

"That's not an option." He flashes his pearlescent teeth at me, his smile unfaltering.

"Is it not my decision? Was the Vision not of me finding my Link on my Eclipse wedding night? Of *my* power growing exponentially? I thought you wanted me to grow more powerful, Father." I can't help but grit my own teeth in response.

"It would be wonderful if you did, Nolan, perhaps you'd finally manifest your Eclipse Gift that has disappointed us by refusing to arrive in your first 26 years." He says this knowing how much it will hurt me. It's been a sore spot since I was a kid. He's never missed an opportunity to remind me how *disappointing* it is that my Gift has never reared its head. Maybe it never will, that would be fine with me.

Unlike him, my only goal in life isn't to become more powerful.

Just when I feel my temper growing, he continues speaking.

"However, we've discussed it as a committee and determined that you growing more powerful is no longer as important as the possible allies we could gain from your marriage, so from this moment on, it's no longer just about you finding a Link. We're looking for a wife, if she happens to be your Link, then let's consider it an added bonus."

Time stops. The world tilts on its axis.

"You can't do this." My fist meets the wood and I'm seeing red.

Vesto nudges my leg again, reminding me to calm down.

"Of course I can, besides, what's the big deal, you are attracted to these three women are you not? We've all seen you with them at the balls. There is still a chance that you find your Link, we're just helping to narrow the pool. Trust me, you will come to like this idea, I know you will. There's no sense in us arguing over it, that would be a waste of time." He stabs more fruit with his fork and starts to chat with his advisors again so casually that I almost don't even realize what he means.

Then it dawns on me.

He plans to use Royal Magic to change my mind about this.

He knows it will work, and that's why he doesn't even want to "waste" the conversation on trying to convince me. He knows I'm going to take his side because he is going to plant the false stories in my head. Stories about my own heart. My own mind.

No. I want to scream it across the table.

No.

I need to find a way to rid myself of his control. He cannot do this to me again. If I were to take off my bracelet, as uncomfortable as it would be, I would still need to find a way to explain it to my father. He would know immediately.

I'm trapped.

But, I remind myself to breathe. Slowly. In and out. I'm trapped, but I'm not hopeless. For now I will have to fake it. That will have to do until I can find a way to get rid of the Royal Magic. I need to remember my goal for today was to buy more time.

"You're right, I like them." I exhale another breath. "I'll consider your choices, just let me have the one on one dates to be sure, and the ball, then I'll announce my decision." I say, schooling my features. Vesto gives me a wink.

"When is the next ball?" My father addresses Vesto now.

"In four days," he says proudly, I know he's excited to plan this one.

"Let's do it tomorrow night. Speed this along," my father says, and I watch Vesto's eyebrows raise, earning a glare across the table from Tilda.

"Tomorrow night!" He nearly chokes on his hot beverage before collecting himself. "Yes, yes of course, your Majesty."

"Then we'll have the final three's families brought in, we'll need increased security of course." My father now turns to Cyrus, who has been unusually quiet this morning.

"On it, your Majesty." Cyrus offers with a firm nod.

"Well done, boys, what else is there to discuss?" my father asks us now. There is so much. Too much. But we decided on a plan before coming in here, and so I speak up.

"We'd like you to teach us more about Royal Magic. Now that I'm getting married and gaining more responsibility, I'd like to start learning about the Palace and how my council and I can be helpful with your agenda, Father." I force a saccharine smile on my face, attempting to match the look my father always wears.

"I never thought I'd hear those words from you, Nolan. How delightful," he says. "It's about time. After your wedding, I'll teach you everything you want to know." I can't help but notice the spark in his eyes.

What is he planning? Why *after* my wedding?

Cyrus must notice the look too, because it's now him nudging me under the table. We finish our breakfast as quickly as we can. I can't help but feel that we've only seen the tip of the iceberg, that there are unimaginable secrets below my father's surface. Secrets I must now make it my goal to uncover.

We're halfway down the path to Cyrus' cottage when we run into the Shadows, all three of them. They were on their way to the market, but Vesto insisted that they join us for *scheming,* as he calls it. That's how I find myself seated next to Darby, our knees nearly touching as we cram in around Cyrus' table, devising a plan for finding where my father is keeping the Storytellers.

Vesto's vision of the past placed the Storytellers underground, but I've never seen anything unusual below the Palace, so we've narrowed it down to the two underground passageways we've never explored before: one leading to our supply reserves, the other to a series of allegedly abandoned caves.

"And what's to stop us from just going there to have a look around now via portal?" Romina asks the group, leaning over the map that we've spread across the table.

"If anyone were to see us, which they wouldn't, we

could just say it was for the Prince's protection," Seline offers, but I'm hardly listening as my hand wanders over to rest on Darby's leg. She knocks her knee into mine in a silent acknowledgement of my affection.

I consider this a small victory.

"Those parts of the Palace are off limits, we have magical wards in place and the main entrances are guarded," Cyrus declares, but I shoot him a look.

"Are you not my head of security, Rus? Can't you just have the guards let us in?" I ask him.

"I certainly could, but we would need a good reason why. A reason that we'd be okay with the King finding out about," he reminds me. Of course, it all goes back to my father. I exhale a big sigh. Now that I've had my eyes open to my father's corruption, I am growing increasingly aware of his control over my life.

"The Prince wanting to look around isn't reason enough?" Seline challenges him, and that's when Cyrus looks at me. We both know it would raise questions for my father and we don't want him looking into this too hard.

"Oh! What if it had to do with the ball?" We all turn to Vesto, who is squirming excitedly in his seat. "The King said we had to move it up to tomorrow, surely he'd buy that we are doing a venue scout."

"You plan to throw a ball in the supply reserves?" Darby asks with interest.

"Better... a cave rave!" Vesto shares.

"*A Cave Rave Ball?* Never been to one of those!" Romina catches his enthusiasm quickly.

"Think of it, we could go scout the caves tonight for

the location and the supply reserves to find decor for the ball, then tomorrow we throw the ball and while everyone is distracted we can sneak off again and keep exploring, it buys us two chances to find them," Vesto explains. It's not a bad idea, not bad at all.

"Great. Let's split up and search both tonight. Then tomorrow at the ball, we can follow up on any leads we discover," Darby says, as she slips her hand into mine below the table, sending a smile across my face. Yes, this is how it should be, us working together.

"We should also start to think about our cover for staying at Court after you announce your final three, Nolan." Romina adds. My smile falls as she then clarifies. "Certainly people will wonder why we're still here after you announce your final three suitors, and we need to stick around until the end to protect you." At the mention of me choosing the final three, Darby's hand stiffens in mine and I use my thumb to gently stroke the back of her hand in an attempt to soothe her.

Seven women remain. Three are shadows. I'm meant to pick amongst the other four. And my father and his council have made it clear who I'm supposed to choose.

"Oh yes, Mina! We had a plan for that!" Vesto exclaims before turning to Cyrus.

Cyrus clears his throat, leaning forward. "We figured you could publicly align yourself with other members of Court, so there would be no questioning why you were still here." He glances at me as he says this, looking for my reaction.

So the Shadows are to align themselves with others. Interesting.

Does he mean, romantically?

"Taking ourselves out of the running, you mean?" Darby asks, her expression unreadable as we hold hands under the table.

"Essentially, that was our idea at least," Cyrus responds.

"Or, maybe one of you could stay in the final three," I say, giving her hand a squeeze. Everyone turns to look at me then. I know what they're thinking, and I don't care.

"But Nolan, that's not what we all agreed to," Vesto warns.

"We can't," Darby says, her voice soft but firm as she removes her hand from mine, sending a shock straight to my heart.

"It would be better for us to appear as though we're otherwise committed, so we can stay here and keep an eye on you while you pursue your final three." Romina chimes in.

"We should make it clear at the ball, while all of Court is there to witness. Let the gossip spread naturally, right Princey?" Seline adds, earning a nod of approval from the group.

The others keep talking, but I'm only partially aware of them as the unmistakable feeling of my chest tightening steals my concentration. Darby took her hand from mine while reminding me that her boundaries are firmly in place.

What does this mean? Is she just playing along with a plan? Or does she no longer have strong feelings for me? Or worse, she reciprocates my feelings but is choosing to put up walls nonetheless.

Surely the connection we felt last night couldn't be so easily severed.

I need to speak with her alone. As soon as this meeting is over.

"So who wants to fake date!" Vesto poses to the group, capturing my attention back.

"You think they should be seemingly *committed* to you?" I ask, with the beginnings of what can only be described as jealousy.

"Better that way, no? Fewer people to deceive," Vesto says with a shrug. He's right, if they are going to pretend to be with members of Court, it may as well be people who are in on it, so as not to confuse anyone else.

Having been on the receiving end of false affection, I would not wish it on another.

"So, Seline and Rus?" I offer the idea despite the fact that I can't picture them together, and no one would ever believe it. I fill my cup with water and take a long sip to try and calm my nerves.

"Been there, done that," Seline scoffs.

"Wait, actually?" Vesto exclaims before I do. I'm shocked, truly.

"Well technically, Darby and I were there together," Seline says next, and I nearly choke on my water, looking to Darby for confirmation. Darby and Seline... and Cyrus?

They were all *together?*

"When was that?" The question is more of a demand as it leaves my mouth.

"After the Grand Reveal Ball." Darby turns to me then, her eyes wide but unashamed as she offers up the detail. After the Grand Reveal Ball I was with Amarie. I swallow again. Alright. Maybe that's why Darby didn't want to give me a hard time about what she saw. And it was before things between her and I really advanced anyway.

I wonder if she ever would have told me?

Would I have told her about Amarie if she had not seen it for herself in Vesto's memory vision?

Once she knew, I made a point of telling her that things between Amarie and I were just physical, but she offered no such information on things between her and Seline or Cyrus.

Could she have real feelings for either of them? She did say she likes men and women.

"So Darby and Rus, then?" I ask, waiting to see if her expression gives me any clues.

"Sure, why not," Cyrus says, while Darby's face remains unreadable.

How could he say that?

He knows how I feel about her.

I feel my own face heat with anger, I quickly pour myself some more water as a distraction.

Darby's eyes land on me and it's clear she's trying to gauge my reaction to all of this. Does she want me to be jealous? Is that her goal? Is she trying to push me away?

Why? Why must she do this?

But there is a little voice at the back of my head that does know why.

She's doing this because I'm meant to choose another. Because she does not believe that she can be my Link, and while I may not agree with her, I do intend to go along with my father's plans for long enough that he doesn't see the need to alter any more of my memories.

I will need to appear as though I'm choosing *his* ideal top three. I'll need to go along with all of this for as long as I can. So really, this plan is a good one. Let everyone at Court think Darby and the other Shadows are out of the running. Yes. Cyrus will be doing me a favor. And I'm not asking him to date her, just to make a bit of a show at a party so that she can stick around, so that she and I can have more time together.

This is a good thing. There's nothing for me to be jealous of.

They were *together* once, no big deal. She told me that she didn't have a real connection with anyone else. I'm sure it was just a physical thing. I can't be upset about that while I've been with others.

I swallow my pride and nod for them to go on.

"I'll find someone else," Seline informs us. I notice Darby's expression changes at that, wait... Could Seline be the woman from Darby's past? Now *that* wasn't just physical. That relationship meant something, at least to Darby. But she would have told me if it was Seline she was talking about, right?

I shouldn't get ahead of myself. I'll just ask her about this later. She promised me honesty, I'm sure she will tell me whatever I want to know. That is, if I do want to know?

"Mina and I will put on a show, won't we?" Vesto and Romina decide to pair off together. They are trouble together, but it's cute in a clearly platonic way. They seem to be having fun together, not like the rest of us with our complicated love lives. I envy them.

"Great, that settles it. We'll all make our new partners

known at the Cave Rave Ball!" Romina adds with a flourish. "Now, shall we go start our search?" Everyone begins to gather their things to head out, but I ask Darby if we can speak privately.

She hangs back. Cyrus notices us lurking in his seating area, he nods his head at me knowingly and follows the others out, his screen door slamming shut behind him.

When everyone is out of earshot I turn to Darby, finding her fiddling with a loose thread on her olive green sweater set.

"So, you and Seline, and Rus..." I say, turning to her.

"Yes." She looks up at me now. "I know he's your friend, I should have told you myself. Sorry you had to find out like that." Her jaw clenches as she anticipates my reaction, but I'm relieved to hear her say this. I appreciate the apology.

"It was just a one time thing?" I find myself wanting to know.

"Twice. Once with Seline, once without," she clarifies, sending a twisted pull of jealousy straight through my gut. She must see it on my face, because she continues. "It didn't mean anything, Nolan. Like with you and Amarie... it was just physical."

Relief crashes over me. Yes of course it's not ideal that she was with my friend, but I'm happy that it's nothing serious. Nothing more.

"Thank you for telling me." I move towards her, ready to take her in my arms, but she steps back.

"It doesn't change our situation." She tucks a loose

strand of her rose gold hair behind the delicate piercings in her ear as her face hardens again.

"And just to be clear, how do you see our situation?" My voice cracks slightly as I say this and the display of emotion surprises her, but I'm not embarrassed, I'd rather be vulnerable with her and get to feel what I'm feeling instead of feeling nothing at all. "You weren't exactly there to talk things through when I woke up this morning," I remind her.

"We have feelings for each other, but we can no longer act on them. If we do, you'll never find your Link."

Hearing her say this angers me.

I want to show her how it could work between us, but how can I show someone something they are not yet ready to see? Why is she so insistent that it couldn't be her? Why would she deny us both the opportunity to be Linked?

"If you can't put distance between us, then I will," she then adds, and my heart begins to pound rapidly in my chest. Maybe if I give her a taste of that outcome, she will realize that it's a terrible idea.

"My father said I have to pick Amarie, Lucci and Brianna as the final three." I take a step away, putting distance between us, just like she asked. "I'll have to marry one of them. Even though I had hoped for a world in which it would be my Link who I married, my father has since made it clear that he does not care for Vesto's vision coming true. He doesn't care if I grow more powerful or find my soulmate...all he cares for now is that I take a wife." I pause, giving her a chance to absorb what I'm saying. "And that she is one of those three. Another

Royal. He said she needs to be a Princess." I drive the point home by turning away from her. I wonder if she'll move towards me.

"You should. That makes sense," she counters without moving a muscle.

"So you agree with him? I should marry one of them?" I turn back to face her and refuse to let my hands reach out and touch her as they so badly want to.

"Yes," she says while finally inching towards me.

"I take that type of commitment seriously, Darby. Once I marry, that's it for me." I move to meet her, entering her space until our bodies press together. "I'm going to spend the rest of my life with my partner. Loving them. Cherishing them. Bringing them pleasure. No one will worship my Queen more than me." I watch our chests rise and fall in unison as we stare each other down.

The tension is thick, the air around us growing heavy until, like a storm hitting, it snaps. Her mouth is on mine in an instant and my arms are wrapping around her, dragging her up the front of my body to bring her as close as I can, lifting her straight off the floor as her legs band around my waist. I'm certain that if I release my hold she will flee this room and that will be it. I squeeze her tighter. Using the passion in my kiss to express what words cannot.

But I'm also angry with her for being so stubborn. I'm angry she's trying to put distance between us. How can she say that when this feels so good? When this feels so right?

My lust-fueled brain clears enough to remember I had decided to let her see what it feels like to push me away.

359

As her teeth sink into my bottom lip, tugging it lightly in a way that sends the blood straight to my dick, I exhale a breath and come to my senses, breaking our kiss and easing her back down onto the ground.

"You want distance?" I manage to rasp out. She looks up at me, her eyes glowing with hunger, but she nods, ever so slightly. "Fine then, have your distance."

It takes every ounce of my will power, but I pull away from her and head out the door, following our friends down the path to the caves, never once looking back.

32

DARBY

I want to tell him I didn't mean it. I don't want distance between us. I feel awful, putting the same walls up between us that Seline did to me. And yet, I must. We are not meant to be together, we are meant to *work* together. That is what I must keep telling myself.

Luckily, by the time I catch up to him at the ominous mouth of the underground tunnels, the group has decided to split up. I venture off towards the caves with Rus and Romina while Nolan heads to the supply reserves with Seline and Vesto. We enter a dark passageway similar to the cobblestone tunnel that led us to the Palace from Harville. It is funny to be back in such a similar setting to when we first arrived. It feels familiar, and yet everything is different now.

I am different now.

The deeper into the tunnel we venture, the colder it gets. Romina and I exchange a look as we both take note of the steep change in temperature.

"The guards are just up there," Rus tells us as he takes the lead, using a small light orb to guide us through an increasingly narrow passage. We reach a set of guards, their light gray uniforms nearly camouflaging them against the stone walls.

"Harland," Rus addresses the hulking guard to our left and I note a deep purple bruise below one of his piercingly light teal eyes. "The ladies and I have been tasked with scouting the caves for the ball tomorrow night," Rus explains.

I almost forgot how good Rus is at lying. It's funny to watch him do it so effortlessly.

"Yes sir." The guard who must be Harland doesn't even bat an eyelash as he motions for the other guards to let us pass.

That was easy. Too easy.

We wander down an even more narrow passageway, the walls so tight that my elbows scrape against the chilled rock and Rus has to hunch over more than usual. The stone ground below our feet turns to hard packed soil and a familiar musty scent fills my nose, reminding me of that cellar we staked out, not too long ago.

"If we throw the ball down here, we'll have to do something about the smell," Romina says.

"And the temperature," Rus adds. "Come on, the abandoned caves are through here."

At a fork in the path, Rus leads us to the left. I see light ahead as we follow him to the mouth of a frozen river which winds through an enormous underground atrium. Pausing at the foot of the frozen water, I take in the sight of this massive cave. The stalactite covered ceiling is taller than the height of the Winter Palace, with ice-coated stalagmites rising just as high to reach them. At the very center of the ceiling is a perfect rectangle of frozen glass, allowing warm light to filter in amongst the stones. The reflection creates a natural sparkle against the ice.

It's beautiful down here. We stand there, basking in the sight of this forgotten beauty.

"Why was it abandoned?" I ask Rus.

"It's been off limits for as long as I can remember, I don't know why," Rus supplies, while using the toe of his leather boot to test the ice. He nods, finding it strong enough to hold us, and Romina takes that as her cue to push past Rus towards the center of the atrium. She gazes up at the glass ceiling, squinting her eyes.

"What is it, Mina?" I follow her gaze.

And then my jaw drops as Romina begins to use her Solar Magic to extend a ray of bright white light towards the glass ceiling. I watch in awe as she melts away a thick layer of crust and ice to reveal a stunning stained glass mural of a half owl, half woman rendering of The Friend: The Goddess who protects Humans.

"It was a temple," I say, nearly breathlessly as Rus steps forward to join me at my side.

"It's said that Queen Lydia was religious. Perhaps the King hasn't held up that practice in the Queen's absence. It would explain why he wanted everyone to forget about this place." Romina turns to Rus whose face has gone pale. "Are you okay?"

He gazes up at the ceiling.

"How could we just *forget* this?" The look of wonder on his face morphs into that of concern.

"I wonder if the King will let us host a ball down here..." Romina muses, her eyes darting upwards.

"Maybe he'll just use Royal Magic to wipe the memory of it after the ball is over," I say, thinking out loud.

"That's awful. How often could he be doing that? How much... how much don't I even know about my own life?" Rus looks even worse now, I notice his breathing quicken. "How is Royal Magic so strong? I always thought....it was supposed to be a good thing. An equalizer. Royal Magic makes power equitable for all. I thought it was the answer to our problems. But clearly the King is using it to alter our memories, to control his people... It makes me sick."

He's right. It feels so wrong. And it's all the more reason we need to figure this out. We need to save the Storytellers and stop the King. The People of Kadneria deserve their memories.

They deserve to know the truth of their own lives.

"Hey, Rus, just breathe." Romina places a hand on his back. "We're going to stop him. This will not continue." I watch Romina soothe him, and eventually his breathing returns to normal.

"Come on, let's keep going," I urge him.

Rus collects himself and steps forward, offering each of us a hand. Romina goes first, carefully sidestepping a slab of rock to land safely on the other side of the frozen river. I'm up next, but as I step forward to take Rus' hand, the rock slips out from under me and I fall forward, landing flat against his chest. He wraps his arms around me to stabilize us, preventing me from sending us both tumbling over. His familiar eucalyptus smell fills my lungs as he looks down to make sure I'm okay. I give him a nod of thanks, then carry on, following Romina.

A few steps later I glance back over my shoulder.

Rus is no less attractive than he's ever been. His wavy blonde hair is pushed off his face and his impossibly blue eyes nearly match the color of the frozen water below the ice. And yes, of course, my body is attracted to him, the memory of his strong arms and soft tongue still send a shiver down my spine. But if I really think about it, he does not pull at my heartstrings.

No, with Rus, I don't feel that completely over-whelming gush of magic like what I felt kissing Nolan earlier today.

Maybe that makes Rus a safer choice for me. Things between him and I have clear boundaries. We are physical and nothing more. I wonder what it would be like to enter into a relationship like that meaningfully. Instead of having that arrangement thrust upon me, like with Seline.

"It seems empty," Romina voices from up ahead, pulling me back to the present. I shake my head, hoping Rus didn't catch me staring at him. We press on, making our way to the back of the cave and scanning the walls for anything unusual.

"It goes on like this for a while," Rus explains, nodding up ahead. Who would have thought there was this massive cavern just below the Winter Palace? And making it off limits? This has to be more than the King abandoning religion. Surely there is something hidden down here. As we wander deeper, I close my eyes, listening for sounds that might lead us in the right direction.

That's when I hear it. The same *humm humm humm* that we heard from the vials of fermenting HelioX that day. It's faint, but unmistakable.

"Mina, do you hear that?" I call to her. She stops in her tracks as she realizes what I'm talking about. The sound grows closer as we approach the far wall of the cave.

I press my hand to it, finding the surface frozen– but there's got to be something behind this wall.

I trace my hand up and down the jagged surface until finally I find what I'm looking for: The faintly etched lines of a doorway. I reach for my own magic then, my Lunar connection to water allowing me to coax the ice into liquid. It melts away from the spot on the wall where I can now make out the marking of the Royal crest.

The Sun, the Moon and the Second Star, connected by a crown.

I think back to the trap door which led us here weeks ago, and I tap on it twice. The stone moves, making the door more visible, but in doing so it reveals something else. I take a step back, inspecting what appears to be a stone lock. Romina and Rus crowd in behind me.

"It's a blood lock," Rus tells us. "We use them all over the Palace for high security. I have clearance to open most of them, but not this one. This one requires Royal blood."

"The King's, I'm guessing, but would the Prince's work?" Romina asks.

"Let's hope so," Rus says, before turning to look back at how far we've traveled into this cave. "Want me to go find him?" It would take a while for him to track Nolan down then return here. Before I can offer as much Romina is already using her magic to open a portal.

"I'll just send you to the entranceway, before the guards," she says, nodding for Rus to enter the giant magic swirl of shifting light that now hovers in the air before us.

"Alright then, one Prince, coming right up." Rus salutes us before stepping into the portal.

"What's going on with you two?" she asks, as soon as he's out of earshot.

"Nothing," I tell her honestly. There is nothing going on with me and Rus anymore. Even if we still find each other attractive, we haven't been alone since that morning in my room, way back before Nolan and I... whatever we've done.

"He can't keep his eyes off you, or his hands," she says, and I think back to my fall on the ice. Could she be right? Have I totally missed Rus' attention being on me?

"Really? I hadn't noticed," I tell her, looking around to make sure we're truly alone. "I've been too far in my own head, thinking about everything with Nolan. I pushed him away Mina, am I just as bad as Seline?" She's the only one who knows me and my history well enough to share this with.

"You're doing the right thing Darbs, even if it hurts. You have to stay away from Nolan," she tells me. Instead of comforting me, her words have the opposite effect, as if her acknowledging my pain only serves to strengthen it. My chest aches with the realization that I'm choosing the hurt this time. I'm causing it.

Before we can say anything more on the subject, Rus

and Nolan come tumbling through the portal, crashing on the ground in front of us.

"I'll never get used to that," Nolan says as he stands, dusting himself off and offering Rus a hand.

"Welcome, Prince," Romina smiles at him. "Think you can help us with this?" She points to the lock carved into the cave's stone wall. Nolan approaches it tentatively, giving it a once over before turning back to us.

"What are the chances my father will find out about this?" he asks, while unsheathing a small jewel-hilted dagger.

"High. We can blame it on innocent curiosity?" Rus suggests.

"I don't know..." Nolan hesitates, turning the dagger in his hand.

"You can't live your life in fear of him, Nolan." Before I realize it, I'm at his side, putting a gentle hand on his back. "This is important. It's the right thing to do." He looks at me, and our eyes latch onto one another. For a single breath, there's no one else.

Just the two of us here on the brink of what could be a huge discovery.

"You're right," he says, breaking the tension between us as he slices his hand open then presses his blood into the wall in one swift movement. I'm still holding on to him as we're transported to the other side of the stone. And this time, it really is just the two of us.

Where did Romina and Rus go?

"Holy Foe!" Nolan exclaims, as we take in the sight of a dark chamber, the humming even louder now. "Where are the others?" He looks around but comes to the same conclusion as me. It's just us.

"I was the only one touching you, maybe you're needed to get others in." We keep our voices low, unsure of what we might find down here. I spark up a new light orb, allowing it to float ahead of us. It's funny that I keep trying to avoid being alone with him when it seems that fate has other plans. "Want to have a look around?" I ask, eager to get moving.

"What if someone sees us? I could shield us but... it would be logged." He looks down at his wrist, his disdain for the silver bracelet more present than ever.

My hand absentmindedly floats to my neck, twirling my grandmother's gold medallion as I consider our options.

We could carry on without a shield and risk running into someone or... perhaps my mother's Stellar magic could come in handy once again to help us shield?

"Let me try something..." I close my eyes, rubbing the pendent to release its magic, the gold medallion warms in response. What if I were to bond it with my own power? Something I'm sure wouldn't be drawn from Royal Magic. We're surrounded by ice down here, and so I dig deep within myself searching for that connection to water that being a Lunar affords. As if on cue, several handfuls of snow lift from the ground around us. "Nolan, come stand by me."

He does as I say, getting closer. I reach out for his hand, placing it on my hip as I picture drawing my mother's shielding ability from the medallion and weaving a tapestry into the snow around us, then draping it over us, like a blanket. There's a crinkle of magic as it falls into place around us, ideally this will shield us from view. That being said, I've never done this before, so we'll have to proceed with caution.

"Wow," Nolan says, pinching my side.

I roll my eyes in response.

"What? I'm incredibly impressed by you," he smiles back, before remembering the distance he agreed to and adding, "Sorry, I shouldn't have said that. Distance and all..."

"It was a compliment, not a proposal," I say to lighten the mood as I tug on his hand and lead us down the corridor. We follow a winding maze of underground tunnels, the humming growing louder as we march on. Finally, we approach an antichamber.

Silently communicating, we inch our way around to peer in, praying that our shield succeeds in hiding us from view. What we find nearly knocks the breath out of me.

There before us stand two white cloaked chemists, much like the one we observed in the cellar all those weeks ago. Their attention is fixed on a table filled with vials of that same purple substance - *the still-fermenting HelioX*, only this time, they are actually depositing a clear liquid into the vials.

It has to be the mystery ingredient Romina couldn't place, I'm sure of it.

My eyes drift past them to a one-way glass similar to what we used in the Prince's blind dates. Beyond the glass is the unmistakable, yet incomprehensible sight of *hundreds* of Sprites: their usually bright green skin now a shade of gray, their small bodies crowded together as they churn in a cramped circle releasing a magical frost into the air.

"Foe," Nolan mutters under his breath as he rubs his eyes. "I don't believe this."

"What are we looking at?" I ask him, not able to process fully myself. Just then, one of the two chemists taps on the glass in front of him, signaling to another white cloaked chemist on the inside who is using some type of large suction tool to collect a thick clear liquid from inside the chamber and pass it forward to the others.

What the Foe is going on here?

"Sprites can manipulate weather. It's how he's keeping Royal Magic from overheating. That's why it's always so...Cold," Nolan provides, and the realization absolutely guts me. The Royal Magic overheats. The Sprites can keep it cool. But, by choice?

There's no way they've opted into these working conditions, have they? And why do they look so pale?

I lean forward, nearly tugging the magical blanket that shields us straight off Nolan. He catches on to my movements and scoots forward to follow me. Holding my breath, I get as close as I can. From here it's clear to see that the Sprites are *chained* together. No. There's no way they opted into this. My stomach churns as the feeling of wrongness threatens to drown me.

And what's with the suction? Is the mystery ingredient something that they are siphoning *from the Sprites*? Some sort of chemical reaction to their cooling ability? How would they know that it could be added to HelioX to make it impossibly stronger?

Just then, one of the chemists begins to push a cart filled with vials. Nolan and I step aside as the chemist approaches us, flattening ourselves to the wall. I feel Nolan's grip tighten on my thigh as the chemist comes closer.

Will the shield hold?

We exhale as the chemist skirts right past us.

Good. He can't see us.

With a silent nod, I gesture for us to follow, and we slink our way quietly down the corridor behind the chemist and his rickety cart. which bumps against the uneven stone ground. We follow him into another chamber. This one is similar, but behind another one-way glass is what we've been looking for: The glowing silver Eye that makes Royal Magic possible. It resembles a giant tuning fork with glowing magical energy gathered between its two prongs, like electricity trapped in a glass bowl. Below the Eye, two ragged elders march in a circle, black spoons dangling from the belts of their worn tunics.

Elders. Their bodies frail. Their eyes hollow.

Are those the Storytellers?

They must be.

Did they know Grandma? Mother?

One of the chemists rings a bell and the Storytellers perk up, their eyes now at attention as they reach for their spoons and hurry to press their thin bodies to the thick glass. They insert their spoons into perfectly fitted holes in the glass.

We watch in shock and awe as the chemist doses out HelioX for the Storytellers. My stomach flips once more, now threatening to dispose of its contents. I can't watch anymore of this. Nolan must realize, his hands wrapping around my waist as my knees turn weak below me. "It's okay, I've got you," he mumbles in my ear, his arms tightening around me.

"Let's get out of here," I tell him, and we retrace our steps as quickly as possible, eager to reunite with the others and try to make sense of everything we've just discovered.

33

DARBY

We're gathered in Nolan's library with Rus, Romina, Vesto and Seline. The wax candles are burning low and my second glass of whiskey is doing little to calm my nerves as we continue to comb over our findings.

"So to recap, Sprites are being used to cool the Eye of Royal Magic from overheating," Vesto says, his face paler than usual as he tops off my drink from a large silver decanter.

"*Hundreds of them*," Romina adds, her mismatched blues eyes still blown wide with shock, none of us can believe this.

"And somehow, in doing so, they are creating a clear liquid that is being added to the HelioX, making it impossibly stronger than usual, and *that* even stronger version is being used to subdue the long-lost Storytellers who are feeding the false truths into the Royal Magic somehow?" Vesto finishes, refiling Nolan's glass as well.

"That would explain why HelioX is here at the

Palace," Seline offers from where she's curled up in the corner on a plush velvet chair. "And why is it stronger than anything we've seen before."

"How would anyone even know *to try* adding the Sprite's magical residue to HelioX!" I'm still stuck on this.

"We all know that the King was an Alchemist. And, we know he didn't just work with metals–he made tonics and medicines too. If anyone were to be tinkering with HelioX, it would be someone with his skillset," Romina is quick to reply from her seat on the divan she's splitting with Rus. She gets an idea then, "Nolan, you said that the King does maintenance on the Royal Magic once every few years. Those Sprites must have been newly recruited, right?"

"They already looked so pale Mina, I can't imagine what shape they'd be in after a few years..." I don't need to finish the sentence for everyone to follow my train of thought.

Cooling Royal Magic, and as a result, all of Kad, is taking a drastic toll on the Sprites. It's costing them everything. To force them into this work against their will is absolutely disgusting. This cannot go on. I think back to the lovely rosy cheeked Urma, who sold us enchanted items at the Marketplace.

Could she meet a similar fate?

"We must free them." Nolan is the one to say it, but it's as if he read my thoughts. Am I relieved he agrees? Maybe, but I don't see a world in which he couldn't. How could anyone stand for this injustice? How could anyone allow this to happen? What is wrong with the King?

No, freeing the Sprites is the least that we can do.

The bare minimum.

They *must* be freed.

Nolan stands from his chair by the fireplace. "Let's go, we can't let this go on any longer." Rus and Vesto rise with the Prince, ready to serve him, ready to stand by his side. Even if it is the bare minimum, my traitorous heart still swells with pride as I watch this beautiful man lead others and do the right thing.

"As much as it pains me to admit this, we can't just go down there and free them." Romina rises to stop them. "Where would the Sprites go? How would you explain it?" She looks around to make sure she has all of our attention. "We need a plan. We need to secure safe passage for the Sprites outside of Kad until we deal with the King." Romina's face falls into a concentrated frown. As usual, I hate that she's right.

"And we need a distraction, you said there were hundreds of them? Can't exactly just march out of the caves undetected..." Seline adds.

"We need to get the Storytellers out too. And we need to get them *off* the HelioX." I hear my own voice trembling with passion. We made huge discoveries today but very little progress. I'm tired of feeling helpless. I'm ready to act. Nolan sits again, this time he reaches for my hand offering a squeeze I can only assume is meant to reassure me.

"Okay, one thing at a time," he says.

Vesto and Rus both follow Nolan's lead, taking their own seats. Silence falls as we all consider the growing issues at hand.

"If we can convince the King to allow us to host the

ball in the caves, two of us can sneak off and administer the antidote to the Storytellers." Rus leans forward, his long arms resting on his knees as his jaw works, a plan forming. "It may not fully relieve them, but it would offer a moment of clarity before they are inevitably dosed again."

"That's better than nothing! Perhaps a moment of clarity is all they need!" Vesto adds. I can tell he's trying to be positive.

"Assuming the Sprites are the source of that ingredient, once they're gone, the King won't be able to make such potent HelioX, he won't be able to keep using it on the Storytellers, or anyone else." Romina thinks out loud as she pulls out her notebook and flips back to the pages where she began researching that very ingredient weeks ago. "You said it looked like a clear liquid? Was it slimy? Sticky? Perhaps when we administer the antidote, we can also collect a sample." She trails off as she buries herself in notes.

"Where are we going to relocate the Sprites? We have to ensure their safety so that my father can't go after them again." Nolan removes his hand from mine now so he can run it through his hair, the dark circles under his eyes remind me that we've been up all night, and yet I can't imagine going to bed with this unresolved.

I feel the weight of eyes on me and look up to find Rus staring at the spot where Nolan's hand was recently making contact. His eyes flick to meet mine before he quickly looks away.

"I'd suggest Crichton, but given their track record, I doubt they'd take kindly to the Sprites," Rus sighs. He's right. Crichton, like Kad, is fueled by prejudice towards those with lesser magic. I rack my brain to think of a more accepting group of people, somewhere nearby.

It's hard to do.

"Oh!! What about the Sea Nymphs! Surely they'd have empathy for the Sprites, you know, being another group of Non-Humans and all," Vesto offers. "Nolan, you could talk to Lucci!" he adds.

Could Nolan talk to Lucci? In doing so, he'd have to reveal his father's secret. That type of information could have serious repercussions if it landed in the wrong hands.

Can we trust Lucci? Rus is following my wavelength.

"Can Lucci be trusted?" Rus' posture stiffens, he's back in business mode.

"Well, she is someone he's considering *marrying*," Romina reminds us, as if this is obvious. "Perhaps this is exactly the type of test you've been looking for, Prince, finding a partner you can trust." Romina leans back casually, finally looking up from her notebook.

"This isn't a test, this is real life, those Sprites need our help," Nolan counters, and I couldn't agree more. My face heats and I find myself angry with Romina. She's always looking for ways to test others, doesn't she know that this isn't a game or an experiment? Their lives are at stake. Ours might be too. Who knows what the King would do if he found us meddling in his plans. It wouldn't be the first time he disposed of those who stood in his way.

Romina must sense our seriousness because her face softens.

"Of course, I just mean, perhaps she can earn your trust this way," Romina says as a peace offering, and Nolan leans back as he considers it.

"I'll have a one on one date with her in the morning. I'll find out if I can trust her with this," Nolan declares before taking a sip of his whiskey. "If we free the Sprites, and the Storytellers, we're going to need all the allies we can get to stand against my father." The weight of what he's implying sits there in the room, all of us understanding that this choice will change everything.

"If you choose Lucci for your final three, her family will be invited to Court." I turn to Nolan now, speaking directly to him. "If you think Lucci can be trusted, we can make our case to her family to get an official blessing from the Sea Nymph leaders to welcome the Sprites peacefully. It could be the beginning of your alliance with them," I say, as my mind races with the possibilities.

"That feels like a good plan!" Vesto adds from where he now sits on the floor with his legs up against the back of a chair, his eyes drifting shut.

"Depending how our date goes." Nolan's face hardens again.

I wonder which part of this is most upsetting for him: The reality of what his father has been hiding from him? Or the fact that it's his father who did all of this to begin with?

"Vest, any helpful visions?" Nolan asks.

"Too tired," Vesto mutters.

"If I were Lucci, I'd make you agree to marry me in exchange for harboring your Sprites," Seline muses with mischief in her eyes. "It's a better political move, and she's smart; might want to be prepared to face that option, Princey."

"Choosing my final three, fine, but I refuse to marry for political gain. I was promised a chance to find a real connection, not just..." He stumbles to go on, slamming his fist down on the arm of his chair. I reach out to comfort him this time, unable to stop myself.

"Nolan, this is so much bigger than you. I'm sorry that it's not what you hoped for, but you are in a position to help people. If marrying Lucci is what it takes to free the Sprites, maybe that's more important than finding your Link." I watch his eyes glaze over as he takes in my words. "You said you had to marry one of them anyway," I remind him, and his whole demeanor changes as he pulls away from where my fingers rest on his forearm.

"It will not come to that. I won't accept it." He rises from his seat and paces to the window. The dark sky has begun to shift towards lightness, indicating that morning is just around the corner.

"Nolan will talk to Lucci, Vesto, you'll make sure the ball takes place in the caves?" I ask, and Vesto nods before an idea occurs to him and he sits up again.

"You don't think...No. Never mind," Vesto mutters.

"What is it, Vest?" Nolan urges him to continue.

"You don't think our parents know about this, do you?" He gestures between himself and Rus. "I mean they are the King's Council, but... I just can't picture my mother agreeing with this, especially how he's using Royal Magic. It's an abuse of the innovation she is sworn to protect." Vesto sounds uncharacteristically sullen as he says this. I shoot a look towards Romina.

"Vesto's mother Tilda is the Innovation Liaison," Romina reminds us, and of course that makes sense based on the story Vesto shared with us in the forest. His mother Tilda had a Vision of the Eye that would be used for Royal magic, she used that information to earn a spot on the King's Council and guarantee a better life for her son. But at what cost?

"It's possible he's altering their memories as well," Nolan offers.

"You need to speak with them, see what they know, or what they remember," Romina chimes in.

"I'll prepare extra antidote, just in case," Rus announces.

"And then what? How are we going to free the Storytellers? What if Lucci says no to helping with the Sprites?" I can feel the room is losing energy, everyone looks exhausted, but we can't stop now. "We need another plan, we need to do more!" Once again I find my temperature rising with my passion, but it's Romina who steps forward to try and soothe me now.

"Darby, it's going to take some time to work this out, we don't have all the answers right now. But we will soon enough." She kneels before my chair and meets my gaze, offering a sense of reassurance that makes my earlier frustration with her fade away.

It's then that a thick snore escapes Vesto who has fallen asleep right there on the floor. Romina rises, looking toward the window where the first light threatens to make an appearance in the sky. "It's almost sunrise, let's try to get some sleep."

I glance around and find that Seline has also dozed off in her chair in the corner. No wonder she's been so quiet.

With Vesto passed out on the floor already I must admit that Romina is right. The unanswered questions threaten to make my heart explode, but we need to rest up for tomorrow. There's so very much to do and I can't shake the feeling that we're running out of time.

34

DARBY

We manage a few hours of rest before Vesto and Rus appear at my door to let me know our presence has been requested by the King. He can't know what we've discovered, can he?

Is that why he's requesting us?

Before I can question it more, Romina appears with a mug of coffee for me and an angry-looking Seline in her wake. I accept the mug with a smile of gratitude, since it's nearly midday I was worried the kitchens would be out of the caffeinated substance.

"You had to wake me?" a groggy Seline says, as she twists her long hair into a loose braid. Her outfit is a simple dark gray woven tunic with thick leather leggings that reminds me of our Shadow uniform, while Romina's opted for something a little fancier, a violet sweater with a matching skirt that is much more suited to the style of this Court. She's even got makeup on.

I look down at my own outfit, an emerald green

sweater top with matching loose flaring pants that could pass for a skirt. My hair is tied up halfway and decorated with a matching green ribbon.

"Yes, the Prince is out on his dates now, the ball is tonight, we have work to do," Romina scolds Seline.

"As I said, the King wants to see you, but the good news is our Cave Rave Ball has been approved!" Vesto adds, with a glimmer in his eyes. "I told the King that I had a vision of everyone loving the Cave Rave Ball so much and praising him, their favorite King, for the festivities, *happy Court happy sport* and all that, he ate it up! Anyway I'm off to finish the preparations!" Vesto departs, but we idle in my doorway as I steal sips of the hot beverage. I'm in no rush to leave my room, and they can tell.

"Come, no sense worrying about it when we can just go find out for ourselves," Rus offers, sensing my hesitation about standing before the King.

I finish my coffee and say a quick prayer to The Friend, The Foe, and The Frequency. Something tells me I'm going to need their help before this day is over. Maybe for once, they'll actually listen.

As usual, the King has chosen his lunch hour for our visit, as though we're not important enough to deserve our own allocated meeting. That's fine by me. I'm finding it hard enough to look at him as it is. How can he just sit there and enjoy his lunch knowing that Sprites are dying for his own ambitions? That Storytellers are being coerced into performing a once sacred act that is now being abused?

This man *is* an abuser. We don't even know the full extent of what he's using Royal Magic for. I wonder what his goal is? Why do all of this? And to what end? To live a life where no one questions him? To drug or brainwash all who might oppose him so they don't even have the option of their own free will?

My anger is bubbling up and threatening to boil over. There's a familiar flicker in my chest, a ball of light fighting to break out. Usually this is when I lose control, but I can't right now. The fate of too many depends on me keeping my cool.

I swallow the outburst of magic down.

"By tomorrow, we will know the Prince's selection for the final three, and their families will be invited to Court." The King licks his fingers clean of sauce from the meaty rack of ribs he's feasting on. "Before that happens, I'd like you to conduct a security sweep of their rooms. Make sure the Ladies aren't hiding anything." He looks down his nose at us between bites. I notice that Tilda is absent from the meeting today, but the rest of his council joins him. "With your set of skills, that shouldn't be an issue, I imagine?"

"Of course," Romina answers, even though it's not a question. It's an order. He wants us to snoop in their rooms.

"Good, now tell me what I need to know about the two Royal Families and the Sea Nymphs–" The King stops abruptly and appears to struggle swallowing his food. We exchange a look, unsure how to help him as he begins coughing. Rus and a few other guards spring into action, approaching the King.

I recognize one of them as Harland. His black eye looks to be healing. Before they reach him the King holds up his hand, signaling to pause. "Do we have more of my wine, Ernest?" The King turns to the man next to him, the one who looks like Rus. *Ernest* wastes no time refilling the King's chalice from that same silver thermos. The King takes a sip before speaking. "Well, Shadows? Strengths and Weaknesses." The King carries on, as if nothing happened. Rus and the guards settle back into position on the edge of the room.

It's clear the King has full confidence that Prince Nolan will not be choosing Ingrid. Seeing as the King told me his preference for the final three on the night of the *ABC Ball,* I can assume this has been his intention for a while.

I wonder why.

Why let his rival's daughters come to Court in the first place?

Why try to ally one of these families with his only heir?

What does the King have to gain from any of this?

We've done our homework on these families as part of our research in coming here, so it's without hesitation that we deliver on his request. We tell the King what he wants to know, including the fact that Amarie will be joined by the current monarch of Langha: her older sister Queen Amandala, and her wife Queen Tori, their strengths being that they are beloved by their people, known for being equitable and just rulers despite the fact that Queen Amandala took over her Queendom at a young age after the untimely death of their parents. Langha's weakness will undoubtedly be the fact that while visiting Court, they'll be separated from their magic crystals. There's no way the King will allow them to use crystals while here.

Princess Brianna of Crichton will be joined by her mother and father, the Queen and King of Crichton, who, much like the climate of Crichton itself, are known to be brutal, yet beautiful. They value strength and power, and generally look down upon weakness or otherness. Personally, I view *that* as a weakness, although it's a different weakness I share with the King. The people of Crichton are eager to form an alliance with our continent, seeing as they sit isolated on the other side of the Sea Nymph's island. And you can guess how they feel about allying themselves with a non-Human species.

As for the Sea Nymphs, while their royal structure isn't as clearly defined, Lucci will most likely be joined by her parents, and her older brother Sabastian, who currently serves as Primary. The Sea Nymphs have many obvious strengths, and yet the prejudice many hold against them is certainly a weakness. A union between Prince Nolan and Lucci could change the way the world sees their people.

We get further into the details too, briefing the King on each of the families' likes and dislikes, their food and drink preferences, whatever he wants to know. Not a moment too soon, he dismisses us to begin our search of the Ladies' rooms.

❄

I'm elbow deep into Amarie's mattress, feeling for anything unusual, when I hear voices coming. Instinct takes over, and I go completely still. Maybe the passersby will move on. I remain frozen, but instead of moving on, they get closer. Louder. Foe.

I duck under the bed just before the door opens and Amarie and Nolan barge in. She closes the door behind them and whirls on him, her back to the bed where I cower below the cover of her flowing blankets. We were told that the Ladies would be having high tea with the Prince today, creating the perfect opportunity for Romina to search Lucci's room while Seline searches Brianna's. Of course, that left me with Amarie's– Amarie, who was *not* meant to be in her room right now!

"Finally! Some alone time!" she exclaims, as I hear her shuffling closer to Nolan. I almost gasp but my hand flies to my mouth to cover any sound from escaping. Are they going to kiss?

It's one thing to tell him to move on, it's another to witness him do it... again.

"That's not why I wanted to come here," Nolan says, as I watch his feet move away from her. "Amarie, we've known each other for years and still, I don't know if we've ever just sat and talked. I thought maybe today we could just have a chat." He takes a seat at the foot of her bed and the frame sinks a bit, but doesn't crush me. Thankfully.

"Have a chat?" Amarie blinks her eyes a few times, trying to understand. I don't know whether to be relieved or disappointed. He's doing what I said, he's trying to see if they can have more than just a physical connection. "Um, okay," Amarie settles on.

Her feelings on this are unclear due to her signature monotone. She sits down beside him. They stew in an uncomfortable silence. Then, she shifts to look at him. "What would you like to *chat* about?"

"I read a book on Langhan Crystals. They're pretty neat," Nolan offers.

"*Pretty neat?* Who says that?" she responds.

"Me. I just did." He's defensive now, and I hear her stifling a giggle.

"Right. Sorry." Her apology carries little weight. I roll my eyes from below the bed, these two really do seem to have little going on between them outside of their physical connection. She takes a steadying breath then continues. "To be honest, I much prefer the Crystals to your Royal Magic. They are something you can gain for yourself, earn for yourself. Here, everyone has the same magic, and that's nice but, it's just being handed to you." I can't see her face but I imagine she looks at him with some sense of trepidation as she says, "I hope it's alright that I said that."

I hear Nolan relax, audibly releasing a breath. "Of course, I appreciate your honesty. Sometimes I feel like no one is truly honest with me." His words strike me in the gut. I wish I could be more honest with him, truly I do, but there were things I had to conceal, and there is still more to my story I cannot share with him, at least not yet. His weight shifts again, I assume he's turning towards her as he says, "Perhaps there is more we can learn from one

another, would you teach me more about the crystals?"
My ears perk up at that.

"You want to know?" Amarie says with what I
imagine is disbelief, despite the fact that her monotone
makes it hard to determine how she's really feeling.

"I do, one day this Kingdom will be mine, I want to
choose what is best for the people, maybe our system as it
currently stands isn't fully that." He's taking a risk in
saying this, but he must trust Amarie.

"Can I trust you?" she asks in response, surprising me.
Here I was questioning if he could trust her and she's
asking the same of him.

"Of course," he says, and the energy in the room
shifts, somehow I feel more intrusive about hearing this
than I did watching them have sex in Vesto's memory
vision.

Foe, how do I keep getting myself into these
situations?

Amarie stands then and crosses to her closet. She
reaches up for something I can't fully see, then returns to
the bed and sits back down above me, beside Nolan. "I'm
not supposed to have these here with me, as you know,"
she says softly, as I can only imagine she proceeds to open
something and show Nolan the contents.

"Wow," is all he says as the room begins buzzing with
a magical current I've never felt before, it spreads through
the room and tickles the back of my neck. This must be
Crystal Magic. *Amarie has Crystals with her after all.* They
are interrupted by three quick knocks on the door.
Romina– she's come to collect *me,* just like we planned.

"One moment!" shouts Amarie, as Nolan clears his

throat. She stands abruptly and hurries back to her closet, tucking away the box before heading to the door to greet Romina, who, to her credit, quickly makes up an excuse for her presence and is even able to inspire the Prince and Princess to head back out. After they've all cleared the room, I slide out from under the bed. Now that I know Amarie has Crystals with her, it's time to decide what to do with that information. Should I tell the King, as is expected of me?

My gut says, probably not.

Considering the conversation I just overheard, I doubt Amarie has bad intentions.

Perhaps if she were to marry the Prince, they could actually do some good together and find a way to blend their magic systems to create something more humane than whatever the King is up to. And if the King found out about Amarie harboring crystals, I fear he would do something terrible to her. I will not be the one who sets *that* fate into motion.

So no, I won't tell.

Hopefully, he won't find out on his own.

Not too long after, Vesto visits us in Romina's room to give an update on the Prince's dates as we get ready for yet another ball.

"Ingrid and Nolan officially parted ways, but he agreed to let her join Court, as a thank you for the information she shared about HelioX," Vesto explains, as he hands over our latest outfits: long sheer robes in various colors that will be worn over our bathing suits for the Cave Rave. The ice is currently being melted down to create hot tubs for the event tonight, I'm told less clothing the better. Of course, it sounds like another one of Vesto's ideas. "That means that after the ball tonight, the official *final three* will be announced as Amarie, Lucci and Brianna."

"Lovely. Perhaps I'll saddle up to Ingrid then," Seline says, as she collects one of the robes from him, it's an endless trail of sheer black lace that will suit her perfectly. She strips off her oversized sweater to reveal a night black string bikini, before wrapping the robe around her and giving us a twirl. Vesto nods in approval, trying hard to conceal his flushed cheeks at the site of so much skin from Seline.

"Why would you do that?" I ask her, more curious than jealous, it's amazing how my feelings for Seline have truly been subsiding these last few weeks. I think I'm finally in a place where I can move on.

"She can be my reason to stay at Court," Seline says, as if it's obvious. Of course, this was part of our plan, to cozy up to members of Court tonight so no one questions why we're still hanging around after the final three are chosen. "Plus, I've grown rather fond of her," Seline adds with a genuine smile that stops me in my tracks.

I've never heard Seline say she's fond of anyone.

In our three years of seeing each other on and off she never said she was *fond of me.*

I swallow hard.

This is good. This is fine. I'm moving on. And so is Seline.

Vesto clears his throat, reminding me to choose one of the beautiful robes from the selection he holds out before me. I waiver between a pink silk robe with a feather trim and a shimmering gold one that sparkles like the flakes of gold in Nolan's chocolate brown eyes.

Stop thinking about him!

"Maybe I'll go pink tonight! I do love feathers," Romina says, as she swoops in and grabs the pink one.

Gold it is, then.

"Rus has prepared the Antidote. Mina, I'm thinking it should be me and you who sneak in to administer it?" Vesto asks next, earning a nod from Romina. "The Prince can get us past the blood lock then we'll trail off as if looking for somewhere more *private.*"

"What about all the guards? You'll need to use a shield," I add.

"I can shield," Romina boasts, in a surprisingly cheerful tone.

"And I may or may not have requested the cave be filled with a certain Forest Cushion Potion," Vesto adds with a sparkling smirk that hints he's not new to the inhibition-lowering herb.

"You didn't!" Seline playfully swats at him. "Oh this ball is going to be fun!" she exclaims.

My eyes dart between the three of them to find smiling faces staring back at me. I'm shocked by how happy they all seem.

"How can we have fun when the Sprites are dying? The Storytellers are being drugged and abused, and the King is brainwashing everyone!" Romina puts a steadying hand on me before I even realize it's me who is shouting.

It's hard to keep a handle on the feelings that are pouring out of me.

"You're right Darby, but selfishly, I also thought the Forest Cushion Potion would help us get through the ball and take our minds off everything," Vesto adds with a shrug. "Someone once told me that enjoying life is also an act of rebellion." He beams over at Romina, and I do remember her saying that.

"We all have a part to play tonight, let's put on a good show so that no one suspects anything," Romina adds with a wink at Vesto.

She's right, we do have an important role to play tonight. This Court loves to gossip, if we can succeed in distracting them with our displays of affection then no one, including the King and his guards, will notice what we're up to. And ideally, no one at Court will question why Seline, Romina and I are going to hang around after the final three suitors are announced. At this point, Nolan may have already spoken to Lucci. The antidote is already made, the Cave Rave Ball is approved by the King...our plans are already in motion. We actually have a chance at pulling this leg of our plan off, then we will figure out the next steps.

So why can't I shake this aching feeling in my chest?

Why does it feel like the closer we come to achieving our goals, the farther it will push me from Nolan? I think about his words from earlier, his voice still ringing in my ears.

"I take that type of commitment seriously, Darby. Once I marry, that's it for me."

It wasn't just his words. It was the passion with which

he said it. The hunger in his eyes, he was begging me to hear him, to see him. He was talking about his feelings for me.

"I'm going to spend the rest of my life with my partner. Loving them. Cherishing them. Bringing them pleasure. No one will worship my Queen more than me."

"Our final ball. I can't believe it," Romina says, coaxing me out of my daze as she fixes the final touches of gemstones along her cheek bones. She looks gorgeous. I then turn to face my own reflection, dusting a little more glitter on my eyelids. If it's our last ball, then we might as well go out with a splash.

35

DARBY

The caves have been completely transformed. I don't know when Vesto had time to do this, but it looks incredible. The frozen walls are shimmering, and remarkably not melting despite the wet, warm air that fills the cave. Sparkling lights hang amidst the stalactites like chandeliers. Where the frozen river once flowed, we now find four large hot tubs, carved from ice, their bubbling pools illuminated from within by soft purple orbs. In fact, the entire cave is glowing in that same purple hue. To top it all off, one glance up at the atrium's stained glass ceiling shows me the Moon and the Second Star sitting directly above us like sisters in the sky, presiding over tonight's festivities.

Barefoot, swimwear clad Lords and Ladies have already begun to find their spots in the various tubs, while others make their way to the glowing dance floor. Trays of drinks float freely around the cave and the Palace's band takes up their spot on a stage made of ice blocks. As the music begins to play and guests start to dance, it's clear that this cave is abandoned no longer.

To my right is Amarie, effortlessly chatting up a group of Lords and Ladies, casually tossing her honey blonde hair over a delicate shoulder as she speaks. She'd make for a wonderful Queen. She navigates this environment easily. And while she may be a bit harsh at times, at least she's honest. This Kingdom could use more honesty. But would Nolan choose her? It didn't sound like they had much to talk about.

Rus catches my eye then. He's pacing in the corner. I notice he is wearing his usual navy blue attire, a pair of swim trunks hanging dangerously low on his hips with an unbuttoned linen shirt barely covering his inked abdominals. Despite his handsome appearance, he seems nervous, and I understand why. Before I can approach him, Brianna appears at his side. Her petite frame is so small in comparison to his large, hulking presence. She turns to speak with him, her back facing me, so that I cannot tell what she's saying. She often uses him as a security blanket—which makes sense, given that he's tied to her sister. It must be nice to have a small piece of home when visiting such a foreign Kingdom. Kadneria and Crichton couldn't be more different. I wonder if she's homesick, and if so, would she ever agree to stay here in Kadneria to be with Nolan?

Next, I scan the cave for Lucci. She's talking with Romina and Seline by one of the floating bars. I admire the details of her pearlescent pink bathing suit top with a matching sheer skirt, and note her naturally iridescent scales on full display against the thin fabric. Her aquamarine eyes shine brightly as she tucks a strand of dark hair behind her pointed ear. She's smart, loyal, and one of the most beautiful females I've ever seen.I try to picture what their kids might look like if she and Nolan were to have them. Would they have scales like their mother? Chocolate Brown eyes like their father? Would they grow up on land or sea? There's a sharp pain in my stomach as I entertain the idea of Lucci and Nolan becoming eternally tied.

No. My body seems to say. *Not her. Not someone else.*

The King appears at the top of an ice carved podium, ready to make his opening remarks, as usual.

"We have gathered tonight in my private caves for our final ball of Prince Nolan's marriage season!" As his voice is magically amplified, everyone stops their chatter and turns to face him. "After tonight, my son will select his final three suitors!" the King adjusts his robe, a silver silk wrapped tightly around his body. "And as this season has been unprecedented, we will continue to switch it up and surprise you. After tonight, Nolan will get to spend the night with each of his Ladies. After those three nights, we will gather under the Eclipse for his wedding!" Cheers of surprise and delight erupt all around the cave. The King has decided that it's not just *any* Eclipse, it's this coming one. Of course he is making the marriage season work for *his* own agenda. Nolan's wedding will take place four nights from now. After he has the chance to be intimate with each of his final three. That was always part of the plan, wasn't it?

"Now, enjoy a night of music and mischief!" the King declares, hoisting his glass high above his head. The crowd toasts with him just as a poof of pink mist is released into the cave. The pleasant smell fills our noses and the guests recognize the unmissable grassy scent of Forest Cushion Potion, resulting in a round of cheers. It's about to get wild in here, I can tell.

I inhale deeply, the potion tickling the inside of my nose. This will be good for me. I'm going to need to clear my racing thoughts if I'm to accomplish anything tonight.

"Darby, a word?" I feel Nolan's voice fill every pore of my skin before looking up to see him before me. His torso is bare, and I drink in the familiar sight of his tattooed, chiseled body.

"Darby?" he says again, and I realize I've been staring at him. I nod, accepting his request and he leads me to one of the cave's swirling walls which forms a carved out area; it's more private.

"How'd it go with Lucci?" I ask, gazing up at him. His face is as handsome as ever, and somehow the lighting down here makes his brown eyes seem almost purple.

"She agreed to help us, as long as her family approves," he says softly, and I can't help but exhale a sigh of relief.

"That's fantastic. I really do like her."

Except for when I entertain the thought of her as your bride.

But I don't say that part out loud.

"We'll appeal to her family, I'm sure they will agree to do the right thing," I tell him, as my fingers float up to touch his abdominals.

Wait, what? I can't touch him like that right now.

I snatch my hand away. The inhibition lowering potion is clearly already working on me.

"So tonight, you're going to fake it with Rus, right?" Nolan asks with tense shoulders.

"That's the plan," I say, swallowing.

"And what about us?" He cocks an eyebrow and it makes my stomach flutter.

"There is no more us, Nolan," I tell him, despite myself.

"Why? When did you decide that?" He turns his back to the party now, caging me in more to the cavern. His chocolate scent hangs thick in the warm air between us. "It's like we both walked away from the other night with completely different ideas, I thought we were growing closer and you thought it was what? Goodbye?" His eyes are searching mine frantically now as if trying to find something to hold on to.

"Yes. How many times do we have to have this same conversation?" I'm growing frustrated now, why can't he just believe me when I say he has to choose someone else? That I'm only going to distract him? Why is he making this so hard?

We can't get married.

I'm a Shadow. He's a Prince.

It's as simple as that.

"As many times as it takes for it to make sense!" He lets out a frustrated sigh before continuing. "I just don't believe that you can't be my Link, and if you push me away again, I will move forward with one of the final three my father chose for me. I will marry one of them... and then it will be too late. Then it won't matter if you were my Link or not, and that would be a tragedy." His eyes well with wetness as he says this and it totally wrecks me. I feel my heart leaping, trying to exit my chest and reach for him, to soothe him. It's as if my very soul wants to take hold of him. But I can't let any of this happen, so I cross my arms over my chest.

"You know what would be a tragedy? If those Sprites continue to die. If those Storytellers spend one more second of their lives in captivity. If your father continues on with whatever evil plans he is working towards... that would be a *tragedy*, Nolan. If you and I can't be together so that *those* tragedies could be prevented? Well I could live with it. Could you?" I glance up at him as he crowds in even closer towards me, heat radiating off his body as our eyes meet.

"Why can't we have both? Why does freeing them mean we can't be together, Darby?"

Because he doesn't know the real me.

That's what I want to say.

And why can't I tell him?

He knows how corrupt his father is now. He's earned my trust. Why can't he know that I was born a Story-teller? That I still aspire to be one? Why can't I just tell him that?

He's looking at me with so much hope in his eyes. His face right now is so tender, so full of expectation. It's a look I know all too well. As if his soul is now mirroring mine. I see in him the longing for connection I've always experienced. The hope that he will find in me that piece he's always been missing. And as badly as I want it too, what if we're wrong? What if we're not each other's Link?

What if we've just been caught up in the circumstances of crossing paths again, and our true purpose is, as I've said before, to work together, not to be in love?

I fail to voice any of this out loud before Nolan continues.

"Let's do the Linking ritual." His voice steadies, a deathly calm washing over him.

He can't be serious, can he? You only get to do the Linking ritual once. After that, it is forbidden to ever try again. That's why you're supposed to be sure before you begin, and what if we're wrong? If there is even the slightest chance that we are not meant for each other in this way, a failed attempt would prevent Nolan from ever having a Link in the future. And sure, he's going to marry someone anyway, but despite what he says, marriages *can* be ended. There would still be hope for him finding a Link in the future even if she isn't one of his current suitors.

If we mess this up, he'd never have that opportunity.

I can't allow that to happen.

"Darby, I know you're afraid, but please..." he continues on, and of course with the potion lowering my inhibition he's definitely reading my fears, but I need to hold on. I need to show him another way for us. I close my eyes tightly and try to picture us as allies. As friends. As collaborators who work together to bring down the King. And nothing more. I try to picture it, so that I can try and convince him as well as myself. Opening my eyes, I attempt to sound like I believe it.

"Nolan, what if we were not brought together to be Linked? What if our purpose is to work together to take down your father?" My voice falters, giving me away.

"I don't doubt that it is, but again I ask, why can't it be both?" His arms are wrapping around me now, he's pulling me in to press against his warm body and immediately I'm reminded of every time we've ever touched, ever kissed. "Let's do the ritual, Darby. It will end all of this. The marriage season will be over."

"Only if we're right," I say from somewhere below his bicep.

"Of course we're right. How could we not be?" He pulls me tighter into him and as I catch a glimpse of the party behind him, my eyes snag on the King. He's looking right at us, his expression colder than the ice sculptures. I pull away from Nolan immediately.

"Nolan, your father would never allow it. He is adamant on who your real options are."

"Fuck him," Nolan growls in response. "He's spent my whole life controlling me, this is the one thing I will not allow him to decide."

"But what if he uses Royal Magic on you again?" I shudder to think of the King using the Storytellers to remove Nolan's memories of *me*. Would he go that far?

"I feel you in my bones. I see you in my dreams. I could never forget you, Darby. " Nolan collects me in his arms again but the unmistakable feeling of fear creeps up the back of my neck. What if the marriage Season did end now, would we still be able to achieve our goals? What about the Sprites? What about the Storytellers?

"But maybe you *should* forget me. It's all too complicated Nolan, and there's too much at stake." I pull away again, taking his hands in mine. "You need to see our plans through, you need to stop your father, and that means finishing out your marriage Season." It's then that the idea occurs to me. Nolan's wedding is in four nights. *That's* the perfect distraction. *That* is when we could get the Sprites and the Storytellers out without the King noticing.

"In fact, your wedding *must* happen because that's our best chance to get the Sprites and the Storytellers out undetected!" I tell him with renewed energy. Renewed hope. But instead of finding joy in this newly realized plan, Nolan's face drops completely.

"What I'm hearing over and over again is you saying 'no'. You don't want to try to make this work between us. You don't want to do the Linking ritual. You don't want me." I can hear the heartbreak in his voice and it twists in my gut like a knife.

"Nolan, I—" I'm not sure what to say, but luckily he continues before I can.

"I don't know how many more times I can handle you pushing me away, Darby." He leans in closer now, his voice nearly a whisper in my ear. "And while this doesn't mean I'm going to stop feeling for you, the way that I do, I fear I've reached my limit of how much rejection I can take tonight." He pulls away, offering one last glance at me before turning back to rejoin the party. "You win Darby. We'll do this your way."

And as I watch him stride over to meet Vesto and Romina to begin carrying out our plans, I can't help but feel that I haven't won anything at all. Instead, I've lost something irreplaceable.

36

DARBY

Nolan has gotten Vesto and Romina into the chamber undetected and Seline and Ingrid are making their interest in one another known to all of Court. The whispers are already carrying through the cave amidst delighted squeals. Good. Our plan is well underway.

I'm doing my best to remain calm after my fight with Nolan. Putting my Shadow training to use, I force my emotions down, down, down, where they cannot stop me from carrying out my mission.

Of course the potion isn't helping, neither are the whiskey shots I just threw back with a group of Kadnerian art collectors. As I stumble away from the bar, I bump shoulders with someone in a silver silk robe. The King.

"Shadow," he greets me.

"Your Majesty," I reply.

"You and my son were looking rather close earlier." He smells of liquor and smoke and I've never hated him more than I do now.

"As you know, I have his trust, I was just giving him a final push to make his selection," I tell the King without hesitating.

"Good, I'd hate to have to intervene with his thought process. However, don't think I'm above stepping in if it looks like he's going to make the *wrong* decision." There's an unmistakable threat in his tone. He's admitting that he will alter Nolan's mind if necessary. It's hard to think clearly beyond the thick cloud of hate for this man, but I can't help but feel that I'm missing something.

What is he planning? Why does it matter who Nolan chooses?

Why can't it be me?

"You can trust me with your plans," I say, trying to convince us both.

"Can I? Hard to trust you when you're still not taking advantage of my Royal Magic." His eyebrow raises as he delivers this statement like a punch in the gut.

"Just trying to do a good job, your Majesty." I swallow, praying for this conversation to be over soon.

"Then convince him to announce his final three officially so we can bring in their families and carry on with our plans. He's already dismissed the red head, we know three of you are Shadows—what's he *waiting for!?*" For the first time ever the King's composure is slipping. I thank the Forest Cushion Potion for this. I'm sure he's just revealed more than he meant to.

It's the *arrival of the families* he cares about.

Not Nolan's wedding. Or his wife.

Collecting himself, the King takes a deep breath and smooths out his silk robe. With a curt nod, he turns and walks away, his face twisting into a fake smile as he greets a hot tub filled with his cronies. I'm not surprised to see Ernest nearby, silver thermos in hand. I should stay and observe more but I need to shake off the thick layer of disgust that conversation left me with.

Through my hazy vision, I spot Rus in one of the hot tubs. It's time to give this gossip-loving Court something new to talk about. I plant myself down on the ground beside the tub, feeling the cold of the cave's floor kiss the back of my bare legs. My robe slides gently off my shoulders and the flutter of gold fabric catches Rus' eye. He looks up at me, his gemstone decorated face spreading into a smile.

"Hi Goldie," he says, as his hand lazily runs through his blonde wavy hair. He nods towards my golden robe. This is so classic Rus.

"Hi," I say back. We haven't talked much recently. He hasn't shown up at my door.

"It's been a while," he says, as if reading my mind.

"It has," I respond, before chancing a look over my shoulder at the neighboring hot tub where Nolan is sliding in between Brianna and Amarie.

"Ready to put on a show?" he asks, and I nod before he reaches up for me, his large hands wrapping around my waist as he pulls me down into the bubbling hot water, placing me directly on his lap and leaving my now discarded robe in a golden puddle at the tub's edge.

I snake my arm around his neck and make myself comfortable. It's easy to be affectionate with Rus. He's familiar at this point. He smiles up at me, our faces now close. Yes, to the outside eye we will certainly look *comfortable* with each other.

Stealing another glance back at Nolan's hot tub, I notice as Brianna's mouth drops wide in shock at the sight of me and Rus together. A heartbeat later, she looks over to Nolan and slides on to his lap as if to emulate my current seating position. Amarie takes the hint and exits the tub.

That's interesting, is Brianna trying to get a rise out of me?

There's no way.

No... wait, is she trying to make Rus jealous?

"What's that about?" I ask, leaning down as I whisper into Rus's ear. To the untrained eye it would look like I'm flirting with him.

"She's always had a crush on me," he responds, his voice gruff.

"But... She's Cleo's sister?" My interest is piqued, this sounds even more complicated than my own love life.

"Didn't say it was reciprocated." He schools his features, and I notice his arms tightening around my body, his hand coming to rest on the curve of my ass.

"Do you think she's trying to make you jealous?" We turn to look at her in unison, finding her arm now slung around the Prince's shoulders, her perky boobs pressed up in his face. Nolan doesn't seem that upset about it, that or he's avoiding looking our way. Rus exhales a big breath before fixing his gaze back on me.

"I promised to help her make the final three, which technically, she's already done since there are only six left and three of you are Shadows." He scoops me up and shifts me so that my weight is more evenly distributed across his lap, his arms wrapping around me comfortably as he whispers in my ear. "She should be more focused on him. Not me. If she was, she *could* actually win this and be the future Queen. I can't help but feel that would be good for my people."

There's a quiet desperation in his voice that reminds me how much Rus cares. How deeply he yearns to help people. His people. And all those who are wronged or disadvantaged.

"I bet that, if she thought it would make me jealous, she might actually seduce *him*. That's not a bad thing, is it?" he says softly, his breath hot on my neck.

With Rus there's always a dark cloud, it looms over him like an ever-present reminder of the love that was taken from him. When Nolan does marry someone else, I'll walk around with a similar cavern in my chest. Maybe Rus will be my companion then. My someone to talk to about the unique brand of pain we've both experienced. I've already lost so much of what was supposed to be mine. Lost before I even got to have it. My family. My future. And now Nolan. Maybe these are comforts I never deserved to begin with. Maybe that's why they will never be mine.

But Nolan deserves more. He deserves to be happy. Maybe Brianna could give him that.

"What's she like?" I ask Rus as the tub's bubbles start up, surrounding us with a steady vibration. It feels good against my tense muscles.

"Bri? She's smart. She's kind. She used to be shy but she's growing out of it..." There's affection in his voice as he continues on, telling me more about Bri than I ever realized. Yes, she would make for a good Queen one day. I'm sure of it. Nolan and Bri have much in common, they could be a great pair.

"Let's give her a little push then," I tell Rus. His eyes meet mine in challenge.

"What kind of push?" There's hunger in his expression as he catches on to my meaning.

"You know what I mean," I say, and so he lifts his hand from the water and grazes it down my cheek bone. We lock eyes in silent agreement. It's time to really get our show started. I inhale deeply, allowing the effects of the bubbling water, the potion and the drinks I've had to work their magic to calm me and to release my inhibitions. It's then that I feel Rus' hand traveling up my inner leg below the surface.

He looks up at me for permission to continue. It feels strange. Cold, despite the warm water. There's no spark, but it's just for show so I nod in agreement. Next I collect his hand from my cheek and take one of his fingers, bringing it to my lips and then pulling it into my mouth, sucking slowly. In unison, we look back over at Bri, who as expected, has been watching us. She pouts before taking the Prince's finger and putting it in her own mouth, sucking on it as well. Finally Nolan looks up, just for a second, to meet our watchful eyes, but it's only that one second before Brianna grabs the Prince's face and starts making out with him, passionately. A cough escapes me.

"You okay?" Rus says for my ears only.

"Yes, that worked faster than expected." I attempt to

play off my cough as a laugh. It's taking all of my training to ignore my true feelings on watching Nolan make out with someone else.

"People are taking notice, should we continue?" he mumbles in response. I almost forgot that I'm meant to be convincing all of Court that Rus and I are an item now so that I have a reason to stay until Nolan's wedding. The thought makes me instantly tense again, but Rus must notice because he starts tracing soothing circles on my inner thigh. While it's not giving me butterflies, the contact certainly grounds me. Nolan is no longer an option for me. I've got to stick with the plan, and so I nod yes and Rus starts kissing my neck. For show of course, but it feels nice. No life altering sparks, but that's okay. Besides, not everyone gets to have that in their life-time even once. I'm lucky I ever got to experience it at all.

His hand roams between my legs again, an unnecessary detail considering no one can see below the bubbly surface of our tub, but I find it feels good. Okay, it feels *fine*. It doesn't really feel like anything at all but I assume he's doing this for my benefit. He's probably trying to help me not overthink all of this.

He must know I'm on the verge of spiraling over the fact that Nolan is in the tub next to us with Bri and Sprites being worked to *death* just one tunnel over. Among other things.

"Hey, Goldie, stay with me," he whispers. "We will figure it all out. Don't worry." Yeah, he's definitely trying to keep me calm. As usual, I appreciate him. I feel like I *should* try to touch him. That's what someone who wasn't hung up on Prince Nolan would do. Maybe if I go through the motions my heart will start to believe it.

Under the surface, I shift my body to rub against him. He grips my ass tighter. Yes. Good. I continue to press in to him, rubbing myself up and down his lap. I can feel him growing harder beneath me. So he *is* still attracted to me. That's interesting. I wonder if... I wonder if being with Rus would help ease the pain of this mess we've all made.

"No Darby, not here." He places a hand on my hips to stop me. Again. Just like that night in my room when I reached for him. The rejection stings. Again, he's not letting me touch him. Why not? He can touch me but I can't return the favor? Am I not deserving of this either?

"You never let me," I mutter, my face an inch from his.

"It's not that... This time I'd love for you to touch me, but I'm afraid if you start doing that I wont be able to control myself and I don't think me fucking you in a hot tub in front of the entire Court is the type of *performance* the Prince had in mind."

I don't have time to digest his words before there's a splash in the tub. We turn to find Amarie has joined us.

"So wait, is this really a thing?" she says, her monotone taking on a little more emotion than usual, most likely due to the potion they're pumping in here. "Seline running off with Ingrid I get, I don't think she was ever interested in Nolan. Then Romina and Vesto disappeared together an hour ago looking like they're having the time of their lives, and she's never looked that way with the Prince. But you...?" Amarie's eyes indicate her unspoken question.

"What does it look like?" I play with Rus' wet blonde hair as I speak.

"I can see what it *looks like*, but that doesn't make it make sense," she continues, inching closer to us. "At the last ball you had your tongue down the Prince's throat, tonight you're grinding up on his bodyguard. I'm just not sure what to make of it." She crosses her arms in front of her ample chest, it's accentuated tonight by her flimsy bikini top.

What is she up to? Why is she trying to stop me and Rus?

This could have been my chance to truly put some distance between me and Nolan.

"Why does it matter?" I respond, anger heating my words.

"I've known Nolan a long time, and we have a history, but I thought he seemed different with you, like you might actually be his Link, and I know that deep down, that's what he's always wanted." Her words resound in my head, forming an echoing loop. It's one thing to suspect there might be a real love connection between me and Nolan, it's another thing to hear Amarie say it.

"It's...I'm not." My voice is a whisper and I can't manage to meet her eyes.

"Whatever you say," she responds, and after a frustrated huff, she raises her perfect body from out of the tub and struts off, but not before tossing a look of disappointment over her shoulder.

Interesting.

I would have thought she'd be happy to know I'm not standing in the way of her and Nolan being together.

Could it be that she actually thinks him and I are Links? Could she have been putting his potential happiness before her own?

Suddenly, it's impossible for me to focus on Rus. I need to go, I need to get out of here. I take his hands in mine and unhook them from around my body as I remove myself from the tub.

"Where are you going?" Rus asks, but I have no response for him as I climb out and actually use Royal Magic to dry myself off, reaching for my golden robe and wrapping it tight around me. I spy Vesto and Romina out of the corner of my eye. They made it back. Romina gives me a subtle nod as if to let me know it went smoothly, before reaching for Vesto's hand and racing him to a nearby hot tub.

Fine, good. Let them have their fun. I'm glad the Storytellers got the Antidote. I should be happy about this progress but instead I feel my heart growing heavy. I can't believe this is what became of the last surviving Storytellers. They've spent the last 15 years trapped in a cage, being fed a highly addictive substance which alters their minds. That's no life at all. What would Grandma think if she knew? If she were alive today?

My feet are moving without my head's direction. I come to a stop before Seline and Ingrid. I watch them twirling on the dance floor with a look of genuine happiness in their eyes. Genuine connection. I've never seen Seline like that. It's certainly not how she ever looked at me. So she *is* capable of connecting with someone then? Just not me.

Again, I wasn't good enough. I pivot and turn again.

There's only one person who ever thought I was worth a real connection. One person who ever wanted to make it work with me. And if I really think about it, he's the only person I ever felt that way towards either. So why have I been pushing him away?

I need to find Nolan. My eyes sweep over the party. He's still in the tub with Brianna, thankfully they are no longer kissing. I make a run for it, nearly tripping into the hot water as I kneel down beside him on the tub's edge.

"Nolan, can I steal you for a minute?" I try to summon my courage despite my shaking hands.

Nolan looks up at me then, his eyes are tortured, as if he's running through an internal debate of his own, but then Brianna inches closer to his side, and he exhales a breath, wrapping his arm around her.

"No actually, I think I need to stay right here," he tells me as if in slow motion, "I'm sorry, Darby."

Of course.

It's too late.

I pushed too far.

He told me he couldn't take any more rejection from me, and now it seems he's not going to risk it. I did this.

"Are you sure we can't just talk for a second?" I try again, my voice quivering.

"I meant what I said earlier," he tells me as I take in the sight of him and Brianna in the hot tub. What if he actually chooses her? What if he marries her? How would I feel then? And as if he plucked the idea right from my head, his face changes, and he stands from the hot tub and the room spins.

"Actually everyone, I have an announcement." He

turns away from me to face the gathered crowd. The music dies down so all can hear as Nolan makes his declaration. "Why wait? Why declare a final three? I've made my choice. I've chosen my Bride!" The cave erupts in excited chatter as the King comes out of nowhere, racing to Nolan's side.

"Wait! We *need* a final three. We have to invite their families, and the overnights—" The King's composure is slipping as he urges his son, but Nolan turns to face the King with a cold smile painted on his face.

"No, the overnights won't be necessary, but please invite the families anyway– the more the merrier. It's going to be a *fully Royal* Wedding after all." My heart stops beating as Nolan reaches a hand down towards Brianna, coaxing her to stand on her own wobbling legs. "Princess Brianna of Crichton, will you marry me?"

I don't know what happens next.

I don't even realize I'm walking away until I round the corner of the cave's exit. My emotions are amplified by that Foe forsaken potion, and the drinks, and the mess of this situation. All the feelings are threatening to drown me. I need to get out of here before I burst into tears.

"Darby, wait."

There's a voice behind me and my heart leaps.

I turn to face him. Expecting Nolan.

But it's not Nolan, of course. It's Rus.

He's come after me again. Like he always does.

I'm sure Nolan must have seen him leave after me. How's that going to look?

I guess it doesn't matter. Nolan didn't want to talk

anyway. Nolan just asked Brianna to marry him. His marriage season is over.

We are over.

"You don't need to try and save me again." I push out the words, fighting back my tears.

"But...when I see you like this... I can't help it." He's closer now. "I know things have been weird between us but, I still feel drawn to you," he adds and while I'm aware of the comfort he's offering me, it's not enough. Rus doesn't love me. We don't have that soul deep connection.

But could we?

Sure, I'm torn up over Nolan now, but will I ever heal from it? Will Rus heal? Could we pave a new way together? I wonder if he's over Cleo. I wonder if he could teach me how to get over someone you never really got to be with.

"If she were here, would you still be coming after me?" is what I say instead.

"She isn't here." Rus' jaw ticks.

"But if she was." I hold my ground.

"I don't know, Vesto had a vision that she was but... I don't believe it," Rus admits. Wow. Vesto had a vision that Cleo was here? I guess that would make sense, there's no way Cleo wouldn't come now that Nolan is going to marry her sister. For the Royal wedding.

"Rus... that's... that's wonderful," I say as my thoughts continue racing. Cleo is coming. She'll probably arrive with Brianna's family. Rus and Cleo will reunite. Yes, he doesn't love me and he's certainly not over her.

I step away from him.

"No Darby, don't." He reaches for me, trying to pull

417

me towards him. "You're upset, I can't let you walk away upset." I let him take hold of me. It's then that I gaze up into his big blue eyes. I don't know who I was trying to fool by entertaining the idea of Rus and I together. We're alike, yes, we're two bleeding hearts, but he doesn't love me - and more importantly - I do not love him. I love someone else.

"You can, Rus, because *this* isn't our love story. I don't think it ever was." And with that I slip from his grasp, sprinting out of the caves before a single tear can escape my welled up eyes.

37

DARBY

Alone in my room, it all comes crashing down on me. It isn't just that I've pushed Nolan away and now he's going to marry someone else. It's everything.

We still don't know what the King is working towards, and even if we can use Nolan's wedding as a distraction to free the Sprites and the Storytellers, what happens after that?

How will we defend ourselves against the King's inevitable wrath?

What will become of the people of Kadneria once the foundation of Royal Magic is destroyed? My hand wanders to the medallion around my neck. How much of this did Mother suspect when she sent us here? Why haven't we heard from her since our arrival?

Anger bubbles over in me as I rip the necklace from my neck.

What good is this anyway?

Sure it helped me shield in a practical sense, but when

has my mother ever shielded *me* from anything? There has been so much in my life that she *could* have protected me from. Instead she pushed me towards pain. Towards rejection.

"Nolan, can I steal you for a minute?"

"No actually, I think I need to stay right here. I'm sorry, Darby."

Foe, I must have looked like such an idiot.

I toss the necklace to the ground with shaking hands, or maybe I place it gently as my own body crashes to the floor. It's hard to say which, as my vision is completely hazed over and I curl inward, desperate to slow my heaving chest.

"Nolan, can I steal you for a minute?"

"No actually, I think I need to stay right here. I'm sorry, Darby."

The moment continues to play out in my head.

Over and over again.

My mortification grows with each replay.

He's going to marry her. Even though marriages can be ended, he would never, he's too loyal. He's going to commit his life to the Princess of Crichton. To Brianna. She will be his Queen one day.

"Nolan, can I steal you for a minute?"

"No actually, I think I need to stay right here."

What if *we* were truly meant to be Linked?

Now neither of us will ever know.

And still, I'll remain here. Working alongside him to right the wrongs of our shared past.

The tears overwhelm me. I'm crying so hard it hurts.

What if I can't do it? What if I'm too weak? Too ruled

by my own emotions that I fail at the task I've waited my whole life to accomplish.

What if I can't save the Storytellers?

What if I can't bring down the King?

What if more Sprites die due to my own short-comings?

The thought is too much to bear. It works like a battering ram, breaking down any remaining hold I have on the darkness that's been threatening to consume me all evening.

My sobs turn deeper as my heart hollows out.

I don't deserve a Link. Especially not someone as wonderful as Nolan.

Nolan deserves more than this. He deserves more than someone who crumbles like I do. He deserves someone who can actually complete their mission. Someone who can do what they planned. Not a failure like me.

It's no wonder nobody loves me.

And I'm alone. So alone.

This is how it's always been.

This is how it always will be.

I don't know how much time passes as I lie there curled up in a ball on the floor, but at some point I become vaguely aware of Romina crouching beside me.

"Just... trust me," she whispers, before opening a portal and pushing me into it.

And I fall into the blackness, once again.

38

DARBY

It's hot. Burning hot. And not the humid heat of the forest in the summer. This is dry heat. I can practically feel the moisture of my skin evaporating. My skin. I reach down to feel my exposed skin. My fingertips grazing against my bare stomach. Where are my clothes?

My eyes blow open to find nothing but sky before me. The Sun and the Second Star are all I see. They burn directly above me, their heat stronger than I've ever felt.

And the sight of them?

They are bigger and fuller than I've ever seen them before, in a sky so brightly blue it's almost white. I blink my eyes, struggling to adjust. I'm overwhelmed by the sight of endless sky and impossibly bright light.

Where am I?

I scan my body once more.

There is something prickling at my back. It's then I realize I'm laying on the ground in a dust so thick it could be sand. Maybe it is sand. I sit up slowly, my head pounding. I rub my eyes to clear my vision as the sight comes into focus: Desert. There's desert all around me, stretching onwards in every direction. An endless sea of sand interrupted every so often by a small prickling cactus.

What the fuck am I doing in a desert?

My hands travel back to my body, discovering that I'm still in my bathing suit from....from what exactly? Why was I wearing this again? I look down to find a golden robe tangled around my waist. I straighten it out, tugging the thin fabric up against my torso, protectively. I guess it's not so bad, any more clothing than this and I might overheat.

For Foe's sake, it's hot out!

Sand sticks to the sweat which coats the back of my legs and I curse my body for giving away that moisture. In Shadow training, we were taught to keep moving no matter what. And so I must rise and I must get going... but where to?

I manage to shift onto my feet, wobbling at first. A gentle wind blows towards me, kissing my skin with the faintest glimmer of relief against the heat. I let my eyes flutter shut, drinking it in. The breeze continues, as if nudging me to get moving, so I decide to follow the path of this breeze, walking where it leads me. One foot in front of the other.

Am I alone?

"Hello... anyone out there?" I call into the void. My words fall flat against the sand. It's then that I realize how much my body hurts and my face feels sore from crying. I reach out to feel the dried tears on my cheeks. My eyelids are swollen.

Why was I crying?

The answer escapes me, hiding somewhere just outside of my reach as the breeze abandons me. Suddenly, I'm all too aware of the heat again. It's hot as a flame and it threatens to consume me. I need to find shade. Soon.

And so I continue walking. Slowly. One more step. Then another.

Keep moving.

The walk is endless. The sand burns my feet. I try to swallow the pain, using my Shadow training to trick my mind, but my mind is not having it. Not when I'm alone out here with my own thoughts.

You're a terrible Shadow.

You don't even know how you got here.

You're failing your mission.

Where is your team?

You weren't good enough for them.

They left you. Abandoned you.

Alone.

You deserve to be alone.

The day stretches on in an endless parade of boiling sand. At this point my feet are so blistered they've lost feeling. I'm parched. My hand grazes my lips, finding them impossibly chapped. It hurts to swallow, my throat is coarse, as if I've been drinking the sand. Maybe I have. I need water.

Water.

That's interesting.

There is something familiar about it. Don't I have power over water?

Yes. Water. A connection to water.

Surely I could conjure some water... couldn't I?

I'd just need to find a plant. A cactus. I scan the desert once more, this time in an attempt to hone in on the small green plants I'm sure I've walked by at some point. There! I spot a small patch of them, just a stone's throw away. I pick up the pace, using what's left of my energy to hobble over, falling on my knees in the sand before it. I hold my hands out in front of the cactus.

How does this work again?

I glance up at the sky. The Sun and the Second Star hang directly above me in the same spot they've been all day, as if no time has passed since I first woke up here. But that can't be right? I've been walking for what feels like hours, maybe even days.

The Sun and her sister shine impossibly brighter then. They seem to be taunting. Teasing. There's something missing here.

The Moon.

The thought wobbles into focus. That's right. My power comes from the Moon. I'm a Lunar. It's flooding back to me now: I'll need the Moon in order to charge my power because currently, my power is drained. How did that happen? I don't remember using it up last night... What did I do last night?

I stare at the cactus, forcing my eyes shut and digging deep down into myself, grasping at any bit of power I have left. I need water. I have to find *something* in myself and latch on to my connection to the water in this plant. I must.

But there's nothing.

And there's no one to help me.

"Help *us*." I hear a whisper on the wind but turn my head to find nothing.

I'm all alone out here.

I fall back into the sand, using my arms to block my eyes from the burning light. Something sharp and metal brushes against my face and I glance at my arm where a silver bracelet hangs loosely, and on it: a charm. A heart with a crown.

The Prince's heart.

The memory comes flooding back: The Cave Rave Ball. Nolan. Brianna. The way I let it consume me. The way I let loneliness claim me. The intrusive thoughts built and built until they swallowed me whole and I was left in nothing but a puddle of darkness on my bedroom floor.

Is that why my power drained? That can't be right. How would my own thoughts drain my power?

"Help us!" I hear again. This time when I look into the distance I see a group of people walking towards me. Their clothes are ragged and their pace is slow. The closer they get, the more they start to look familiar. I sit up and rub my eyes to confirm what I'm seeing.

Yes, that's Romina! And Seline!

I muster all my energy to stand and launch myself towards them— falling into Romina's arms in a blistering hug.

"All you've ever wanted to do is help people. Now is

your chance. Help us." Romina's nails sink into my skin, I squirm below her grasp. It hurts. I pull back and look up to tell her as much, but I find I'm no longer in Romina's embrace. Now it's a scowling Rus who gazes down at me. He looks angry.

"You told me you enjoyed helping people," he says, nodding to where Seline, Vesto and Romina stand behind him. Romina? How did they change places so quickly? "Help us."

"She's all talk," Seline coos, as she and the others crowd around me. I dig deep inside myself again, I must have something left to help them. Some connection to water...

"Coming up dry?" There's a taunting voice behind me. I turn to find Nolan. Nolan is here. My heart leaps as I reach for him but he turns away from me. "You can't help us. You used up all your power. You're burnt out." His tone is cruel. Cold. Calculated. He signals to the others. "Come on everyone, there's no use."

Wait! I try to call after them as they begin to sulk away but no sound leaves my mouth. I keep trying, keep digging deeper and deeper into myself searching for any ounce of magic, but he's right, I'm empty.

"She inspired herself into thinking she was worthless, not deserving of love." I hear a raspy voice I don't recognize. "And now she has nothing left, she can't even help them."

Romina, Seline, Nolan and Rus disappear into the sand. My closest people have abandoned me because I let them down. I couldn't help them. I shut my eyes and turn inward, falling to the ground but it's not sand below me.

427

It's soft?

When I open my eyes I discover a plush pillow below my head. More alarmingly there's a thick weighted blanket covering me. I'm not even sweating. The temperature is perfect. I take a deep breath and inhale the sweet scent of lavender and mint— what the Foe. Did I ... have I died?

"You're not dead," that same raspy voice says from somewhere on my left. I shoot up in bed, my eyes blowing wide. There's a woman sitting on a wooden chair next to the plush bed I'm dozing in. She's incredibly thin with sharp features, her eyes are bright turquoise, her curly hair a mix of the same color and shining silver gray. Her deep voice is in contrast to her frail frame, and I find myself gasping with surprise as she hops up from her seat and prances over towards the edge of the bed with a burst of energy. No, she's not frail at all.

"Of course I'm not frail. I'm not even *that* old," she says, and I cover my mouth in horror. Did I say that bit about her being frail out loud?

I sit up, taking stock of the room I'm in. The bed frame is made of driftwood, the linens are cream colored. The room is mostly neutral tones with hints of turquoise decor that match her eyes. There is a beautifully tiled turquoise pot in the corner of the room where a large cactus grows. Next to it, an oversized window is covered by turquoise and yellow woven curtain shades that block out all light.

"They said I had to help you manifest your Gift, but they were wrong, weren't they?" she says as she leans over me, her thick layers of beaded necklaces clacking together as she moves. "I sifted through your mind. Your Gift isn't missing. It's all over the place! No, you're just a mess, and they sent you to me, thinking I'd clean it all up. 'Oh Candace! Oh Candace, please, we need you!' Always on clean up duty aren't I?" She summons a glass of water from thin air and hands it to me. "Even after all these years I still don't know how to say no to them. So I guess I *am* stuck on cleanup duty. As for you, well you really need to learn how to control your Gift, darling."

I look at her in disbelief. I have no idea what she's talking about.

She sifted through my mind?

That wasn't real?

It certainly felt real.

"What?" I ask between sips of the coolest, most crisp glass of water I've ever tasted.

"Your Eclipse Gift," she says without flinching.

"I don't know what you mean..." I avoid her gaze, her eyes too piercing to look at directly.

"Oh, so you don't listen then? Didn't hear a word I just said?" She sounds more impatient than angry, I think.

"I was listening, it's just, I've never manifested an Eclipse Gift..." I sit up more, my voice returning.

"But you *have*, and it's a mess, as I just said, you don't even realize you're using it, and using it, and using it all wrong. You've drained yourself, you've given others your thoughts involuntarily, you've convinced yourself of things that aren't true. That is not what your Gift is meant for."

She stands now, making her way to the curtains which she pulls back gingerly. The sight steals my breath away. Out there beyond this room is nothing but desert, miles and miles of desert, and from here where I sit comfortably, I can finally appreciate how beautiful it is. I glance up towards the sky where the Sun is finally beginning to set, dipping down to the horizon. Soon the Moon will take its place next to the Second Star. Soon I'll be able to recharge my power.

My power...and my Eclipse Gift?

The unmistakable feeling of hope begins to grow in my chest for the first time in a while.

"Don't you know?" She stares back at me. "Haven't you felt it?" She finishes tying back the curtain shades and I consider this.

"You've given others your thoughts involuntarily," she told me, that's interesting...I'm not a Mentalist, am I?

And I'm doing it wrong by giving my thoughts away instead of reading other people's?

My mind briefly floats back to Nolan that day many moons ago when his Dreamseeing first manifested. He was so frightened by being able to see people's fears. I wonder if he just got used to it? Or has his gift somehow been suppressed by his lack of memory?

When I see him again, I will ask.

If I see him again...The thought causes a sharp pain in my chest but I need to stay focused on the here and now.

"You've convinced yourself of things that aren't true. That is not what your Gift is meant for." Well that's an interesting clue. It's a clue that unlocks something from the catacombs of my mind. Somewhere buried deep in there is my Storyteller training.

There was this story, more of a legend really.

Of Storytellers who were born with an Eclipse Gift that could aid in their Storytelling. They could Inspire others. The gift would allow them to give energy to ideas, to set thoughts into motion, not meant for planting ideas in people's heads but to breathe life into thoughts that were already there as if watering the seeds of imagination and encouraging them to grow. To blossom. To flourish. But it was a very rare Gift, one of the five most powerful Eclipse Gifts. Only those destined for greatness would receive it from the Goddess of The Frequency.

That couldn't be me. Could it?

"And why not you?" The strange woman is prancing around the room again.

When have I ever *inspired* anyone? I think to myself but she responds out loud.

"Well you certainly *inspired* yourself to believe that you were worthless, unlovable and destined to be alone, none of which is true, by the way. Especially considering we all know you are destined to be Linked." Her tone is drier than the desert. "Unless you think you know better than Us," she adds with a taunting smile as she reaches the door.

Than Us? Who is she talking about?

"Get dressed, we have company."

39

DARBY

I find a set of breezy white linen pants and a matching top neatly folded at the foot of my bed and change into them. Then I visit the washroom to freshen up, before making my way down the hall of the home I'm in, following the sounds of chattering voices. Padding down the hallway, I soak in the cool floor beneath my bare feet. So different from the torturous desert sands that scalded my skin not long ago.

How long was I out there? *Was* I actually there?

I round the corner to discover a sprawling dining room. The sparse but elegant decorations perfectly complement the sight of the desert outside the oversized windows. Everything is beige or white, except for all the colorful tiled pots, each boasting a more lavish cactus than the last. Not unlike the turquoise pot in my room. At a large whitewashed wood dining table there are three women - *Candace*, and two others. As soon as I enter, they turn to face me. My eyes immediately land on the older of the three, a curvaceous woman with gray-streaked rose gold hair, wrinkled olive-toned skin, and gold-rimmed hazel eyes that I still see in my dreams. She rises from the table to meet me.

"Grandma." The word leaves my lips before my brain has fully even caught up to speed. Then I'm in her arms, burrowing into her softness as she strokes my hair.

"Arabella. I've missed you." She squeezes me tight, her voice slightly softer than I remember, but her presence still calming.

Arabella.

The name echoes in my ears.

It's been so long since anyone called me that.

I pull back to take in the sight of her. This can't be right. She's dead.

And now.... Wait a second.

Have I died? I know Candace dismissed the thought earlier, but I don't know if I trust her.

What if this is the afterlife?

What if that's what the journey through the desert was all about?

And I'll never see Romina or Seline again...Or Nolan.

Nolan. Oh no.

THAT'S IT? I'm DEAD?

The look of panic must be painted on my face, because Grandma squeezes my hand.

"We're all very much alive. But I'm afraid I have some explaining to do, come sit." She leads me to the table to join them. Candace gives Grandma a nod to go on.

"I'm sorry that we kept this from you Arabella, but please know, there was no other choice that would guarantee your safety. Lemonade? Candace makes a mean one," she asks, gesturing to a pitcher of lemonade I hadn't noticed before. Candace pours the beverage into glass chalices for everyone and I can't help but stare at my Grandma, sitting in front of me 15 years after her death, offering me lemonade like that's the most normal thing in the world.

What the Foe is going on here?

A heavy crystal glass is placed down in front of me and she continues.

"When the King turned on the Storytellers, I enlisted myself to serve the Goddesses in exchange for your protection. I knew that you were our only hope, that your gift would one day save the Kingdom, and save *our* people. Everyone had to think I had died, but I am sorry that we led you to believe that..." She takes a sip of her own drink. Grandma smiles at Candace. "Tastes great, much sweeter than last time, thank you, Candace." As if the taste of the lemonade matters right now?

My mind is traveling at a mile a minute.

She enlisted herself? What protection? When have the Goddesses ever protected me? And she knew about my Gift all along? Why didn't she help me learn how to use it? Is she going to help me now? Why did I have to believe that she was dead? Who else knows?

"Wait so. Did Headmaster – I mean, Mother, she knew?" is the mess of a sentence that I end up stringing together.

"None of us wanted to keep this from you," Grandma replies. My very much alive Grandma. This is going to take some getting used to.

434

"Well she did it anyway. I can't believe it." I'm so angry. Why? How?

Mother kept this from me for all these years. There's so much that she hid from me. That she took from me. My blood begins to boil, and it's Candace who speaks next.

"Is that really going to solve anything, Arabella? Getting angry with the people who actually just want the best for you, who have done nothing but try to protect you?" Her words cut through me. "It would be far more productive to focus your energy on reversing the impact of your own actions." She almost rolls her eyes and it makes my temper rise even more.

"My *own actions?* Are you kidding?" I turn to face where she sits next to me. "Who are you anyway?"

"I thought you said she was smart and observant?" Candace twists in her seat to face Grandma now.

"She is," Grandma's eyes are rich with concern.

"Well then she's just being ridiculous. It's easy to put the blame on your mother so that you don't need to take responsibility for yourself. Sure, she lied to you, and maybe that wasn't the best way to go about it, but she was trying to protect you and your Gift. It's *you* who has been harming yourself with this negative self talk, this questioning of your own value... " Candace says to me, and all hope I had for calming down has gone out the window.

"Me!?" Who is this lady? Why is she so brutal?

"Oh you weren't expecting tough love? I'm sorry, but the whole Friend thing didn't work for you so now you're stuck with The Foe." Her eyes shine as she says this, and I force myself to meet them, blinding as they are. It's then that my brain finally manages to catch up with what my body already knows. There's an energetic pulse surrounding her. Almost intangible, but if I really pay attention, I can feel it. Candace is no ordinary woman.

Candace is The Foe.

A gasp escapes my lips as it all clicks into place. Was it impolite to curse in *her* name in front of her?

Grandma stands up and rushes to my side, resting her hands on my shoulders. "Arabella, take a deep breath, there's a lot to process here but we need you to get up to speed, we're running out of time." Grandma's voice is steady and unwavering, it calms me, a little.

"We are here to help you harness your Gift, so that you can combine your power with your Link, and stop Godwin, before it is too late." This comes from the third woman, who I had almost forgotten about. My eyes float to her. She looks to be about 40, and I can only describe her as hauntingly beautiful. It's as if the memory of her high cheek bones and big brown eyes stays with you even when you look away. There is an elegance to the way she carries herself, like royalty. Even the soft smile she offers me lights up the room. Something about her seems alarmingly familiar.

"Have we met before?" I look at her more closely now. There's a dimple in the left cheek of her otherwise perfectly symmetrical face.

"*I enlisted myself to serve the Goddesses in exchange for your protection,*" Grandma just told me, and there's only one other person I've heard of doing that.

The Queen. Nolan's Mother.

She smiles at me as if realizing I just figured it out on my own.

"You can call me Lydia," she says kindly.

Queen Lydia.

"He misses you so much." The words leave my mouth before I even realize it. "How could you leave him?" The hurt bubbles to the surface and I realize it's not just Nolan's wound, but my own. I turn to Grandma. "How could you leave me?"

Grandma reaches for me again, taking my hands in hers.

"We did what we had to in order to protect you both. It wasn't easy, but love never is." She looks over to Lydia and a deep emotion passes between them. Clearly, they have bonded over this. My own heart thumps in response.

Love never is easy, is it? That I can understand.

"You knew I had an Eclipse Gift? Even before you..." I don't know how to say died, because well, she's not dead. "Before that day with the King?"

"I didn't know what it was yet, but I knew you'd have one of the five," she tells me.

"How could you know that?" I've already met The Foe, learned Grandma is alive and survived some sort of subconscious desert nightmare, and yet I have a feeling that whatever is coming next is going to push me over the edge completely.

"Because we are *LeSang*, and all EclipseBorn LeSang are one of the five: Inspiras, Augmentors, Visionaries, Chronos and Dreamseers. One Gift from each of the five original houses of the Gods and Goddesses." My Grandma tells me this with the same voice she once used in our lessons. Back when I'd absorb her every word. And yet right now, I can't make sense of a single thing she's saying.

"What. The. Foe," I respond.

"Excuse me?" Candace scowls at me, but I continue.

"We're LeSang? What does that mean?"

"We didn't get there in your training before we had to stop," she says, putting it lightly. "LeSang means *of the blood*. God's Blood. Our great ancestor was descended from a Goddess."

"Of course, it's prohibited for us to mate with mortals now, but we do what we can to protect the lines who carry on. It's why we offer the Service Agreements," Candace adds, nodding towards Grandma and Lydia.

"So you are.... And that means he is..." I'm looking at Lydia, my mouth agape as I realize something horrible. "Are Nolan and I related?"

"Of course not! You know how many Gods and Goddesses there are? Enough to ensure none of the LeSang are related, that's for sure...although it would strengthen the line if you were to mate with another, which is why the Goddess Amira often ensures they are Linked." Candace appears to like this idea and I'm distracted by the sense of relief that's pouring through me. I take another big sip of my lemonade, trying to process everything they are telling me.

The Foe is sitting next to me.

Grandma is alive.

She's working for the Goddesses.

Nolan's mother is too.

And we're all LeSang?

And then I realize. The Five: Inspiras, Augmentors, Visionaries, Chronos and Dreamseers.

"Nolan, Rus, and Vesto...is it a coincidence?" I look up at the three women now.

"Of course not. Power is attracted to Power." Candace says this as if she's annoyed with me for needing the clarification.

"Why is this not a known thing?" I fire back.

"It's one of the secrets the Storytellers keep. Your friends do not know," Grandma says.

"And how do you decide who gets what gift?" I'm swimming with questions, grasping for whatever feels most urgent to know.

"We don't..." Candace glances up at Grandma where she still stands behind me. "You've told her our history?" Grandma nods, and then Candace continues, sitting back in her chair to get comfortable. "Long ago, after the war and all that, when the Humans asked the Gods for Magic, we agreed, but it was complicated." She gesticulates casually as she speaks. "Tarajian performed the ceremony during a celestial event so that the magical frequency would be more potent. She had all the Gods and Goddesses, Old and New, gathered to share their power. But, Tarajian is an overachiever. She used herself to channel the magic. *She became the Frequency itself.* It was too much. Nearly exhausted herself, and you know what that's like, don't you?" Candace gives me a pointed look, "Perhaps you should pay *her* a visit too." Then she continues, "From that point on, Humans were born Lunar,

Stellar or Solar. But there was a side effect. Those born during an Eclipse would sometimes also inherit extra magic. An Eclipse Gift, as you call it, a bit of extra magic from both the Old and the New. Over the years we've found it's even more potent in those with God's blood. We've noticed that family members tend to inherit the same gifts, generally."

"But... you told me that..." I'm digging up the memory as I twist in my seat to face Grandma. "Eclipse Gifts are rewarded to those the Goddesses see fit. You said it was a privilege to receive one!" A shadow crosses her face as she considers her response.

"It is a privilege. And, as I always say, even the past can surprise us." As she says it, those very words echo through my memories.

"So Eclipse Gifts are a mistake?" I turn back to Candace now.

"Just because we didn't intend to give them, does not make them any less of a Gift. Tarajian, Rominanna and I have committed our lives to ensuring Humans do not abuse the power; we monitor and protect the balance."

Rominanna.

Romina?

"Of all the shocking things you've told me, that may just be the one that—" I don't even have the words. Romina?

"I'm sorry but the whole Friend thing didn't work for you so now you're stuck with The Foe." Candace said earlier.

"She's the Friend." I conclude on my own.

"She's been protecting you ever since I signed my

Service Agreement." Grandma settles back into her seat across the table. I watch as Lydia places a gentle hand on her arm. They've been through a lot together, haven't they? Lydia and Grandma both made the ultimate sacrifice in order to protect me and Nolan. Is that why he and I feel so connected? Because the Goddesses are meddling in our families' lives?

"So what now? You're going to help me learn how to control my Gift and then what?" I say, trying to remain calm.

"You are to use your Gift in combination with your Link. You will grow even more powerful then. Together, the two of you can override the mind control of the King and stop his abuse of power," Candace offers, and my brain snags on a detail.

"You mentioned a Goddess named Amira? She makes the Links?" Pain is blooming between my temples. I rub them gently as I speak. "So she can just choose whoever she wants?"

"Amira is one of the old Gods," Grandma supplies. "She has the ability to see souls. She finds the souls that complement each other and helps create a path for their destinies to intertwine."

"Right but... she could choose whoever she wants and then alter their fate to meet?"

"No, that wouldn't work." Lydia chimes in now. "Your souls have to be a fit for each other, she can discern this, but she does not decide it."

"Well then I'm afraid we're out of luck." I lean back in my chair, crossing my arms now, hoping to create some distance between myself and the burning gazes of these three women.

"Why is that?" Lydia studies me from across the table.

"Becuase I don't have a Link, and if Amira cannot choose one for me, I don't see how this plan could work. We'll have to form a new one."

"You do have a Link, and I think you know that. I think this is your fear talking. But we need you to be brave. How is anyone else supposed to believe in you if you don't believe in yourself?" Candace says.

"What about the Blood Oath I took to never form attachments? I received the Shadow Mark." I lower the waistband on my linen pants to show them the ink on my left hip bone only to find... nothing.

"Rominanna made it appear that you had, but in fact, you did not perform the full Shadow Blood Oath ritual, a simple illusion really," Candace says casually, and yet my world tilts further off its axis. *What? I didn't? How could Romina let me believe this for... 15 years?*

I look to Grandma for guidance. The love in her eyes as she gazes back at me is the only thing keeping me steady as everything I have known to be true is going up in flames.

"The Goddesses have been watching you, Arabella, they've been working to protect you almost all your life," Grandma tells me. "You can *Inspire*. It's the most special Gift a Storyteller can have. You can change the world."

"But I'm not a Storyteller anymore, I'm a Shadow now, that's what happened when you..." I'm scrambling to make sense of this all, but Grandma puts a hand up to silence me.

"You will always be a Storyteller. It's in your heart." All three women turn to look at me now. The clear passion in their eyes overwhelms me.

"What if I can't do what you need me to do? How can I change the world when I can't even...well I've already fucked up enough. And a Link? There's no way I have a Link, if there was a chance for us to be together, I've already blown it." There's doubt in my mind. So much of it. And with these three women looking at me with so much expectation, well it's just three more people who I could let down, actually, two people and a Goddess. Even worse.

"You made it this far." Grandma nods towards the window.

"And we're here to help you now, Arabella, if you'll let us." Lydia's words are tender, I appreciate her softer approach. "Just because you have the power to change the world, doesn't mean you need to do it all on your own."

I let her words wash over me and find comfort in them. Okay. Yes. I could use some help. I notice a tear streaking down my cheek and use my hand to wipe it away. The release feels good. Like the beginning of something bigger. A letting go of something I didn't even realize I was holding on to. A few more tears trickle down.

"It's Nolan, isn't it? He's my Link?" I look right at Lydia to find her own eyes welling with tears. She smiles at me and nods.

"I pushed him away," I tell her. "He asked the Princess of Crichton to marry him." My tears have escalated to include some snot. Grandma hands me a linen handkerchief, and I accept it.

"Well they aren't married yet, we still have time," Candace offers, and the seeds of hope are planted in me once more.

"He's a Dreamseer," I tell them.

"We know, but unfortunately, he does not," Lydia says, her grief painted on her face. She stands from her seat and raises a hand toward me. Unsure what to do I stand and take it. Her hand is warm like Nolan's, but delicate. She wraps my arm around hers and leads us over to stand by the window. At first we stand in silence gazing out at the desert. Lydia's head hovers somewhere above mine so that I cannot fully read the expression on her face. Clearly this is where Nolan gets his height from.

"I know you have questions about my son," she says gracefully, "Please. Ask away."

I wonder about the terms of her own Service Agreement with the Goddesses. How much has she been able to do for Nolan from a distance?

"I understand him not remembering when it manifested but...how is it that he hasn't realized he's a Dreamseer? It's been ages..." My voice wobbles as I ask, giving away how nervous I am. It's not everyday you watch your almost lover propose to someone else, fall into a pit of despair only to be rescued by your dead Grandma, a Goddess and the long lost Queen of Kadneria. At this point I could laugh at the absurdity of the last 24 hours. Or at least, what I suspect may have only been that long.

"Godwin...he changed." Lydia's voice drops as she turns to me, as if this conversation were meant for only the two of us. "He lost his way. Nolan was at risk. If

Godwin realized how powerful our son was, I feared he would do something terrible. I had no choice but to ask the Goddesses for help. They subdued his Gift in exchange for my service. So that Godwin could not exploit him."

"They... wait what?" I know this is not how one should speak to a Queen but I'm too shocked for manners. "*That's* what you asked for in return for your service? You could have asked for anything! Nolan deserves to know he is a Dreemseer! It's his Gift!"

Lydia's eyes flit briefly over to the table where Candace and Grandma are chatting, when they land back on me, I can sense her concern.

"I was desperate. Perhaps I should have phrased it differently, but unfortunately, I did not. What matters is that Nolan has been safe."

"Safe and subdued. How can he ever be his true self with this essential part muted..." I force myself to turn from her deep brown eyes. They remind me too much of him. Instead I focus on the vast stretch of sand outside the window.

"In your own way, your Gift has been muted too." Lydia steps closer, she places a gentle hand on my shoulder. "Perhaps it was always meant to be this way. So that you two could come into your full power together, and grow even stronger because of it."

We stay like that for a moment, gazing out the window. I'm turning over the thoughts in my head when Candace calls out for us.

"Ready to get on with the plans?"

"Right then." In my peripheral I notice Lydia nod her head before turning back toward the table. I follow her back and find my seat next to Candace.

"The King is using Royal Magic to control people's minds. We need Nolan to use his Gift to see the truth in their hearts, and you to Inspire them to let those ideas rise above Royal Magic's influence. Once you are Linked, your powers will be even stronger when used together," Candace tells me. "It's quite straightforward actually."

So they want us to combine our powers, and that makes me remember what Candace said. The line would strengthen if Nolan and I mated. Is that the only reason we are destined for one another? Are the Gods and Goddesses to make a weapon out of our connection?

"So we are pawns in a game of Gods? Amira Links us together to *strengthen the line?*"

"Again, Amira does not choose, she only helps guide. Besides, he is your soul's mate, your Link, a match for your power, mind and heart, isn't that what you always wanted?" Candace responds. "Does it matter why?" And she's right. It is what I've always wanted. So why am I fighting it? Am I just looking for reasons to walk away before this dream can be taken away from me somehow? Before yet another hope can be shattered?

"But what if..." I start to say, but three sets of eyes bore into me again, cutting me off.

What if he doesn't want me anymore? What if he actually marries Brianna? What if things between us are beyond repair at this point?

"He's your Link, Arabella, it's going to take more than one fight to keep you two apart." Grandma tells me.

No, I can't walk away.

I couldn't even if I wanted to. The thought of never seeing him again was worse than thinking I might have died. I feel called to Nolan. I crave him.

Even if it comes with some complications, Nolan is still the one for me.

And I am the one for him.

We will figure this out, together, and we will not be pawns.

"You've got this, Arabella. We're going to help you. It's all going to be okay. You just need to believe in yourself, and give it your best shot," Candace tells me, and it's the nicest thing she's said so far. Perhaps the nicest thing she'll ever say, considering they call her The Foe for a reason. I take a deep breath, and allow all their words to sink in. In some ways, it's just another mission. A new task at hand.

"You should get some rest, we'll start our training in the morning," Lydia announces.

"We're running out of time, we should start now," Candace challenges.

"A few hours of sleep aren't going to change anything, besides, I'm going to place her back in the timeline exactly where she needs to be." Lydia responds with a Queen's authority, and I can infer that she is a Chronos.

Incredible. I've never met one before.

At least not one that I'm aware of.

Candace nods in reluctant acceptance of Lydia's suggestion, and I find that my eyes are suddenly heavy, the weight of this conversation has left me exhausted. I hug Grandma once more, and make my way back to my room. There is hope rising in my chest again. Hope and determination.

I wake up to a tingling sensation. Opening my eyes I find the room in darkness, and yet, there's a feeling I can't ignore. Like pins and needles in my hands and toes. I sit up and pad my way over to the curtains. Pushing them open to reveal the vastness of the desert outside my window. An ink blue sky, and up there, shining brightly next to the Second Star: the Moon.

She's nearly full. I close my eyes and allow her light to wash over me like a long lost lover's embrace. Finally the pins and needles subside. I can feel the blood pumping through me again. I can feel my wells of power beginning to restore.

I leave the curtains open and head back to my bed. Laying down gently with my body angled so the Moon's milky glow can still kiss my skin. It's a soft sensation that attempts to cool me as I lay here sprawled out like a starfish. I try to get comfortable but the blood pumping through me is picking up speed and my heart is racing.

There's so much pent up, so much I've been holding in:

Anger over all that has transpired. Over all that was revealed today.

Hurt, for the way I left things with Nolan. For the way I failed the Sprites and the Storytellers. For the way I failed myself, allowing myself to believe that it was all over, that there was no more hope, that I couldn't just ask for help.

Help. What a concept. Will these women really help me? Have others tried to help me? My thoughts drift to Romina. We have been through everything together. But she's only been protecting me because she is The Friend. I always knew she had secrets, but I never suspected she was an actual *Goddess*. I wonder if she really cares for me, or if it was all just an assignment for her. I can't help but feel angry with her. There's been so much deceit from the person I trusted most in this world.

It was her who sent me here.

"Trust me," she said, before I fell into the darkness.

I'm clearly here for a reason. And if what they say is true, then I'm going to need help because I have no idea how to use my Gift for anything other than what I've managed to use it for so far.

And being LeSang? That is a lot to unpack.

But if I can Inspire then...well that's a Storyteller's gift if there ever was one.

Does that mean I will get to be a Storyteller again?

I glance out the window again to find The Moon and the Second Star twinkling in response, as if they've heard me. The increase in their brightness sends a jolt of energy through me. It feels good. A spike of adrenaline.

"I'm going to be a Storyteller again," I say aloud for no one to hear but myself.

Because voicing it helps it feel more true.

And if I'm to be a Storyteller, then I'll no longer be a Shadow.

And that means that perhaps Nolan and I could actually be together.

That we could work together to take down his father and reestablish Storytelling in Kadneria. And it wouldn't just be about working together. We could really *be* together.

It's almost too wonderful to imagine.

"He's your Link, it's going to take more than one fight to keep you two apart." Grandma's words drift back to me now.

I am going to trust this. If I can convince myself that I am unworthy, then why can't I convince myself to believe in this?

Besides, there's no way that I can brush aside the feeling of connection between Nolan and I. True connection. A soul deep tether. And how can *he* ignore it if, all along, I've been struggling to ignore it myself? This is unignorable. This is real. He is already a part of me. And I am a part of him.

Ritual or not, he is my Link, and finally, I am not afraid to admit it.

Another wave of power washes over me, and I close my eyes and allow myself to feel it all. From behind closed eyes I see each emotion in vivid color, watching in awe as the yellow of hope mixes with the red of hurt, the blue of longing, the pink of love. It's a beautiful swirl of emotions, like a painting. I let go of everything I've been holding on to, my walls crumbling, and it feels good. So good. I feel a hand graze my upper thigh and for a second my traitorous heart imagines that it belongs to Nolan, but he's not here. It takes me a second to realize that it's my own hand which has started to trace slow circles on my sensitive flesh. I make myself comfortable against the soft sheets as my hand begins to roam closer and closer to that deeply Human part of me which is now aching. I think back to all the nights in which I longed for touch. Nights when I went searching for someone, anyone to fill the void of connection.

But what if I had just poured my precious energy into myself?

Has this body not earned some tenderness?

I feel the unmistakable crinkle of magic brewing in my sternum. It's not unlike the way I've felt before having a magical outburst, only this time, I'm in control. I am connected to this brewing magic.

You deserve to feel good.

You deserve to show yourself care.

Yes. This is it. This is how my Gift is meant to be used. To create light. Not to send myself into the darkness. The magic bubbles over and I open my eyes to see my entire body is faintly glowing, sparkling even. My own hand finds my center, slipping inside to feel the soft wetness. I begin to explore, collecting moisture and tracing it up towards my clit. Pressing firmly. A breath escapes my mouth as I discover new parts of myself. Some feel better than others, but there is no shame holding me back. I continue to explore. To try. I have always turned to others for pleasure instead of taking care of myself. But instead, I can make *myself* feel good. It's not so complicated. And as the feelings swell within me, I turn my energy inward, saying thank you to the body which has stood beside me through it all, the body that has been there for me when even my mind turned to darkness. With one step in front of the other we made it through, and as I continue to worship my own body, with my own hands, I feel myself crack open, breaking apart in a crescendo of energy, and reforming into something entirely new.

A smile spreads across my face as I think to myself: Wow, *I did that.*

I did that for me.

EPILOGUE

Nolan, after the cave rave ball

The cave is a mess. This night was a mess. My life is a mess.

At least the ball is over.

I reach for a half-empty bottle of wine, pulling it straight out of the hands of one of the Palace staff who have begun the post-party clean up. All my friends have retired for the night, so have my suitors. Luckily, they didn't question that I wanted to be alone tonight, seeing as I'll be spending the next three nights preparing for my wedding. To Brianna. And yet, I can't imagine her being my wife. Or my Link. So why did I ask her?

What am I going to do?

It's clear we need to make it to my wedding. Darby was right, the wedding will be the perfect distraction for my father. It will be under the full eclipse that we can sneak the Sprites and the Storytellers to safety.

But how am I going to manage until then?

My head and heart are both hurting. Maybe more wine will help.

I bring the bottle to my lips and chug down every last drop. Wiping my face, I toss the bottle to the side. It clatters to the cave's floor, shattering into a million pieces. Just like my heart.

I'm so angry with Darby.

And yet I can't stop thinking about her. Foe.

This is all wrong.

Maybe it wouldn't be so bad to lose a few more memories.

Maybe forgetting the pain of my past was more of a gift than I ever realized. Yes.

I pivot, propelling myself forward towards the far wall of the cave. Glancing around to make sure no one is watching, I press into the recently formed slice on my hand. The wound hasn't healed yet. All it takes is a little urging for a drop of blood to surface. I press my hand against the wall and open the blood lock, sending me to the other side.

The internal passageway is quiet. My father clearly told his chemists to take the night off. I wonder how many of them are members of our Court. Have they been right under our noses this whole time? Were they at the party?

I drift through the halls until I find the antichamber I'm looking for. The lights are dim, but I can make out the shape of the two Storytellers, slumped over by the glass, resting.

I approach them. Eagerly.

"How's the antidote?" I whisper to them.

The younger looking one of the two inches forward, his eyes heavy as he makes an effort to look up at me with dull green eyes. All he can manage is a nod.

"We're going to get you out of here," I vow.

"How can we thank you? We will be forever in your debt," the man finally says, his voice a strained croak.

"No. You won't owe me anything, this is wrong, my Father is wrong." I kneel to meet his eye level, pressing my hand against the glass as if I could touch him. He bows his head in response, a tear forming in my eye at the gesture.

"But I will ask a favor, if you feel up to it," I add, before I can think better of it.

"Anything," he says, gazing up at me.

"Help me forget her." As the plea leaves my lips, there's a chuckle behind me that makes the hairs on the back of my neck stand up.

I turn to find my father standing at the antichamber's entrance in his silver robe.

"That can be arranged," he says, as his face twists into a wicked smile.

ACKNOWLEDGMENTS

Thank you reader. I so appreciate you taking a chance on an indie author and I hope this is just the beginning of our journey together. As a dyslexic person who couldn't read until the 4th grade, I'm amazed that this book exists and so thankful for the people who have supported me in creating it. Thank you to the educators who took the time to teach me when my learning style was different from the rest of the class. Mrs. Mattingly, wherever you are - you changed my life by teaching me how to read. Thank you to my mom and dad who taught me how to believe in myself. Thank you for seeing me as a storyteller and for telling me to never give up. Thank you to my brother, watching you fight to get your films made has been inspirational. You were my first friend and my forever collaborator and I'm so lucky to have you in my life. Thank you to my entire extended/blended family, I could not have done this without ALL of your support, from Paige pitching my book to stores, to Judy calling to remind me that "the world needs artists", and everything in between. Thank you to the Chicken Girls, over 25 years of friendship have made me who I am today. Molly is the person who got me into Romantasy, and she changed my life. Thank you to the Beta and Sensitivity readers: Maggie, Molly, Lindsey,

Vijay, Quinn, Susannah, Asher, and Kyla. Nicole, Gabbie, Ruby and Sidney were the first to read and give feedback and their enthusiasm means everything to me. Sam and Kat took the time to write *pages* of thoughtful notes. Thank you Chloe, Anika, Lucie, Julia, Heidi, Bela, Steph, Dan, Pri, Zoe, Levi and all the friends (and acquaintances) I bombarded with google forms to Beta test my promotional material. Thank you Jocebed for the early edits. Thank you Joe B. for coming on as a proofreader but staying as an editor, world building consultant, and support system. Thank you Sami for the extraordinary cover art. You are so talented and I'm in awe of the work you do! Thank you Claire for lending your talent to this world. Thank you Torii for the marketing tips! Thank you to the real Tara, Candace and Romina: my first three therapists. I learned so much from each of you and I would not be the person I am today without the work we did together, even when it was really hard. Thank you to everyone I've ever been romantically involved with. Whether it was a long term relationship or a short term situationship, I never take connecting with another human being for granted, and this story was born from what I learned about love in my 20's. And last but not least, thank you Daniel. I haven't felt lonely since the day I met you. Your endless love and support make this all possible. Thank you for being there by my side on the worst days, and the best.

I love you.

ABOUT THE AUTHOR

Janey Feingold is a Brooklyn based writer for page, stage, and screen. She is passionate about coming-of-age stories that use magic and romance to talk about vulnerability and mental health. ROYAL MAGIC is her debut, indie published Romantasy novel.